THE FALLEN

THE FALLEN

BY JUAN MARSÉ

Translated from the Spanish by
Helen R. Lane

Little, Brown and Company   Boston   Toronto

FIRST AMERICAN EDITION

English language translation Copyright © 1979 by Little, Brown and
Company (Inc.), Boston.
Originally published in Spanish under the title *Si Te Dicen Que Caí* by
Organización Editorial Novaro, S.A.

Library of Congress Cataloging in Publication Data
Marsé, Juan, 1933–
    The fallen.

    Translation of Si te dicen que caí.
    I. Title.
PZ4.M364Fa [PQ6623.A745] 863'.6'4 79-13856
ISBN 0-316-54676-3

BP

Designed by D. Christine Benders

Published simultaneously in Canada
by Little, Brown & Company (Canada) Limited

PRINTED IN THE UNITED STATES OF AMERICA

If they tell you I fell
On the battlefield
I lie in the place appointed me.
On the march home the flags of victory will wave
In the joyous cadence of peace. . . .

— Falangist anthem

THE FALLEN

I

ITCHY tells how, on raising the edge of the sheet covering the drowned man, he revived in the swampy, stagnant pool of his wide-open eyes a section of the city with wretched vacant lots and lopped-off geraniums, pierced from one end to the other by the keen whining of a knife-grinder, a remote mirage transfixed by the blue shriek of truth. And he says that despite the elegant silver-haired temples, the suntanned skin, and the gold rings that the corpse still had on, he recognized him; as he put it, everything had been deceptive little bits of mirrors in those days and in those streets, including the rag-picker who after thirty years reached his final corruption disguised in dignity and the trappings of wealth.

His own mother had a belly flatter than an ironing board and yet they used to call her "the Pregnant Woman," Itchy remembers: those tongue-wagging neighbor women with curlers in their hair, suffering from acute cases of unreality, carting buckets of water from the public fountain weighted down with wasps and gossip, that contest of vicious backbiting, on that autumn afternoon when suddenly he felt a bubble of light

3

burst inside him and he said to himself I'm a grown-up now, I'm a memory, and you won't be able to handle me, you hags. Nonetheless, and for a long time afterward, appearances would continue to justify the opprobrium of the neighborhood and the stupefaction of the son, who that very night as he lay on the cot would see her once again, a great belly dressed in mourning coming toward him in the half-shadow of the room and her following behind it, swaying like a doll on feet spread wide apart. In his confusion he could not decide whether he was waking up from a dream or stepping into one again. Dawn had just broken, and at that hour hunger always kicked him in the belly, awakening him and leaving him sitting up in bed, and then he could see how everything was shown up as an illusion by the still-uncertain light filtering through the closed shutters: that gunman riddled with bullet holes leaning over as though to tie his shoe, with a fedora sliding down over his forehead, once again became his father's jacket hanging on the chair; that exploding grenade, that silent red burst of flame spitting out shards of glass and splintered wood would soon be the sun stealing through the cracks in the worm-eaten shutters; and that Mauser hanging on the wall a stain left by the dampness. But his mother, clinging desperately to the bars of the bed, continued to be mysteriously pregnant. Her face was contorted with pain and she was groaning, her legs spread wide apart; he could see her belly, as swollen as though she were in her ninth month, thinking this is it she's going to give birth right here, standing on the tiles. In her helplessness, he thought he could see another person tucking up the skirts of her mourning dress as she strained till her veins stood out, panting: then there gently slipped from between her legs a shapeless mass that she barely had time to catch in her hands. Thick trickles of blood dripped down from her thighs onto the floor, and her fingers were like pointed red fish. Exuding a deathlike sweat, an infinite fatigue, she huddled up next to her son in the bed, enveloping him in a heavy smell of dried vegetables, of freight cars rotting away on abandoned tracks.

4

The second episode that would make him rub his eyes occurred a few hours later in Java's junk shop. Luis and Martín were already sitting on the sidewalk outside waiting for him, and the others arrived a little while afterward. On entering the cellar he came across a huge pile of little paper birds, so tall it almost reached the ceiling. He had never seen so many paper birds at once, and of so many different sizes. They were made out of the pages of Republican magazines, the same ones that Java's grandmother kept stored up at the back of the junk shop and still hadn't dared to sell; but Java said no, in an annoyed tone of voice and without deigning to look at him, don't start imagining things so early in the morning, I bought them from a paralytic who lives in Ensanche, and added:

"You're always thinking up stories, Itchy. You're going to end up going out of your mind."

He was in the kitchen, washing a used condom under the water faucet and then blowing into it to see if it had holes in it. Leaning against the brick wall, almost hidden by bundles of dusty daily papers and old film weeklies printed in blue and sepia, the grandmother was stooping over to pick a tin plate up off the floor. There was always some sort of plate lying around the place with remains of food getting moldy: in case the cat came back some day, Java used to say, as though he'd been caught red-handed at something. But there hadn't been a sign of a cat around the shop for over a year. So that seemed even odder than seeing a used condom there.

"What's more, cats don't eat with a spoon," Itchy said.

"Just one of Granny's peculiar habits," Java said, disentangling a handful of cords. "Go on, clear out, I've got work to do. Are you deaf or something — don't you hear them calling you there outside?"

He joined the gang on the sidewalk, and they immediately moved over to make room for him, some of them rubbing their hands together impatiently: go on with the story from yesterday, Itchy, come on, tell us the rest. Unpaved streets and broken sidewalks where grass grew: that was what this neigh-

5

borhood was like. The mountain of refuse on the corner of Camelias and Secretario Coloma looked higher than before and full of delightful surprises, but it was just that the level of the water in the gutter had gone down after the recent torrential rain. What was peeking out of the mud was not an old shoe but a poisoned rat. The sky was still a huge spiderweb. The storm had passed, but a dark, shadowy drizzle was still falling, an endless, tangled curtain that blotted out the leprous façades and windows that still had pieces of broken glass and charred boards over them. Tell us, come on, tell us. From now on, kids, danger will await us everywhere and nowhere, the threat will be constant and invisible. They say that spring will smile again in some faraway place, and they also say that she'd been a spy and knew too much, and that many years after the last grenade hidden in the grass beneath her feet exploded, on that afternoon as she crossed the vacant lot in the company of a person unknown, the dust raised by the explosion was still falling on the scars of her emaciated, syphilitic body, because she was a whore of the most miserable sort, kids. The grossly fat proprietress of the Continental Bar soon appeared on the corner where the refuse was piled up, hiding a loaf of white bread between the lapels of her black raincoat. Her heavily made-up green eyes cast a sidelong glance at the rat that was spinning on its hind legs, not knowing which way to turn. At the foot of the almond tree on the Can Compte lot, Itchy recounts, there are some cartridge boxes that have fallen to pieces from the rain and a rusty Mauser with a split breech: that means that the stores of ammunition aren't far off. The rat zigzagged across the gutter, squealing, and found all the drains plugged up with mud: Java came to the door of the junk shop and looked at the woman, half-closing his gummy eyelids.

In the middle of the gutter, the fat woman in the raincoat spun on her high heels like a black toy top with a hood, her eyes following the rat's last desperate trajectory. She agilely skirted the puddles of water and came over to the shop.

Even before seeing her open her mouth, Java had already gotten a whiff of her vulture's breath.

"Hi, sonny. How about it?"

"I can't," he answered. "I'd like to go on doing it, you've been very good to me and my granny, but I just can't."

"Think it over. Don't be stupid."

"There's lots of t.b. around, ma'am."

"You always come away with a little something from that house. Look what I got," she said, allowing the toasty-brown end of the loaf of bread to peek out from between her lapels. "Is it more pay you're after? Do you want me to tell them so?"

"No, there's more to it than that. I just can't so soon again. I swear to God, I just can't."

"Don't be such a ham."

"Besides, it's never the same girl. I have to show them what to do every time. It's a terrible drag. Really, I'm starting to develop t.b."

"All right," she said. "They'll pay you more — I'll see to it."

Java turned his drowsy eyes away and signaled to Itchy, who interrupted his story and got to his feet, telling the others: To be continued later, clear the hall. They all ambled after him to the rubbish piled up under the newly painted Falangist yoke and the arrows, the black spider stenciled on the board fence of the Europa soccer field. Luis and Tits had already squatted down and were beginning to dig through the garbage: their hands came up holding red corkscrews of orange peel, eggshells, and pale white remains of heads of escarole. Itchy's dull voice was heard announcing Susana's parents have come back to their house, look how well they're eating again. From the door of the junk shop the house on the Calle Camelias was not visible, but Java could see in his mind's eye the garden gate, open again as always, the air full of the fragrance of the linden trees, the gravel free of dead leaves, and the hammock hanging once more between the palm tree and the eucalyptus.

The fat woman looked at him, waiting for an answer. Curls

as black as charcoal over her forehead, traces of lipstick on the thick cracked mouth, red lips with more lips piled on top, and streaks of mascara on the bags underneath the green eyes. A broad face totally devoted to a calculating but affable coquettishness.

"How about it?"

"It's never the same girl," Java said again. "But they always keep asking for *me*. Why is that?"

"Because that's the way they want it," she said with her big toothless mouth. "I have to follow orders too, sonny."

"It's a crock of shit, ma'am. Sometimes the girl refuses to do all the things she's supposed to, or else she doesn't know how to."

"I do what I can. I make every effort to choose the best ones. Okay then, everything'll be taken care of. But make sure you show up this afternoon, you hear? At four on the dot. Give yourself a good scrubbing beforehand, and remember: if you keep your trap shut you won't get flies in it. That's the number one thing to keep in mind."

"I'm more deaf and dumb than my granny, ma'am."

"Okay then, see you later."

A little girl rode by on a man's yellow bicycle, pedaling in a rage, crying, a frail, musical lament. She looked at Java, her eyes begging for help, threw a folded newspaper at his feet, and rode off down the street full of puddles, weaving and lurching, perched precariously on the narrow saddle, with her moth-eaten red muffler wound around her neck and wearing socks reaching up to knees that were purple with the cold. A child's jacket with the seams popped out constricted her bosom. It was a fall day with high clouds in the sky that looked like a fire or the reflection of a fire far off in the distance. The proprietress of the Continental Bar stopped on the corner and pinched off the end of the loaf of bread to give it to Itchy, who was holding out one hand and propping himself up on his gimpy leg with his other withered arm, looking like an inmate of Cottolengo Charity Hospital: a pitiful victim of meningitis, his head shaved bare and legs as thin as wires — an incurable case, my good lady — and the poor bastard really did look like one. Before disappearing, the fat woman turned around to wink at the ragpicker: make sure you show up.

And he goes on to tell how, once she'd turned the corner and couldn't see him any more, Java gestured with his arm that had the black leather wristband around it, up yours you bitch, and how Itchy then explained: but he'll show up just the same, kids, I know where he's supposed to go and I know he's interested and he'll be johnny-on-the-spot, even though right now he's turning up his nose at the deal. Crunching the crust of the soft bread between his teeth, he added in a serious tone of voice: I know why they want him to get himself good and clean beforehand, how much they pay him to go there, what kind of a job he's been hired to do. And the gang, more and more intrigued, in chorus: sit down and tell us all about it, Itchy, what's the password? what does she mean about giving himself a good scrubbing beforehand? Let's take up the details one by one: he knows the address by heart, there's no password, he's not scared, and this time he's not even going to take his razor with him in his pocket.

He'll hitch a ride on Streetcar Number 30 and jump off at the corner of Bruch and Mallorca, and then walk for a ways in the direction of the Paseo de Gracia. With his muffler wound around his neck and his belly empty, with his legs trembling a little, like on the first day, though not from fear this time, but lack of strength. This is the fifth time in less than two weeks that he's gone to this secret rendezvous, and of all of them he remembers the first one especially, that afternoon when he was out in a different place than usual, far from his own part of town, through Ensanche, underneath wide balconies draped in flags and bedspreads, with laurel leaves and dried palm fronds hanging from them. As always, he was carrying his sack over his shoulder and his balance-scale fastened to his belt, but he had a suspicion that it wasn't precisely to sell him waste paper or rags or bottles that they'd asked him to come. Had he

9

known exactly why they had wanted him to come, he would have washed himself from head to foot and rubbed the crusts of grime off his feet with pumice stone, that's for sure, and Granny would have given my head a good scrubbing, she'd have rid me of that smell of bad weather in my clothes, and I wouldn't have jerked off for at least a month beforehand. But all they'd told him was: for so much dough at so much an hour, show up at such and such an address. And he wondered why, what it would turn out to be, a trap, one of those torture chambers that still existed, run by the secret police now, according to Mingo's father? Some sort of black market deal, a nice little widow in need of consolation? Somebody in search of news of a relative who'd disappeared at the front, or blood for somebody with t.b. maybe? It was a bit windy out. Unshaven pedestrians looking all about out of the corner of their eye popped up around corners like phantoms and crept off down the street, hugging the walls as though looking for a hole or a crack to take refuge in, as though the streets threatened to be suddenly inundated by flood waters. Behind the leafless acacias ghostly buildings in ruins loomed up. Balconies stripped of all their decorations bared their twisted iron railings, red with rust, and windows gaped open emptily, like toothless mouths. He saw women standing in line in front of a coal-dealer's shop, their feet wrapped in a rustle of dry leaves, and a gang of prison laborers shoveling rubble into piles underneath the metal skeleton of a garage, amid a luminous red dust. The number written down on a piece of paper turned out to be the same as the one on a very tall front door, leading into a long entryway with carved walls and a carved ceiling, with a marble staircase winding around the shaft of the elevator, which wasn't working because of the electricity rationing. Windowpanes of polished glass that the bombs had left intact: second floor, first door, opened by the fat woman greedily chewing on something: you were right to come, my boy, you won't be sorry, grabbing his hand and leading him down a dark corridor on the walls of which there filed past huge armies marching to battle, cavalry troops sweeping down in bloody charges, mounted on thoroughbred sorrel horses rearing up on their hind legs amid clouds of dust, and phantasmal armor, shields, swords, flintlock pistols, damascened steel daggers. An enormous old-fashioned apartment, engulfed in a pungent penumbra, with the clatter of dishes ringing out from somewhere in the inner courtyard. White slipcovers like shrouds over the straight-backed chairs and the easy chairs, repeated in the mirrors. Opening a door paneled in wine-colored velvet, the woman showed him into the room and the door closed behind him like a trap shutting, leaving him all alone inside. It was a bedroom illuminated by a gaslight, with an old folding screen decorated with cherubim that were flaking away and little pearl-colored clouds scaling away, women's clothes spread out on a divan, heavy reddish-gold drapes, and beneath his trembling feet the huge rug showing a blurred dawn breaking over a beach and pale-faced men of some long-ago century with manacles on their wrists, standing next to a Capuchin monk. He then spied the bare shoulder of a girl who was sitting on the far side of the bed, peeling her stockings off her legs with painful concentration, as though she were skinning herself; and suddenly she looked at him over her shoulder, like a rabbit just before it is seized by the back of its neck. . . .

But this time it will be different. Wanting badly to urinate but deliberately holding back. Today he has half an hour to kill and he'll go into a nearly empty bar, order a sack of French fries and a glass of plain soda water at the counter, and then go to the can: straddling the toilet with his pants down, he pulls the chain and washes his cock and his balls with the running water, wanting badly to urinate but still holding back. He slowly chews a few French fries that taste like wet cardboard as his wet groin transmits to him vague fears of venereal disease and tuberculosis. Standing in front of the counter again, gazing at a plate full of stale little meat pies, he feels eyes like sharp pins stuck in the back of his neck staring at him, turns around, and sees him: it wasn't that he was all that handsome or sickly-looking, not all that slender or young or vain, with a supercilious, lewd expression on his face, with the hair on his narrow head slicked down with brilliantine and the little black mustache of a would-be ladies' man just above his pale mouth, it wasn't that exactly, but something much worse; and what's more, sitting in a wheelchair, his legs wrapped in a blue wool laprobe, his hand leaning on the ivory handle of his cane. From behind the marble table strewn with dominoes, he scrutinizes Java through the steam rising from the cup of camomile tea that he is holding up to his mouth and blowing on. Java turns his back to him and looks at the little meat pies again: they cost too much, what are you staring at, you fairy, I can't afford one. A shrill screech like a bird's cry makes him turn around again: the wheelchair is now being pushed toward the street by a girl he hadn't noticed before, a gray shadow in the coarse gray cotton smock of a maidservant or a poor pupil in a boarding school.

On the corner, an old man leaning on crutches is painting black brush strokes across a stencil he is holding up to the wall; when he takes it away, the spider remains, dripping signs of mourning, black crape like a black pool of vomit exploding on the wall. Java winds his muffler around his neck another turn; the wind rumples his hair and curly locks fall over his forehead. Passing in front of La Provincial, the government administration building, turning around, the wheelchair following him at a distance of some twenty yards, beneath the acacias. The girl pushes it along as though walking in her sleep, her feet shod in flimsy rubber sandals with thick khaki-colored socks. He has never seen the concierge in the entryway; her booth of carved wood, as solemn as a towering confessional, is covered with dust and abandoned, and the elevator doesn't work. He dashes up the stairs and raps on the door, takes his comb out of his pocket, and runs it hurriedly through his hair. Before the door opens, he hears three shrill bird's screeches with silences between come up through the elevator shaft.

"You're early today," the proprietress of the Continental

Bar says, half-closing her eyelids daubed with gray makeup above her green eyes, taking him to the little parlor with the furniture that smells of linseed oil and the colored glass window overlooking the patio. She leaves him sitting stiffly on the divan, on his best behavior. Ten minutes later, the door opens again and the fat woman ushers in the whore, a real prize: not a platinum blonde, skinny and pale, with enormous eyes and a drooping mouth like a fish, nor a hooker with red shoes and a skirt slit up the side. Worse than that. This time they didn't even introduce her to me; the fat woman went away, closing the door behind her, without saying one word. Hi, I said, raising my butt an inch or so off the divan. Hi, she answers in a hollow voice, then a few sidewise glances at me, sitting down on the other end of the divan. She crosses her legs, opens her purse, and takes out a cigarette.

"What's your name, kid?"

"Daniel."

"Daniel what?"

"What's *your* name?"

Her attention at that point seemed to be entirely concentrated on putting the contents of her purse in order. She wasn't old like the ones the other times anyway. Nice-looking knees, stockings darned so often they were nothing but a bunch of holes desperately sewn together, with socks over them. House shoes with tassels. A short pleated skirt, an orange-colored scarf, and a brown mackintosh carelessly draped over her shoulders. She looked like an ordinary housewife who had popped down to the corner grocery store for a minute to buy something.

"Ramona," she answered, as though talking to herself, and leaned back on the divan.

"Was it the proprietress of the Continental who got in touch with you? Where, if I may ask?"

Casting furtive glances at him, she closes her eyes as though trying to keep herself from swearing: she's just gotten a fair idea of how old Java is.

"Nobody told me it was going to be with a little kid. Who lives here anyway?"

"The only one I know here is the proprietress of the Continental."

"Have you been here before?"

"Yes."

"Is it true they pay what they say they will?"

"Yes."

Looking at him through the blue smoke of her cigarette, half curious and half uneasy, blinking her eyes as though she were having trouble seeing him clearly, rubbing her tongue over her teeth: how old are you, kid, and as Java smiles and says nothing, she imagines she sees a pale rose growing bigger and bigger on his forehead. The door opens and the fat woman comes in, carrying a tray with two little glasses of milk and two tiny tuna sandwiches on it. Java, rising to his feet with a note of false authority in his voice: not even real coffee today, ma'am? quickly reaching out for the sandwich, and without waiting for an answer, saying to his partner: no need to gobble it down, we've got plenty of time. The fat woman goes away but returns a few moments later, with a half dozen meat pies on a plate this time. You won't have any reason to complain today, she says, and Java thinks to himself, scowling, I'll be damned, the same ones as in the bar. Ramona devours her sandwich, almost turning her back on him, crouching over like an animal, her fingers nervously plucking the crumbs off her skirt, not missing a single one.

"Can we expect to get paid quite a bit?" she asks.

"It all depends."

"Who is he?"

"I don't have any idea. Do you know what you have to do?"

"Yes."

"And do you agree to do it all? Just don't start telling me later . . . "

"All I want is to get it over with as soon as possible."

The chattering of maids and the sound of dishes and

silverware rattling suddenly fill the inside patio. Java is just slipping two meat pies into his pocket when the fat woman opens the door again and peeks in: come on, she says without entering the room, and they follow her down the dimly lighted corridor. At this point Java notices that Ramona has slipped her ice-cold sweaty hand in his, and squeezes it tightly. Once in the bedroom, she stands there looking at the two gas lamps with yellow shades, one on the night table and the other on a little round pedestal table; they make a continuous buzzing sound, like bumblebees that give off light. The slit between the pair of honey-colored drapes affords a glimpse of a little paneled door, engulfed in shadows. Ramona's eyes remain fixed on that spot for a moment once the fat woman has gone away, leaving the two of them alone. But immediately thereafter her spirits seem to revive; she opens her purse, takes out her cigarettes and matches and puts them on the night table, removes her shoes, and begins to undress. Java sits down on the bed and takes off his shoes, allowing his gummy eyes to wander over the rug with the worn design showing manacled men with their backs turned toward the firing squad. It must be very near the seashore, he has always thought, because you can see rounded moss-covered boulders in the sand and it's almost as though I could hear the sound of the waves, the foam licking the feet of those who have fallen in the first round of fire, they look so real. He indicates by signs to Ramona that she should take her clothes off slowly, he situates himself behind her, and as he embraces her he removes her sweater, whispering in her ear, let me do it, I know how they like it done, the slip over the head, the skirt falling on the floor, and then the bra, and her standing there very quietly, looking to one side, letting him bite her on the nape of the neck. Her white body exudes an effluvium of sweat and cheap soap. As he caresses her breasts, moving his hands now with an exaggerated slowness, an obsequiousness directed toward a third presence, Java's fingers will become aware of a delicate relief, like that of a coin, on her skin: scars. Okay, your turn now, he murmurs, go to it, whereupon she turns around, thus showing him her belly, and clumsily bumping her hipbone and curly hairs as stiff as wire against him. She finishes undressing him with cold, distracted hands, like this? come on, baby, bite me, groan, scream if you want to have a hot meal today, girlie, come on, that's it. Rubbing the fronts of their two bodies together for a considerable time, but comically immobile from the waist up: locked in embrace as though to rest or reflect or just stand there for a while, listening to the spiteful serpent-hiss from the gas lamps. Ramona with a mute question in her eyes.

"Is he there?"

"I don't know."

"But he must be watching us. . . . "

"I suppose so. Now let me do things my way."

Guiding her rigid hand toward his member, gently pushing her shoulders down, and then her slowly kneeling down so as to bring her mouth to the proper level, but not being able to go through with it, holding back. Drawing her mouth away like a prude. The trembling of her lips, the nervous resistance of her head turned to one side, that stubborn insistence on turning her eyes away and looking somewhere else: damn, Java thinks to himself, another one who's going to give me a hard time, the idea crossing his mind that she might not be a whore like the others, but one of those war widows whom poverty and her starving little kids have forced out onto the streets to pick up a little money every day. If not, why that anguish in her eyes, why those whiplashes of fear?

The deal was that the performance was to go on for no less than an hour, and he'd already acquired a certain technique: letting himself go with the very first orgasm, so that afterwards, firmly installed on a lesser level of excitement, he could control the slowly mounting curve of his partners' excitement and prolong it without letting it slack off, without ever letting up on them but without hurrying them either, keeping them going steadily at it till the end of the time agreed on.

"Not that," Ramona said, with a little laugh, feigning poised self-assurance. "Anything but that."

"Don't hand me that, you."

Bathed in sweat, her body gleaming like dirty snow in the lemon-yellow light from the gas lamp, lying face down and clutching the pillow, thrusting Java away for the second time with pleading eyes. Not that. You have to let me do it to you, don't be a prude, come on. Panting. The living flesh of his member, moved not by any sort of desire but rather by a triumph of blind will, could not manage to penetrate between her contracted buttocks. Come on, don't tell me this is the first time. Suddenly she hides her head in the pillow, which she squeezes tightly in her folded arms. Java casually presses his hand down on the wet cloth, clacks his tongue, surprised and annoyed, and then bows in the face of the evidence.

"It's all over. Come on, don't bawl, damn it."

But that wasn't why she was crying: because of what she'd done, or what she'd allowed to be done to her. Freeing her from his embrace, muttering in a low voice why the fuck do they bring me these dumb bitches dying of hunger, he turns his back to her and waits for her to get over her little crying spell. He lights a cigarette, lying face up looking at the ceiling, staring into empty space: there was worse to come yet, and he was thinking of asking her, listen, baby, how long have you been in this business? when he hears, loud and clear, the double shrill bird's screech behind the curtain.

The curtain is now drawn back a couple of feet, revealing the paneled door, standing slightly ajar. Ramona sits part way up and sees something that causes her to collapse on the tear-soaked pillow again. A shudder runs down her body, as she huddles up close to Java, hiding herself. He then turns his eyes toward the curtain and stares too, without turning a hair, at the vermilion nest of shadows with a wax mask that appears to be floating in them and hears the peremptory order issuing from between two chromed wheels: put your cigarette out in the porcelain ashtray and thrust your aching groin in between her ice-cold buttocks again. The onlooker remained there, frozen in the accidental, inhuman immobility of a mannequin. The shawl had slipped from his knees and lay on the floor. He raised his chin in the air, a gesture that betrayed his habit of being in command, and he repeated the order, pounding on the floor with his cane. Ramona whispers hide me so he doesn't see me, lying on her side on the edge of the bed, receiving him now as though falling with him into a well, moaning. Her eyes, accustomed to his contempt now, finally close. Let's hurry up and get it over with, Java mutters in her ear, help me, nibbling at her tense neck, please.

Not only will she not look toward the curtain again, but she will also try to hide her face the whole time, as if a glare were coming from that direction that hurt her eyes and her memory. What the devil's the matter with you? he says as he penetrates through concentric tendernesses that he was not expecting, though without managing to touch the bottom of that sudden humiliation and that fear so unusual in a whore. Ramona's hands finally running over him, abandoning herself to his assaults, raising one trembling leg like a wing but still hiding from something. Accustomed to receiving the stream of commands that come from the curtain, Java will go on telling her what she must do: moan at certain moments, and scream, curse, bite, hurl insults at others. In any case, she will stubbornly continue to hide her face, even when she rolls down onto the rug with him, dragging the luxurious bedspread along with her, or when she crawls along on all fours receiving blows delivered half in pretense, and pretending in turn to be protecting herself with her arms but doing such a bad job of it that he has to order her in a low voice: whimper, scream, cry, and make it good and loud or I'll have to beat you for real. He cuffs her three times but her moans are feeble and genuine, and hence not believable, she lying on the floor looking at him like a scared rabbit, and he thinking to himself this isn't going to go over at all, feeling almost sorry for her: her rosary of vertebrae, her little head with straight close-cropped hair like a boy's, the pitiful nape of her waif's neck. A little while later he will see her kneeling on the bed putting bright-red lipstick on her mouth, what are you doing? perhaps to give herself a moment's respite, with her back to the curtain of course. But just then three imperious raps with the end of the cane on the parquet floor: put that lipstick down, and the new order: spread her legs apart and bite her you know where till she screams like a madwoman, carry her over to the chair and dress her in the cope, put her hands behind the back of the chair and tie them together with the purple cord, and suck her tits while she throws her head back and kicks her feet violently. That might turn out better, but then, crawling along as he whips her with the cord, what does she do but halt motionless again, curling up in a ball on top of the men executed by the firing squad, with her head buried between her arms. Sweating, Java pulls on the cord and she digs her knees in the blood-stained sand, between the shattered head and the fallen top hat, who would ever think of going to his death wearing a top hat? crouching down with her hands on the nape of her neck until her forehead touches her knees. Then, standing next to her, spreading his legs, Java aims carefully and empties his bladder on her hunched shoulder, at last, what a relief, on the back of her neck and on her head. She shudders on feeling the hot spurting stream falling on her, she is aware of it trickling down her sides and her thighs, dripping off her hair, her nose, and her chin. Obeying another sign, Ramona was obliged to get up, let him grasp her by the hips, and slowly slide down the whole length of his body, down to where his legs spread apart. Java would be aware of the cheek wet with tears and urine and sweat lying against his member, and would be obliged to center her head with his hands, force her, hold her down. Ramona resisting the whole time, till she heard more thumps of the cane, demanding more action. Java's member burns indifferently an inch or so from her mouth. On her knees, bent double, she finally yields to the pressure of his hands.

Feigning sudden accesses of tenderness during the act, Java was to weave a shining dream amid that reality that continued to be hard and burdensome: unable to tell whether they were hers or his, he could hear intestines groaning with weariness or hunger, vaguely feel her mouth contracted by nausea, and at a certain moment, purely by chance, his hand came across another scar lying curled up on her shoulder like a pink lizard, near her neck. Then an emptiness suddenly takes possession of his cock in her hot mouth and it goes limp. Ramona raises her eyes and gazes at him with a questioning, far-off look. Java tries to blot out from his mind the image of the scar, he covers it with his hand, but it is no use. Crawling on her hands and knees, panting with fatigue, she runs her tongue up the length of his body several times. Finally she manages to get her teeth into him, going beyond her own fear, and Java pushes her over backward; they tangle with each other as in a fistfight, seeking each other out and pushing each other away. Again he orders: scream, you bitch, insult me, but she merely says in a very soft voice kill me, twice at the end, kill me, and he never could decide whether it was real or fake.

A little later they discover that they are alone. Ramona runs to the bathroom and locks herself in, and he puts his clothes back on. When she comes out, she refuses to look him in the eye; she is still trembling, and in a hurry.

"Who pays me?"

"You're in quite a hurry now. But just let me say one thing first. You sure made me sweat for my money."

"Not him, I suppose?"

"No, the proprietress of the Continental."

Dressed now, they sit on the bed waiting. Ramona chain-smokes furiously. Java takes a meat pie out of his pocket and eats, staring pensively into space. They hear a knock on the door, go out into the hall, and the fat woman, after handing each of them a sealed envelope, takes them to the outside door.

Out in the street, before separating, they discover that the sidewalk in front of La Provincial has been blocked off: it is occupied by some twenty men in blue shirts who have jumped out of a truck, formed ranks, and are singing. A goodly number of passersby have stopped and raised their feeble voices in chorus with theirs, arms upraised, and the new shirt that yesterday you embroidered in red will be what I'll be wearing if death overtakes me and I never see you again. They have to wait till they are finished, spring will smile again, and just as Java is about to bite into the last meat pie they hear a voice at his side:

"Don't you two know how to salute?"

"Yes, sir," Java says.

"Let's see that arm go up, you little cunt!"

"Yes, sir."

"None of that sir stuff! Up with that arm!"

"Yes, comrade."

He was already standing at attention when the blow landed on his face. Ramona, with her chin tucked down onto her chest, still smelling of urine, also stretches her arm up toward the bare branches of the acacias standing out like spider legs against a leaden sky; with her eyes lowered, she seems to be not so much saluting as pushing away someone she doesn't want to see, someone she doesn't want to listen to. Hiding the meat pie behind his back, with his mouth full and his eyes wet, Java waits for the ritual hurrahs.

II

THE white Simca 1200 GLE, license number B-750370, had only one pane of glass still in one piece: the rear window. Sticking three or four inches out of the water, with the light of dawn already striking it, its black vinyl roof and fine shiny paint job still had all the elegance that had one day doubtless bewitched its owner into buying it. The snout of the motor was submerged in the water, at the foot of the rocks, and the surging tide broke in swirls of foam over its upraised white tail. One of the rear doors was open and the waves were playing with it. Inside the car, two identical boys' faces were glued to the curving back window, their round eyes gazing at the murky nothingness of their underwater surroundings; their bodies floated weightlessly above the upholstered seats, as in a vacuum chamber or an aquarium, amid swaying seaweed and a transparent jellyfish or two. The glass in the side windows seemed to be made of dirty snow: shattered into a network of a thousand cracks. One of the rear wheels, with a racing hub and a radial tire with a white stripe, was resting, with no air left in it, on a submerged rock. The only part sticking completely out was the tailfins, whose blinking lights, in the ten seconds immediately following the accident, had been beaming reflections back in answer to the dawn, inhuman winks, signs of technical survival despite catastrophe and death; looking perfectly placid, moreover, as when the car ate up the miles or parked at the door of the club.

It had the appearance of an animal peacefully quenching its thirst at the foot of the cliff, some twenty yards below the sharpest curve at Garraf. The breaking waves kept pushing it slowly to one side, as though to frustrate its stubborn insistence on drinking at that particular spot. On the right side of the body, a little above the arbitrary waterline, was a huge dent with the paint still flaking off it and various holes through which splintered wood stuck out. Inside the car, all the naïve requisites of ostentatious luxury: a clock with an illuminated dial, a locking glove compartment, a cigarette lighter, a padded inside roof panel, reclining seats. The man lying face down across the steering wheel, just behind the shattered windshield, had had a radio installed in the car so he could listen to music. His wife had insisted on having real carpeting put in, to impress the neighbors perhaps, and he had acceded to her wishes. She was now huddled up next to him, barefoot, with her skirt and her hair rising up toward the roof, swaying back and forth with the drifting currents. Fastened to the dashboard was an exact photographic reproduction of the twins floating behind them in the back seat with their faces pressed against the rear window.

On the surface of the water near the car was a thin streak of oil, as slimy and undulant as a snake. A little farther away, among the rocks, a half-inflated rubber swan was pecking about here and there, obeying the ebb and flow of the waves. A big blue ball was also floating in the water, next to an empty suitcase drifting along with its lid open, and around the car, spread out over an area of some fifteen yards, children's colored T-shirts and women's print dresses, straw sunhats, beach towels, sandals with wooden soles, two sailor caps, tourist brochures, and highway maps. Lower down, in somewhat deeper water, a school of slender, steel-colored little fish with black stripes were swimming round and round the car. From time to time, all the fish darted as one to the open door and tugged at the ends of frayed red strings of coagulated blood floating like ribbons around the heads of the man and the woman.

And he tells how, at the top of the cliff, the ambulance attendants saw a young blonde covering her face with her hands, leaning across the steering wheel of her sports car with the rear end smashed in.

" 'That madman' — that's what they said she was shrieking as she sat there weeping," Ñito reports. " 'He wanted to pass me, he got it into his head that he had to pass me,' she screamed. 'That was the one thought in his mind, the minute he got slowed up behind me in Sitges, the poor crazy bastard.' "

"This mania people have for getting places in a hurry," Sister Paulina sighed. "What a pity."

Every day, from about three in the afternoon till it was time to recite the rosary in the evening, during those stifling September days, the old caretaker would sit in his blue workclothes in front of a glass of yellowish liquid, in the dark, dingy, stuffy room that Sister Paulina insisted on calling a pharmacy, though it was nothing but a sort of bad-smelling storehouse for potions and vials. There the nun made up her formulas and sickly-sweet syrups and harmless and nameless concoctions consisting mostly of artificial coloring and a few drops of alcohol. There was an opening with a grille over it up near the ceiling, level with the street. As the sun beat down on this side of the hospital, near the morgue, it got hotter and hotter and the big, round, plain face of Sister Paulina, with the sticky, bland goodness of a peeled potato, seemed to give clearer and clearer evidence of its silent vegetable nature, so as to allow him to talk and drink his syrupy liqueurs. The nun didn't even appear to be listening to him as she busied herself writing down orders in a little book, walking back and forth between the shelves and the table with a sigh, dragging her leaden feet hidden from sight beneath the long skirts of her habit. She always occupied a tall straight-backed chair on which she merely rested her buttocks rather than actually sitting down on it, across the table from the caretaker, who sometimes helped her sort little boxes containing ampoules for injections and pills, so as to be able to stay awhile longer and go on drinking and chatting. Although she occasionally moved her big moon face with the heavy-lidded eyes, floating weightlessly in the half-shadow, and looked at him without his realizing it, usually it was only to reproach him for some vulgarity he'd committed: her little gray eyes never showed the slightest gleam of interest, the least sign that would betray the passage through her mind of a memory that begged to be shared.

"I wonder who his wife was," the caretaker said. "One of those orphans from the Casa de Familia, I'm sure. There was one of them he was quite taken with, let's see, what was her name. . . . "

We're going to operate on her, she likes getting it, hey, Luis, hand me the sweet potato, I can't hear her heartbeat. Gluing his ear to her right tit, squeezing it: auscultating it, Amén stammered. Sister Paulina cleared her throat, banishing evil thoughts: you're a bunch of filthy pigs. Pressing the hard belly with his fingers, feeling the bones of her pelvis. Touch here, doctor, the assistant said. Hmmm, we'll have to open you up right away, señorita, and with burning, lightning-quick hands he pulled her skirt up to her waist. Juanita, her name was.

"I don't think so."

"How about their families? Hasn't anybody come for them?" the nun said.

"Nobody's going to come claim their bodies; they don't have any relatives," the watchman said with a wry smile. "But those quacks are looking for me to do autopsies on them anyway. Dr. Malet told me to do one on each of them."

The nun wanted to know if that included the children, and the watchman said yes, them too, what a bunch of vultures.

"When one is dead, the soul is the only thing that matters."

"If you say so, Sister."

Innocent creatures, she thought, little angels, and stricken with grief, her mind imagined the fall through empty space, the car suspended amid fragments of the wood rail and stones, the wheels spinning in the air, and the terrified faces of the twins glued to the window. The caretaker ventured to say that when the mother was little, she might have been one of those girls that used to be very fond of playing doctor-games, of playing at being the prisoner of the slum kids from Guinardó, in an air-raid shelter at Las Ánimas. The nun claimed she hardly remembered their old parish and didn't want to hear any more wild tales and tall stories, Ñito, the few teeth you have left are going to fall out, even that silver one. But he went right on, as though he hadn't heard her, you ought to go back there, Sister, and continued to dredge up memories, serenely jumbling them all up, the stories and the friends around the bonfires, the oath they swore on the skull and how mysterious the city was when he was thirteen, with its starving cats and its screeching streetcars. I'm too old, she said plaintively. If you have time, he said and then didn't finish the sentence: if before you die you take a stroll down that way, he meant, if your old legs can take you back to our part of town and you stop to look at the church, then you can't help remembering that that ugly red-brick church sits on top of the cellars and the air-raid shelter that were once our territory. A wide strip of land running down the middle of the block from Escorial to Sors, with an entrance on both streets, a path covered with gravel, a chapel with hydrangeas pressing against the sides, with muddy corners planted with lilies, and a faucet without any water. At that time this nun was a kindly catechism teacher, a plump, affectionate woman, like a mother to the children, not very young anymore, interested above all in religious ceremonies and the girl orphans' choir, and so she knew very little about the rowdies and their stone fights. But she will remember that around the crypt of what was going to be the new church there were only the shafts and the excavations for what were later supposed to be the solid cement pilings, the foundations of the future great parish church, because the Republic or the war interrupted the construction work, so that the tiny original little chapel, scorched by fire and riddled with bullet holes, still was used for services despite the cold and the damp and the few people that it could hold, so that, remember? at Christmas you had to stand right in the doorway to direct the choir. Go back there some one of these days, Sister, and you'll see that on the steep streets that the kids slid down in their infernal soapbox coasters — even though today these streets are paved, even though modern apartment houses have gone up and there are more bars and shops along them — everything is just the same as always. That old stench of miserable, lice-infested vagrants, that offensive smell of a wretched prison cell lingering in certain doorways, has never disappeared. And on certain corners you will still see the black spider that the rains and the streams of piss of thirty years have not completely erased, presiding over the same mountain of garbage as in those days, though bigger now and more succulent, because nobody's dying of hunger anymore — that I'll admit. And you'll also remember the boundaries of the neighborhood, the invisible but very real limits of the slum kids' territory, the bloody and imaginary line that separated them from the stuck-up kids from the Palace of Culture and La Salle, the ones who wore golf knickers as they played around with their little silk-

27

worms in their mansions and gardens on the Avenida Virgen de Montserrat.

The slum kids roved about in the vicinity of the Europa soccer field and the vacant lots at the top of Cerdeña, completely undisciplined, with no schooling — lots of them learned solfège before they learned to read and write, Sister Paulina said with a smile. They were worse than the plague, bigger liars than the Devil himself: they smelled of burned gunpowder and the smoke from summer bonfires. They hung out in air-raid shelters half full of dirt and rainwater, that there hadn't been time to seal up yet or that people had forgotten about, and at the beginning they refused to have anything to do with Las Ánimas. Sister Paulina sat there on the edge of her behind, nodding sleepily, but the caretaker was persistent: I wanted to talk to you about that fondness of theirs for inventing tall tales, Sister, a game that didn't cost anything and was doubtless a consequence of the fact that they had no toys to play with, but was also a reflection of their memories of disaster, a muffled echo of the deafening sound of battle. He spoke of cold winter afternoons submerged in the warm sea of acrid-smelling daily papers and comic books in Java's ragpicker's shop, with everyone sitting in a circle around Itchy: with his shaved head with dust-covered crusts covered with sulfur ointment, like fierce hungry green flies, his deformed, mangy hands, his handsome pocketknife with a mother-of-pearl handle. But the best stories were the ones that Java told on rainy days, when he didn't go out looking for junk with his sack and his balance-scale. It was on a day like that that it occurred to him for the first time to introduce into his continuing plot a real person that all of us knew, Juanita, "Wheaty," an orphan girl who'd been taken in at the Casa de Familia on the Calle Verdi. At that precise moment, Java's audience held its breath, not knowing what to think, their eyes staring, their mouths open, their hands held dead still on their knees. In time, he perfected the method: he put all of us into his stories, including himself, and then it got really exciting because there was always the possibility that one of the gang would find himself playing a starring and decisive role in the action when he was least expecting it. Each of us felt like someone who is about to have something terribly important happen to him. As time went by, he increased the number of real persons and decreased the number of fictitious characters, and what's more his stories started having settings and plots involving events that had happened in the city, incidents reported in the newspapers, and even the mysterious rumors going the rounds in the neighborhood concerning denunciations, detentions, and people who had disappeared without a trace. It was a big act, a voice recreating things that we had all heard rumors about: talking about rumors — that's what "telling stories" meant. The best ones were the ones that had neither head nor tail, the ones that you had no trouble at all swallowing because nothing made any sense in those days. In fact those kids' fantastic stories had their roots in a much more fantastic world than the one their imaginations created. Once their capacity for utter disbelief was ruined the only thing that held their attention was the workings of sheer chance and the totally improbable: Amén assured them that he had seen pregnant women giving birth to floods of rice on Montaña Pelada in the moonlight, with their legs spread apart like old women taking a pee standing up; right there in the ragpicker's shop, when Java and his granny weren't there, Itchy said he'd heard the rasping of a file and the clinking of a spoon against a dish; and Luis swore that in the Roxy Theater he'd seen a guy from the secret police get riddled with bullets from a hunting rifle. At times, sitting around in a circle listening to the ragpicker tell the most incredible tall tale, the misty air brought to their ears the ghostly sound of the foghorn of a boat along the dock, and it was like a siren-call heard in a dream, unbelievable, coming from a world infinitely less real than our world.

"Those are aspirins," Sister Paulina said. "Don't mix all my things up, if you please."

Java used to begin his stories by feeling his way along, searching for some sort of "gimmick," a mysterious boat, for instance, sailing along in the night with its hold full of gunpowder disguised as sacks of coffee; then, if he didn't know exactly how to go on, he'd stall for time for quite a while by hooting "HOOOOOOOOO...," imitating the foghorn of the boat by cupping his hand around his mouth and blowing through it as he thought up the rest of the story, what was going to happen next, how the plot would thicken. And then clutching his knees, balancing back and forth with his legs crossed under his rear end, the pupils of his eyes gleaming in the center of the circle of those sitting around listening to him, the tale full of all sorts of unexpected twists and turns would suddenly start flowing from his mouth, like the swift waters of a torrent, the story becoming more and more impetuous and fast-moving and hard to follow, leaving here and there little puddles of inconsistencies and loose ends that we never thought to wonder about until much later. For example: how could an invalid in a wheelchair get up to the second floor of a building that was really a bedroom if the electricity had been cut off and the elevator wasn't working? Apart from the fat lady whom Fueguiña never got to know, there was nobody in the building to give her a helping hand.... But Java always skipped over such details — maybe even he himself didn't know at the time, and it was a long time before he told us that it was the young girl herself, Fueguiña, who took the invalid in her arms every afternoon on reaching the foot of the stairway after their walk and carried him all the way up, one step at a time. He let himself be carried like a doll, with his short little legs wrapped in the laprobe, with his head with the hair plastered down with gooey brilliantine dangling over her shoulder, with his close-cropped little black mustache on that face as white as wax. We would never have thought that Fueguiña, who was so thin and frail, would have had the strength to carry the invalid upstairs, nor did it ever occur to us that there were so many things she had to do for him: undress him and put him to bed, wash him from head to foot, and help him when he had to go to the bathroom. Because in Java's stories, as we were to realize later, reality was a dark and heavy material that had to remain on the bottom for a long time still, since it couldn't float to the surface yet. But in the end everything always comes out, Sister.

"Their favorite haunt was the shelter of Las Ánimas, all right," the nun conceded.

"But nobody knew it at the time."

"*I* did," she said, and a little cloud of sadness crossed her eyes. "I spied on you all one time, and what I saw was absolutely diabolical."

The sun was no longer striking the outside wall, and the blind panes of the little opening turned an ashen color. After draining his glass the caretaker rose to his feet, wiping his lips with the bloody sleeve of his work-smock. Thank you, Sister, he said, I have to give the dogs their injections and feed them. She watched him walk over to the double swinging door — good-bye Ñito and God bless you — and push it open as though he didn't even see her.

He met Dr. Albiol in the hallway and went through the motions of making a quick draw and firing at him. The doctor laughed and stopped him, you're always kidding around, Ñito, what would we do without you, offering him a cigarette. Anything going on, he asked, and the caretaker answered with a laconic: this morning four came in, car accident in Garraf, a husband and wife and two children.

"What about their relations?"

"They don't have any."

Dr. Albiol stared at him intently.

"How do you know?"

The caretaker began to cough, and went on coughing for some time, leaning one hand against the stuccoed wall. I know what you're driving at, he thought, you're all the same. He wiped his lips, his eyebrows, and his forehead with his blue handkerchief, and turning halfway round, his face flushed, he

31

muttered nobody's going to come, if you want an autopsy just say so, what does one more hunk of meat matter anyway? The doctor asked who's going to do the autopsy? and then without waiting for a reply, with a faint, tense smile, what's wrong, are those tears I see in your eyes? The caretaker walked away. Do you think somebody around here's crying, you asshole?

III

D OCTOR," he said, "come over here and feel this."
Pressing the hard belly with his fingers, palpating the pelvic bones. We've got to open her up right away, the other one said, and she noticed that his hands were more delicate, warmer, as he pulled her skirt up to her waist. Suddenly she heard him call out: Scissors!

Lying stretched out on her back on a hard surface that smelled of burned wood, she saw the doctor's face bending down toward hers, with a flash of silver between his teeth. She gave a tranquil smile, though feeling very nervous inside, seeing him brandish the scissors and hearing him tell her in a cold voice: keep calm, Juani, this isn't going to hurt, it'll be like a dry shave but don't worry, it'll grow back again; who's scared anyway?, with a defiant smile: you're not going to see me shed any tears, damn it, I'm not going to give you that satisfaction. She felt hands separating her thighs, the fingers lingering in the most sensitive areas, the cold contact of the scissors, and the clicking sound of the honey-colored curls being snipped off. She heard a voice say she's a hairy one, as she held her breath, smiling resignedly at the late midsummer night, at the stars. The last curls fell and the hands kept insistently feeling, exploring. Tell me when it hurts, scream if you like, nobody's going to hear you. She struggled violently beneath the straps and thought what filthy pigs, whatever happens I hope they get it over with soon. The doctor mentioned something about ulcers and malignant tumors, somebody said Anastasia, and somebody else answered anesthesia, you dummy, and then she saw a white drop that smelled like snot fall on her nose. She lashed out furiously with her feet until she could breathe again. Keep still, kid, she heard, and the five faces leaning over her moved closer together, forming an even tighter circle. We have to explore further, the doctor said. You told me you'd do it with gloves on, she protested, pressing her thighs together, but four hands immediately separated them again, as the gleaming knife blade passed before her eyes. Juanita stifled a scream as she felt the finger poke around, parting the lips, poking, twisting round and round, sliding over the moist walls. She concentrated, trying to imagine what was going to happen, closing her eyes and dreaming of a gentle weight pressing on her breasts, a caress on her hair, but she didn't feel a thing. On the other side of her tears, up there at the very tiptop of her rage, beyond the branches of the almond tree and the palms stirred gently by the breeze, the twinkling of the stars went mad all of a sudden, the light fell all to pieces. You won't have a sign of it left, somebody said, lie still, if you don't behave Dr. Java will come and operate on you and you'll see what a good job he does.

Juanita managed to raise her head up and stared him straight in the eye:

"You pig!" she spat out, along with a stream of saliva. "You rotten mangy beast!"

"You've had fair warning," Itchy calmly replied, wiping the spit off with the back of his hand. "So start talking, sing out everything you know or it's the Red-Hot Iron for you."

"Or would you rather see what the sweet potato feels like?" Luis said.

"This kid likes getting it," Martín whispered in Itchy's ear as the two held her down by the legs. "She'll spill everything she knows, but she wants to feel the sweet potato first. Just the tip. I know her kind very well."

"Don't be a prude, Juani," Tits said, removing the handkerchief. "Sing and we'll let you loose — don't be a dummy."

"Is this what you call playing doctor?" she protested. "You won't trick me into playing it again. And you're the one who wants to be a doctor when you grow up?"

"I'm going to be one. A surgeon," Itchy said.

"Ha ha!"

"What are you laughing at, stupid? Luis, the sweet potato," Itchy ordered, opening his hand with the overbearing imperiousness of a surgeon. "Make it quick."

Luis came over, and she noticed that his clothes smelled like roasted coffee. She pressed her thighs together. With its rough, warty skin, raw, sharp-pointed, and at the same time soft from having been rubbed by so many hands and pockets: that's how she imagined it making its way inside her. All those hands put together didn't have enough strength now to part her legs, all Itchy's diabolical cleverness wouldn't succeed in sticking even the tip up her. Wait, wait, I'll talk, she said in a feigned tone of urgent supplication, but untie me, let me rest a little. . . . Luis lighted the butt of a cigarette in the flame of the candle. The sound of distant orchestras came through the night, a medley of lively dance tunes coming at the same time from several of the nearest streets: Legalidad, Providencia, Encarnación, and Argentona. Sirens were screeching at the various carnival attractions and stands in the Plaza Joanich. Standing next to the wall around the Can Compte lot, a toothless silhouette standing out against the starry sky, they gazed with drowsy eyes at the little orphan girl tied with snakeskin straps to the fire-scorched door stretched out over piles of bricks, in

35

the middle of the field sown with rubble: a barren, desolate wasteland, ancient trees half-charred by lightning or bombs, a plot of ground that in places looked as though it had been mangled by teeth and claws. At times the air still seemed to be full of ashes and smoke. Bindweed hung from the wall like dusty, antique lace, and the prisoner was screened from view by the foliage of an old almond tree whose trunk had been riddled with bullets: around each hole, a heart and a name engraved with the point of a knife — Susana, Menchu, Fueguiña, Virginia, and Trini. Squatting on his heels alongside Juanita, Martín was toying with the knife. In a soft voice almost like that of a lover, he said to her don't be afraid, Java's still in the car, he may not even come by this way. Tits and Amén sat down next to Luis, who was passing out cough drops. Leaning his elbows on the improvised operating table, Mingo was looking at the prisoner's white panties, pulled down to her knees that were dirty from the dust of a prie-dieu. In all their faces there danced the yellow light of the candle in the middle of the bidet, standing upright in its pool of melted wax. Goddamn, Juanita, you're great, Mingo said — I didn't think you'd hold out this long.

"Just let me catch my breath, you creeps," she said. "Hey you, will you cover me up?"

Mingo pulled her skirt down. From nearby came the chirping of crickets, and from afar the music of the carnival. Martín stood up, scratching his skinny chest with the little ball of camphor hanging from around his neck swinging back and forth across it, and gazing grimly through the clear night air, his eyes sweeping across the scraggly weeds and the whitish, sepulchral empty plot of land that stretched from Legalidad to Encarnación, to the ruins of an ancient farmhouse sheltered by four palm trees. Beyond the gullies and the burned fields there could be seen palisades and tangled barbed wire fortifications that looked as though they had been felled by a hurricane. From the Calle Escorial, sticking out above the wall, a street lamp bathed in a blue light the rusted chassis of the Ford sedan

36

with its four doors removed, an abandoned hulk, a snail shell rusting away from the rain. Inside it was a shadow lying on frayed burlap sacks, holding a lighted flashlight. Martín touched its shoulder: Java, he said, are you coming or not? I'm coming, he answered, sitting up with a thoughtful look on his face, his thumb hooked in the big brass buckle of his wide belt. On joining the others, he leaned his foot on the edge of the porcelain bidet, his elbow resting on his knee, glancing first at the flame of the candle and then looking the prisoner up and down from head to foot: her coarse blue uniform, her little white schoolgirl's tie, the chaste little bun of hair at the nape of her neck, her lowered panties, the dirty scapulary tied across her face. She looked at the ragpicker with her cold eyes and her ears as bright red as hot coals, with a hypocritical smile tinged with both fear and cunning.

"I was hoping I'd see you, you bully. What do you want to know, come on, what is it you want to find out?"

Java said nothing. It was Martín who answered:

"Is it true you found ammunition buried here?"

"Go fuck yourself," Juanita said.

"Is that the way they teach you to talk at the Casa de Familia?" Amén said.

Martín cleaned the blade of the knife on the edge of Juanita's skirt. This is our turf, he said, talk or we'll take out your pendis.

"Mark her up, Martín," Tits said.

"First we'll put matches under her toenails."

Luis took the box of matches out of his pocket. Fear mounted in Juanita's eyes, still fixed on Java, and she blinked: I heard something like that at Las Ánimas, she stammered, but I don't remember exactly what. . . .

"Spill everything you know," Itchy said, brandishing the sweet potato, waiting for a signal from Java. "What was it you heard?"

"That one of the kids from Las Luises had found a hand grenade."

"Where?"

"Somewhere around here — how should I know?" Juanita began wriggling frantically on the planks. "Untie me, you, I'm starting to bleed."

"Listen, kid, do you go to Las Ánimas a lot?" Itchy asked.

"Sure, why?"

"Louder — we can't hear you," Luis said, scratching his asshole with his finger. "Talk or we'll torture you. Who was it who found ammunition?"

"Listen, have you got ringworm?" she answered, with a look of mock pity on her face. "Do you want to know how to get rid of it real quick?"

"We're the ones who ask questions around here," Itchy said.

"Well, you're not going to get a word out of me, you rowdies, you good-for-nothing slum kids."

Itchy thought things over for a minute, walked around the bidet, and looked at Java, trying to read his face, his odd silence: his dark hands hanging down motionless in front of his knees, the colored bandana knotted around his neck, the blue sailor jacket, the impassive face in the light of the candle. What was Java, their pal with the gummy eyes, waiting for, why didn't he question her himself, since it had been his idea to take her prisoner?

"Let's see," Itchy said, walking back over to her. "Which of you guys have been to Las Ánimas, aside from Amén and Tits?"

"I have," Mingo said. "I went there once."

"What was going on?"

"It was as dead as a tomb. Prudes and mumbo-jumbo."

"But they've got Ping-Pong tables and soccer equipment, with jerseys and shoes with cleats and all that sort of stuff," Tits said. "And they've got a stage where they put on plays."

"Yeah, but they make you swallow communion wafers and stuff catechism down your throat all day long in return."

"It's not all that bad," Juanita said. "Ask Amén — he's an

altar boy. And they give you a free afternoon snack. Hey you, keep your hands off me!"

"Okay, but who was it that first talked about going there?" Itchy said in a furious tone of voice.

"Java."

"What for?"

"So we could get in good with the orphan girls, don't you understand, stupid?" Martín said. "To interrogate them."

Java didn't say a word during this discussion. He had sat down on a big jagged stone underneath the almond tree and was watching Juanita. From far off in the distance there came through the night air a loud explosion of voices and applause from some street where people were celebrating, but the musicians must have gotten tired by now and the melody gotten lost somewhere en route: the only sound that reached their ears was the monotonous beat of a bass drum and the throbbing of a double-bass, a muted pulsation that seemed to come more from the darkness than from the orchestra. Luis said: "My old lady would like to see me go to Las Ánimas — she says it would keep us off the damned streets."

Freed from the table, with her hands tied behind her back, Juanita was pushed by Itchy to the center of the ghostly band, alongside the bidet with the candle. His final push left her lying sprawled on the ground. Java aimed the flashlight around. Itchy kneeled down in front of Juanita and the candle flame illuminated his shaved head and the crusts with sulfur ointment on them to cure them. Who found the ammunition? he said, spill what you know, you miserable little wretch. Java stood up. Martín roared: she took us for patsies, threw himself on top of her, and the two of them rolled around in a little pile of fine plaster dust. Juanita remained on all fours and for a moment he clung to her buttocks, wriggling frantically, thrusting his pelvis at her like a dog. Kicking out with her feet, she turned around, biting Martín until he leaned all his weight on her and she fell flat on the ground and stopped moving. She slowly shook her head and spat on the ground, and then, even more slowly still, gave Java that smile of hers that was like a grimace. Moving closer to her, Java blinded her with the flashlight beam, but she continued to stare at him defiantly, her mouth contorted and smeared with dust and bloody saliva. He bit me, the beast, she said, licking her lip and spitting.

"Let her go," Java said.

Martín moved to one side, on his knees. Juanita had already gotten to her feet, and he shook the dust off her skirt and her legs with his hands. You animal, she murmured, standing there above him, you beast.

"Come over here, closer to the candle," Java said. "What's your name?"

"You know very well what my name is, ragpicker."

"What's your name, I said."

"Juanita. You over there, get this filthy stuff out of my hair. Take it easy, you brute!"

Martín wiped the dust off her hair. Luis said: 'La Trigo' — 'Wheaty.' Juanita la Trigo, they call her."

"Why do they call her that?"

"On account of the color of my hair," Juanita answered, shaking her mane. "Can't you see? Geez, what big rough paws you've got! Come on, let's get this over with. I've got to get back to the Calle Sors — the señorita will be wondering where I am. What a lot of work for just two lousy Merlin comic books!"

Tits immediately answered: just one and that's all, pug-nose, and she protested indignantly: you told me two, damn it. Itchy intervened, saying sure you can have two, dummy, but first you have to let yourself be fucked.

"Not on your life. Who do you think you are anyway?"

"But all you girls let yourselves get felt up by the Dondis at the entrance to the Casa de Familia."

"That's a lie. I wish I'd gone to the Fiesta Mayor, you pigs."

Java, who was walking back and forth around Juanita and the candle, said without looking at her: "You'll get what you were promised, it's going to be one 'Monito,' plus one 'Fifi' for a tip. Okay?" he said, stopping in front of her and smiling at her. "Do you like big fiestas?"

Something in that smile made Juanita think: yes, he could really hurt me now, and nobody would hear me scream, nobody would come to my rescue if he made me bleed to death.

"Yeah, they'd be great if you could stay all night and dance . . . ," she said. "But as I told this guy while we were coming here, the señorita only lets us stay a little while. Just long enough to walk around and see the streets all decorated, the bands, the girls' dresses. . . . "

But she'd had a good time anyway, she added, first they'd gone to the parish church and from there, along with the priest and several catechism teachers, they'd gone out wandering along the streets; the priest had gone up onto the orchestra platform to open the fiesta, and Pilar, Virginia, and Mari Carmen had gone up onto it too, and the priest had delivered a nice little sermon, or rather a speech, saying that it was a source of great satisfaction to the parish church and to God too, since it meant that the parish church was again being asked to participate in the wholesome joys of the people, that he understood that they had need of a little diversion after the many misfortunes and sorrows brought on by the war, and when he mentioned those who had fallen in battle some of the women burst into tears, but the priest grabbed a trumpet out of one of the musicians' hands and began playing it, and everybody laughed like crazy and said how about that, to think that some people claim he's a Red.

"Don't you have any father or mother either?" Java asked.

"I'm an orphan, like all the girls at the Casa de Familia," Juanita said in a rather irritated tone of voice, spitting out the words. The Nationalists shot my father, if you want to know the truth, but he deserved it. Anyway, what else is it you want to know? Martín told me you wanted to know about the ammunition. . . . Is that what this is all about or isn't it?

Java removed his bandana from around his neck, and she said, intrigued: are you going to blindfold me? He knotted it

41

around her neck, and even after she could no longer see anything, she could smell the same cologne that Lieutenant Conrado used, that Fueguiña sometimes deliberately spilled on herself. They spun her round and round like a top, and she could
feel a hand hurriedly fumbling around under her skirt, guess
who it is, she whirled round and round, kicking with her feet
at empty air, lost her balance, and felt Java's hands hold her up
by the waist: take it easy, Juanita. And Itchy's voice: is it true
that a Moor raped you in your town, you tramp, right in front
of your father? And bursts of laughter.

"Shut up, you assholes," Java said, but she noticed that his
tone of voice was not very forceful. "Don't be scared, Juanita.
I'm going to take the blindfold off now and you can go back
and dance some more. You can trust me. I only want you to
tell me one thing."

"If the señorita discovers I'm not with the others, she'll kill
me."

"Tell me — who's the directress of the Casa now?"

"Señorita Moix. She's an old lady now, and she can't see
worth a damn, but she knows everything that goes on. Fueguiña and I always manage to sneak away somehow. . . . Fueguiña's luckier, of course — she's got a job outside the Casa."

"Do all of you work?"

"Do we work? No, we practically sit around doing nothing
all day — all we do is sew, do embroidery, wash and iron, and
scrub floors. Oh yes, we also make paper flowers — the ones to
decorate the streets for the fiesta. We slave from morning till
night, kid. Other girls are luckier and have jobs on the outside.
They work as maids, or practical nurses — like Fueguiña.
Lolita's attending a dressmaking school. . . . "

Someone — not Java — grabbed her by the shoulders and
spun her around again, and a voice said: can you see anything?

But the ragpicker's voice, so close to her ear, was the only
one that made shivers run down her spine: "The directress
who ran the Casa before — what was *her* name?"

She began to tremble again, even worse than before. Her

head, with her eyes blindfolded, came up again for a moment, as though she had heard a signal in the night, beyond the music of the crickets and the orchestras. The loudspeakers in the nearest street were broadcasting the nasal voice of a vocalist.

"What was her name?"

"How should I know? I first arrived at the Casa four years ago, just after the Moors had invaded our town. . . . When they brought me to Barcelona Señorita Moix was already in charge. . . ."

"But you must have heard the other girls talk about her," Java insisted.

Juanita heard an irritated voice rising from the ground below her, Itchy's voice: what's your game, Java? What's the point of all this talk about some other directress? What are you getting at, what do you want to know, what does all this have to do with our ammunition? But the ragpicker paid no attention, and in the same icy tone as before he said once more: "You must have heard the other girls talk about her — I'll bet anything you did."

"The señorita doesn't want us to talk about that other directress who was there before. There may be a few girls who knew her, the older ones, but it's forbidden to even mention her. I don't even know what her name was."

"Why is it forbidden?"

Juanita sighed. She could feel that all of them except the ragpicker were tense and nervous, because none of them was saying a word: they didn't understand the questions he was asking her. This is a real drag, Itchy said. She heard the click of the jackknife opening.

"Talk or I'll brand you," Java said. "And I'm not fooling, kid."

"Because of something bad she did once," Juanita whispered. "They say that one night she cut the heads off all the dolls belonging to the littlest girls in the Casa. And what's more, they say she's a whore now, like Menchu."

"Just one more hooker, eh?"

43

"That's right."

She felt Java's fingers on the nape of her neck, the handkerchief slipped down over her face, and the first thing she saw was Itchy, sitting at her feet, watching the ragpicker with a bored and impatient look in his eyes. Well, I'm glad that's over, Juanita said, how about untying my wrists now? — I think they're bleeding. Can I go now? Luis offering her a cough drop in the scabby palm of his hand: would you like a cough drop? clawing furiously at his hind end with his other hand. Put it in my mouth, yeah, like that. Hey, do you really have ringworm?

"Have you heard anything about her?" Java said. "Do you know where she's living now?"

"Ask Fueguiña — she used to be friends with her."

Java turned his back to her, and walked away toward the chassis of the Ford. Itchy said to himself: this whole thing is a real bore, and gave Juanita a push, forcing her to sit down on the bidet. The candle flame burned between her knees. Java had stretched out inside the car again, and was indifferently watching the whole scene. Luis and Tits tied her up by the ankles. Mingo held her arms behind her back and Itchy moved her thighs closer together around the flame. We'll see if you sing now or not, he said, we'll see if you tell Java where that whore is living. And turning his head in the direction of the Ford: Is it important, Java? The ragpicker puckered his lips and Itchy said: You see, bitch? Spill what you know.

"But how can I tell you anything when I didn't even know her? You're beasts, I swear — nothing but beasts."

"She's getting uppity, Itchy," Tits said. "Shall we take her panties down again?"

"We're going to burn your cunt, kid," Mingo said, blocking Martín's path as he tried to come closer, warning him: "Stay right where you are. Don't be scared — nothing's going to happen."

With bulging eyes she watched the flame of the candle just

a few inches away from her dust-covered thighs dripping with sweat. Struggling frantically, she managed to free one hand and scratch Tits's face, whereupon he rolled on the ground.

"Juani the fearless."

"We're going to put the sweet potato up your ass."

"I don't know anything, I tell you — not one thing!"

"We'll see about that," Java said, shining the flashlight on all of them. They blinked but continued to hold her down just the same. Juanita's panting breath almost extinguished the candle flame. "We'll see about that. If you tell me the truth, we'll let you go. Do you know if she had any sort of noticeable mark, have you ever heard the orphans at the Casa talk about any kind of scar she had? . . . "

"What animals you are, I swear," she groaned, and then more or less recovering her equanimity: "What did you say — a scar?"

"Yes, a noticeable mark of some sort."

"No. Like I said before — ask Fueguiña. I don't know anything." All of them protested again, not knowing what Java was up to: you gummy-eyed bastard, tell us once and for all what you're trying to track down, who this whore with the scar is. But all Java would say was: untie her and let her go. Juanita smiled through her tears, rubbing her aching wrists.

"The way you look, nobody's going to ask you to dance," Mingo said to her. "I'm sure you know that if you talk about what's happened here, if you say one word about it to anyone, I'll slash your face with this knife and shave you bald."

"Is that so?" Juanita purred. "Is that all? That's all you wanted out of me? You think you're really smart, don't you? You pigs."

And turning halfway around, she headed toward the gap in the fence leading to the Calle Legalidad, making her way through the rubble, stumbling but self-confident. Luis hurried after her, scratching his ass, and when he tried to grab her by the hand she eluded his grasp in fury. But she said to him: I know a cure for ringworm that never fails to work; I'll make you a string of garlic cloves to hang around your neck, even though you don't deserve it, you beast.

It was during that same night that Java was to begin to interrogate all the orphan girls, searching for a clue that would lead him to the "Red" whore. It must have been in the summer of '40. Street by street, beneath the eyes of the slum kids with pockets full of gunpowder and strips of snakeskin for belts, for almost an hour he prowled the streets of the neighborhood crowded with people out celebrating, to no avail: he met orphan girls from the Casa several times, but never ran into Fueguiña.

They shoved their way into the crowds, forming a wedge and pushing, raising the girls' skirts, pulling their hair. They sailed paper streamers from one sidewalk to the other and from balcony to balcony, above the heads of couples and bystanders who were inching along, squeezed from both directions. They stopped for a while in front of the platform on the Calle Sors, admiring the wild drummer. On the corner of the Calle Laurel, in the middle of a knot of excited girls who were licking ice-cream bars, a young poorly dressed artist was painting pretty pastel landscapes and auctioning them off right there. An old vendor who had set up his cart with anise cigarettes, cigarette holders, and bottles of vermouth was roughed up by a Guardia Civil, in civilian clothes, who lived in the neighborhood. Almost no one paid any attention to the young merrymaker with a knapsack and a shaved head slowly leaning over the sidewalk: he looked as though he were bending over to pick something up but in reality he was falling. They picked him up with a cut on his forehead, and the daughter of a neighbor, a girl in a tight green dress, brought a glass of milk that the stranger refused to drink.

A burst of applause came from the other end of the street. With his hair slicked down and the emaciated face of a tubercular, a handsome gigolo of a dancer was whirling about elegantly with his blonde partner in the middle of a circle of onlookers. In front of the door of the parish house, the orphans from the Casa de Familia were dancing with each other, clutching green plastic coin purses. When Martín asked them, they said they didn't know where Fueguiña was, laughing like mad things, but here's Pili. . . . In a dark and deserted alleyway a couple were kissing and they stopped to scrutinize his hands with their sharp eyes, accustomed to hunting cats in the darkest shadows. The bells of Las Ánimas struck twelve. The silent shadow whose path crossed theirs at this moment was Margarita's sweetheart: he passed by without seeing them, with his white face with smallpox scars that was as hard as ice. Itchy crouched down as though he had heard a bomb whistle. "Taylor" was walking along absentmindedly, his hair looking like patent leather and his arms far away from his body, as though he had swollen glands in his armpits, and passed by so close to them that they caught the smell of sweat and leather.

After midnight, Java proposed forming two groups and meeting up with each other later. Except for him and Mingo, they all turned up an hour later at the attractions on the Plaza Joanich. They asked for a rifle in the shooting gallery and for a *real* they shot at a bottle of anise until the gallery owner caught them using bullets that Amén had in his pocket and took the rifle away from them. As they went up Escorial, stoning the solitary lamp on the corner of San Luis, a sudden wind blowing up out of the darkness knocked Itchy backward; it was like a ghost, he would explain later, a tall pale man who was coming toward him with his head bent over in the darkness; for an instant he could see the steely brightness of his eyes, his open sailor jacket and his tall bare tattooed chest; golden curls peeked out from under his beret and his beard was as blond as honey. They met as he turned the corner and he strode quickly away in his ragged blue espadrilles. He tried to add, although he couldn't or wouldn't, that he seemed to emerge not from the night but from a shipwreck, a storm, or a tavern at the port with its stained bar counter.

"It's him," he said. "The sailor."

"I didn't have time to see him," Amén said. "What a scare!"

"It can't be — he's in France," Martín said. "He went on a freighter."

"Well, he's come back."

"Can he be the one who brings black market coffee to the clandestine roasting place where you work, Luis?" Tits asked. He was convinced it was.

"Yes, it's a sailor who brings it all right, but not that one. This one is from the underground, you guys, what do you bet? — he's bound to have a set of papers from the Republican Army; my father has one."

Nope, Itchy said, starting on again, I tell you it's him and he's come from Marseilles, he always wanted to be a sailor. He was about to tell Java about it, but they didn't see him that night. When Mingo joined them he told them what had happened with Fueguiña: they had finally met up with her on Torrente de las Flores, but Java was more enigmatic with her than with Juanita, and didn't even ask her about the ammunition. Apparently he didn't recognize her immediately, it wasn't like the first time he saw her, that gray shadow in a gray smock and rubber sandals. She'd been dancing, he said, with a guy wearing balloon trousers, a guy named Sergio, whom Java knew from having sold him Doc Savage comic books. He held her very tightly but she didn't seem to notice. Above her lively head and her black hair parted over her forehead and pulled back into two thick braids, the strings of paper fringes and garlands and colored bulbs stretched to the end of the street. The ragpicker's greedy little eyes wandered over the pitiful little flowered skirt and the miserable red pullover, with worn sleeve ends and covered with a light, luminous fuzz. Taking advantage of a pause in the music, he invited her to dance but she refused. Mingo didn't know how Java got rid of the guy, all he saw was that he whispered something in his ear, and then both of them went into a dark doorway together and in a little while they joined her again, whereupon Sergio, limping a bit, took her in his arms to dance. It was a slow number.

He didn't finish it. Mingo said it was as though he'd been seized with a terrible pain or had suddenly gotten a kick in the balls: he turned tomato-red, stifling a scream, let go of his partner, and went limping home, hugging the walls like a hurt dog. She wasn't surprised or anything, just a little bit annoyed. When the next dance began, she allowed Java to hold her as tightly as Sergio had, with a vacant look on her face, as though unaware of her body. He supposed that Sergio had had a cramp in one leg. His voice was like his look: troubled, fixed, studiedly indifferent.

"What's your name?"

"María."

"But they call you Fueguiña. Why?"

"I don't know."

"Don't you remember me?"

She shrugged. Her eyes peeked over Java's shoulder with their dull swampfire light.

"No."

"Have you ever eaten tuna pies?" Java said, hugging her a little closer. "I've been looking for you all evening."

"Liar."

"Why don't you have a uniform on like the other girls?"

Those who worked outside of the Casa de Familia, she explained, those who worked as maids or did housework by the hour, could wear street clothes. "Who knows where you can be," she hummed under her breath, "who knows what love adventures you're having." Yes, she took care of an invalid, a wounded war veteran, several hours a day. The directress of the Casa was nice, she treated them well, she probably was somewhere on the streets with the other girls, maybe looking for her, it was getting late.

"What was the name of the other directress, before this one, the one that had scars and everybody says was a big Red?"

"Señorita Aurora."

"Have you ever seen her again?"

"No."

"And you don't know where she lives?"

"No."

"They say she's a whore now."

Fueguiña shrugged.

"That's what they say."

He stepped on her foot unintentionally and smiled to excuse himself, clasping her less tightly. He could then see her strange smile with teeth missing, her broken and decayed teeth. She looked at him fearfully and he stared right back at her. It all happened so fast: they turned out the lights and there she was with a little lantern in her hands, she said I'm going for matches, and Java was still waiting for her. Not a sign of her. After the lantern dance, when the vocalist had already left the platform and the orchestra was playing the last tango, the women suddenly began screaming and the couples started to run in all directions. Crossing a curtain of smoke, the musicians jumped into the gutter with their instruments. In a few seconds the crowd had moved onto the sidewalks, and the deserted platform, with smoke pouring out the bottom of it, with flames here and there, and then explosions: the next day's skyrockets went off, and the sacks of confetti for the end of the fiesta and a few folding chairs were on fire. In just a few seconds a gleaming tongue of flames devoured the draperies decorating the platform. The cries of fire! fire! could not be heard as the flames flared up on one side of the platform, doubled back, and licked the piano. They felt the heat of the fire on their faces, like the breathing of a wounded animal. They threw buckets of water on it and the smoke rose, dense and white, toward the starry sky. Java struggled through a double wall of men who smelled of tiredness and sticky sweat, a muscular tension that in an odd way made them brothers with each explosion of fireworks. On stepping up to the sidewalk in order to escape the stream of water running down the street, he caught sight of her head outlined against the flames for a moment, and then her face: lighted up by the flames, among the dense crowd of neighbor women, she was looking on as though it were all a ritual, with her ancient icy eyes noting every detail, every ember that flew up like a bat. The gleam struck her face and she yawned as though for lack of air. Two men were unable to restrain Java, who struggled loose and began to run to the other side of the platform, as the last rockets of the fireworks display went off. When he got to the other sidewalk, Fueguiña was no longer there.

IV

DON'T say: I can't stand any more, Marcos, there's no
way out. Leaning over to light his cigarette between
trembling lips, huddled in a corner of the Alaska Bar. And to
think that in the beginning they all said this can't last, this
can't go on, without suspecting that the echo of their words
would filter down through thirty years to the deaf ears of their
grandchildren. Their minds were elsewhere, they were blind,
very far from seeing themselves taking up arms again, in fact
they couldn't even imagine such a thing: their faces hidden in
knitted balaclava helmets and pistol in hand, pushing the revolving door of the Central Bank or placing a bomb on the
monument to the Condor Legion. Men of iron, tested in so
many battles, weeping in the corners of bars like children.

Palau was the only one among them who probably saw,
amid the burning tears that still clouded his vision of victorious
troops parading down Salmerón, the platinum blonde waiting
for him in the bed at the Ritz, covered with jewels, or the car
of the guy with the top hat, stopped at pistol point on the

Rabassada highway. Don't say that, man, there are a thousand ways to screw them.

The more you close your eyes, the more clearly you can see it. What made them form a resistance group that brought them together again for their first meeting in the apartment near the Fontana subway stop, the very day that the victors marched in, was not reality, but rather the obsessive and suicidal desire to repeat this can't go on, this can't last to each other in a low voice. A sawed-off shotgun, some cartridges, and a little luck are all that's needed; Bundó has a Ford sedan and Palau will dig up his Parabellum that's buried at the foot of the lemon tree in the garden on Los Climent, we have to locate Esteban and get him to come, Meneses will never be a schoolmaster in his village again and is also available, he's got a Browning, and Marcos, if he can ever work himself up to coming out of his hiding-place some night for something other than to stretch his legs or steal candelabra in churches: we have to resist, we have to hold out some way because it's obvious that this won't last much longer and in any case the allies will arrive sooner or later.

"We have to count Luis Lage in, as soon as he gets out of Modelo prison, and Jaime Viñas," Palau said excitedly.

The Ford circling the Plaza Calvo Sotelo in the direction of Pedralbes, one day during that spring that arrived smiling and dusted with sunshine like a cheap whore. The plane trees, a bright green with their new foliage, file by one by one, the ghost of Mary's Bar and its apéritifs, the storefronts with new windows, the silk bedspreads and the red and yellow flags hanging from the balconies, sticking like skin to the dry branches from Palm Sunday. Passing by the scorched door of a church crowded with faithful on their knees: the hymn seems to give wings to the Host, there at the front of the church, above the sea of bowed heads. The fresh ruins of the destroyed church, or at any rate of the part of the church that had been built, the burned apse, the charred remains of the beams, and the broken glass were justification in the end for all the psalms.

They went to Penedés to rescue Meneses from hatred and vengeance and then went slowly back down the Diagonal, as Bundó had asked them to: I have a plan, let's see what you think of it. In front of the Palacio Real a cloud of dust and inside it a century of young Falangist Arrows, parading along with their shaved heads, their black shoulder belts, red berets, and machetes in their belts: there go your sons, Palau laughed, to think that we lived to see such a day. Bundó obsessed by the idea of attacking, now or never, you bastard, his black mechanic's finger pointing past the windshield: the iron gate of the park. Was he really seriously proposing mining the Palacio by making an underground tunnel night after night and blowing it up with dynamite after the armored car had entered? He won't come, don't wait for him, Palau would say; thinking about liquidating him is like jerking off just because.

You're right, there are other ways of fucking them — Esteban Guillén at his side, so handsome, elegant even, though his belly was rumbling with hunger. "Cleaning out their banks, their factories, their supply offices, their billfolds."

"That's first on the list" — this was Palau. "Without dough we won't get anything done."

"Listen, we're not highwaymen" — this from Meneses with his white face with smallpox scars and his black, almost feminine eyelashes, a suitcase on his knees and two suitcases full of books in the baggage rack. And in his memory a blackboard and *clear out, Red* written in chalk on it, a people with a weathercock as a landmark and black war widows, a pretty woman leaning against a wall covered with lilacs. Saved from hatred by his friends, almost weeping when it came time to leave, huddling in the back of the car with lowered eyes, raising them only for an instant to look for the last time at the gang of kids around the car, the white schoolhouse, and the white road. The electric lines overhead hummed of faraway places and the future. A kilometer from the town, the young girl in mourning, with a black scarf on her head, was waiting at the foot of the whitewashed wall of the cemetery. Amid the sound of locusts chirring, as though life about her had suddenly been paralyzed, an interminable embrace, a few farewell words, I'll be back to get you, the wind combing the tall cypresses.

Many of them did not approve of the fact that Bundó had contacts with anarchists in exile in Toulouse, but he argued:

"We're all equal now."

"We'll never be equal with you anarchists, I told them," Palau said as he sat facing me in the Alaska Bar, trying as best he could to light my trembling cigarette. "Except for 'Taylor' and Guillén, you know what they've been and how they are. Braggarts. You were different, you wool-gatherer, they got you involved too, you were okay at the front but they corrupted you here in the rear guard. The anarchists' playboy. And look what you've turned into. Scared shitless."

"They want me to join the group. . . . "

"I told all of them no straight out. And I told them I didn't know anything about petitions and blowing things up and all that, and I got straight to the point. Our first obligation is to empty their wallets, and I still say so. Goddamn anarchists, I told 'em."

"What does all that matter now, Palau, how long are we going to go on arguing about the same thing?"

" 'Let's see if we kiss ass, eh Palau?' Bundó and Fusam told me — they were fit to be tied. You should have seen them."

"You fool. While lots of you guys were hiding out here, ours were organizing the resistance in the concentration camps — guys from POUM who were going to end up in the gas chambers of Mauthausen and Dachau, did you know that? What do you say to that, you braggart? Did they have balls or didn't they? Let's just see if we can stick to the ideas we already have, if we're all equal."

" 'I'm not a man with ideas, you show-off,' I said to him."

"You're the one who's a show-off," Fusam said laughing. "The minute you come by five *duros* you're in the Bolero with a whore. You're mad."

"Where do you expect to get information, you ignoramus?

Where do you think the factory-owners' girls go, to mass, dummy?"

Following the apprentice of the Munté jewelry store without letting himself be seen. Through the half-open door of room 333, you can see a blonde stretched out on the bed, asking for her breakfast by telephone — without thinking there's a man hidden in the hall, without wondering if he's an old trade union hand, a Socialist, a mere separatist. What's the difference now, show-off, what distinguishes us now, what separates us?

"Of course not, there are still classes, you anarchists."

"Get me the desk," she says, laughing, shaking her platinum blonde hair back, baring a white throat. A silk peignoir and lips and fingernails painted blood-red. The Pekingeses trotting all over the bedspread lick her pink ankles and her satin slippers.

"Hello, is this the desk? The apprentice from the jewelry store is coming; have him come straight up."

She gets up and sees the patent-leather asphalt of the Gran Vía through the window. What does a de luxe mistress think as she watches the rain fall from a window of the Ritz, on a cold winter morning, toasty-warm with her centrally heated room, her Pekingeses, her mink stoles, her colored turbans? She is merely thinking how things were seven years before, a red-headed girl tottering around in green high-heeled shoes that some soldiers wrapped up in blankets have given her; the truck bristling with guns stopping in front of the garden of Las Ánimas, the young militia-girl with her foot on the running board, her red scarf around her neck, her curly black hair; the orphans pass out dippers of hot coffee and cigarettes. The littlest one, about seven, looks with hypnotized eyes at the dying fire. All around, the militiamen are discussing why the North was lost, damn it, death to priests, you, guard, how about sucking me? They see the motionless child taking care of the fire with her strange ashen gaze, come here, one of them says, twirling the little gold chain with the cross on his finger, and tell that redhead to come over here and get warm, there's room for two in my blanket.... And he saw her come closer, when all of them were sleeping, and let herself be embraced under the blanket with the ruby cross around her neck, and the little one standing by the fire again looking at him with her blue-green eyes and saying if you let the fire go out, soldiers, I'll light it for you again....

Wasn't that the night they came for you, Marcos, and by a miracle you escaped, taking advantage of the confusion that was created when they discovered what was up?

Hadn't that horrible atmosphere of suspicion and a spy mania already been created among the comrades at the Hotel Falcón, with everybody going round whispering and watching each other? Wasn't there already a Russian agent after you, who said that it was all an anarchist plot hatched in the hotel, don't you recognize yet that the source of your fear is a dead issue now, that you could get out of here and try to cross the border?

He followed the apprentice without letting himself be seen, his eyes hidden under the brim of the hat. He was in the habit of entering the most crowded places without faltering, with a dead Lucky stained with coffee hanging from his lips, with his long blue overcoat belted at the waist and the falsely imperious look of a functionary on his horse face. If necessary, he would even show his old badge of an agent of the Generalitat. He pretended to be tying his shoe behind the big plant with leaves like fish gaffs, at the end of the carpeted hall on the third floor of the Ritz. Waiting. The kid knew the way by heart. Hearing dance music from behind some door or other, a woman's wild laughter, a clink of champagne glasses. Walking down the hallway, the apprentice shivered: there must be a blonde behind each door, half-naked, with high black silk stockings and embroidered garters.

The kid knocked on door number 333 and Palau didn't take his eyes off him.

The gray façade of the Falange headquarters in the Eighth District, Plaza Lesseps, in the late afternoon, the smell of roast chestnuts. The rattle of streetcars and blue sparks from the trolley grazing the cable. A bomb bursts under a window of the headquarters, the red flame spits out glass and fragments of stonework. The sidewalk outside the Roxy strewn with handbills. In the vestibule of the moviehouse, sticking his head between the curtains to see the stage, a policeman will discover something suspect. He enters. Two men with their hands in their pockets and their tickets between their lips, one of whom is pale, tall, and hunched over, with this blue jacket of mine and this cap with blond curls peeking out of it, I am hugging my automatic with a silencer under my armpit. The other one has on a beige raincoat that conceals a sawed-off shotgun. In the last row of seats the policeman sees a woman with short, powerful thighs with her skirt tucked up, slapping a boy seated at her right. Just as he is about to intervene, he hears the click at his shoulder. He turns around quickly. I spy the desperate gleam in his eyes, still blinded by the bright images on the screen, when suddenly he sees the open raincoat and the gun pointing in his hand. The hail of shot hits him in the chest like the stream from a hose. The woman and the child scream and dive on the floor between the seats. Covering the comrade's exit, then running after him. A little later, clinging to the curtain, the policeman would go out into the vestibule with a drawn face, intensely black lips, and cheeks like paper. The pink-cheeked young Arrow who has come with the order to pick up the handbills stares openmouthed as the policeman lets go of the curtain and slumps down till he is on his knees, holding his arms out toward him, his belly soaked with blood. The fat Arrow steps backward. The policeman lowers his head and belches twice, a trickle of blood comes out of his mouth, and he faints.

Looking at the end of the passageway out of the corner of his eye, the apprentice's left ear rings. As the door opens, the shadowy silhouette of the blonde with her peignoir open.

"From the jewelry shop."

"Well, finally," pulling the peignoir shut. "Wait a minute,

handsome." Turning halfway round she goes in again. From the door the apprentice sees her vigorous buttocks beneath the silk, the dimples when she walks, her ankles as pink as strawberries and the little dogs frisking about them. She tries on the earrings in front of the mirror, and looks at herself with self-satisfaction, surprised, amazed almost: those red cherries that were her first earrings in the Dondis' grocery store, the grace when she walked in her pleated skirt amid the smelly sacks of chickpeas and lentils, an attractive girl from the neighborhood, a redhead drinking orchata with the boys from the Calle Verdi. The pink ribbon in her hair, the little open blouse, the knitted sweater. And knees secretly tanned on the roof-terrace of the Casa, but always with the dust of a prayer-bench, like a stigma, and the boys' jokes, you're a knockout, kid.

"Do you still go to confession at Las Ánimas, Menchu? Is it true that while you were sleeping in the subway one night during the bombardings, they caught you with your panties at your feet under the Dondis' blanket?"

"A rotten lie."

"And does the directress know you use lipstick?"

"They say the biggest Dondi boy has t.b. and it's your fault."

"That's just gossip. We were never sweethearts."

"It's too bad it's all over, isn't it, kids? We'll never go back to the refuge with Menchu, we'll never hear the sirens again."

"I don't really want to, man."

"How good you are, Menchu. When are we going out together, hmmm?"

Sticking to her like flies to honey, inviting her to drink orchata, pretending to themselves that they were getting her drunk.

"Hey, baby, an orphan's got a right to live too."

"On Monday I'm going to begin working at some people's who've got a telephone in the bathroom, just imagine, and two cars" — one of the boys tries to rub her knees full of dust and she moves away, her violet eyes blink and she speaks as though in a dream, her eyes staring off into emptiness. "One of these days I'll chase this dust off my knees and I'll leave this dirty orphan rat-trap and never come back."

We think yes, we say no. We think, this won't last, let's try to bear up under it. There won't be any more air-raid sirens, that's one thing. The national anthem accompanies the elevation of the Host. There are no more mouths of shelters vomiting cries of mother into the night, they won't come back through the sky to kill kids: from now on, fellows, the threat will be invisible and unending. . . . The one who says this is a boy from Carmelo. There's not very much truth in his stories, for the time being anyway, so this kid tells tall stories basing himself not only on the bloody facts of the past but also on facts yet to come. He talks of bombs hidden in the grass that will explode many years later, of poison scorpions that will survive these ruins and of ineradicable tattoos and scars on the skin of memory. In a little storeroom dimly lighted by a candle, he says, someone sitting in a rocking-chiar is making little paper airplanes with old newspapers, by day and by night, thinking of a pretty sweetheart in rain boots, of comrades that are brave and faithful unto death, of what could have been and was not, of everything and nothing, wool-gathering.

V

WHAT the devil was Java looking for among the little orphan girls from the Casa, they all asked Itchy, what was he investigating and who was that whore, who sent him to meet her and why: he seemed to be playing detective, he asked so many questions of indigents who collected old newspapers, crippled veterans who were out of work, and jerk-off whores from the neighborhood moviehouses.

In some part of her forgetful mind Sister Paulina murmured the names Jesus, Mary, and Joseph as the watchman continued to mutter, always in the same tone: there was no inflection in the questions, no irony or sadness, no emotion at all.

And when and how the search for the redheaded whore began no one knows, nor does anybody know who started it: after the fire on Torrente de las Flores Java didn't see Fueguiña again until one day when he stopped her as she was going out of the Casa de Familia to Las Ánimas to rehearse. No, the nun said, it was in the old church, in the little chapel that had burned down: with that cold coming down from the roof she helped me to change the flowers and the candles and suddenly I didn't see her there, she was in one of the side altars staring at an image of the Virgin and perhaps praying. An image of the Immaculate Virgin that had been mutilated and soaked with rain, yes, they still hadn't repaired the roof. But she wasn't praying. She always had the little notebook of the Salesian Dramatic Works with her and took advantage of her spare moments to rehearse her role; nonetheless that was not what occupied her memory either. He silently tiptoed over to her from the back, guessing, she said, oh now I remember what it was that was burning in her eyes back then: the scorched black walls, the ruined altar, the charred beam holding up the gray sky, the great traces of smoke everywhere. She seemed hypnotized, she said he thought, standing there in the tumultuous shadow of a fire she'd never seen, and he whispered in her ear: they're still looking for the madman who burned the platform down. She didn't even turn around to look at him, and he added: I mean the madwoman, they still don't know it was you, but I'm going to turn you in. She turned around then, with the notebook tucked into her belt, a candle in each hand and in the middle her swampwater eyes, not afraid or anything, dead. Did you hear me, Fueguiña? She raised her eyes in the direction of the piercing cold that was falling from the gap in the roof. But I won't say anything if you help me, he said to her, I swear I won't say a word; I know that this week you're rehearsing the play and I need a role, I'll explain to you what you have to do. (I called to her, Ñito, I wanted to avoid that, come what might, and told her to change the water in the vases, I thought she'd take advantage of it to get away but that one was never very clever, and he went and waited outside and they must have planned the whole thing together, even though she prayed she was a bad lot.) That's right, Fueguiña was a bad lot even though she prayed, that was for sure. Who's playing the part of the Devil, what's his name? Java asked her, holding the vases that she was filling in the font in the sacristy. Miguel, Miguel something or other. I know him, he said, and he must have left immediately because he caught him as he was coming out of the Palacio de Cultura, it wasn't six o'clock yet but it was getting dark already, a good time to pick a fight, to get rid of somebody.

"Everybody's looking for somebody now," Itchy said. "Just look around: news of some relative who's disappeared, or hidden, or dead. You'll always see somebody weeping and searching for somebody."

And how much was he being paid for it, for sniffing about in taverns and whorehouses, for asking questions of his friends the gypsies, the knife-grinders, the umbrella sellers, for seeing whether they knew her or had seen her, for poking around in cheap boarding houses where he bought paper and old clothes.

"There's no secret, kids," Itchy said again. "No mystery. It's all a matter of denunciations, of ratting to the cops, of dragnets and searching all round. What's so strange about that? X's father has turned out to be a Red, they suddenly tell you, and Y, didn't you know? — well, everything he has in his house is stolen, or else: have you heard the news, so-and-so's sister has become a whore, or so-and-so's uncle's been hidden in a wine cask for two years, he does crossword puzzles and they give him his food through a hole. . . . Look at the papers, read the announcements asking for news of sons and husbands who've disappeared. Right here in the junk-shop there's something fishy, I'm sure. Don't you sometimes hear the creak of a rocking chair and the rasp of a file? Have you had a good look at the bone rings Java sells? They aren't made by the prisoners in Modelo; he says so but it's not true. And what about the little paper birds made out of newspaper that suddenly appear by the thousands, as though they'd rained from the sky? Are you going to make me believe that Java has 'em in his sack, that the whole neighborhood has suddenly started making paper birds? I've never seen Granny Javaloyes make a paper bird. And do you know what they say, haven't you ever read one? Well, take one, this one, unfold the paper and read: 'Miguel Bundó Thomas, replacement 41, Red Army, 42nd Division, 27th Brigade, 907th Battalion, 2nd Company (chauffeur) I will be grateful to anyone who can give me news of his whereabouts.' Take another, just any one, any of the big ones, this one: 'Terrible fire in Santander. Jaime Viñas Pallares and Luis Lage Correa have been detained for providing means to flee abroad.' And this other one, look: 'Recovery of stocks and jewels confiscated by Marxism.' And this one: 'Armed robbery in the Hotel Ritz.' And this urinal full of shit and piss that Granny secretly empties in the water-closet, thinking that we don't see her?"

In the autumn Itchy and his mother went away to their town for a few months, both dressed in mourning: the father had appeared one morning hanged in the gateway to the Europa soccer field. For two hours a mongrel dog barked at his old sandals that smelled of vomit, until they opened the wooden door on the Calle Cerdeña. They took him down: a skinful of wine surrounded by clouds of flies, a black tongue that had caused more deaths than the war itself, they said in the neighborhood. Itchy said that when they loosened the cord around his neck he burped, as though he were alive. And that once again he saw, fluttering above his closed eyelids, things that he had seen when his father took him by the hand to the shelter, things that he would never forget: women and soldiers wrapped up in blankets and taking turns warming themselves round a bonfire, women in high-heeled shoes dragging along armfuls of guns. . . . That Itchy had hallucinations, Sister, he was out of his mind from the bombings. In his house in Cottolengo they had spent four days not knowing anything about the father. He seemed very old but he wasn't all that old, he often went on drinking bouts to the Barrio Chino and had no job, it was said that he was a confidant of the secret police; he'd recently been sleeping in taverns next to the radio, in the early morning he didn't dare enter the house and threw himself down on the landing, and his kids used to stumble over him as they went down to the street. One night as we were sitting in the doorway we suddenly heard a deathly noise and the drunk came down on top of us, rolling down the stairs like a bundle.

This time and lots of others we cleaned the blood off his face, buttoned up his fly and his shirt, took him by the armpits and the legs and brought him upstairs without making any noise, leaving him stretched out at the entrance to that little apartment with wretched and filthy walls. His funeral was attended by the miserable ghosts of his nights, informers and dissipated bar-bums, a strange nocturnal fauna, unshaven, with faces the color of ashes and eyes that could scarcely bear the sunlight. Some whores from the Cine Iberia, neighbor women, loaded down with children and very sleepy, dropped by the house to offer their condolences: he was a good man, nobody's useless in these times. That was when Java, on seeing them there without makeup on, with children in their arms, like someone who belonged to the family, asked Itchy: do you know if your father ever knew a certain Ramona, did you ever hear him talk about her any time? No, he never talked about his filthy job or about his friendships with whores. Ramona, you say, so that's her name? No, why, who is she?

Itchy didn't weep over his death, nobody in that house wept, and after the burial he and his mother stayed some time in the town with the weathercock, and when Itchy came back he found many things changed. In the junk shop they told him:

"Hang on to your hat: Java's going to Las Ánimas now!"

"That can't be" — with his ringwormed hand scratching his bare shaved head, dressed from head to foot in clothes clumsily dyed black, he seemed to just be coming out of some sickness or some danger. He stuck his hand in the mountain of paper birds and added: "I can't believe it."

"I swear on my mother's head that it's true," Mingo insisted. "And he goes to mass."

"Mumbo-jumbo *habemus,* Itchy."

"Hey you, divide up the licorice and shut up, Tits," Mingo said. "Seriously, he goes almost every day."

"What about you?"

"We do too — only less often," Luis said.

"And what the hell does he do there?"

"He plays Ping-Pong, sings in the choir, shoots the breeze with the girls, asks questions, looks, and keeps his mouth shut," Martín said. "He wants to be an actor, he says."

"He's delighted, he goes to spy on the rehearsals without them seeing him," Amén said. "He sits down on the last bench, in the dark, but quiet as a dead man."

"He'd do anything to get a role in the play."

"He's already done it," Martín said. "He had his plan."

It was six o'clock in the evening and he was running through the icy streets with his black fists in his armpits, but it wasn't hunger or cold that was making him hurry. He went to meet him as he was coming out of the Palacio de Cultura with his briefcase and his album of champions, and he stopped him and said: are you Miguel, the one that plays the part of the Devil? Yes, what's up? Come on, and he took out his razor but didn't open it, he trapped him in the darkest part of the Calle Larrad and gave him a kick in the balls. When he'd thrown him on the ground he kicked his kidneys and ribs, leaving him almost breathless, so he couldn't shout. Are you the one who's going around saying that Luis's mother jerks guys off in the Roxy? Sitting on his chest, he carefully hit him in the eye with his knuckles: if he was blind he couldn't be the Devil. Without malice, Sister: he only wanted to put him out of commission for a while, he had nothing personal against the kid and so he invented that story about avenging the mother of a friend. Don't you know that mothers are sacred, kid? He reflected, standing there looking attentively at those swollen eyes, those split eyebrows, the puffy face, fearing the possibility that he would recover in a few days. So he decided to make sure: he held him face down in the grass, sniffling alongside the open album and the many chrome reproductions that weren't pasted in yet and were scattered all round him, and first he picked them up and put them in the album one by one, and the album in the boy's briefcase, which he left within reach of his hand; then he stretched his arm out on the ground, put his foot over the elbow and stamped down hard, just as he doubled it back, a

66

pull, and then the cracking sound: this time he did scream, but he says he waited a little; Java had already let go of his arm and as he set him free he fell backward, as though he were made of rags, and fled down the street, along the sidewalk with the dark street lamps; it was very cold, a night not fit for a dog.

"It's because he's got the hots for Fueguiña," Martín said. "He's doing it all for her."

"That's not the reason," Itchy said gravely, lost in thought. He looked at Granny Javaloyes enveloped in her big shawl at the back of the junk shop, sorting rags out from a pile of papers, sitting underneath the calendar that had frozen forever in June of '37, the month that it turned a bit yellower each year. With her busy hands occupied, she was holding two copies of the magazine *Crónica* in her teeth. Itchy asked her by signs if she wanted them to help her for a while, and her answer was to hit the crook of her elbow with her hand: clear out of here this minute, it meant. Itchy turned to the others: "It's not that. He's trying to get close to the orphan girls, wherever, including at Las Ánimas. Come on, Granny's pissed off."

Before getting up he looked at the door at the top of the stairs; the street and the night, the invincible cold. Then he looked at Tits and Amén buried up to their necks in the mountain of little paper birds, and said what a bore the town was, I was anxious to get back, where's Java, is he coming today or not?

"No, not now. Come on," Martín said. They said good-bye to Granny, using signs, and she didn't even see them. "You still haven't been to the place, you'll like it."

Itchy didn't answer. They set off at a fast clip, the whole noisy bunch of them. In the Calle Camelias the night or the nostalgia for other less inclement nights wafted an odor of jasmine from the iron fences to the sidewalks.

"Getting to be a friend of Señorito Conrado's," Amén said. "That's what he wants. And to make friends with the catechism teachers so as to get cans of milk and clothes out of them."

"What do you know about it, dummy?" Itchy said. "I see you still don't know which way is up."

"Well, spill it, what are you waiting for?"

"We're there," Mingo said. "Silence."

It was right there on the Calle Escorial. A sign riddled with holes and spattered with handfuls of mud on the wall of the nun's nursery school, stamped next to the black spider, and it said in blurred letters Expiatory Chapel of the Souls in Purgatory, and on the side the enormous columns like severed trunks, in a row touching each other, forming a barrier that had to be scaled. Two yards beyond was the shelter, whose entrance in the form of a horseshoe curved backward over the red earth, between a mountain of bricks and debris left from the interrupted construction work: beneath the starry sky its mouth gaped open as though sinking in quicksand. Inside, the little wooden door, and one of the boards was removable: that's how we got in, Sister.

"Ammo? . . . ," Itchy asked.

"Naw. A broken wheelbarrow and picks and shovels," Amén said. "But nobody but us knows about it."

Once they were all inside they nailed the board back in place, with real fury: the cold lay in wait on the other side of the rotten boards. It was warm there in the darkness. I'm going to tell you what's up, Itchy said; do you remember that Sunday morning this summer, before the fiesta, when a taxi came? Yes, they remembered: they'd never seen a taxi in that wretched street, much less parked in front of the ragpicker's shop; so many fumes were coming out of the gasogene motor that they thought it had been damaged. It came from Las Ánimas. Señora Galán takes her son to mass every Sunday, Amén said. But only on Sundays: on Tuesdays and Fridays they stay in their private chapel in their apartment on the Calle Mallorca, isn't that right, Tits?

They were helping say mass; Amén went on Tuesdays and Tits on Fridays. They always came back after tucking away a keen breakfast, with toast and butter and cups of milk, and with cookies and chocolate in their pockets, and they told endless tales about the lady's immense apartment, so many sailboats and lanterns and furious waves in the colored glass windows and pistols and swords and daggers with the dry, black blood of centuries on the walls; Amén swore that on Lieutenant Conrado's desk were five silver bullets molded in a paperweight in the shape of five roses, and an autographed photo showing Juan Centella, with his white turtleneck jersey, his knickers, and his boots, driving a powerful motorcycle.

"Come on, shut up. Quit jabbering and let Itchy talk."

The lady got out of the taxi and behind her there appeared a waxen hand dancing inside the khaki sleeve, handing her the little package wrapped in tissue paper and tied with a purple ribbon. The lady had an embroidered black mantilla over her shoulders and on her head was a little blue hat with violets and the veil drawn back. She stroked Amén's hair. The others drew closer, but they had eyes only for the package dangling from the loop around her finger.

"Does a deaf ragdealer-woman live here?"

"Granny Javaloyes, yes, ma'am," Martín said. "But she's not here."

"How about her grandson?"

She had a clean little porcelain face and smelled marvelous, we all remembered, and Tits confirmed it, stumbling and feeling his way through the shelter: I knew her a long time before you did. Her son remained seated in the back of the taxi, his eyes with the haughty, gloomy look scrutinizing the door of the junk shop through the window. She went in, Itchy said, reminding them, but I had gone on ahead without her seeing me so as to tell Java he had a visitor, it's charity from the parish, I said to him, you're in luck, and I hid behind the sacks to see what they were bringing him: I hope it's canned meat, I thought. And the rest of us waited in the street next to the taxi, waiting for the paralytic to lower his chin and smile at us, his hands resting on the handle of his cane and the little towel around his neck like a scarf, why is it he always wears towels instead of scarves? Because he must like it, manias, whims of an invalid. Until he finally lowered the window and said come here, and asked us our names one by one and invited us to share his blond-tobacco cigarettes. He had a sleepy, very bored face, but was very lively despite his misfortune. Luis, who always claimed that he had wooden legs, simply went over to see if he could get a look at them, and finally got around to asking him if it was true that his socks and his shoes were painted on, the animal.

"And what did the lady want, Itchy?" Luis asked, feeling the damp wall of the shelter. "Java wouldn't tell us."

It was a narrow tunnel sloping downward: four yards inside there were walls and a brick roof, and then everything from there on was dirt. Be careful not to get lost, you leadfeet, Mingo said, and in the light of the flashlight he could see the muddy water on the ground, there where the sloping part ended and there was a bend to the right. To the left was a cave three yards deep: a lateral passageway where the work had not gotten much of anywhere. They passed in Indian file over the plank thrown across the mud, with Mingo and the flashlight in front, and Amén tagging along last, making a nuisance of himself, humming, we're going to tell lies, tra-la-la, laughing like a rabbit, do you know who discovered this shelter?, and Martín's voice: Java, but it seems that Fueguiña already knew, but then she usually knows more than she lets on. But go on, Itchy, tell us. Let's sit down here and smoke a fag first. Wait just a minute though so you can see how great it is.

She'd been sitting on the pile of magazines all this time, the ones that Java's granny wants to burn, and in such a natural and even elegant pose in her maroon tailored suit that you could see she was used to making visits to the poor. And Java sitting on the floor next to her, looking at her delicate hands as they undid the little purple ribbon and pushed aside the tissue paper: three pastries with cream filling appeared, in a cardboard box, in the lady's lap.

"You're to share this with your friends, but keep one for

your granny," the lady said, her smiling blue doll's eyes blinking. "Come on, eat a little as we talk."

She told him how they were sending us food, clothes, and medicines from Las Ánimas, we even have a little dispensary and all, she said, and a list is being made of the most needy families in the neighborhood, and you and your granny. . . .

"Didn't you also have a brother?"

"He went away. On a boat, he always wanted to be a sailor" — and then, chewing without interruption, on his guard: "Did you only come to ask me how many of us there are here, ma'am, is that all?"

"I also came to ask a favor of you."

"Sure."

Then she lowered her voice a little, but kept on smiling and blinking. First she asked him if he knew that the Center was engaged in helping the parishioners, and not only with food and clothing. . . . She soon interrupted herself and came to the point:

"For some time the Congregation has been looking for a girl you know, you've been seen with her. She's someone we want to help and we don't know where she lives."

"Ah," Java said, grabbing another piece of the pastry from the lady's lap, looking at her lively and mischievous eyes, her little teeth with gold fillings. "Of course I know lots of people, you realize, we ragpickers get inside all sorts of houses and talk with everybody."

"That's why I thought of you."

She was going to ask him to denounce somebody, I bet, Luis said. But Amén and Tits protested: how can you think that of the lady, she's as good as they come. And what else, Itchy? you've left the best part in your craw: who was she? A whore, you dummies.

"A girl," the lady said, "a poor misguided girl who has suffered a great deal. Her name is Aurora Nin."

Java shook his head.

"I don't know anybody by that name, ma'am."

71

"It's certain that she goes by another name now, and she may even have dyed her hair. She'd be very afraid, poor thing."

"Why?"

The lady hesitated a few seconds, tilted her head to one side with a sad look, and sighed.

"Because of something bad she once did, my boy. But that doesn't matter now. She's all alone and without resources, she needs our help and we know she's hiding. Before, when she was a well-behaved girl, she used to come to the parish church, but now it must make her feel ashamed to see people she knows. . . . "

The lady explained herself, moving her hands and her eyes a great deal, happy to see him eat with such gusto and enjoyment: a new endeavor on the part of the Center, saving those unhappy girls if there's still time to, getting them into the Foundation for the Redemption of Sins, in Gerona, but she also had a special interest in helping this Aurora because she had had her as a maid when she was a young girl, and she was always very nice, and she was fond of her. And he must know her because someone had happened to see them together in the Calle Mallorca, one afternoon when there was a Falangist gathering.

Java's jaws stopped moving, he remembered, his mouth full of cream with just a little taste of cinnamon, and he raised his head and his eyes got smaller, thinking like he does when he tells a spy story and suddenly his powers of invention fail him and he wants to stall for time; there was almost nothing of the pastry left now, the little bastard.

It's not certain that Second Lieutenant Conrado, who was waiting in the taxi, was the instigator of all that. It didn't even occur to us that he might know something, or that someone from the Blues lined up standing at attention who might have seen them could have said something to him. A poor hungry couple, smelling of urine and with upraised arms, forced to salute right in the middle of the street is something that today might give you some idea of the intolerance and humiliation of yesterday, but at the time it would have meant very little to an onlooker: a couple of stinking citizens in a crowd of stinking citizens, that's all. Unless they knew her from before. . . . That was why Java asked: who says they saw us? and the lady said a former chauffeur of ours, but it's all right, my son, perhaps he was confused. Hmmm, Java said, was your son also on intimate terms with her? he said absentmindedly, but the lady was reflecting now, her eyes almost blank, choosing her words: and when what happened happened, she said, when Aurora's uncle plunged our house into mourning, you mustn't believe that that made us any less fond of that girl. What happened, ma'am? Ah, my son, let's not speak of unhappy memories, in those days the hour for vengeance for so many things had come. . . . And returning to the reason for her visit, she kept asking whether the two of them had seen each other again or whether he knew where she lived. It wasn't, she said, that she thought that he might have done something bad with that bad girl: he was almost a child, she knew; perhaps he only knew her from her buying bottles and old paper from him, or simply because he hung around the Barrio Chino with his pals, or perhaps she was a friend of his brother's. . . . No, ma'am, my word of honor, I don't know her.

The darkest part was the cave to one side and we used to sit down in a semicircle in front of Martín, who would lean his back against the wall at the back. Luis lighted the candle stuck into the skull and put it in the center, Mingo turned off the flashlight, we all held hands, and Martín passed out a few pinches of cut tobacco and cigarette paper. We had lots of meetings there, Tits brought tomatoes and onions sometimes and we made salads in a cookie tin and then smoked and talked till very late at night; at other times Amén swiped a can of condensed milk from the Center and we made ourselves little swallows of it with lots of water, and added a little bit of the licorice dissolved in water to a bottle of orange soda: that was our coffee.

"Great for telling stories, I bet," Amén said, rubbing his hands. "You'll get lots of inspiration here, isn't that so, Itchy?" squatting on his heels, his hungry eyes leaping from one face to another in the candlelight: masks in the emptiness, and the cold and the fear waiting on the other side of the rotten boards, there in the street. Luis coughed a lot in there and didn't talk much; we seemed to be able to hear the echo of bombardments and air-raid sirens still. On the walls of earth where the shadows swayed the notches made by pickaxes could still be seen, an area scraped clean, a stone with black and green flakes that could be removed: in behind it was a little oven, and it was there that we hid the candle and the skull, the matches, a Prince Albert can with gunpowder, two Bill Barnes novels and a copy of *Signal* with Messerschmitts in color. The rhythmical, guttural, persuasive voice of Itchy, more and more mysterious: well, even though you don't know her, remembering, you were the right person to ask, do us this favor, the lady said, because you must have seen any number of things going from house to house as you do, you doubtless know so many of these unfortunates.

"Don't fail to tell me if you run across her or have news of her," she added. "The parish will find some way to repay you, and I for my part will do so too, as a personal thing."

The pensive faces nodded.

"Hmmm. Little by little your ass gets soaking wet, that's the trouble. We'll have to bring some sacks."

"Some bricks to sit on would be better. Let's go now," Mingo said, getting up. He turned the flashlight on and blew out the candle. "Leave everything the way it is, we'll be back soon. Follow me, Itchy, the best is yet to come."

With their eyes wide open so uselessly in the dark, feeling their way forward, their memories recover fleeting childish visions: big trucks with their lights off filed furiously through the night swept by antiaircraft searchlights, right there in front of the star-studded mouth of the shelter; the militiamen play football with the skull of a murdered bishop, they say. And suddenly, the wall at the very back scraped bare: it's awfully little, Itchy said disappointedly. It was as though they hadn't had time to finish it, as though the end of the war had caught them by surprise and they had thrown down their picks and their shovels right there, and a rotten wicker basket, and a wheelbarrow with its load of earth, and run happily home. Itchy sniffed: turds, that's the end of that right now, anyone that shits here we'll make eat his turds. The rats scampered after them, you could hear their little paws splashing in the mud. Mingo aimed the flashlight at the base of the back wall. There was a hole the size of a small barrel. This way, follow me, and he knelt down and stuck his head and shoulders through, holding the flashlight pointing backwards so that he could see.

She also asked him why we didn't go to Las Ánimas, not as altar boys like Amén and Tits, but to have a good time and make friends, Itchy remembered as he crawled along on all fours after Mingo and then on his belly: their heads touched the ceiling. So if it's true what the lady told him, that her Aurora had been so good that she even came to be the directress of the Casa, though it was only for a few months during the war, then it's clear why gummy-eyes is suddenly taken with a desire to be in a play at Las Ánimas: he wants to get what he can out of the little orphan girls and then go tell the lady. She herself suggested the idea to him: one or another of the older ones perhaps might know where she lives, and then she added: "and what's more it won't do you any harm to go there from time to time, you need a bit of discipline, my boy; at least there you won't learn anything bad and you wouldn't be roaming the streets all day. . . . "

"Sermon *habemus*," Amén said.

"She handed him a bunch of bullshit, 'just imagine, you'll be doing a work of charity,' " Itchy said. "But what interests Java is dough, or what dough can buy him."

"A small-bore shotgun," Luis said. "That's what he asked the lady for."

75

"You made that up, you dummy," Martín exclaimed in annoyance.

They advanced slowly on their bellies, helping themselves along with their elbows. The passageway was recent, and it smelled of cat-shit. You've worked hard, Itchy said, and Amén, at the tail end, piped up: three nights in a row. And where does it go to? Wait and see. The light from the flashlight swung rhythmically in Mingo's hand, picking out earth and more scraped, dug-out earth: a roof and narrow side passageways with tool-marks. It's twenty-four feet long, Martín said, we're getting there. Behind him, his mouth glued to his buttocks, Luis and his dry cough. You're rotten, kid. And when she said good-bye and left the junk shop, Java stayed sitting in front of the remains of the pastry, his belly full, the little shit, as heavy as a boa constrictor digesting a cow and enveloped in the lady's perfume, in the kindly echo of her voice.

"She came out calling to her Conradito: 'Conradito!' " said Tits. Who was sleeping in the taxi, Mingo remembered. And they had been able to get a good look at him: his well-polished boots, his belt, his little gold star on his chest, his paralyzed legs, and his towel crossed over his chest like a silk scarf. She again stroked Amén's head as he held the door of the taxi open, standing at attention like a bellboy. And then, surrounded with fumes from its gasogene engine, the taxi disappeared around the corner of Camelias, going in the direction of Cerdeña.

The end of the passageway: the old wood of a trunk nailed shut, picked out by the flashlight, blocked the exit from the other side. Mingo pushed the trunk aside and slivers of light came into the passageway. He turned off the flashlight, and holding it in his teeth, his voice cracking, he said: Java? and they heard footsteps and a curse on the other side. The trunk grated on little grains of sand and they came out one after the other, like rabbits from a hole. Blinded by the light, Itchy couldn't see anything or anyone yet. They nudged him in the ribs:

"Wake up. You're in the dressing room of the theater."

It was a part of the crypt, or what would one day be the crypt, nestling among the foundations of the unfinished building weighing heavily over their heads, the future church. He saw a subterranean room with columns, a high vaulted ceiling, with brick walls covered with unfinished patches of cement, and a floor of hard red beaten earth. It was in the shape of a half-moon, in this part anyway, because there was a temporary parapet, a curving wall of bricks, with an opening and a sack over it that served as a door, separating the part of the crypt that was used as a dressing room from the rest of the theater: the little stage and the little orchestra section full not of chairs but of church benches, with backs and prayer benches. Itchy smelled cocoa butter, sour sweat, hair of old ladies. He opened eyes as wide as saucers: leaning against the walls, in violent colors in the strong light, flat and naïve, were landscapes painted on large canvases mounted on strips of wood, gray, snowy mountains, green and leafy groves, flower gardens with fountains of clear water and boxwood arches, houses in fertile valleys in the distance, streets with lighted lanterns, façades with doorways and balconies and little walkways that led nowhere. There were also red and black curtains, trunks of cardboard and plaster trees in the shape of half-circles, old chairs, rickety armchairs, and candelabra, an old divan upholstered in green silk, trunks and wooden boxes full of velvet and gauze with spangles, a console table with wigs and beards, notebooks from the Salesian Drama Collection, a bidet, mirrors, and a bronze bell on four piles of bricks. Itchy whistled in admiration: better than the flea market, he said, and on turning around he saw him from the back, looking at himself proudly in the full-length mirror: dressed in red from his ankles to his sulfurous horns, in red tights and a flowing red cape with a high stiff collar, Satan himself rehearsing wicked gestures of power, clenching his black-and-blue fists with skinned knuckles still stained with the innocent blood of Miguel:Java.

77

VI

A T the beginning all they had was an old revolver with a pearl butt and a loose cylinder. The first contact was finally established at the entrance to the Diagonal subway station: two union organizers from the old days who recognize each other, without having to give the password. But Bundó was to find out later that Palau had trailed him that far, and then immediately disappeared down the stairs of the subway on seeing that the two of them were embracing.

"Hello. It's about time you made up your minds to come," Bundó would say. "How many of you are there?"

"Three. Sendra, Fusam, and me."

"That's all?"

"Be thankful for that. Headquarters didn't even want to send us, especially when they found out about Artemi. It was Sendra's doing."

"Few of you and not in agreement," Bundó said.

"Be patient. The first thing to do is establish contact. Sendra will tell you, let's take a walk."

They went through the center of the Paseo de San Juan,

amid children and pigeons. The itinerant photographer was standing eating his lunch, with his lunch-basket on the back of his cardboard horse. They went into the Alaska Bar and chose a table with no one around.

"Is this a safe place?" Navarro said suspiciously.

"None of them is and all of them are, you'll realize that after you've been in Barcelona a week. What will you have?"

"Wine."

"Are you sure Sendra will show up? He doesn't know the place."

Navarro smiled self-importantly: "He followed us. You'll see him coming in through that door any minute."

Tasting: wine from the region, how well it goes down even if it's watered; almost three years without having any. With Sendra you feel safe, he adds; I think sometimes that he can even make himself invisible, Bundó, no fooling. You ought to have seen him guiding us with his fieldglasses and his knapsack full of flares, we didn't meet a single three-cornered hat. And he thinks: from Perpignan to Berga, passing by Puigcerdá, crossing the Sierra de Montgrony to Montemajor and then along the Guardiola road, he remembers: at a time when they didn't have bases yet, going ahead of the best guides and opening up one of the routes that years later the guerrilla fighter Massana was to use so much. And his work in Toulouse from the beginning, recruiting comrades from the mixed brigade scattered in camps in Algiers and Barcarés, in Montpellier and Carcassonne, comrades mistreated by the Senegalese and then slaving away in factories and vineyards, in mines, on dams and highways, receiving miserable pay, yeah, sweet France. And he thinks of the stormy meetings in the Sindical on the Rue Belford, forming the first group that he wanted to sneak back across the border, of the interminable discussions with those who were wary of Sendra because of his Communist past, and of Sendra's final decision to go ahead with the plan and come anyway, without meeting up with a single three-cornered hat, he's got guts, Bundó, you'll see when you know him.

He always left with two or three *pesetas* for a tip, sometimes a *duro*.

"Thanks, miss."

His eyes glued to the low-cut neckline until she closed the door, smiling at him. Waiting at the elevator, the errand-boy watches out of the corner of his eye the gray bulk kneeling behind the flowerpot. He can barely make out the gray hat, the dark glasses, the chin beard and the big mustache, the brazen fool, he always did like disguising himself as a clown. He would stand there tying his shoelace till the door of the elevator closed.

Patting the Star in the bottom of his overcoat pocket. The coast is clear. Straight to door 333, which does not have the safety latch on. He enters and closes the door with his foot, sticks the barrel of the pistol in the blonde's belly, and she walks backward until she stumbles over the little table. He holds her by the wrist and with his other hand, without letting go of the pistol, he puts his hand over her mouth and stifles her scream. He bumps into a large flower vase with his elbow and it crashes onto the rug.

"Take it off, beautiful."

"What do you want?" she says with fear in her eyes. "Who are you?"

"And the earrings too. I won't hurt you. Hurry."

She jerks the bracelet off, the earrings, the medal on a gold chain. Struggling, she knocks off his dark glasses: his grotesque gaze above the mustache and the false nose rests for a few seconds on the blonde's fresh red mouth.

"What are you going to do? . . . "

"It won't hurt much."

"No, oh please no. . . . "

The blow hits the left side of her head and she falls onto the rug with a dull thud, her open peignoir revealing a round thigh with iodine on it. Without taking his eyes off her, moving quickly: putting the jewelry in his overcoat pocket along with the pistol and the soft hat, picking up the glasses, taking off the

80

cardboard nose and the mustache and hiding all of them in the other pocket before leaving. At the door he takes off the over-coat, turns it inside out and puts it back on again, with the plaid lining showing now. The thigh slightly raised, moving. The inner surface of the thigh like caressing, luminous silk. The trembling of a tendon.

Juan Sendra probably hardly remembers us, much less Pa-lau, the brazen fool. Entering the Alaska Bar his sad boxer's eyes look at Navarro and Bundó as though he didn't see them; he asks for a beer at the bar, keeping an eye on the street and the few customers, and then comes over to them without look-ing at him, on his way to the toilet. Only when he comes out, after casting a careful glance toward the street door, does he make up his mind to sit down with them, grumbling.

"You're a tough one to meet up with, for Christ's sake."

"The contact's in Modelo," Bundó says.

"I know."

"He'll be getting out soon, and Lage surely will too. On the other hand the old man, if he's still alive . . . "

"Don't worry about Artemi; he won't talk," Sendra inter-rupted him. "I know him. Let's get down to practical matters. I don't have much time."

Bundó rapidly reviews the situation: Lage and Viñas in prison; the only safe base they had, a garage in San Adrián, was lost when they nabbed Artemi; but there's another car besides mine, an old Wanderer; few arms, less munitions, and no dough at all. We began with a sawed-off shotgun, Palau will tell you. But Sendra stares at his hands. In short, Bundó adds, we have Meneses, Palau, and me here, waiting for you to come. Waiting years and years.

One day, years later, the plastique would also arrive, in the hold of a ship, camouflaged as sacks of coffee. And Sendra would add, without irony now: What about Ramón?

"He's all right. Living with his cousins in Vallcarca, Ac-tive."

"I can't imagine him without his long black skirts."

Naturally. Congregating by the railing of the Vallcarca bridge, ragged urchins with small-bore rifles are shooting at rats, like rabbits carried along the current. Without a cassock and without a breviary, naturally, hurrying by them, his pipe smoking like a squid shooting out its ink, tall and taciturn, with a beret and a leather jacket. Look, that guy's a defrocked priest, one kid says to another, if he took off his beret you'd see the shaved place on his head, he's dressed in ordinary clothes, I'd swear it's him.

"And what about Palau?"

"He's too independent, Sendra. People here are changing. Let him tell you himself, let him talk to you about his reversible overcoat, ask him what he's doing, how he's been spending his time while we waited for you. . . ."

I'm not about to play guessing games, Arsenio, Sendra interrupts. He wasn't willing to recognize the change that was beginning to take place in all of them, or else he couldn't see it yet: he had blinders over his eyes, like all the exiles. And even though he was later to forbid personal activity, he would never really understand this change, he was too political to understand it. We'll talk about all that, he added. What's happening with Marcos?

He would have to notice it, he would have to say there's one missing, he would ask: what's happening with the sailor, is he still in his rathole? and Bundó would tell him, that same day or some other day: he's a shit, Sendra, that's what's happening. When he found out that Artemi Nin wasn't with you in Toulouse but here in Modelo and getting beaten up every day, he goes and shuts himself up in his hole again, may I be struck dead if I'm lying, it was he himself that put up the wall, I don't know where he got the iron bars and the cement. He goes out on some nights to stretch his legs in the neighborhood, they say, and he even goes to the port, he's out of his mind, he says he doesn't want to hear about anything and then suddenly one night he appears and asks for a submachine gun. He doesn't know what he wants, I think he's sick. I'm not sick, but don't count on me if I have to risk my neck, I'm not even up to distributing handbills on a bad night when it's freezing and there's no moon, I'm not even up to that. Palau is the only one who knows what's happening to me, he understood me from the first day, there on the balcony.

Open onto the Calle Salmerón, despite the cold. His hands in his pockets and the big cigar in his mouth, looking at the soldiers parading by amid stopped streetcars, coming down from Lesseps with their flags and rifles and people pouring out into the street to clap them on the back, look, to shake their hands, to throw flowers at them, look how many blue shirts, how many bastards had them all ironed and waiting, that windy and cursed twenty-sixth of January. Crying like a baby but smoking a Havana, that was what he was doing, and his kid clinging to his legs and crying at seeing him cry. Shhh, little one, this isn't going to last, *foc nou i merda per els que quedin* — we'll really fuck over the ones who are left. The victors passed by, and the wind whipped the broken blinds on the façades of the buildings. His ashen horse face bathed in tears, his black velvet eyes brimming with tears on turning around to look at me from that balcony jutting out over the *vivas,* the anthems and the songs, and me buried in my armchair at the back of the room: the last one, he said, brandishing the cigar, and you're going back to your rat-hole, poor sailor, they'll be wanting to track you down even more than the others. I probably didn't have the strength left to smile, but I smiled anyway: what did you mean, man, that this was going to be your last cigar, you're too much of a show-off, Palau, you've always liked living well and in a certain way it's saved you from so much intolerance, so much humiliation.

There in that old apartment on the Calle Salmerón, close to the Fontana subway stop, they would establish a new temporary base of operations, when he and his wife and kid had moved to the La Salud district and Palau was sleeping heaven knew where. The building threatened to fall to pieces, and was destined to be torn down, but when the Organization decided to send the first group, Palau still had the key to the apartment. But Sendra was nonetheless mistrustful.

"When we leave we'll throw the key away in the sewer and not mention it again," he said. "I'll look for a safer place."

They will arrive one by one, after midnight, sitting down around the table stained by the light from the Petromax, a kerosene lantern with red fringes that projects a rain of blood on the walls. They will make sure that not a speck of light escapes through the cracks in the shutters nailed shut. Someone will crack the usual joke, are there any recluses today, and as always the defense would come from Palau, leave the kid alone, you jokers, the less he goes out the better for all of us. And Navarro nervously: "Okay, are you with us or not?"

"Sure. All you have to do is send me a message. Have your girl with the bicycle bring it."

"Hmmm, you don't know what you want, Marcos."

Sendra staring at us with the battered eyes of a famous boxer. Are you sick? he finally said.

"I'm okay."

"Sit down. And the rest of you shut up. Give him some tobacco."

He opens a little suitcase on a chair, he doesn't see their curious looks pinching my nerves, he doesn't see that they're laughing up their sleeves, that they're making fun of the beard and the tattoo, that they're scaring him with their clumsy jokes: clapping their pistol-finger in his shoulder to surprise him or snapping their fingers next to his ear, you're always distracted, you've got no reflexes, what will you do with a submachine gun if your eyes can't stand the sun any more? Palau shrugs, settling the plaid overcoat thrown across his shoulders. He lights a blond-tobacco cigarette and throws the package on the table, shut up and smoke, you jokers. Navarro's knotted hands of a lathe operator pass round the Afare papers: only if you have to go across the border, meanwhile you'd do well to bury them.

"Since when are you anarchists so well organized?" Palau says.

"We're all equal now."

"You'll never be our equals."

"Lower your voice, animal" — this from Fusam. "We've gotten together to see what needs to be done, not argue about the same old thing again."

"It was a joke, you," Palau said, patting the pocket where he had put the identification papers. "I'll always keep it with me; it'll bring me luck."

"Anyway, Palau is right," Bundó says. "Are we starting that shit about bureaucracy all over again?"

This time they wanted to do things right, Sendra would say again and again, though he has to keep repeating it for a long time afterward, on that night when he divides the plastique in two on the table. Prepare it, Marcos. Navarro, bring the mechanical pencils. And you, bring me the plan.

"Do things right?" Palau says. "Fine. With the Germans at the frontier. Haven't the Nazis fingered all of you from the Sindical yet?"

Sendra doesn't answer. He sits wearily down at the table and opens the plan that they put in front of him, searching for district thirteen with his finger.

"I think they'll even get into the country," "Taylor" says dreamily.

"I hope so. If the Germans crossed the Pyrenees, we'd become guerrillas," Navarro says, still dreaming.

Knead the plastique into two thin layers. The real article. It was probably stolen in France, like the dynamite for the first jobs and that rudimentary material for making all sorts of explosive articles, all stolen from under the Germans' very noses, in the mines and at the work sites where dams were being constructed, where comrades still worked. Sendra asking Palau if he'd gone to the British Embassy for the leaflets.

Palau grumbling: did you take me for a bellboy at the Ritz?

I wasn't able to, I had to take the kid to the movies today. Moreover, what do we want all those mountains of paper for anyway, frankly, Sendra, we've got to break more eggs, do more damage, I'm tired of painting posters and distributing handbills. . . . Sendra must have noticed my clumsy hands, the damn things aren't coming out right, and it's such an easy job.

"This isn't kid stuff" — Bundó to Palau — "wait and see, don't be the first one to pull out."

"Do you think that present is nothing?" the hunchback says, pointing to my hands.

Fusam, all hunched over, running zigzag down the middle of the Calle Mallorca, the open skirts of his black overcoat fluttering like a crow around his hump, avoiding the bursts of machine-gun fire from the policeman posted in the door of La Provincial. Somehow intuiting the explosion about to take place suddenly behind his back, the cop throws himself to the ground, leaving off shooting for a few seconds, which the hunchback takes advantage of to reach the corner. Almost at the same time, a black vomit of glass and shattered wood leaps out into the street through the door of the vestibule, falling on the policeman stretched out on the sidewalk. Huddled against the wall on all fours, two women scream. The first Falangists come out the door of La Provincial, unharmed, coughing. Wriggling around the corner, Fusam reaches the black Wanderer cruising along the sidewalk with the door open, and my hands don't tremble as I pull him in by the lapels, with Palau patting me on the back as a sign of approval: a little more practice and you'll be like you were before.

Palau showed his big yellow teeth like dominoes in the top balcony of the Gran Price; how he liked these boxing nights when our fear allowed us to mingle with the crowd. He handed round big fat cigars and Romero kept shouting throw him a left hook, to the liver, to the liver, nudging Meneses in the ribs with a laugh.

"They told me you've gone and gotten your Margarita. I

trust you're not taking her to the Shanghai — they might recognize you."

"It's called the Bolero now," "Taylor" says.

"It doesn't matter, it's still the same owner. And to get back to what I was saying, the sailor certainly behaved well the other day. But," Palau said, looking at Navarro with a skeptical expression on his face, "that's also risking your ass for very little, you know. There are things that do more damage and bring better rewards. . . . "

Jaime Viñas, having difficulty being heard amid the crowd's booing of the referee: for example?

"Drop it," Navarro says. "Don't you see he's just shooting his mouth off?"

"How'd you like a punch in the nose, Navarrete?"

"Come on," Jaime says in a low voice. "Listen, anything's better than a cell in the slammer."

Palau discovers that the lace of his left shoe is undone. He kneels down, smiles under the brim of the hat, suddenly stands up, sticks the barrel of the pistol hidden underneath the folded overcoat on his arm as with the other hand he neatly relieves him of his billfold, murmuring: like this, I keep telling my kid: Mingo, if you want to see the end of ridiculous people, just take their wallets away from them.

"You're always up to something, Palau — there's no changing you."

VII

THEY were working their way through the hall on their knees, coming toward him dragging their feet wrapped in ragged strips of cloth behind them.

"Dr. Malet is looking for you, Ñito," the first one said, wringing out the mop in the bucket. "He wonders where you've been."

"Ha. None of his business."

"He seemed hopping mad. He said that when you're not in the bar he doesn't know where you are. Careful where you step."

"On your aunt's ass — go tell her," the caretaker said, stepping on the scrubbed part and leaping like a monkey.

"Watch what you're doing."

"I am."

"You're in a bad way, old man," the other one chimed in, settling her knees more comfortably on the soaking-wet cushion. "You clumsy thing. You could be more careful."

The caretaker continued on his way down the hall between walls with white tile, and then through a side passageway to the exit of the clinic. He walked along with his head down, rubbing his unshaven face, yawning. Students patted him on the back as they ran by, and nuns and nurses in a hurry went on ahead of him. On the stairway of the Faculty of Medicine the sun blinded his eyes: he never noticed anything until he reached the bar, the street and the bar itself were nothing more than a continuation of the inside corridors, the invisible passageways of time. He chose a table in front of the silent television set and saw the end of a blurred football match in the rain, on the muddy field of a faraway country. The nurses' heels rang on the wooden floor, at the tables were caretakers eating sandwiches and students chattering together, and on the walls was a ghostlike landscape, a pale grove of trees against a background of gray drizzle. When the broadcast was over, the muddy field that made movement difficult lingered in his eyes, grotesque figures struggling in a nightmare of silence; his numb, bloody fingers on the plastic table top painfully unwrapped the tissue paper around the piece of pie that Sister Paulina had swiped in the kitchen; then he turned his head toward the man at the counter with a mute plea in his eyes: Just one, Paco. Here too the students come up to him, as in the corridors, asking him for the mimeographed tests, and his hand takes the sheet of paper out of his pocket and puts the tip away, and if it's a girl his hand moves very, very slowly in order to give his eyes time: the knees, the little short skirt, the breasts compressed by textbooks, would you like a cough drop, miss, they make you kiss your sweetheart better, ha . . . ."

"Just one little beer, don't be mean, Paco."

"No, no more credit. Listen, Dr. Malet and Dr. Albiol have been asking for you."

"Were they together?"

"No."

"Buzzards," he said, chewing on an ice-cold mouthful, some sorry thing from the big hospital kitchen right in the middle of the pie. "They can go to hell."

He got absorbed in the television program, his eyes parched

by an emptiness: I'm going to have to go back to Sister Paulina and her concoctions, well, it's better than nothing, they ought to take that guy to Lourdes and be done with it. He fell asleep in front of the gray images of cops and robbers, seeing the other invalid in the other wheelchair: the same way of propelling himself, elbows flapping in the air, stretching his neck and nodding his head like a thirsty tortoise, anxious to get in front of him and get a good look at his waist and ask him: "What's your name, kid?" perhaps smelling his leather wristband and his scale hanging from his belt. "Well, listen to me carefully, Java" — maybe his fly — if the bishop comes out that door instead of this one turn the chair around. But hurry. Yes, sir: he could still see Tits peeing endlessly beneath the stars, leaning against the trunk of an acacia in the Calle Escorial. "How good you are at stories, you fairy, it's like a movie." "There are movies that are true" — it was Martín's voice. "What happened?"

"Not so fast. They haven't done the autopsy on them yet."

Paco stood there watching him with his hands in the sink, that persistent vacant smile annoyed him: if he's already tight, what does it matter, and took the bottle and the glass, left it on the table filled to overflowing with cognac and went back to the counter without saying a word. But he caught the happy blink, the gratitude behind his eyelashes. What happened, tell us.

"What happened was that we were all in Lourdes pushing the wheelchair, pushing the lieutenant in uniform to the very center of the plot and a fucking mess. There wasn't any miracle at the end. . . . But things don't begin here, but before the trip, in the bishop's palace, that was where they got acquainted: the two of them are part of a delegation of parishioners who are organizing a pilgrimage to Lourdes and are waiting to be received by the bishop in a carpeted reception room. What silence in this palace, what a hissing of prayers and what murmurs of velvet, what silken noises. At times that plump catechism teacher who's the daughter of a sergeant pushes

Conradito's wheelchair, with an embroidered white mantilla on her head. . . . "Señorita Paulina, that's who," Amén's impatient voice interrupts. He is sitting in the fork of the acacia tree, holding up the starry night with his heavy adult's head. On the sidewalk, Mingo and Luis have already gotten everything all mixed up, asking what was he doing there, Itchy, how did he manage to sneak into the bishop's palace? Didn't he know the invalid by then?

There's nothing like being crippled to inspire confidence: limping and showing a stiff, twisted, crazy hand: a poor paralytic, a helpless, pitiful creature. But he was also accompanied by the catechism teacher, helping to push the wheelchair with the lieutenant in his dress uniform: shiny boots, corduroy trousers, the black patch with the yellow star pinned on the left-hand side of his jacket. "So they met each other there, then?" Tits said, clinging to the trunk of the tree and shaking his cock before buttoning up. "Wasn't the first time they saw each other in a bar, one day when he invited him to have tuna pies, don't you remember?" "Shut up, tramp, don't interrupt."

No, the Lourdes part would be before the tuna pies, one day when he dropped by the parish house because he'd seen some yellow papers in the streets with the announcement: "Pilgrimage to Lourdes with the ill." And he wanted to escape from here, to go to France, and he thought: if they see I'm crippled. And he presented himself at the Center limping and with the crazy hand that he couldn't hold down, which suddenly began trembling, a Quasimodo, kids, somebody with meningitis like the ones in Cottolengo Hospital. He made a very good impression, but they told him he couldn't go, the number of places was limited, they were full up, another trip. It was that catechism teacher. And as he was going away, terribly disappointed, she called him back, do you want to earn some cash, come tomorrow morning at ten, you'll be a stretcher bearer, we're taking sick people to the bishop's palace and there's always a need for a little help. Out of pity, as a favor so he could make a little dough: and that's how it happened.

"Okay, okay," Luis said. "We're in the bishop's palace, go on."

Hushed footsteps, murmurs beneath the richly carved ceiling, red curtains, old chairs, lamps without bulbs: with paschal candles, the bishop's palace with restrictions on electricity? I can't believe it, Itchy. You turn your head from one side of the reception room to the other and look at everything, standing fascinated in the center of the big carpet that gives off a smell of good beeswax, in the very center of forces, of powers that he still knows nothing of. How are you dressed? the same worn pants as always, that colored bandana knotted around your neck, the leather wristband and the hunting jacket dyed blue. Other groups were waiting for an audience too: a half-dozen nuns, two little country priests, Brothers in white chin-cloths accompanying schoolchildren, a little boy dressed in his first-communion admiral's outfit, with ruffled shirt and patent-leather shoes and all the rest.

A little door opens and a tall, smiling priest appears, pointing at us authoritatively with his finger: Parish of the Expiatory Souls in Purgatory? this way, and we followed him, and another carpeted hall, another antechamber, another smaller reception room with tall chairs, curtains, and doors padded in velvet. Crystal lamps and the smell of perfumed wax. Las Ánimas isn't a parish yet, sir, the young catechism teacher explains; that's our fondest wish, but all there is so far is the chapel. And the priest, smilingly: I know, my daughter, but we will soon begin the work again, His Excellency has a great interest in it, you will soon see this holy wish realized. And now if we would be so kind as to wait here, His Excellency would be out immediately. And he goes off, swinging his arms, looking like a bell in his wide, rustling cassock, and disappears through the door. We all keep our eyes glued on that door, in a group on one corner of the rug, as if we were surrounded by a flood. Limping, you help the catechism teacher place the invalid's chair facing the door, but there's another one and you don't know which one His Excellency will come out of. Then for the first time the lieutenant exchanges a glance with him, a few words, and from then on he won't take his eyes off him. Like this, look. With his hands between his thighs, under the blanket covering his legs, that's how he looks at him. . . .

"What do you mean? Had he realized that he wasn't crippled, had he discovered him?"

"Maybe. But that wasn't why he was looking at him so hard."

And he realizes. Suddenly his hand starts trembling, his eye, his cheek give a nervous twitch: he is playing his role. But the other eye, a terrier's eye, meets the lieutenant's insistent gaze.

"Super," Amén said. "Java knows all the tricks."

"Shut up," Luis protested. "Go on, Itchy, it's great."

The door silently opens and the purple-clad figure of His Excellency is framed in the doorway for an instant; a short little man with a belly and no neck, smiling, with his head tilted to one side, an Excellency who looks as if he had a broken neck. Pinned to his chest is just one of his many decorations: the Medal of Military Merit. He was probably not fifty-five yet, but it was impossible not to see him already in his eighties, and still vicar-general of the military forces. Behind him is a yellow and violet glow, the light of his private apartments or his office: ah, so there *is* electricity there, how can that be? The reverend prelate slowly moves forward and behind them there appears the tall priest, who closes the door and follows him, swaying from one side to the other to the rear of him as though he were afraid His Excellency might fall backward. The committee of parishioners has lined up behind the lieutenant. Java leans one hand on the back of the wheelchair, the other one with the trembling held up very visibly: may they have pity on me, in Christ's name may they have pity. The bishop stops in front of them with his hands crossed on his fat belly and his eyelids half-closed with simple goodness; some of them kneel and kiss the pastoral ring and the bishop bends down, lifts them up one by one and begins to speak: have a good trip to Lourdes, pack love and faith in your bags. He takes a friendly interest in the sick who have come as representatives of the others: Conradito first, praise for his glorious lieutenant's uniform, the universities have been the salvation of Spain, the blood so generously shed by young men like him will flower in benedictions, how are those legs, my son? They don't get me very far even with wheels, Your Excellency, but God will provide. Ah, that's the way, don't lose your good humor and please convey my benediction to your mother, what a wonderful woman and what a saint. Peeking timidly over the head of the lieutenant, your mad hand attracts the bishop's attention as it trembles and contracts like a pitiful claw. But before the prelate can say anything, to your great surprise, Conrado is already introducing you without too much formality, smiling familiarly at the bishop, almost winking his eyes: this is the lad I was talking to you about, Your Excellency, he's so anxious to go to Lourdes that he's invented himself a paralysis. . . . Blessings on your youth, my son, faith moves mountains, the bishop says to him looking at his mouth, and the mad hand quiets down and is still, you let your arm fall to your side and rest. All sensations except hunger disappear from your body. What has happened?

With his hands again crossed on the purple sash, His Excellency steps back and his eyes inspect the group, looking at them in silence one by one, his head gently bowed and with a beatific smile on his face. His humble, kindly eyes do not linger for long on any one of these faces anxious for his blessing, or on any of the bodies tortured by illness and suffering: it is evident that his paternal love is equal for all, that he has no favorites. When his eyes meet yours they linger even less: an imperceptible blink, and on to the next person. Then he steps back a few paces more to have a look at the entire group, and with his loving glance he embraces all of them. They bow their heads and kneel, and he gives them his solemn blessing.

"Could Conradito have believed that he was going to be cured in the pool?" Amén asked. "And that Java's gummy eyes would be cured?"

"Shut up, once and for all, or I'll make you eat the gummy stuff in yours," Martín said, and cuffed him over the head.

His Excellency retires to his apartments, still assisted by the tall, nimble priest. The latter returns to the reception room to see the visitors out, and standing at the door of the antechamber as all of them are filing out, when you pass by he says: wait just a moment, my son, His Excellency has expressed the desire to converse for a time with you, wait for me here. I'll get to Lourdes, you think, I've got it made, I've got it made, standing all alone in the very center of the elegant rug, at the very point where the complicated, beautiful, symmetrical arabesques meet. But you are not taken through the door that you thought you would be. You start losing the limp and the tremor as you walk down another corridor with stained-glass windows where sailboats are breasting furious waves and huge armies in perspective are campaigning amid clouds of gunsmoke, and shields, swords, and damascened daggers, following the long-legged priest, who will say nothing else to you, not even as he closes the door behind you. Red damask on prayer benches and cushions, a reception room with a gleaming chandelier in the ceiling, tall shelves of books, deep armchairs, a picture of Pius XII and a huge crucifix on the wall, the bloody feet among candles and jars of dizzying flowers.

Buried in the armchair, you pass the comb through your mussed hair, take out a toothpick and clean your nails. A door opens and in comes His Excellency: a cope with pretty edgings on the front, a mysterious shield on the back. He advances like a tortoise over the soft rug and a multitude of little birds sing in the ample folds of his cope. He sits down, ramrod-straight, before him. He has risen respectfully, and the bishop gives a nod to indicate that he should sit down, and they remain there, face-to-face, looking at each other in a kindly way. He hopes in vain for a few words from the man in purple, but the latter says nothing, his hands hidden beneath the cope; the same gentle little smile, the same little head tilted to one side, his eyes of a dreaming bird, his venerable double chin. He smells of after-shave lotion. Java melts, smiles in confusion, hopes in vain that he will say something to him; it is hard to sustain the bishop's innocent, almost childlike gaze. And he turns his eyes away for an instant to look at the swan-necked lamp, the tall draperies, the peeling mother-of-pearl cherubim, the gramophone and the pile of records without jackets. Virelays, he thinks, Salves, solemn stuff on the organ.

"What parish are you from, my son?" — finally his nasal, quivering cavernous Easter Sunday voice.

"I don't know, Your Excellency. You see, I'm from Las Ánimas, in the precinct of La Salud, but since Las Ánimas isn't a parish yet . . . "

"So that's why."

"There's another one near there, in Guinardó, they call Christ the King."

"I know it. A mission parish." A pause and then: "What's your name?"

"Daniel Javaloyes. But my friends call me Java, Your Excellency."

"Call me Fermín."

He nodded affably without his expression changing. Another silence, a very long one. You'd think the palace was asleep, there's not even a fly to be heard. Five minutes go past, perhaps ten: sitting very rigidly in the chair, staring at him, dressed in his ample silk cope, he looks like a little porcelain figurine. Java suspects that it's necessary to say or do something, he doesn't know what. He takes the comb out again and runs it quickly through his hair. At one point His Excellency says: Are you thirsty, my son, do you want something to drink? and his face lights up, two roses appear on his cheeks, beardless still. We might take a glass of sherry; it's a digestive. He moves slowly, his hands peek out like two little white rats from between the embroidered edging of the cope and run playfully toward the bottle and the glasses lined up on the shelf. His rosy cheeks swelling, he blows on some little motes of dust on the surface of the two glasses he has chosen, fills them half full, offers Java one with the fingers of a celebrant, raises his own: may you have a good trip, may the Virgin grant what you ask, my son. I'm not going to Lourdes, Fermín, he says mournfully, they say there's no room for me. What's that? — don't worry, I'll arrange it.

Sitting there looking at each other, the sherry warming his insides, tickling his heart, silence between them: it becomes so long this time that it is clear that the bishop is waiting for something, but what, Java ponders the urgency of doing something, asking him something, but what, kids, what?

"To enter the seminary" — it was Amén's shrill voice, mingled with the rumble of the black car painfully making its way up the Calle Escorial: a girl's face glued to the window watching the rowdies sitting on the sidewalk. "Saying to him: I want to be a fisher of men."

"No. Asking him for an Arrow's shirt and a machete," Tits said absent-mindedly, looking at the red glow in the back of the gasogene. "But it doesn't matter, go on. What happens then?"

What happens is that the bishop asks him: "Do you like music, my son?"

"I should say so."

"What sort of music?"

He says after a few seconds' hesitation: "Classical music. Waltzes especially."

The bishop turns his back, goes over to the gramophone and chooses a record, blows the dust off it, puts it on the gramophone, brushes the needle with the tip of his finger, and with the greatest of care allows the point to enter the groove: "Tales from the Vienna Woods." And loud — it echoes through the whole reception room as His Excellency, again in front of him and very quiet, looks at him, smiling affectionately, looks and looks at him, endlessly. I have to do something, Java cries to himself, but what, dear God, what? And the waltz fills the air with its sweet strains, falling on their heads like honey, and suddenly, overwhelmed by the evidence, as though he had had a revelation, he finally understands, everything is explained. And he slowly rises to his feet, walks over to His Excellency, and offering him his hand, palm up, says to him: "Most Illustrious and Most Reverend Bishop, may I have this dance?"

Having arrived at the other end of Escorial, on the short steep incline of La Travesera, the rear-engined gasogene farted and gave off sparks and bits of burned charcoal. Don't let it distract you, Itchy, don't stop now.

Have you ever held a bishop in your arms? They smell good: of virgin wax, of parquet floors of the houses of rich people, of spikenard and funerals, of Floid after-shave lotion. Sticking his arm out from under the cope, he held him by the waist and with the two of them on tiptoe, eyes closed, flying, flying gloriously all over the room to the point of dizziness as they followed the rhythm of the waltz, His Excellency's cope opening like wings of fire and the edges swaying and brushing the honey-colored draperies, the velvet armchairs, and the green divan and the folding screen and the men shot at dawn, he whirled him around and around till his mind went blank, till the yellow towel worked itself loose and also began flying through the air. He whirled as though on little invisible wheels beneath his silk skirts, his head thrown back and his eyes closed in ecstasy. He unctuously murmured the words *in te confido non erubescam* in Latin and leaned his forehead on his partner's shoulder, with his brilliantined hair, his little black mustache, and his face white as wax. . . .

"But he didn't get to Lourdes," Itchy said. "The lieutenant did, though, but there was no miracle: they took him seated in his wheelchair and that's the way they brought him back. Nothing."

Mingo had gotten up from the sidewalk with a yawn, with the night dew on his buttocks. He squatted there, rubbing his frozen backside. Amén had loosened his new transparent plastic belt and took a pig bone out of his pocket and proposed a game of knucklebone before going to sleep. Martín, Luis, and Tits suggested different plots, but nobody was interested in going on, though Mindo kept saying: so he didn't get to Lourdes.

"He got something much better" — did you already say that? "He got Conradito to notice him" — have you said that yet? he thought, gulping down the last mouthful of pie, the last sip of cognac. And what happened to him a few days later in the Continental Bar, buying old paper, his surprise at hearing the proprietress say: do you want to earn a couple of *duros* without very much work? well drop by tomorrow at such and such a place and at such and such a time, and I'll introduce you to a little girlfriend of mine, yes, that's how he casually began his career, one day when he was acting as a stretcher-bearer. . . .

"I've finally found you, you belly-splitter" — the hearty voice of Dr. Malet, his big hand on his shoulder, in the same good humor as usual — what happened to the errand I sent you on?"

"Nothing yet."

The caretaker got up, gave the inside of his glass an expert lick, took a toothpick, and looking over at the counter waved and said: 'Bye, Paco.

"What do you mean nothing?" Dr. Malet said. "They've done the autopsy already. They're going to bury them and here you are peacefully sitting here, helping your cirrhosis along, ha ha, come on, have a smoke. You're one of the most useless ones around. I was waiting for you in the laboratory" — then lowering his booming voice — "since it doesn't look like they have any family. Ah, you rascal, I bet you share out the bones to pretty girl students who ask for them, am I right?"

"Somebody may still come," Ñito said, moving toward the door, crushing the toothpick between his decayed teeth. With a sudden burst of speed in his legs, he reached the exit and slipped off without hearing Dr. Malet calling him. Buzzards, he spat, buzzards.

He locked himself inside the storage room, saw the filth on the floor, blood and dust, the refrigerator with the corpses stored away in boxes, the dim light of the bulb in the ceiling filtering down on the rigid forms on the stretchers, on the dirty linen. Still together, shoulder to shoulder, the twins had matted hair and wrinkled genitals, as dark as raisins. All he gave her was an absentminded glance that scarcely lingered for a second on her old woman's legs, with their heavy calves and thick ankles. He put the remains of the pie in the drawer of the little table, then washed out some socks, dried them on the cord hung between the standing wardrobe and the hat rack, and in his bare feet, treading an indescribable grime adhering to the tiles, he drew out the drawer of the refrigerator, drew up the stool, sat down and pushed the edge of the sheet back: searching with a strange obstinacy, squinting because of the close focus, his hypnotized eyes ran over the long, serene profile, like someone reviewing the cloudy memory of a life. Gently raising up the lashless lids with his finger, he could read: in all dead people's eyes there were those depths of a muddy swamp, that childhood paradise drowned by the waters. Buzzards, worse than buzzards.

VIII

I SAID I didn't want to see you here tonight." Java turned his head to look at him, whirled around and the red cape fluttered round him, reflected in the mirror. "Oh, I didn't know you'd come back."

"What are you doing dressed as Satan?"

"Lucifer."

"Have they given you a part in the play?"

"Not yet. Don't touch anything," Java cautioned, trying on a chin beard and some pointed mustaches that smelled of spirit gum.

Martín was rummaging through the drawers of the console table, and put on a black face mask; Tits was trying on wings in front of the mirror; Amén was putting on a silver belt with a sword and unsheathing it; Mingo and Luis were trying to plug up the passageway, put the bricks in place, and push the trunk back across the entrance. Java stopped them.

"There's no use doing that; you have to leave right away."

"Itchy wanted to say hello to you, you bastard, that's all we came for," Mingo growled. "And to show him the shelter."

"They mustn't see you here," Java said nervously, as Amén came by, looking at him with a mocking smile. "What are you staring at?"

He threw the mustaches and the chin beard on the table. Amén fingered his horns.

"Flabby as sausages," he said. "You don't look like the Devil, Java."

"You look like Captain Marvel," Tits said. "The cape is great."

"Clear out, damn it."

"You look like a bishop," Amén said.

"Didn't he ever tell you that he met the bishop once?" Itchy said. "I swear. Remind me to tell you about it in a while. . . . "

"Tits, leave the wigs alone," Java said in an irritated voice, pushing him. "Come on, get out, all of you."

"Listen," Itchy said, coming over to him. The bulb in the ceiling illuminated his shaved head, his scabs covered with green sulfur. "Why doesn't the cripple let you be in the play?"

"I know why," Java said crossly.

"He's got it in for you."

"He doesn't. But he'll give me the part tonight, I swear it on my mother's head. I have a plan, I've made a deal with Fueguiña and Juanita."

He had his head bent as though to attack, a faraway look in his little gummy eyes. His droopy cloth horns quivered and he was walking around in the red cape like a villain in a musketeers movie.

"How were things back home?"

"They made me work like a horse," Itchy said as he poked around inside a big wooden box, amid straw and old newspapers wrapped around a half-broken set of dishes. He heard Java roar: get the hell out of here, and said to him: "You sticking around?"

"He turns out the lights and stays hidden in the theater, among the benches," Amén said, "and when they're in the middle of rehearsals he sits down and lets himself be seen, as though he'd just come in the front door; do you get the picture?"

"I'm sorry about your father," Java suddenly cut in. "Did he leave anything before he hanged himself, some letter, an address of one of the whores he knew?..."

Itchy was looking at himself in the mirror now: he spat on the floor.

"He didn't know how to write."

Java got undressed, hurriedly pulling off the red demon-suit. His clothes were in the bidet. Itchy saw it and exclaimed:

"How come you brought that pussy-washer in here? Or isn't it the same one?"

He pushed aside the clothes and saw the trails of powder in the glistening bowl: a dense network of tobacco-colored lines.

"It's the same one," Luis said, sitting cross-legged on the trunk. "It was Martín's idea."

"Okay," Itchy said. "All those orphan girls have dirty cunts and we'll wash them for them. When shall we catch one of them, Java?"

"Take it easy. We'll see."

"You must be good friends with them by now."

"Who me, are you kidding? Come on, once and for all, you guys, scram."

Itchy was poking around among the scenery.

"What about the other tortures?"

"Back over there," Tits said, "well hidden."

"And that bell?"

"The Infernal Bell," Amén said. "Something new, kid. Want to try it out?" he said, grabbing the hammer. "Get inside."

"Beast," Java said. "They're going to hear you. Let it alone...."

He was sitting on the floor putting on heavy rationed boots with cleats on the soles and metal toe-plates: they looked at him enviously. A present from the widow Galán, Itchy said, and Java got up and signaled to him. He raised up the sack covering the little door in the brick wall and went out onto the unlighted stage. Come on, he said, and Itchy followed him: there was enough light filtering through the sack for them to see the deserted board stage, the tiny prompter's box, lined with red cloth, the dented zinc footlights, and beyond that the dark theater with the mass benches lined up, without a center aisle. Java pushed him toward the dressing room again: you've seen everything, now beat it, you guys, and he stationed himself next to the trunk, with a brick in each hand, ready to close up the narrow passageway as soon as they left. The last one to go through was Amén, and Java stopped him to search him; he had a devil's wig under his sweater; Java discovered it because of the holes in the sweater. Bring it here, you bastard; you're going to end up in the reform school.

I was dying to see you, but we obeyed you, gummy-eyes, we left you alone in there, we heard you close the passageway off like a madman and push the trunk back. We left through the entrance to the shelter on the Calle Escorial. It wasn't cold at all and the stars were shining; it wasn't very late: there was time to sit on the sidewalk under an acacia and tell each other a story. We saw two women in mourning with sacks on their shoulder; they disappeared, bending low, around the corner of the Calle Laurel. Then Amén took off his plastic belt and proposed a game of knucklebone: when Java wasn't around we often amused ourselves playing the most childish games.

But it was no use: what we would really have liked to do was to see you act, you clever bastard. So we separated and I went with Tits to his house on the Carmelo road; there were windows lighted in the huts, radios blaring, a baby crying: dinnertime, no doubt. I said goodbye to Tits and went back to the shelter. I crawled through the passageway on my knees in the dark, a rat ran over my leg and with one blow I sent it flying through the air, then I took the bricks down and pushed the trunk aside. They were already rehearsing on the lighted stage, reciting their lines slowly and emphatically; I recognized the director's voice: Wrath inflames my breast, my fire is that of hell; I rage, and hence, Let others rage as well! I was dying to see you act. On the brick wall that separated me from the stage there were holes the size of coins, used to tie down the flats on the day of the performance; I chose the lowest one, sat down on a cardboard tree trunk, and closed one eye: I could see "Wheaty" — Juanita — as the Virgin awaiting her turn in the wings, with her hands together as though she were praying, but yawning, five shepherds around the fire and the cooking pot, with sheepskin coats and tambourines, and the prompter in the box, the oldest girl from the Casa and responsible for bringing the others back safely to the Calle Verdi before midnight. There was no sign of Fueguiña. I wondered where the one who was giving the orders could be hidden when the heavy honey-colored drapes moved a bit and from between them came the high double bird's squeak, then the silver pommel of a cane, and finally the lieutenant in his wheelchair, with brilliantined hair, a black mustache and a face as white as wax. His tight jacket with square shoulder boards gave him the air of a fragile, obstinate hero. The top button of the jacket was unbuttoned, revealing the fine cream-colored towel around his neck.

He directed the play from there, firmly and with authority, at times brusquely invading the stage with his knees thrust forward in his wheelchair, handling it with diabolical skill and speed, so as to situate a character helpfully, correct some detail of a costume, a fold, a wig. He had his notebook in his lap, on the maroon robe tucked around his legs, with the cane in one hand and a bamboo pointer in the other. Lucifer's tardy arrival wasn't normal, he said: where can he be, he always arrives late but not this late, followed by his favorite swearword: damn.

"He won't come."

I was dying to see you, you joker: how you got up from the last bench, where the shadows had hidden you up until then, how you came confidently striding down the side aisle, how you said:

"He won't be coming, sir. He's got a broken arm."

"Oh hell," the little shepherds said in chorus.

"Something's always happening to him," the prompter said.

"He's a very frail boy," "Wheaty" put in.

The director rolled the wheelchair to the center of the stage and braked, the shepherds moved aside, the little pointer whistled through the air.

"What are you doing here?" he added, squinting to see you better in the half-light of the theater: Java was nervous, as he always was when he saw you from too close up and in public. "Who told you that you could come in?"

"His mother sent me. She says he broke his arm playing leapfrog in the Parque Güell. He won't be coming, he can't play Lucifer."

The director reflected for a few seconds.

"Is that true?" and his delicate hands moved the wheels, the notebook slid from his lap, he abruptly turned his back on you, called to the Virgin and sent her to the telephone in the sacristy to see if it was true. Remember, there was a telephone at Miguel's. The Virgin came back and said, it's true, her hands clasped fervently together, he's got his arm in a plaster cast and is in bed, the Immaculate Virgin lied: as you had told her she should.

The cripple didn't look at you as he said:

"Very well, you may leave then."

"Señorita Paulina has given me permission to see the rehearsals. I'd like very much to be in the cast of the play, captain."

"Don't call me captain. And we don't need you for now, as I've already told you once."

"I'd like to play the part of Lucifer, Señorito Conrado. I know it by heart."

You were already climbing up onto the stage, your footsteps resounded on the boards and you faced him with a smile, sure of getting the upper hand: I bet you gave him a beating in your mind. Your legs parted and firmly planted, your thumbs hooked in your back pants pocket, the red bandana around your neck and your muffler hanging down over your shoulder: "I think it will suit you, sir. Try me out, you'll see how satisfied you'll be."

"No" — without looking you in the eye but nonetheless looking at you. "Don't insist," he said, touching the wheels, going backward, whirling the chair around as though looking for an exit. "No one can substitute for Miguel. . . . Well, let's not waste any more time, Christmas is practically upon us. You'll take his place, but only at rehearsals. That way we can continue. Don't hope for anything else; he'll play the part when he comes back."

"He won't be back, Señorito Conrado. And I know Lucifer's part by heart."

"Let's see — recite me something."

You clear your throat, swaying back and forth and putting your weight first on one leg and then on the other, and finally raising your arm to the lieutenant, at attention as in the movies when they sing the national anthem, you said in a vibrant tone:

"With pride and hauteur you occupy a royal throne that does not belong to you. Wretched one: against Whom did you rebel, master of the shadows? You have an endless number of treacherous vassals, an army that obeys your commands and executes your plans. But what do this throne and these vassals, this army, this empire avail you if you are to see yourself — O shame! O degradation! — humiliated and confused, till you reach the extreme point where a feeble Woman, an immaculate Damsel, a radiant Dawn boldly and courageously stamps the seal on your proud forehead with her audacious foot."

"Rather poor," Señorito Conrado said admonishingly. "You must declaim. This is drama, remember. It's not a speech. But it will do. Come, everybody, to work" — clapping his hands, making the pointer whistle through the air, shouting for the Archangel Michael: he'd sent him outside for a glass of water and he was dallying. Come on, tableau eight, scene ten, a wood, the same ones as before, and Saint Michael! Where in the world did he go for that water, to a well?"

A stir onstage: the shepherds taking their places around the fire, the sound of tambourines, Juanita the Virgin running to look for Saint Michael, and you begging the director:

"Can I put on Lucifer's costume? It'll be more effective."

"All right, but hurry it up."

And you didn't even see me, you didn't look around once as you got hurriedly dressed in the dark, almost next to me: you were mumbling stanzas, lisping like a pious old woman telling her beads. And running onstage again with your proud red cape, your horns, your chin-beard, and your splendid mustaches. The director looked you over.

"The tights fit too snugly. But it will do. You begin. End of scene nine, do you know it, do you remember it?"

And with his arms crossed, in the middle of the stage, his head down as though he were going to attack, you, Lucifer, remember:

> *If who I am you fain would hear*
> *Listen now, and give me ear!*
> *I am that great favorite*
> *Who at the king's right hand did sit,*
> *Banished from his sovereign's court*
> *To the abyss condemned forevermore....*

"Stop!" the director cut in. "It isn't necessary for you to begin so far back, just recite the end so as to give the shepherds their cue."

Java Lucifer:

> *... know then that before you here*
> *Is your great enemy Lucifer!*

Shepherds:

> *Flee, all, flee!*

Archangel Michael appearing, brandishing his sword:

Shepherds, flee not, stay!

Fueguiña, but this time looking magnificent, kids: a helmet with a red plume, a white tunic reaching halfway down her thighs and cinched in at the waist by a wide, shining belt, high boots, and a blue and white cape over her shoulders, and to top off such a stunning sight, her bare arm upraised, holding the gleaming sword. And declaiming:

> *And you, monster most hideous,*
> *Would you create a world aflame*
> *To quench your burning thirst?*
> *Flee, villain, flee, in heaven's name!*

Java Lucifer:

> *Stay thy hand!*
> *Raise not your voice in victory*
> *I find your tone patentory.*

Director: Peremptory.
Java: " . . . Excuse me: peremptory."
The pointer whistled through the air. The Archangel Michael took advantage of the pause to take a lipstick out of her sash and furiously repaint her lips, with her sword still held on high and her proud legs planted wide apart. Her mouth between her rouged cheeks was like a red carnation and it seemed as though you flung yourself so precipitately and unexpectedly on this flower, obeying a muttered murmur of the cripple, that you frightened her and her lipstick fell to the floor. When you fell at her feet as the planks of the stage creaked, raising clouds of dust, your clutching hands searching for a grip on her legs, dragging yourself across the stage amid curses and the brimstone of Hell itself, you rascal, sinking your

fingers in the flesh of her thighs, pulling on her skirt and casting sidewise glances at the director from time to time, you sly wretch.

Archangel Fueguiña:

> *Proud, daring breath of hell,*
> *Would you dare oppose as well*
> *Heaven itself? O too-proud one,*
> *Claim not victory till battle's done!*

Java Lucifer:

> *Appease not my wrath!*

Archangel Fueguiña:

> *Lay not a finger upon me!*

And you clutched her as though she were a greased pole, slipping and snorting, using your hands and your knees and your elbows, until you buried your face in her bosom and then, slipping down again, arrived at her crotch, as she — how well you must have rehearsed her on the terrace of the Casa de Familia! — wriggled and writhed so as to thrust you away as she showed the whites of her eyes and raised her head and her gleaming sword heavenward, throwing herself completely into the role.

> *"Prideful one, with vainglorious breath . . . !"*

Java Lucifer:

> *Curses, curses!*

Director: "No, no, the line is 'I am vanquished, vanquished, Michael.'"

Archangel Michael:

Be consumed in flames, infidel!

Director: "More feeling!"
Shepherds:

"Ay, ay, ay!"

Virgin Juanita:

O Virgin!

The director shouted Cut! pounding on the boards with the tip of his cane. Moving forward in his chair with his mouth open as though he were gasping for air, he wheeled himself through the terrified shepherds, gently admonishing: "You've lost your place, Lucifer. This is where you say, let me see" — leafing through his notebook with his delicate, agile fingers, still panting. "Yes, here we are: 'A vengeful serpent shall I be!' Once more now, from the beginning, and don't rail like that, Michael, my girl, more tenderness, eh? firmly but with great tenderness, this is the eternal struggle between Good and Evil, between Beauty and Ugliness, let us say. Do you know what I mean?"

"Yes, sir."

The director took his place once more between the backdrops.

"And you on the other hand, Lucifer: with fury, with vengeful wrath, with genuine passion. Don't be afraid you'll hurt her; make your entrance decisive."

"Yes, sir." Taking advantage of the pause, Java had lighted a cigarette and was blowing spirals of smoke at the ceiling.

"All right then. Begin with 'Daring mortal, hold your tongue.' Look alive, shepherds. Open the trapdoor. Ready,

Saint Michael. And *will* you put that lipstick down, once and for all!"

The curtain was gaping open a bit and revealed the backdrop, a paneled door. Hunching down between the two wheels, looking at them over his pale hands crossed on the head of the cane, the cripple pressed his skinny bare feet tightly against each other, sheltered in a vermilion nest of shadows. The shawl had slipped from his knees and was lying on the floor. His drowsy eyes, small and wet, seemed like two points of light eaten away by an acid. He thrust his jaw forward, a gesture that betrayed his habit of taking command of a situation, and repeated the order, pounding on the floor with his cane: no smoking. Java obeyed, drenched with imperceptible sweat, a coldly rehearsed humiliation.

Java Lucifer to a shepherd:

> *Daring mortal, hold your tongue*
> *Or your funeral mass will soon be sung!*

Shepherd:

> *No, no, I pray, stay your hand*
> *Has such a beast e'er roamed this land?*

Java Lucifer:

> *You shall be in these precincts*
> *Food for ravening wolf and lynx.*

Archangel Fueguiña:

> *Stay thy hand, monster from Hell.*

Java Lucifer:

> *Your effort, Michael, is in vain!*

> *Hear, I pray, of my great pain:*
> *It passeth all my powers of thought*
> *To dwell on evils I have wrought.*

As you declaimed this, I saw the Archangel raise one leg and scratch her knee absentmindedly. The bird squeak could again be heard behind the curtain, and the imperious pounding of the cane.

Archangel Fueguiña:

> *Do not let madness o'er you tower,*
> *Challenge not the Divine power!*

Java Lucifer:

> *A vengeful serpent shall I be!*
> *Furies inflame my wrathful breast*
> *And my heart is filled with restlessness!*

The Archangel again raised her leg to scratch it, just as you flung yourself upon her, obeying the obscure command issuing forth from behind the curtain. She brandished the sword proudly above your head, but this caused her to lose her balance, and the open-mouthed shepherds saw Michael and Lucifer roll on the planks of the stage in a whirl of capes that formed an incandescent white and blue flame. Lying on her back on the stage, with Lucifer standing astride her belly, she nonetheless contrived to shout:

> *Alas for thee, Lucifer!*
> *Rage on, spew forth your contumely*
> *But respect the awesome mystery*
> *With not a trace of Adam's sin!*

You catapulted into the air, gummy-eyes, and the Archangel sat up with her sword on his, and when you attacked again she exclaimed:

See how the mighty arm of God
Hath cast you at my feet!

And you fell back defeated, groaning, as she put her foot on your head and you crawled away, ripping at her high boots with your claws, not to mention her little tunic all in tatters, and the wide purple girdle, seeking a support amid your agony, and casting glances at the curtain from time to time, from which there came the sound of the cane pounding once more. Sitting hunched down in the wheelchair the cripple was squinting his eyes the better to capture all the details. From his air of a cultivated gentleman, a person would have sworn that he did not like this at all, but his glassy stare was focused on a distant point in space and his long fingers kneaded the towel-scarf around his neck with incredible swiftness; it was as though he were looking without seeing, draining his strange blindness to the bitter end. A person might be inclined to think that he was also indignant, that something about this fight between Good and Evil disquieted him, and he was sweating nervously, rigid in his wheelchair, mute and blind, in torment as though aware of a sudden pain in his legs.

Lying there on the stage on your back, and with the foot of Saint Michael on your chest, you nonetheless raised yourself up a little bit to clutch at her girdle and say:

Curses! Vanquished am I
I declare that I shall be, forevermore,
Your willing slave, Lucifer!

And dragging yourself along, like a fiery crocodile, you disappeared down the trapdoor. How good, oh how good you were, gummy-eyes! And the director gave you the role. He made you sweat for it though; I went home because it was very late, but I found out later that you were obliged to go through the scene with the Archangel five times more.

That winter had a special odor of mud and decayed leaves, of wet shoes drying next to the brazier. The rains and the intense cold spells coincided with Martin's best stories: they listened to him buried to the neck in the warm mountain of papers and surrounded by the sound of water dripping from the broken drains. The ragpicker's shop was the navel of the world. Itchy's shoes smoked there next to the brazier, but he didn't notice, as he lay on his belly on top of the newspapers scratching at his infected knuckles. Java's granny came out of the kitchen with half a dead cigar stuck in her lips, with a pot full of soup, but on seeing all of them congregated there she went back to the kitchen again. That afternoon Mingo came running in, half-dead with cold and snot hanging down to his lips; he had come from the shop, with his apprentice's smock and his thick muffler across his chest like two cartridge belts; he had to go take some jewelry to somebody's mistress, he said, a platinum blond who lived in the lap of luxury in the Ritz with two dogs. He'd been there several times before and this was the errand he liked best, because the whore always gave him a *duro* as a tip, and he said that one day she opened the door in a transparent nightie; he could see her ink nipples and her black stockings. Java himself said that she was a fabulous whore, and swore that a big-time black marketeer had fallen in love with her at first sight and had taken it into his head to put a signed check down her bosom, leaving the amount blank, and that she had put a nine with sixty-nine zeroes after it, as many as would fit on the check. Among the jewels that Mingo had for her was a solid gold bracelet with a little scorpion hanging from it, also solid gold and with joints that moved. It could practically walk. Mingo allowed each one of them to hold it in his hands for a short while, and that was when Java told them about scorpions: when they are trapped by fire with no possible escape they turn on themselves and kill themselves by poisoning themselves with their sharp stinger. He also said that scorpions are evil creatures that bring bad luck and stand for the hatred between brothers, and the capacity in man to destroy himself — do you remember your spiel, gummy-eyes, and how you promised us a story about all this?

Then there were the first fumbling experiences with the jerk-off whores at the Roxy, the visit as a spy to the Continental Bar, entering with the sack made of mattress ticking over your shoulder and the scales dangling from your waistband, singing "papers, bottles" with the deep voice of an adult; that first meeting with the one-eyed man who turned out to be looking for her too, and the first sparks from Fueguiña that were to lead to a big fire, gummy-eyes. Did these things really amuse us? Did we really find them as exciting as the movies at the Rovira or the Delicias? Pulling the cart along day after day, going through the streets ringing your bell hanging from a red rag and a dried rabbit pelt, your eyes glued on balconies and windows, at times in the company of your granny, who followed along after you to keep watch on the load, both of you deaf to your endless cry of "Raaabittt skins takeeeen here . . . !" that penetrated all the houses, all the shops and taverns of the neighborhood, along with the name: Ramona.

"Ramona. I haven't seen her again, kid, she doesn't show herself around here," the proprietress of the Continental said. She was drinking a cupful of malt, as thick and black as tar, for breakfast. She poured some cognac into the cup and as she put the bottle back on the shelf, with her back to Java, she looked at him over her shoulder, with a twisted smile on her lips: "You liked her and want to do it with her again, right, you rascal?"

"That's not the reason, ma'am. I have a message to give her. Where does she hang out? Where does she live?"

"I don't know" — and again the wry smile. "What did you do with her, handsome?"

Java shouldered his sack again and muttered something or other crossly, leaning on the counter with that indolence of his that lay coiled up in his lower back and his long legs. The proprietress stared at him, uneasy now: "Listen, did you catch something from her?"

"No, no."

"It would surprise me if you did. Because you can say for her that she's a nice clean girl."

"Do you know if she had steady work at anyone's house?"

"Not that I know of. I was saying to my brother just yesterday: it's been months since we saw hide nor hair of her. It's as though the earth had swallowed her up. You look tired, boy. Do you want a beer? Now that you've dropped by, I've got a rabbit skin for you. Wait a minute."

It was early in the morning: an atmosphere of ashes mingling with the light, chairs legs-up on the tables, the greasy floor strewn with olive pits and half-swept sawdust. The proprietress's brother had the broom in his hand and was sitting at a table talking with Señor Justiniano, who was wearing his black army coat today. Above their heads, in the dark balcony upstairs, a young girl was breakfasting on canned sardines set out on the marble table, her gaze still focused on the labors of the night before.

"It's strange that she hasn't come back here, isn't it?" Java said, sticking the bloody rabbit skin in his belt.

"Did she swipe something there in that room?" the proprietress said.

"No, no."

"You never know with her kind."

"Where did you meet her?"

"Right here. She used to come here to begin her night. She would eat something and hardly ever spoke to anybody else. If she didn't latch onto a client right away, she went around looking for one. Finish your beer," she added, lowering her voice, catching the black look of the one-eyed man out of the corner of her eye. "He doesn't like minors to hang out here."

"I'm working, I've got my Cadillac outside. Who is that guy anyway?"

He turned around to look at him and saw the patch over his eye, his gray temples, his bitter mouth beneath the hairline-mustache. His huge jaw, a square monument to the habit of command, thrust forward a bit as their eyes met and his slowly turned away. Java deliberately turned his back on him. Lowering her voice still more, the proprietress said: "Don't you know him? He's a friend of the man who pays, you'd do well to stay on good terms with him, don't ever have a run-in with him, don't ever argue with him, sonny, and if you happen some day to find him sitting next to you at the movies, be on your guard, get up and get your arm up good and high to salute when they play the Falangist anthem, without horsing around and with your mouth shut tight, they're in command now." "I know it, ma'am." And in a whisper she added: "He's the one who tells me when there's work for you, he's very particular about the day and the hour and there's hell to pay if the girl doesn't turn up."

"Don't you make the arrangements directly with that other man?"

"I've never even seen him. I make the arrangements with this guy."

The delegate from this section of the city, she said, and as justice of the peace in the neighborhood his word is law, but basically he's a petty political boss, one of many. You'll see him around here recruiting kids — hasn't he ever stopped you in the street to talk to you about going to a Youth Camp? — he must respect you. He's sort of bad news, I must say — every month he comes by to collect for Social Aid and the Falangist contribution from this district, he never fails to drop in at every bar along the way, but in exchange they let me sell blond cigarettes and all that, if you know what I mean, sonny. What do you expect? — he's one of them and with what they get out of me somebody must be making a bundle."

"Don't exaggerate, ma'am," Java said. "And have a little patience — these are bad times."

"No, we've already got each other's number, he and I. Because if I owe him favors, he owes me some too. And I keep my mouth shut — I know what's good for me."

Java had raised his head to look at the hooker upstairs: she was eating with her sleepwalker's calm there upstairs, without paying any attention to anything or anyone. Java could see the one eye of the delegate in profile, a black, insistent eye. He had gotten up from the table and was now walking toward the door, followed by the proprietress's brother.

"I just tend to business," she said, seeing him leave out of the corner of her eye. "They say to me, on such and such a day at such and such a time you bring the couple, it's him that gives me the key and the money. I go on ahead and open the door for you, and when the whole business is over I pay, I clean up a little, I lock the door, and head for home."

"Doesn't anybody live there? Haven't you ever seen the mother?"

"No. I think she lives in an apartment higher up, or else lower down, I don't know which. The entire house belongs to the widow and she has all the apartments rented except two of them. The son only sleeps in the one you saw from time to time, along with a girl who takes care of him; they used to live in that apartment but they moved when the father died, it seems to me. And listen, there are still valuable things in that apartment — you should see how it's decorated!"

"While we're on the subject," Java said, "isn't there anything going on over there now, ma'am?"

"No, not a thing. I'll tell you when there is — I'd rather you didn't come around here" — and again there was smiling mischief in her painted eyes. "You'd like it if it was with that Ramona, wouldn't you, you rascal?"

"I just wanted to see her, that's all."

"One thing you can say for the girl, she's clean. It's noticeable." She drained her coffee and put the cup in the sink. "Wait and see. Balbina!" she shouted to the girl on the balcony. "Have you seen Ramona?"

Straightening up as though she were waking up, the girl shook her permanent: nope, she said, puckering up her mouth with no lipstick on. Java had already started up the stairs, and could see the gaping hole in her stocking at the knee and her flesh bulging though it like a tomato, her full hips clad in stiff satin trailing on the stool, freckled hands and the prettiest face imaginable. He stood there at her side.

"Are you a friend of Ramona's?"

"What is it you want?"

"I have a message for her, and I don't know where to locate her."

"She used to live in a boardinghouse. But she's moved. And what's more she owes me fifteen *duros*."

"But where is she now?"

"Did she tell you? Well, she didn't tell me either," she said, shrugging her shoulders and looking at Java with a twinkle in her eye. "I didn't know you liked pretty girls. . . . "

"Have you known each other very long?"

She waved her hand vaguely, accompanying the gesture with an insecure little pout: and how, we've known each other for a long time, kid, ever since we were both virgins, laughing it up and eating all we wanted to, you can imagine how long ago that was, Itchy, choking with pleasure as they wolfed food down, what good luck to find her, with her hearty babyish laugh as she remembered it: from when the two had different names and different cunts, and different work too: maids in a country house in Gracia. Two little servant-girls like two rosebuds, working for a couple with one daughter and a couple of very old grandparents. The civil-war shit had been going on for a year, terror had already made its way into all upper-class houses, and one fine day the family decided to go live in town and closed the country house. They were left without work. It was the second time for Ramona: she'd already been a maid in another house just before the war began, and something happened there with the young son who was in the militia, Balbina could imagine what without her friend ever telling her: at the time Ramona was still madly in love, for the first time, with a nice boy who soon died on the Aragón front, not of machine-gun bullets but of cold. They'd been sweethearts since they were thirteen and they really loved each other, a story to bring

120

tears to your eyes, kids. So those first days without a job, lost in the midst of the civil uproar, with nothing left but a sweet-heart in the front lines, if you want to write me you know where, but very soon not even letters get through and the trap closes: everything seemed to have been planned so that they'd open their legs, and they did open. Balbina began a long time before Ramona, but she doesn't even remember it any more, she takes her johns to the mansion where she'd been a maid, she has a key and a clientele of fascinated soldiers on leave, all excited and hot to trot, crouching between her legs, so scared they were almost like little kids. Before the mansion was con-fiscated by the anarchists, she got pregnant and one night dur-ing the bombardment of '38 she meets Ramona sleeping in the subway station with a man: this is my uncle Artemi, she says to her, and Balbina, who always thought that Ramona didn't have a family: don't make me laugh sweetie, or I'll have a mis-carriage, it's certain that your legs are open wider than an um-brella too. And what about that cross set with rubies that you're wearing around your neck — are you going to tell me you got it for nothing? It is a night of alarms and omens: among the crowd lying there half asleep, a little girl squats down and urinates with her panties off, and the butt of a pistol peeks out from between the lapels of a jacket worn over a mechanic's overalls. There was no salvation for either of them by that time, and they met again after the war was over. They shared a rented room together and had some pretty well-off johns, but not for long: Balbina catches herself a fiancé, a real one, and thinks that she'll be able to get married, and Ramona goes off to live in a roominghouse. She didn't seem the same, according to what Balbina told me, Itchy: she'd dyed her hair blonde, she was so skinny and sad and full of scars, what with her uncle in jail and her nerves shattered by that strange fear, those gory nightmares that didn't let her sleep. After a while we rarely saw each other, Balbina concludes, sometimes here or in the Alaska, where of course she never had a cent.

"A mansion in the Calle Camelias that was closed, with

white roses and a palm tree in the garden," Itchy said, blinking in the sun, shading his eyes with his hand. "With a little girl who was eight years old then and is around thirteen now. Well, Java, that's it, the same mansion and the same little girl who smells of tangerines, the same black crock that runs on gas and alcohol and farts like Granny."

"Hmmm. I don't put much store by what a hooker says," Java answers. "When they opened the house up again they were still eating pork sausage from the country: remember the skins we found and the escarole and the tangerine peels?" Itchy insisted. "It's true — that hooker wasn't pulling your leg."

"Maybe," Java said, poking at his teeth with a toothpick. "Hey, is all this washing that your mother's done?"

"Yes, all of it," Tits said.

They were lying sunning themselves on Tits's flat roof, with the wash flapping over their heads giving off a fresh odor of bleach. They could hear voices of women down below in the yard. Java shredded the toothpick with his teeth, lost in thought, and then spit it out.

"We'll have to tell the others," he said. "It'll be tonight. I'll bring Fueguiña and she can be the Virgin."

"Wouldn't the girl from the country house be better since she knew the hooker?" Itchy asked.

"Some other time." Java crumbled three cigarette butts slowly, the cigarette paper hanging from his lips. "Susana's a dummy."

When he went out to work with his granny and the cart, they ate together sitting on the curbstone of some street, wherever they felt like it: chick-pea or lentil soup that the old lady brought along in the lunch bucket. She liked it a lot when they went out to sell old paper: they ate in a tavern on Paralelo, where the old lady, an inveterate smoker, bought herself big cigars. When he went out hunting up things on his own, Java always planned his route so that siesta time would find him near Itchy's or Tits's, in Cottolengo: tiny roof-terraces with wet sheets flapping in the wind and sending forth whiplashes of bleach in their faces, with a blue spring sky where heavy kites made of newspapers swayed back and forth.

"In the street from dawn to dark — he only comes home in time to eat" — the complaints of the neighbor women coming up from their sinks, coiling about in the air along with the one song being played by all radios at once, joyful refrains like spangles in the sun, like little silvery fish biting their own tails. "You're right, of course, but they're less trouble that way, my dear. That grown-up kid of a junk dealer does as he pleases with them" — voices beaten along with the wash, along with the cries of birds like arrows in the sky, and the noisy shouts of children and the barking of dogs from the neighboring hillsides. "And the other one, the 'Pregnant Woman's' son, there's one for you. They sometimes go to the parish house now, but I'm certain it isn't to learn their catechism; don't fool yourself that it is."

"Damn," Tits grumbled. "They're magpies."

"Which one is your mother?"

"The one that screams the loudest."

"Well, at any rate I know where mine is when I don't see him, now that he's an altar boy."

"That one," Tits said.

"Come on," Itchy said, getting to his feet. "Should we tell Luis too? He's got a terrible cough — you can hear him a mile away."

"That's your cough drops for you," Tits said as they went down the stairs. "The more of them he eats, the more he'll cough. They're infected — they say that girls with t.b. make them these days — the laboratory doesn't have to pay them as much."

"At ten o'clock tonight," Java said as they separated. "Listen, Tits, don't forget the piece of rail and the rope."

That night when Itchy arrived at the dressing-room Fueguiña was all set to play the Virgin, sitting rigidly in a chair. With her hair hanging down her back, her feet bare, and with a white tunic and a blue mantle with nothing underneath, as was plain to see. They had lighted candelabra and placed them strategically about. Java turned out the overhead light and placed two candelabra on the floor, one on each side of Fueguiña, who didn't seem afraid, but then she never complained. All she said was how come here? — it'd be better onstage.

"We'll rehearse here a little first," Java said. "Pretend that your name is Aurora."

"You told me you and I would rehearse alone. . . . " and then, mistrustful of the others, looking at the box of matches in Amén's filthy hands: "Do they have parts to play too?"

"We aren't going to rehearse *The Shepherds* today," Java said, repositioning the candelabra. "This is a new play that Itchy's invented. We want to surprise the director — you'll see. I'm sure you'll like it. Give me your hands first, come on, don't be afraid."

"And I'm to be tied up all through it?" she said, giving him her hands.

"No," Itchy said, as smooth as silk, approaching her with the rope on his shoulder. "Not all the time — it's up to you. You'll see, it's a very special play," the little bastard said: that shaved head of his, and inside that crazy imagination of his, do you remember, gummy-eyes? — just look where it's gotten him. "It's not written out," he said, "but we know it by heart and you'll soon learn it. It begins like this: imagine that you've got your hands tied behind your back and they want to make you talk, they're already preparing to torture you. Get up."

He took her over into the corner and seated her astride the bidet, amid an unbearable smell of urine; he made her put both hands behind her back and started to tie her wrists together. And at that point she glared at him with eyes that were suddenly furious.

"Not you," she said to him, and then looking at Java: "I don't want anybody touching me but you."

Heaven only knew how she had managed to steal out of the

124

orphans' home; they thought it might have been like this: the girls did the washing for Las Ánimas and other parishes, altar cloths and cassocks. At times the wash was so big that night had fallen before they'd finished the ironing; they had two irons heated by coals and one of them was lent by a neighbor, so Fueguiña went out to return it and didn't come back to the Casa de Familia right away.

"Are you ready, Aurora?"

Java kneeled and tied her wrists behind her back, carefully mussed her hair, opened her legs wider, and leaned her farther backward. She closed her eyes: she was riding against the night and the wind of a memory. That's fine, he said, bring the candelabra closer, Itchy. Ten candles in two rows, five on each side of the bidet, casting a bright glow on her apple cheeks and her sand-colored eyes. What shall I pretend to be? she said, why am I sitting on this thing? and Luis said, laughing: imagine that you're horseback riding, and behave — where did you expect us to get a horse, dummy? Assisted by Mingo and Amén, Tits brought the can of gunpowder with considerable ceremony, as though it were a viaticum. Java took the can, made Fueguiña get up for a moment, and carefully laid down a fine line of powder around the semicircular edge of the bidet. Then he had her sit down again with her legs spread, with the inner side of her thighs touching the trail of powder, a black snake with two heads. That's fine, isn't it, Itchy? Java said, and lighted the paschal candle with a silver band around it and passed it before the eyes of the prisoner. They all sat down silently on the floor. Is this okay? she said. What do I have to do? following the flame with eyes that revealed neither fear nor curiosity, what do I have to say? Whatever you want, Itchy said in a low voice fraught with mystery, but pretend you've been kidnapped by Moors who'll torture you if you don't talk. And he stretched out on the floor like an old dog, holding his chin with his scabby pink hands, looking at her sleepily, purring: come on, gummy-eyes, interrogate her, how exciting to have girls in your power that way, bite one of her tits, make her sing. Another furious glance from her: is that your role, you bald-headed mangy thing, to sick him on me? Yes, Aurorita, that's always my role, making bad guys be even worse, I like that. And now answer what they ask you if you don't want to see your delicate skin branded. Her name was Aurora then.

Aurora? she said, the one from the Casa de Familia, years ago? The very same, Java said; sing, cough up, Itchy said. I can't answer that, I was little then, ask something else. No, that has to be the question, she had the very same job you have now, she was a maid for the same man, Java said, brandishing the paschal candle, bringing the flame closer to the powder. Not exactly the same, she just went to make his bed in his bachelor apartment, she never went to the apartment on the Calle Mallorca, which is much bigger and takes much more work to keep up. But I remember, don't push me, Fueguiña said, playing along with the game, though dubiously: should I answer or should I hold out? Talk, damn you, spill it: what happened when his militia service was over? No, smiling maliciously now, what a sly fox she is, adapting herself to the role of the heroine who isn't afraid that they'll fuck her over, I don't know anything, you bastards, I was a little kid then. And Itchy: spill it, or we'll put the Malayan Boot on you. And Java: what can you tell us about her? Nothing. You knew her. Yes, but there's nothing I can tell you, I only remember her very pretty face and her green high-heeled shoes. Java brought the flame up to the edge of the bidet, a few inches away from the powder, and she didn't even blink, though her white thighs became rigid. Lying there on the floor, they held their breath. Burn her pussy hairs to begin with, gummy-eyes, her nipples, mark one of her tits, teach her a lesson. She raised up and her wicked toothless smile hovered for an instant above their heads there on the floor. Is it true that a Moor bashed your teeth in, kid? Itchy grabbed her hair, jerked her head back, and ordered: you have to say I don't know anything once more and then I strip off your dress. That too, pigs, she said. Let her talk now,

126

leave her alone, Java bellowed. Don't be scared, we're not looking very much, Aurora, don't quit now that you're doing it so well. Okay, strip me, but only a little, and not on top, okay? she said, just down below, well anyway, you're seeing everything I've got, you're clever you are, but don't think you're fooling me, okay, that's enough, that's good enough, is this part of the play too, you sly one, couldn't I wear the devil's red tights? We'll see, but sing now, spill everything you know about the whore, come on, isn't it exciting?: all of them admiring you as they lie on the floor around the bidet, a few inches away from the tunic in tatters, with their mouths hanging open and their eyes on fire, Martín's fierce mustache coming unglued and hanging down in a corkscrew, Luis with his face hidden in the cape and racked with coughing. Talk, you bitch, we know that you were good friends, that she liked you a lot and sometimes let you sleep in her bed.

"I was so small then, I was so afraid of the bombs, I swear to you I was dying with fright."

"Aren't you afraid now?" Tits said.

"I'll never be afraid again."

"Ha! Don't you know that the war isn't over yet, that there's still an underground? Who can say: I'm not afraid?"

"I say so," Fueguiña replied.

"Ha ha. A poor orphan without a father or a mother, a dumb kid from Murcia who has to take an invalid's pisser out a hundred times a day so he can piss."

"Is that true, Fueguiña?" Itchy asked.

"All I do is hold his cock."

"That's a lie" — this from Tits.

"I'm not from Murcia. I'm from Lugo and my name is María Armesto!"

"That's a lie."

"Shut your mouth, Tits," Java said without looking at him. "Enough of this nonsense. Let's go on, Aurora" — as he brought the flame closer to the gunpowder again. "Are you going to talk?"

"No."

Luis's deep cough distracted her, as Java, with no ill-humor in his voice, playing his role rather poorly, said: You'll sing — a tango even — as the flame touched the powder and it suddenly went fffuuuuu . . . ! like a rocket going off, and the blue explosion going off between Aurora's knees, with two little black puffs of smoke rising to her face. You bastards, she exclaimed as she saw the two angry little flames advance along the edge of the bidet toward her thighs: two swift spiders taking off in opposite directions, turning to smoke and leaving a tobacco-colored trace. She made no attempt to get up, to struggle with her bound hands, moving not a muscle, not a hair. With her chin on her breast, she silently watched the rapid advance of the two trails of fire and saw them reach her flesh, and only then, when it appeared that they would bite into her flesh, did she part her legs a little more, remaining rigid as she saw them suddenly die out a few millimeters from her skin. What balls this kid has, Tits thought admiringly, and even Java seemed surprised. She calmly raised her head then and looked her inquisitor straight in the eye.

"I talk when I care to — get that straight," she added as she shook her black hair. "I don't really remember very well, you must mean Menchu, another one who ran away from the Casa to be a whore, or so they say. The bigger ones all talked about it, but I wasn't old enough to work outside the Casa. . . . "

"What about Menchu?"

"She told me she got along with all the girls, that she had a sweetheart whose name was Pedro, and that she did day-work. She went to Señorito Conrado's every day to make his bed for him, she'd been doing it since she was fourteen, when he was in school and his father was still alive, before the war. And then the whole family came to be very fond of her. He wasn't a cripple then and they say he was very good to her, that he gave her presents."

"And why was that?" Itchy asked. "Why should he be good to a housemaid, why should he have given her presents?"

"Don't scream at me, damn it. Why? It's a sin and I'm not going to say anything about it."

"Talk!"

"Well, she and her sweetheart used to see each other in secret in that apartment where she went to clean every day, and Señorito Conrado knew it. He knew that they kissed each other and touched each other there, and even though he knew it, he never gave them away, he never told his mother or the directress of the Casa. Why . . . ? Ouch, don't pull my hair like that! Her sweetheart came there in the morning after Señorito Conrado had left, he found her sweeping or changing the sheets on the bed, and that was where they did everything with each other. And she took her pleasure, they say. That's all I know. Hey, let go of my hair, you brute!"

A comfortable, youthful little apartment, an attractive one, with furniture made of steel tubing and lots of books, cut crystal ashtrays and cushions with Cubist designs. When Aurora went to clean it afterward, he had just come back from the nearest café and was holing up to study. He discovered it one day by chance, Sister, it's as though I could see him: stooping down at the foot of the bed where he lay stretched out hours and hours, studying for a career that he would never have, far away as yet from the glorious uniform and the wheelchair and the machine-gun bullets that were to go on destroying him year after year as though they were termites, I can just see him kneeling on the rug with his head lowered, lost in thought, hypnotized by the metallic gleam of the lighter that belonged to Pedro and he knew it, looking at it for a long time there next to the leg of the chair, not touching it, with maniacal eyes, joyously bearing up under that burning revelation, that heaven that opened up in his life and held in store a morning of shadows for his body; striding up and down the room, happily tearing at his hair, talking to himself, laughing, crawling into the bed, sniffing the sheets, the towels, the pillow, smelling the odor of her hair, of her skin, like a little dog, measuring in his imagination the hollow of their bodies in the mattress, calibrating their weight, perhaps hearing their moans. With his body on the edge of the bed, weeping with happiness, a thankful prayer on his lips.

"And what else, Aurora," Amén whispered next to the sputtering candelabrum. "What did he do then, why didn't he give them away?"

"Because he's a good man, because he's a gentleman brought up by the Jesuits and is never going to go around telling about other people's sins," she said.

"Even though they commit them in his own house, in his own bed?"

"That's right."

"Don't be silly," Itchy said, screwing up his eyelids like a cat, watching Java lithely pacing round the prisoner, his thoughtful air. He saw him stop in front of her, bend over with the candle in his hand, and allow a few drops of hot wax to fall into the bidet between her pale thighs and sticking the base of the candle into it. The flame threw sharp shadows on the walls. What are you going to do, she said, you know I'm not afraid of fire, but don't let anybody else but you touch me or I'm leaving. "Go on, spill it if you don't want to be the Marked Woman," Itchy added.

"Don't threaten me, stupid."

A top-floor apartment in the Calle Cerdeña with a little terrace full of geraniums, from which Pedro and Aurora, locked in each other's arms, saw the Europa soccer field and the cinder paths of the Hispano-France factory. The apartment of a rich bachelor, a nest for a twenty-year-old body that as yet had become passionately interested in nothing and no one. There were hunting trophies, tennis racquets, cups won in shooting matches, maps of African campaigns and a collection of riding boots set out in neat rows along the wall, the caprices of a son and grandson of army officers. Floating in the vengeful euphoria of a penniless young man, Pedro drinks up his cognac and smokes his cigars, sits in the perfumed water of his bathtub for hours at a time, wraps himself in his towels and walks barefoot on his rug and even wears his ties. And he was aware of all this at that very moment, as he held his burning forehead in his hands over a university textbook, or at his mother's, or in the militia. If the Republic doesn't take all this away from him, Pedro said, standing naked in front of the row of suits hung in the wardrobe, I'll take it away from him, the shitty snob, I'll fuck him over. And he knew it, Sister, and put up with it, never complaining of Pedro's swiping things, and what's more he even left cognac on the night table, within reach so that the two of them could drink in bed; he even bought himself a smoking jacket for him to use, and hung a mirror in a strategic spot, and left pornography magazines as though he'd forgotten them in an open drawer; there are men like that.

"I don't know anything more."

"Well then, we're going to make you put the candle out with your legs," Itchy said.

At a sign from Java, he blew out the candles in the candelabra one by one. All that was left was the flame of the paschal candle between Aurora's thighs. Imagine that if you can manage to leave us in the dark by putting the candle out, someone will come and save you. She looked at him suspiciously: what are you up to now, you louse, what's running through your mind as you devour me with your eyes? Talk or put out the candle, damn you, you've no other alternative. Aurora grasped the candle halfway up with her thighs, not quite able to reach the flame; she tried again, parting her legs slowly, on tiptoe, trying several times to go through with it, opening and closing her legs, and the flame flickered, throwing dark shadows behind them, which they watched in silence. After several attempts she put out the flame with trembling thighs, as drops of hot wax ran down them; not a single groan, not even a sigh escaped her. She suddenly found herself in the dark in someone's arms, transported elsewhere, being pawed and then suddenly kissed on the lips, kids, on her feet, tied to a tree trunk with her hands behind her back. She heard the sound of footsteps round about her, a frantic going and coming, laughter, people stumbling, a finger poking at her down below. The surprisingly expert mouth landed on hers once again, and the third time she gave him hers, oh kids, how nice, it slid off hers and then found it again, with the smell of licorice and whispering please let me, I won't say anything, fumbling blindly about, letting other hands slide up her thighs.

"That's enough."

"Matches, right away," a voice said.

"I won't say anything, Ramona, please, please. . . . "

"What did you say?"

And the presents: it began with gewgaws and he finally ended up giving her black stockings, transparent nightgowns and satin slips, garters with lace trimmings, panties and bras, like in the movies, what a guy. Accept it, Aurorita, for when you get married, it's a way of thanking you for your work here, he says. And that's the way it was, Sister, as though I'd seen it with my own eyes: he set the stage, the scene, he took care of the details, he decided on the costumes, always very delicate underclothes, and took care of arranging the meetings between the two of them: Aurora, I won't be home all Monday afternoon, you might come and change the lace curtains, they're filthy. Yes, sir, as you please. . . . Something happened one day that might have made her suspect, but she didn't tumble: in order to scrub the floors she had always filled her scrub bucket in the bathroom next to the bedroom, but after a certain day, just a little after her fiancé lost the gold lighter that she'd given him for his birthday, the bathroom was always locked from inside.

It was as though the finger were exploring a moist flower: silky petals opening one by one. Suddenly it crept into the most sensitive part, and she wriggled: she didn't try to escape from it, it was like a mad limpet and set first her belly and then her heart to trembling. She finally heard the sound of a match being struck and the flame rescued all of them from the darkness. Tied now to the artificial tree trunk that Tits was holding up from behind, and the rope wound around her entire

(

body, from her ankles to her neck. Not fearful, still having her fun, her eyes searching for that mouth, trying to recognize it. It was you, you damned opportunist, she said. All of them going round and round her, one hand and then another, it was you, until Java pushed the hair back from her face and she caught sight of Martín lighting the candelabra again. And now what, you sneaky opportunists? Wasn't somebody supposed to save me, you liars? Not yet, Aurora, spill it if you want to get out of the hundred lashes or be the Marked Woman forever. More pulling on her tunic, the silent, piggy hands, who's touching you, dummy? the mask slipping down over Mingo's nose, the belt in his hand, ready to whip her and his other hand clutching at his pants that were about to fall off.

"We're going to lick the hide off you, Aurora."

"Don't be silly. I'm thirsty, give me a swallow of licorice-water. And untie me now, I don't want to rehearse this stupid play any more, I'll tell Conrado on you" — Fueguiña was really struggling now, and the coils of the rope were sinking into her flesh. "Let me go, you bastards."

Java opened the razor in her face. Leave her with the Mark of Zorro, gummy-eyes, Mingo said, and Martín: we could put a banana up her, just to see how she'd act, and her replying without blinking an eye: you'd be better off eating it, pig, her eyes fixed on the razor. Java very quietly, thinking things over: shut up all of you, and (to Fueguiña) tell me: did she ever figure out what was really happening? Didn't she ever realize that he was setting the scene? Fueguiña struggled in her bonds: scene? what scene? Java put the sharp edge of the razor against her chin, but smiled as he said: don't play dumb, cutie, you're the cripple's helper, you know more about the way he lives than anybody. Ay ay ay, you're cutting me, you brute, let me go, that's all I know, I swear.

"Okay then," Java said, lowering the razor to her breast, sliding the blade under the rope and cutting it. "You're free now. Don't tell anybody anything or I'll really cut you up good. Is it a deal?"

133

"You're crazy." This said as she dressed herself behind the mirror, with Tits crouching down spying on her, and the others putting out the candles. "What I really like a lot is this hidey-hole of yours."

"I'll go along with you to the Calle Verdi," Java said.

"I'm not afraid to go alone. Will you let me have the box of matches?"

When they got to the Plaza Rovira she managed to run away from him. Wait, do you want me to take you home or don't you? It was past midnight and all he could think about was something to eat. The last drunks were pouring out of the bars like rats, listing like ships and hugging the walls, muttering hoarse reproaches and vague insults, vomiting a pestilential wine at the street corners. He suddenly caught sight of her in a dark entry hall, making signs to him, come on, smiling, come on silly, and he thought: she liked it with me, she knows it was my mouth and she wants it again. As he came in through the doorway she drew him toward the dark with her hand, but then suddenly let go and that was the last he saw of her as he felt his way along the walls and the greasy handrail of the stairway, stumbled over garbage cans and heard from somewhere very close to him the sound of crumpled paper and the lids of garbage cans dancing on tiles. His legs coiled around her body as she knelt there, when suddenly he heard the rasp of a match and saw the flame quickly catch in the pages of newsprint and garbage piled up in the center of the entryway. What are you doing, you crazy girl? he said, and she laughingly caught his hands, preventing him from putting out the fire, whatever are you up to? the glow lighting up their faces. The night watchman's stick resounded on the paving stones of the square. All the shadows in the entryway suddenly retreated to the little porter's lodge, impelled by the great flame, redeeming the peeling walls, the warped steps of the stairway, the worm-eaten railing and the blue espadrilles on large pale feet that were sockless. Fueguiña stifled a cry. Surrounded by a thick, evil-smelling smoke, Java saw that he would not be able to put the fire out, and grabbed her hand as she stood there, as motionless as a statue, staring at nothing, and the two of them made their escape at a run. . . .

Now, the tense skin of her hunched shoulders, like a gauze arrogantly covering them, was the only thing about her body that still had a veiled splendor of youth.

They ordered him to put down the hose, to place the head on the wooden block and go find the saw; he obeyed whistling and with a trembling, solicitous hand he parted the black, still rebellious locks curling over the forehead and before the saw touched her he brushed them swiftly backward. It was the only thing he did with dispatch. He could not, or would not, obey when the doctor, busy washing his hands, told him to begin to saw, nor was he capable of introducing the catheter in the arteries, he didn't lend a hand as he did other times when he was perhaps drunker than he was today, but with a swift and steady hand and jokes that were famous among the medical students; he knew the work by heart and might well have done it better and cleaner than the autopsy surgeon himself. And it was only after he'd finished with the twins, so identical in their frozen astonishment, so closely linked to their mother by the fluid of dreams that their rigid, gray little faces suggested, listening to somebody grumbling sew 'em up and see to it that you leave everything all nice and clean because you're doing things badly today, that he began to react, splashing on the floor that cloudy liquid suddenly shorn of a past. The last students left, following in the autopsy surgeon's wake. The four bodies lay with their insides exposed on the marble. He would clean them up good, he would remove all the water from their thoraxes and bellies with a ladle, he would sew them up and then would hose them down for one last time, he would leave them like new even though nobody came to see them, even though nobody asked after them. He had the bottle of formaldehyde all ready. He introduced his hand into the frigid, waterlogged chest and gently cradled the heart in his palm. He changed from scalpel to scissors and then worked busily with needle and thread, this time looking at the expression on the purple face, with eyes that had not closed at all, the death boiling over with intrigues and cock-and-bull stories. He went on with his work, maundering and humming snatches of popular songs, sewing up the skin in a continuous furious suture, not giving his hand a rest, the entire skin from bottom to top, from the pubis to the sternum.

IX

THE baroness received the new lady's maid in the rococo drawing room full of gilded cornucopias, bronze clocks, helmets, and a collection of armor with matching swords. Short and chubby, covered with furs and jewels, sitting on the divan, she rested her feet shod in crimson slippers on the edge of a huge brazier of burnished copper. Her husband was napping in a wing chair, with his glasses and a copy of *Vértice* magazine sliding off his lap, his sleepy hand chasing away a shadow of indigestion at the level of his gray, close-cropped hair.

"Is it the Casa de Familia that sent you?"

"Yes, your ladyship. Señora Galán and the directress."

"I've already spoken to them. They say you're a good girl. How old are you?"

"Eighteen."

"Have you ever worked as a lady's maid before?"

"Yes, ma'am."

At this point the two sons of the baroness entered the drawing room in their embroidered dressing gowns and slippers.

The older one was pale, and hunched over to cough; the other one began winding the grandfather clock with an enameled dial showing two stags fighting. He had dirty fingernails.

The baroness looked at her affably.

"What's your name, my girl?"

"Menchu. . . . "

"We'll call you Carmen."

Below the bottom edge of their dressing gowns, the legs of the two boys were the color of wax. Menchu spied dirt on their ankles.

"You seem very well-mannered," the baroness said. "I want to tell you that I suffer from a nervous ailment. What I need more than a lady's maid is a companion, a nurse. I have relatives in the country that are making a martyr of me. Do you like riding in a car?"

"Yes, ma'am," she said, suddenly very nervous, putting a fingernail between her teeth. A pink ribbon in her hair, a knitted sweater, a pleated skirt, pretty knees still covered with the dust of a prie-dieu.

"Don't bite your fingernails in public; it's nasty."

The husband gets up drowsily from his chair.

"I'm going to the bathroom and have a bowel movement, Elvira."

As the baroness opened a box of cigarettes, a song about Ferdinand and Isabella began playing. Almost everything in this house had been bought cheaply from two friends of the husband who worked in a government office for recovery of goods seized by Communists. With time, Menchu was also to come to know the baroness's relatives.

The enormous car, as perfumed as a fancy bathroom, was a black Buick, pearly with little drops of dew and parked in the yard in front of a farmhouse near Tortosa. The baroness's older son was smoking Murattis, with his hands crossed over the wheel, and in the back seat Menchu was looking at a landscape of vineyards and olive groves through the tinted windows of the car.

"Mama and the peasant will be a while," José María said, getting out of the car. "Come and take a walk, kitten, this air is good for the lungs."

She gazes mistrustfully at the frail shoulders of her young master; she will follow him to the olive grove, she will accept a little bouquet of daisies, a few squeezes, and a kiss with her eyes open, stubbornly fixed on heaven knows what, along a dusty path down which a vagabond is retreating, his dented canteen on his belt gleaming in the sun. Suddenly she looks at her watch and runs back to the car, opens it, picks up a purse, takes out a bottle of pills and hurries to the farmhouse with it.

She meets no one in the courtyard, just chickens pecking at ears of corn, voices behind a side door, which she pushes open and enters. In the middle of a sort of storeroom full of sacks of rice, white beans, potatoes and jars of olive oil reaching to the ceiling, the baroness is having a heated discussion with the peasant couple who take care of the farm. Her muddy rain boots peek out from below her fur coat. She stops talking and sends a furious glance Menchu's way. Menchu, her legs trembling and with the pill in her open palm says:

"Pardon me, ma'am, it's your five o'clock pill."

One must not imagine them in hoods and clutching pistols all the time, sticking together and consuming themselves in the flames of the underground; they also spent a great deal of time alone doing normal things that involved no risk whatsoever: Fusam watering his dozen tomato plants weighed down with heavy soot, next to the train tracks in Hospitalet, watching an old woman in mourning, incredibly agile and with a belly as though she were seven months pregnant, jumping out of one of the freight cars; Palau taking a shower in the bathroom of his house in La Salud, singing a ditty in a voice that is meant to drown out the complaints of his wife in the kitchen; "Taylor" embracing his Margarita inside a black car with lace window curtains, on a sunny Sunday, a prey to a cloud of little kids who'd gathered round; Navarro stretched out on a camp bed in

Bundó's apartment, oiling his pistol if he is alone and if not chatting aimiably with two old maids; Jaime with his brother-in-law the locksmith having his shoes shined just outside the Liceo subway station, watching women walk by waggling their hind ends, and Guillén traveling around the countryside peddling cosmetics, and Sendra in overalls under a car in Bundó's garage, but always at night; of all of them he is the most prudent. Peace-loving citizens.

These periods of inactivity end up exciting them even more, and then their meetings degenerating into violent arguments till dawn. Moreover, this is inevitable: they have been militants in different parties and throw it in each other's faces that they once belonged to this group or that. A youngster from Madrid brought up in the tough anarchist youth group formed by the exiles in Toulouse was to be part of the group for a brief time, a daring kid who had already been through the basement torture rooms of the Department of Security, whom Sendra sent back to Toulouse after three weeks. Navarro was sorry to see him leave.

"He was a good sort. And his father too. I knew him in Montpellier."

"A fool," Palau said laughing. "His father was one of the men who shot up the Sacred Heart in the Cerro de los Angeles. Ha ha. A bigwig, that's for sure. Like Navarrete."

Laughing at the joke, "Taylor" sat sweating beneath the bare light bulb, consulting a map of the outskirts of Barcelona and Palau was perched on the folding chair, with his feet on the table, oiling his Navy Parabellum Special. And Navarro was making an inventory of their very small stock of ammunition. At the beginning of this summer of '44, their base was an abandoned ice factory, in Pueblo Seco. Thanks to Sendra, the liaison with Toulouse was better, but they still had no contact in the city and did not receive very precise orders. Little by little conditions got better, and each time Sendra came back from France he was more elated. "Not a three-cornered hat anywhere en route." "How's my wife?" Navarro asked. "Will another group ever get here?" Fusam wondered. "I don't think it'll be long now, lots of people are getting ready to come."

The night that they waited for Sendra in the factory, after three months with no meetings, their tempers flared again as they talked about the guy from Madrid: Palau the victim of more recriminations: in '34 you and Ferrán tried to prevent them from burning down the church in your village, Fusam recollected. That fool of a Ferrán fell and you took to your heels — are you going to deny it?

"The nuns paid eight *duros* a fire."

"You're a brazen fool. I still remember your troubles in the SIM, when you insisted that we should let that old village priest go. How many more did you help, and why?"

"The priests I saved had voted for the Republic. Did you know that, you old farts?"

"And who knows how many people rolling in dough," Bundó insisted, lying there stretched out on his back on a wooden bench, cleaning his fingernails. "And how did they thank you for it afterward?"

"I don't want their gratitude, I want their wallets. You guys can't understand because you're from the FAI — left-wing anarchists clinging to Federica Montseny's skirts."

"Palau, some day they're going to give you more hell than you ever learned about in church, you'll see."

"All you friends of the great dead anarchist hero Durruti can kiss my ass."

"They say he has a pretty broad brought in from time to time, but only to chat," Bundó said, yawning at the ceiling. "The one who really makes out is his kid brother. . . ."

"You animal," Palau protested. "The worst thing for Marcos wasn't the front, but here, with old Artemi, with your patrols."

"Somebody had to clean out the rearguard, right?" — this from Fusam.

"Too much responsibility for such a youngster. Work that was too dirty for him to do. You're animals."

"If everybody had done their jobs we wouldn't be here to-day cooking up plots and dead broke," Navarro said, looking at him sternly.

"I didn't fight a revolution to get money, you *faieros*. And come off it — we've all bitched enough."

When Sendra arrives the arguments end. Jaime comes in after him with a heavy suitcase and a new pinstripe suit. Sendra stubs out his cigarette in the triangular metal ashtray whose sides read "Alaska Bar." Who brought this here? he asks, clucking. But he changes the subject when he sees Jaime lower his eyes, and turning to "Taylor" he says: "His name is Bernardo Nogueras; you can nab him right in the doorway of his house, you'll see. The other one is a police commissioner; he crosses the Plaza Sagrada Familia at exactly the same hour every day, with an adjutant. I'll take care of him. If Palau can't, or doesn't want to, let Bundó come."

"It's not that," Palau grumbles. "It's just that it's a waste of time. Did you hear the BBC yesterday?"

"The only thing you like to do is throw nails on the Rabassada road and stop cars," Navarro says. "Because it pays off better. I'm coming with you, Sendra."

"Shut up, you show-off," Palau chimes in. "I'm going along, just to show you I'm game."

Kids piling up dry sycamore leaves on the sidewalk of the Calle Sicilia, and rolling around in them. A fine rain is falling. The brown Studebaker with patches of orange paint coming down the Calle Corcega gets ready to cross the Plaza Sagrada Familia. An old woman wipes the nose of a little boy in a school apron, beneath a black umbrella, steps backward in fright, raises her eyes as the four-door Ford sedan passes by, slowly rumbling along the curb.

Fusam at the wheel, Sendra and Palau in the back seat. Suddenly Sendra's voice hisses, come on, put your foot to the floor. As it passes by the Studebaker, the Ford accelerates and the steam coming from the radiator clouds Palau's view through the windshield for a moment. He can barely make out the two occupants of the car: one guy driving, at ease and chatting away, and the other one at his side, suddenly smelling danger. The hump on Fusam's back gets bigger all at once as he turns the wheel and sticks side by side with the other car; the tires squeal. Sendra appears at the window with the submachine gun and shoots. The windows of the Studebaker shatter, as Palau, hunched down in the back seat, empties the Parabellum Special at the heads, less than three feet away, that are already tumbling to the floor.

The Studebaker goes out of control against the curb, gaining speed as it zigzags over the carpet of grass and the nose collides with a tree. One of the back doors opens all by itself; lying in the seats are two men in blue shirts soaked with blood.

The baroness slept far into the morning. Her husband had had a white telephone installed in the bathroom and every morning he took care of some urgent bit of business sitting on the toilet seat. His voice, congested with intestinal pleasures, came out through a little window, crossed the inside patio, and reached the ears of the maid preparing breakfast in the kitchen. After that he went to his printer's shop with his elder son. He earned a pile as the sole printer of rationing cards, but Doña Elvira was never willing to give up her dealings in the black market. That autumn she gave her rain boots away to the maid.

By noon the baroness was bored and had to invent activities for herself.

"Carmen, we're going upstairs and clean the attic."

Beneath spiderwebs and dust, behind a set of bedsprings were piles of old magazines and a complete collection of *Crónica* up to July of '36. The baroness leafed through a magazine with a grimace of distaste, her nostrils filled with the acrid odor of the pages, the plebeian climate of that noisy Republican Madrid, with its taxi-dances and Miss Apricot contests, vociferating little dressmakers and workers on strike, with luncheon banquets in the Casa de Campo, starlets with their uplifted breasts and Socialist summer schools.

"Give all this filthy stuff to the first ragpicker who comes by."

"Yes, ma'am."

By arrangement with the peasants in the Tortosa farmhouse, the purveyors transport the goods by train, but only as far as the vicinity of the Hospitalet station. Poor people who live in misery, women in mourning who run along the rails pushing bundles that roll along the tracks. At night in an old rented mansion converted into a warehouse, with Menchu sitting at a little table noting down the deliveries in an account book. Sacks of goods carried by men and women who receive the sum agreed on: fifty *pesetas* for each 150 kilos, plus the expenses of the journey.

Doña Elvira's tubercular son verified the weight of the goods delivered.

"You're ten kilos short, Petra. And this is the third time."

The woman, who is pregnant, is sorry: she had to abandon the sacks for several hours along the way, kids must have made off with a few handfuls, or maybe even the Guardia Civil. Making dangerous trips in dirty trains with bundles hidden underneath the seats, a poor widowed scullery maid, with a son suffering from the itch, have pity on me, young lady.

"You're lying, you witch" — the man's slap with the back of his hand leaves a star of blood on her lips, a nose like a broken waterpipe spattering the wallpaper with fleurs de lys and the window nailed shut with boards and slats. Menchu wants to intercede in her favor, but the second blow raises the black skirts, baring her flannel petticoat and the red, almost invisible cords amid the folds of flabby flesh around her waist, holding up a pregnant belly made of little sacks of rice, pork, and flour. Who were you trying to put one over on, you old whore?

"Please, José María," Menchu intervenes, lowering the woman's skirt. "Let her go."

The rubbing of the cords, after so many hours, had worn away the skin at her waist; from her thighs great streams of blood trickled to the floor, and her fingers were like slender red fish. From between her legs there slipped down a little bundle tied with a strip of blood-soaked burlap that she barely had time to catch with her hands before it fell to the floor.

The baroness dried her tears of laughter in the foamy lace of an embroidered handkerchief, as the other women stood watching. Rumor had it that she was not a baroness and had never been one, that she was a sly woman who had escaped from a very ordinary family. The salon full of guests, the silver candelabra with black candles on the white mantle of the buffet. Silk dresses, furs, jewelry, red-purple lips and fingernails. In deep bright violet armchairs, three gentlemen talk about gasoline. The maid with the tray circulates amid joking owners of warehouses, tax appraisers, presidents of guilds, paper manufacturers, proprietors of shadow-factories, officials from the Department of Supplies, and matrons who work for charity. A member of the Paralelo chorus was praising the originality of their hostess in everything she did.

The Christmas gift of the baroness to her friends in this 1944 holiday season had been a can of five liters of pure olive oil decorated with a patriotic red and yellow ribbon.

The maid hurries through the passageway to the kitchen; a satin caress clings to the dimples of her high buttocks as the friends of master José María laugh in the shadows, already a bit drunk. An arm shoots out from behind the armor collection and takes Menchu by the waist, pulling her along toward the dark bedroom where the red-hot tips of three Havana cigars gleam. Happy New Year, dearie, the voice whispers in her ear, here's a little present for you — as the cold of the cross slips down between her breasts.

Sendra insisting on controlling all the operations, forbidding any initiative taken apart from the group. In no uncertain terms. Nonetheless, at this very moment in the vestibule of the Kursall movie theater, Palau's eyes beneath the tilted brim of his hat look sidewise at the man in a dark blue twill suit heading for the lavatory. A woman is waiting for him with a little mirror in her hand, touching up her thick, shiny lips with a lipstick. She is wearing a cloche decorated with pearls.

The barrel of the Parabellum is thrust into his back. Sometimes Palau could see how their balls shrank in their open fly, how they wet their pants when you said shut your trap, don't turn around, don't look at me. He relieves them, always from behind, of their wallets, their watches, their diamond solitaires. When I go wait five minutes, he says to him, if you don't I'll have you bumped off, fascist, we know you, we know how many you turned in to the police today. And he leaves him there trembling, goes out into the vestibule, brushing past the lady, pretending respect and a sense of decorum, smiling to himself with his horse teeth.

"I'm beginning to get fed up with jobs like this" — Sendra at the base in Pueblo Nuevo, smacking the palm of his hand with the rolled-up newspaper, without looking at anybody, though everybody knows who he's talking about. "Nobody is to strike out on his own or he'll end up in the gutter with a bullet in his neck, I'm not a fanatic, all of you know how I am. There's no room at my side for pickpockets or thieves, do you follow me? and if somebody wants to settle accounts with a fascist, let him wait for better times the way I'm doing."

Jaime Viñas steals a silent look at Palau, who is sitting poking at his teeth with a toothpick. Navarro and Bundó exchange grimaces. And no excuses, Sendra adds, such as wanting to send a few *duros* to Lage's wife or somebody's widow. The organization is taking care of that already. Palau smiles beneath his aquiline nose: the Red Cross pays more punctually and better, he says to Guillén in a low voice.

Suddenly Sendra turns around and looks at me, a bit down in the mouth: what about you? What did you go out tonight for? Didn't we agree to tell you if we needed you? Don't you know that they're beating Artemi every day and if he sings you're a goner? All right, out with you. No, wait a minute. As long as you're here, have something to eat.

"Even God can't understand you, Marcos," Guillén says.

"Are you trying to get all of us nabbed just on account of you?"

Palau seems to be fighting with his jammed Parabellum Special.

"Goddamn it, my nice big heater doesn't work any more. Some day you're going to get all of us fried, Sendra — next time you go out see if you can't bring me back a good Thompson."

He is thinking of a long, quiet car like a caterpillar slowly cruising along the curb. About fifty yards farther on, that worker with a blackened face who will smell of espadrilles when he gets into the car, is swiftly applying a paintbrush to the outside wall of Pompeya Church. At his side is another worker holding the bucket of tar and a third one is watching the street corner, the deserted sidewalk of Diagonal with twinkling streetlamps. They paint "down with" just above the spider that is already there. The February wind makes the reflections of the street lamps quiver on the asphalt; the Monument to Victory on the Plaza Cinc d'Oros seems to move. The black Wanderer goes swiftly up the deserted Vía Augusta at three o'clock in the morning. Its side windows launch hundreds of white leaflets in the night, which drift back and forth before landing on the sidewalk. At almost the same hour a plastique bomb exploded at the monument to the Condor Legion. "What! Well, it wasn't us," I said to her, and it seemed to be taking forever to get her rain boots, her stockings, her blouse off. "It might have been Quico, maybe he's back. A bunch of madmen." "Why do you go with them, why don't you forget them forever?" Don't cry, damn it, I'm not risking my neck at all, all I do is paint signs and distribute leaflets.

"Leaflets, firecrackers, and pricks in vinegar," Palau always joked, leaning with his back on the bar of the Cosmos this time. "And meanwhile what do we have to eat, huh? Lots of identification papers and lots of trips to France for Ramón and Sendra, and what's the good of it all? That's what I said to them, Mianet, you know how I am. Have another glass of milk with brandy, old stud, I'm paying."

The old man was nodding sleepily above the box of trinkets hanging from his neck. A potbellied whore, stuffed into a tight skirt with a broken zipper down the side, waggles her flaccid buttocks at them. Palau hands Mianet a little cardboard box shaped like a pencil-box.

"Let's see if you can sell it all. Except for the gold scorpion. I want you to put it on one of your love-bracelets and have the name Margarita engraved on it; it'll be my wedding present."

"Is 'Taylor' getting married?"

"Yes, gramps. How time flies."

"It'd be nice to have Ramón perform the marriage ceremony, wouldn't it?"

Palau laughs, staring at the whore and attracting her smiling gaze.

They kneaded the plastique a little reluctantly. They were like drug addicts, like sworn coconspirators, clenching their teeth with a taste of iron on their palates. Above their heads, the statue of Victory was being lashed by gusts of wind and a fine drizzle. Then as the car goes off down the Diagonal toward Pedralbes, a red flame rises at the feet of the monument, without an explosion, a glare reflected in the wet asphalt, followed by thick smoke.

"A dud," Palau was to say as he rolled up the car window. "If this stuff won't go off, balls, can't you see that this whole business is a crock of shit?"

Twelve hours later, Sendra was on his way from Barcelona to Berga by train. He spent the night in the farmhouse where the contact had a store of clothes for the mountains, and arms. The contact was a guy with a pockmarked face that Sendra didn't know. He was there to collect funds and send them to the Toulouse headquarters. But this time Sendra wasn't going to hand over any money — he was there to ask for some.

"You guys in the city are asleep," the other man said. "The money that we get here can't be touched. Do you think we risk our necks cleaning out farmhouses so that you guys can carry off the dough?"

"We need other things in Barcelona."

"I suppose so. My advice is to go to Headquarters and talk with Palacios. I can't go with you, but I've heard that you know the route better than anybody. Don't go by way of Andorra, La Molina is crawling with guards, take the Guardiola road. You'll see Marti in Perpignan."

He went on his way next day equipped with mountain boots, a hunting jacket, a khaki shirt, a cap, a knapsack, field glasses and the Thompson .45. In Perpignan he gets orders to take certain papers to Toulouse showing various routes to follow from Andorra and Perpignan across the Pyrenees, where new bases in farmhouses and refuges had already been chosen. Well, let's see, what else. He also took false identity papers, with the personal data left blank, for the members of the new group that's getting ready to come to Barcelona. . . .

So what, Sendra, I said, what are you hoping to get with all this, and I burst out laughing at it later on, in the hotel for whores. There she was, in her bare feet, struggling with the broken zipper on her curving hips, she said what are you laughing at, brown eyes, what's your name, please forgive me for asking, but a girl never knows who she's got between her legs. The poor thing must still be waiting for me: I tell her I'm going down the hall to say hello to the towel boy, he's a friend of mine, and I leave the room, and listen: it's perfect, kid, it can't fail: there are six of them, plus one at the door, and I think there's another one who serves drinks at the bar. And the customers are loaded. I've got it all planned down to the second and it can't miss. Are you on, sailor?"

"Sendra's going to tell you no, Palau."

"You're wrong. He's already said yes. Or did you think he'd be an idealist all his life?"

X

HE visited Galán's widow in her apartment in Ensanche to talk to her about his granny's cold and the medicine she needed, or to tell her how the search was going, and he always came away with a few *pesetas* or a bar of chocolate. In exchange he had to make up cock-and-bull stories. One day in the middle of December she received him in the company of a number of devout ladies who were making up food parcels for Christmas for the Poor, the great parish festival that was being celebrated this year for the first time. She was presiding over a big table in the drawing room, full of wrapping paper and cans of condensed milk, and tying up the packets already prepared with blue ribbons. Come over here, my boy, do you want a little almond paste? The ragpicker, standing there amid the glass cases with miniatures and those musical clocks slowly ticking, gave her a version of things that was very ambiguous, trying to make his voice blend in with the affable cackling of the benefactresses congregated there: I'm on the track, ma'am, I really am. They were fables made up by himself and Itchy, in turn, in the junk shop; I've found out that she was working as a prostitute in one of those houses, we can tell you for now, the baroness's maid told me so the other day when she sold me a sack of old magazines, she was working at Madame Petit's, and I beg your pardon, ma'am, but that's the name of the place, it would appear that she was very popular because of how well she did the double boiler with customers, shall I explain what that is? as you like then, where were we? after that she was seen working as a waitress in a bar on Paralelo, you can tell her, she was trying to redeem herself, according to what the bootblack in the bar told me. What do you mean, redeem herself? yes, yes, that's right, so as to be able to pull the wool over people's eyes, and as a result the proprietress of the bar had just kicked her out, and do you know why? not for stealing, no, no, and not for being a tramp or being full of lice, that it appears that she more or less is, and not for selling soap on the sly to the artists at the Cómico: but for taking up with her husband, even though to tell the truth the proprietress and her husband aren't really husband and wife either, apparently, they're just lovers, begging your pardon, ma'am, but what dramas one sees going from house to house, ma'am, what messy situations. That one has no respect for anything and manages to hide her tracks and slip away, she's the careful sort, but anyway I'm on another trail now, but there's the problem of expenses, ma'am, with all my money going as it does for streetcars and coffee and tips. . . .

It was that chill December that so often drove the slum kids to sit round the brazier in the ragpicker's shop, to the animal heat that lingered in the corners where old Granny Javaloyes worked with her dead cigar butt in her mouth, surrounded by sacks and piles of rags. On many afternoons when they came in, they saw Itchy almost buried in the mountain of paper and exchanging confidences with Java, instructing him: This time you get right to the bottom of things, you go to her and you say: ma'am, I have it on good authority that she might be the person who's living in the Ritz now as the mistress of a city councilor, or so they tell me, she calls herself by another name now and she's dyed her hair, a delicate business and she keeps an eye peeled for the cops: that you're about to pin her down but you spend a lot of dough waiting for her to come out of the bar across from the hotel alone, or tailing her in a taxi, not to mention the drinks you have to offer the whore who's a friend of hers and the one who put me on the track, you tell her, the one that warned me to be careful because she's very well connected now and receives real bigwigs, the impresario of the Tivoli Theater no less, and a colonel, and the star Carmen de Lis. You ask whether it's true that they get along well together? everybody in Barcelona knows it, ma'am, even the students, he sends her jewels every week and comes and goes in secret, and I won't tell you any more, kid, it's not right. Tell her that's what she told you, don't be stupid, try to get all you can out of her and don't let the cow run dry. And that you've got a lot of expenses and I could use an advance, ma'am, this is really a strong lead, but we'll see, she's a sly one and knows all the tricks, I do the best I can. . . .

He never told the real truth. Not even Java, in fact, knew what it was. As in the stories he made up for his pals, the truth was that murky material that never managed to take wing, to come unstuck from the bottom. Señora Galán kept looking at him, smiling a bit sadly, but still staring fixedly, like a charmed snake: as she listened to the ragpicker's report, she gave the impression that she was waiting for him to slip up and at the same time convinced that this would never happen: she must have intuited that the youngster was not telling the truth, but at the same time she was in some way aware that he wasn't lying either, and that it might be true that he was short of money. Her fragrant pink hand opened her purse before he'd finished, long before he clammed up, and her tired eyes blinked in their remote blueness, and she would say, all right, son, her hand nervously searching for coins, here take this and don't waste it, give it to your granny.

So she was living the life of a kept woman, climbing higher and higher, for example: from being a whore put up in the Ritz with little doggies and a transparent negligee, with a chauffeur and jewels, and then passing from the arms of one black marketeer to those of another and for example: a little apartment in the Paseo de San Juan with cretonne curtains, a bidet and a bar, okay? Keeping company with nouveaux riches in the boxes of the Liceo and the Barca soccer field, surely having an affair with the president of the club: higher and higher, with those who've got hold of the cow by the udder.... A lie, the whole thing had to be a lie: going farther and farther down the drain all the time, more famished, more eaten away by syphilis, more lonely and sick of all the terror, a sad whore in a poor neighborhood who'd never make a career for herself, certainly. Really a bitch of a life she's leading wherever she is, Itchy would say, but that's not the way you should picture her because then there's no color, kid, there's no story. Incapable of up and leaving the neighborhood and her past life for good, even though she promised herself a thousand times, she comes back some nights to slip into the Verdi moviehouse or the Roxy like a shadow, because she can't help it, because she grew up in those streets and the sounds of that neighborhood are the only thing she still has left of it, that prehistoric screech of streetcars and the whistles of the knife-sharpener; out of nostalgia, perhaps, for her lost innocence, because from time to time she passes by the orphans' home that she left one day, never to return. That's how you have to picture her for the lady: a lively one, wiggling her tail, always within reach of our hand but never letting herself be caught, and that's the way you can keep playing in this lottery, don't be stupid. And you can say that you finally found her that night, lying on the sidewalk outside the Continental Bar, drunk and with her head shaved, unknown, at the end of her rope, consumed by venereal disease, kid. But she got away from you: you still have to meet her twice more and lose her again, don't get nervous on me, gummy-eyes, it's all calculated so that the story will be confused and the punishment clear.

Before that, in the autumn, when the kids began to hang out

at the parish house following Java's example, when they were getting to be friends of the catechumens, including Susana, who'd signed up for Theatricals, and everyone was on good terms with them and they could play Ping-Pong and sing in the chorus, it suddenly seemed to them that their stories were disappearing in a dreamy fog. The affection and the generosity shown them at the parish house was like discovering a new world. But that pious seed of goodness could not germinate in untilled earth. Tits wore a jersey given him by Social Aid, with a black and brown diamond pattern, but his ears still leaked pus. With the first cold spells there were still stone fights, and the first one of the season was one of the bloodiest ones that had ever been seen in the neighborhood and it coincided with fresh news about Ramona.

It all began one afternoon when Itchy was setting up his comic-book stand in the Plaza del Norte, on the sidewalk outside of Los Luises where a blind man sold lottery tickets sitting on a folding stool. The kids from Los Luises were going at it with a rag ball and raising a lot of dust. It was a windy day and he looked around for stones to hold the comic books down. Shortly thereafter Luis arrived with his lunch under his arm and a packet of Merlins: Java's got another pile of Tarzans, he said, he's just gotten them for just the weight of the paper, go right now and get them, I couldn't bring all of them. He seemed very tired and was having trouble breathing. Itchy gave him his cough drops, and then went off to Java's and Luis stayed to watch the stand, sitting with his back against the wall. He began to cough, opened the little box of cough drops and tossed four of them into his mouth. He sold a Mutt and Jeff calendar for a *real* and exchanged an old Flash Gordon for two Shadow albums without covers. Itchy likes The Shadow, he thought to himself, he'll be happy. Only a few kids came over to the stand to have a look — kids from Los Hermanos and the Divino Maestro. Some men in berets were sitting on a stone bench in the square, talking together and staring at their feet; seen from the back like that they seemed not to have heads. As if he had been hit in the belly by a stray bullet, one of them suddenly doubled over and fell face down in the dust. Two monks who were playing soccer with their cassocks tucked up took him away. Twenty number being drawn today, the blind man chanted. A woman in a turban and dark glasses crossed the center of the square, waggling her hips. The wind whistled among the ruins of the dye factory on the Calle Marti and whipped the laurel peeking over the wall of the Salesians. Whirling in the dust, the blue cover of *Signal*, showing planes diving, coiled about Luis's feet, as he stood there with his lunch in his hand, without having yet bitten into it: half a loaf of bread split in two with a slice of quince as hard and black as a dried fish. As he was getting ready to sink his teeth into it, with a sigh, he saw three guys with the look of bullies coming toward him. They came up to him and began pawing through the comic books but didn't buy a single one. Two more from Los Luises joined them, waving Ping-Pong paddles, and then another one he recognized: he was from the Palacio de la Cultura and had a shoebox with silkworms and mulberry leaves in his hand. They destroyed the comic-book stand and tore a cover showing X-9. Luis put his lunch to one side. The one with the silkworms, standing there with his legs apart, challenged him: "Who broke his arm? Which of you beat him up, you shitty slum kid?"

"What are you talking about, sissy?"

"You know very well. You're the shits."

Sitting on his heels, swaying back and forth, Luis pushed the closest one and tore the comic book from his hands: kid, he said, they're raffling off a beating and you've got all the winning tickets.

"Is that so? Your mother's just gone by on her way to the Bosque. Did you know she works the last row of the peanut gallery?"

"That whore isn't my mother."

"Yes she is, and she does jerk-off jobs and she's got a scar on her tit."

Luis blinked, momentarily forgetting how much he'd like to blast his enemy. A scar? he said. Are you sure? What happened to her?

They trampled on the stand. With one swipe of his hand Luis knocked the box with the worms to the ground, get that filthy thing out of here, you fairy, he said, beat it or I'll clobber you. The other boy came a few steps closer, followed by his cohorts.

"You've got no right to talk, you lousy bastard. Your father's in jail."

A springtime smile flowered on Luis's pale mouth, and his chest swelled.

"Why, may I ask?"

"Because he's a Red. That's why. And your mother does jerk-off jobs in the movie house for a skin, and everybody knows about it."

Luis stood up, his fists clenched. A painful grimace took the place of the smile.

"Say that again."

"Your mother's a whore."

"So's yours, you son of a bitch."

Luis's head butted him in the balls, and the other boy screamed to high heaven. They rolled on the ground together. The others leaped on top of him and made him let go of his prey, of the flesh that he was already sinking his nails and his teeth into, and they kicked him in the ribs, forced him to the ground and twisted his arm behind his back. They hit him in the nape of the neck and his sides with the handles of the Ping-Pong paddles. The blind man turned his wooden face in the direction of the blows, his profile rigid, obstinate: he could see with his ears, drawing today, he chanted. The men sitting on the bench watched the fight with wet, dusty eyes, and no one moved, none of them came over to separate them.

"This is for what you did to Miguel," the one who had the melodious voice said to him, kicking him. "And this, and this."

When they let go of him he was on all fours, sucking his

split lip with his tongue and coughing. He picked up the comic books torn to shreds and the remainder of his lunch. He was sick to his stomach and covered his mouth with his hand, as the warm blood trickled through his fingers. He went running to the junk shop, wanting to tell Java: they've seen her in the Bosque, they've touched her scar. Before he got there, at the fountain in the Calle Camelias, he stuck his head under the faucet. He began coughing again then, and his chest hurt so much that he had to lean his back against the wall. He was breathing like a bellows, his face was deathly pale, and with his bulging eyes he could not see or answer the person who stopped to ask him what's the matter, son, why don't you go home? It was an old lady in men's shoes. With his eyes closed he let those anonymous hands stroke his head, he let himself be scolded gently, they've insulted my mother, he said, until the old lady went on her way chewing caramels and her sadness. Luis finally got to the junk shop and told Java and Itchy what had happened. Amén was also there, and Java sent him running in search of the rest: first we'll settle accounts with those damned pansies and then we'll see if it's true that it was really her. A half-hour later they were all in the Plaza del Norte with their mufflers crossed over their chests like two cartridge belts and their pockets full of stones, but the enemy had gone to the Can Compte vacant lot in search of ammunition. They found them there. They attacked them with a rain of stones and saw them take to their heels without being able to catch a single one of them; they reappeared later with reinforcements from Los Luises and the battle lasted till nightfall along Alegre de Dalt, Paseo del Monte, and Martí, outside the Remedio Clinic, whose high walls bristled with glass shards and hunks of bottles. The neighbors closed their windows and balconies; it was one of the bloodiest stone fights in memory. Itchy got hit in the forehead with a stone and went around with a bandage around his head for a month. Amén skinned a knee and Martín twisted an ankle. The one who came off worst of all was Mingo: as he was leaping over the wall of the clinic he slipped, catching his pants on the shards of glass, and remaining hung up there for a moment, finding a handhold wherever he could: he kicked and twisted about trying to get free, and they saw him hanging there with his wrist caught on a piece of glass, which finally broke. So much blood spurted out that they thought he'd cut his veins. They took him to a dispensary, and in the jewelry shop where he worked they had to fire him, and he was going about now like a kid in a movie, a wounded Prisoner of Zenda. He was bored without the shop to go to and in order to be doing something he sometimes went out with Itchy to sell bone rings and postcards of film stars in the bars around.

Java for his part went several times to the Bosque in hopes of meeting Ramona, but never did. In the middle of one Sunday morning, Mingo came to the junk shop all excited: yesterday in the Viadé Bar, he explained, a guy who knows all the whores around had bought a colored postcard from him, the one of the German blonde in boots, the guy said it was funny that she looked so much like a whore at the Bosque that he knew. My heart started pounding, Mingo said, and I asked him what her name is. Ramoneta, he said, she always sat at the very top of the peanut gallery but don't go there because you won't find her there, kid, I think she works the matinees at the Roxy now. The Falangist delegate also happened to be in the bar, Mingo went on, and he hassled me: I had to give the money back to the guy who'd bought the card and the delegate kept it. Who gave you this? he asked, don't you know that I don't want you selling dirty postcards around here? I'm not doing anything bad, comrade, I said to him, I got them from the junk shop, they're nothing at all and I sell them for pennies. But the one-eyed son-of-a-bitch hauls off and socks me so hard I'm still spinning my wheels. A really good one. He took all my postcards away from me and said I don't want to see you in bars any more or I'll have you shut up in Durán Asylum. That was last night. This morning I went to the early show at the Roxy, and here comes the good part, Java, because she was there, in the next to the last row.

"Are you sure?"

"I didn't get a good look at her face and she had something around her head, but I swear it's her. I've just touched her breasts under her blouse and her scar with this very hand."

"On her left one or her right one?"

Mingo pondered the matter, his arm in the sling, let's see, he said, sitting down on top of the magazines as though they were an armchair, raising his free arm and waving his hand in the air without looking, as though he were fumbling around in a sack of apples with his eyes shut, let's see, yes, it was the left one.

"She charged me a skin," he added, "and she's great at it. Give me your handkerchief, she said to me, and when she gave it back to me, I said how much? A skin. And then I ran here to tell you, I didn't even stay to see the movie, it had just begun."

On submerging himself in the silvery half-shadow he saw Arsène Lupin shining a flashlight in a dark room: white gloves, silk ascot, top hat jauntily tilted over one eyebrow. The orchestra seats were almost empty; a few couples necking, and here and there a few men by themselves, dressed in stiff raincoats and mufflers. It may well have been colder in the movie house than in the street. He allowed his eyes to adjust to the darkness, standing at the end of the aisle, looking for her. In the last rows various pairs of eyes gleamed like those of a hungry cat, catching the flickering light from the screen; one whore who was eating a sandwich hissed at him, another had fallen asleep with her head on her chest: very short hair, dark glasses, a purple blouse with twisted shoulder pads, as though carelessly hung on a hanger. He sat down beside her with silent, feline movements and slipped his hand in the neck of her blouse. She was breathing heavily as though having a bad dream, with a sack of caramels in her lap. The straps of her brassiere were down, and there was a tender warmth between her breasts. Java's hand closed around her left one, small and warm, and his fingers searched for the scar, although there was no need to: he had just recognized her despite her new haircut, the turban, and the dark glasses.

"What a dream I was having, kid," she murmured as she woke up, still not looking at him but already placing in his fly a hand that appeared to have a life independent of her will and her body, weightless, solicitous, watching Arsène Lupin bow gracefully and elegantly before a lady with luminous bare shoulders. Then she turned around and looked at him. She gave a start. "Well, well."

She took her hand away but Java grabbed it and pulled it toward him. Ramona took off her glasses to see him better.

"Wait." She looked around with the eyes of a cornered panther, her hand resting on his sensitive flesh, causing a gentle abandon to creep slowly over him.

"I was passing by and came in," Java said, leaning over in the seat and kissing her neck. "What a coincidence, isn't it? I'm glad to see you, honest and truly, you please me, I've been thinking of you ever since that day. . . . "

"Even though things went so badly? Have you had a good look at me, kid? What is it you like about me?"

He thought: the way you tremble when you embrace me, the way our teeth knock together, the way you huddle up next to me like a docile, scared puppy.

"Your breasts," he said. "I like your breasts a lot."

She laughed softly.

"What did the guy who was watching say about me? I take it he'd like to see me again."

"I've already told you that I never spoke with him."

"You've followed me, you've come looking for me to take me there again."

"Why are you afraid? What makes you run away from me?"

"Who, me? What a laugh. You see too many movies, kid."

"Well, why don't we do it again, there in that apartment. . . . ?"

"I've never taken a liking to that sort of work."

"You haven't come back to the Continental Bar either. How come?"

"I needed a change of air." She was rigid, all caught up in her rapid calculations, but her hand reacted immediately. "Come on, keep your mind on what you're doing. The movie'll be over soon."

Her thoughts were far away, surely much farther away than the screen, but her hand went on stroking with diabolical precision, impelled by a mechanism at once distant and affectionate. Java noticed Ramona's heart beating beneath her scars, and he got excited, forgetting everything for a while: that they were pursuing her in rage and hatred and he didn't know why, that she was not a whore like the others, that she had two names and a deep-rooted fear still, a sweat of imminent disaster on her ruined skin.

On the screen: a woman screeching, the headlights of a car in the night, stopped along the highway, and a frightened man struggling between his two tormentors; a third taking out his pistol and the woman screaming don't kill him, this isn't Arsène Lupin, don't kill him; and the shots, one, two, three, four, and Ramona's agitated breast beneath his hand, her heart beating frantically now, what's the matter with you? it's only a movie, and her hands suddenly covering her eyes so as not to see. It's all over, he said to her laughing, don't you like scary movies? but she sat there for some time hiding her face in her hands and trembling. Java kept quiet, and it was only afterward, when she began stroking him again, that he said to her: "Don't be afraid of me, Ramona, I want to be your friend."

"I don't want any friends. Give me your handkerchief."

"Not yet. Come on, let's go to your place instead, okay?"

"Not a chance. You don't have enough money for that."

"Please. I'd like it. Ever since that day, I've thought of nothing but you, even though I've been back a couple of times with others. They're no good at all. I've fallen in love with you, Ramona."

"Liar. What a kid you still are." She smiled rather sweetly for the first time, looking him in the eye. "With the body of a man, but still a kid anyway."

"You like me a little, I bet. I gave you pleasure, I bet."

He kissed her on the lips. She leaned her head against the back of the seat with a mixture of fatigue and condescension, closed her eyes, and let him do as he pleased. Java lifted her skirt up, and she opened her legs. The vibrant music announced the end of the movie. The house lights went on: some fifteen spectators stood up, saluting the blank screen as the Falange hymn rang out. Java's handkerchief was still in his pocket.

"You see what happened, with all that chattering?" Ramona looked at him out of the corner of her eye, her arm upraised. "Button up."

"I'll see you home."

"There's no need."

"Look at the state you're leaving me in. Please, let me be your friend. You like me a little, Ramona, don't deny it."

Arm upraised, with the hand open and extended and forming a forty-five degree angle with the upright body. When the hymn was over she looked him in the eye for a second as though wanting to tell him something. Then she put on her dark glasses and smoothed her skirt.

"You don't have enough dough to pay for a room."

"I don't want to go to a hotel room with you, I want to go to your place."

"It's a roominghouse, and it's not possible there."

"I'll sneak in without their seeing me."

"No, I tell you."

He followed her down the aisle and at the door they caught up with the spectators leaving, leaning on each other drowsily, Java following after her with his arm about her waist, clinging to her buttocks, happily, his mouth pressed against her ear: is it true that you worked in a house on the Calle Camelias, years ago? She shared with him his need for warmth, intimacy, company: yes, why do you ask? It was then that Ramona's hand squeezed his in silence, and she turned around to kiss him on the chin. You're a good kid, she said. They came out onto the

Plaza Lesseps, bathed in pale Sunday sunlight. Java tried to take her arm but she wouldn't let him and seemed to be in a great hurry. Suddenly hunger made Java raise his eyes to the big clock on the church: twelve-thirty. At the streetcar stop, a friend of Ramona's made signs with her hand and she said I'm going to go with her.

Java didn't know what to do.

"Why don't you drop by the Continental Bar some day?"

"Why not? 'Bye, somebody's waiting for me."

"Let your friend go on alone. I'll buy you a vermouth."

"Don't be a bore. Some other day."

"Do you come to the Roxy every Sunday?"

They stood there still talking as she let two streetcars go by, but she caught the next one on the run, hopping onto the steps and leaving Java in the middle of a sentence. He was surprised; he'd always thought that she was trying to get rid of him for some reason, that he represented some sort of danger for her. He would never know what had precipitated this daring, unexpected hop onto the streetcar: a blueshirt next to the news stand. Java didn't quite realize what was going on till the streetcar disappeared down Salmerón, with Ramona giving a timid little wave from the back platform. Then as he turned around he saw the blueshirt, but somehow he didn't connect the two of them, and he thought idly to himself, well, well, there's the one-eyed man again, recruiting kids for the youth camps, and immediately forgot him: his square jaw and his black patch over one eye, his little notebook in which he noted down the names and addresses of the kids that surrounded him with ill-concealed impatience to go on with their interrupted soccer game.

But he would not forget the end of his conversation with Ramona, shortly before seeing her hop onto the streetcar: save up a little money and come see me, I can't allow myself to do favors just now. And also: I share my room with another girl, but I'm beginning to get tired of the Barrio Chino, there's a room for rent in the Calle Legalidad but for the moment it doesn't suit me. . . . And he: it doesn't suit you, you say, are you afraid? pretending not to understand, why, have you done something bad? and as she seemed to be deaf, or pretending to be deaf, Java went back to what he'd been saying before: how nice you are, when will I see you again, you can't leave me here like this, like a dog. . . . But I'll be moving soon, she kept saying as though he weren't speaking to her, and everything will change, this can't go on, I'll rent a sewing machine and try working again. You could try, of course, he said, you should try.

For now she was going to stay on in the Barrio Chino: that was what stuck in his mind. He'd had her in his hands and she'd gotten away. But wasn't it better that way if he wanted to get a little dough out of the señora, as Itchy said? He drank his vermouth, all by himself and lost in thought, and once he was back at the junk shop he was still dizzied by the furtive odor of the whore's body in the darkness of the movie theater.

In the Calle San Salvador he met "Taylor" and his girl; they were coming out of a pastry shop, laughing; he had a proud tilt to his face pitted from who knows what adventures, with his revolver under his armpit and his pretty Margarita with her head leaning on his shoulder.

XI

A ND they only send word when they don't know how to
forge safe-conduct passes, for example, or when they
have difficulties with the plastique and the explosives. They
use Esteban Guillén's niece for a messenger, a crybaby who
rides a man's bicycle with her skirts raised up way past everything. "Taylor" would be the one entrusted with visiting the
families of comrades in jail or exile, taking them things to help
out. A hut in Guinardó swarming with mosquitoes, its zinc
walls burning hot in the July night. The table beneath the bluish light of the kerosene lamp, cups of coffee with saccharine
and a pack of cards, and round the table three women in dirty
bathrobes and house slippers, curlers in their hair and their
faces smeared with face cream. Quick, Trini, the Flit, I can't
stand these things another minute. They've broken off their
card game and are looking at "Taylor," so handsome with his
brilliantined hair and his iron eyes, his high, stiff shirt collar,
and a spring to hold the knot in his tie in place. A radio is
playing, the dogs are barking in the nearby kitchen gardens.
Ramón is sleeping on the studio couch with his beret clutched

in his fist and his leather jacket covering his long legs. Meneses looks at him almost enviously.

"Don't wake him up," Trini says as she gets to her feet. "He's worn out from the trip. Do you want a cup of coffee? That's all there is in this house."

"Thanks, 'Blondie,'" "Taylor" says to cheer her up, pinching her on the chin. "Don't be down in the dumps. Palau says we'd be better off having a forced vacation, like your husband. You're not the only one — we're all tired. But Luis will be out of jail when Sendra comes back. Chin up, girl, it won't be long now. I've brought some more leaflets, but don't distribute them in this neighborhood. Here, this'll be enough for you to get by on for a few days."

He slips a few bills into the pocket of her bathrobe. "Blondie" sits down astride a rickety chair, her plump bare arms hanging over the back. Thanks, Meneses, if it wasn't for you ... And then with a sigh: I know you've gotten married, just look how we're showing off these days. Grabbing his hand, looking at the scorpion hanging from the love-bracelet: a wedding present? Yes, from Palau. When everything's said and done he's very nice — look, he's even had the name engraved on it, here, Margarita. "Taylor" would then ask about the little girl and abⁿ ⁿᵉ all about the boy: he's a good kid, he keeps bringing you home coffee from the roasting shop, I see. ...

"They always give him a hundred grams for himself. He only goes there three nights a week now. If you could see how that boy of mine coughs still. I want him to sign up for the youth camps, he'd at least have enough to eat there and pure air to breathe. But if his father ever found out, he'd kill me."

"No, woman, you're doing the right thing. This is going to go dragging on, who would ever have said that a few years ago?"

Poor "Blondie," sleeping with her head on a pillow full of leaflets. She thinks it's useless too, that all is lost, she talks as though lost in dreams: the shootings, the bombs, the underground — and all for what? Before her drowsy eyes pass news items read in the paper, rumors started by neighbor women and spread in the food queues, slogans against the regime painted on the walls of Hospitalet, high-tension poles blown up in Llobregat, a bomb at the monument to the Condor Legion. A policeman murdered in the Plaza Joanich. Another bomb in the cathedral, and yet another one in the Hotel Ritz. The murder of the Falangist Don Bernardo Nogueras. Two Falangists riddled with bullets in the Plaza de la Sagrada Familia, when they mixed up their car with that of a police commissioner. . . .

"I hope Luis doesn't get out of Modelo; I hope he never gets out," Trini whines. "I hope they bring him back to me all paralyzed and crippled and not able to move from this chair for the rest of his life. Anything rather than see the whole thing start all over again. . . . I could bring in enough money to support the four of us."

"Don't cry, 'Blondie.' I've heard he isn't being beaten anymore."

But he is. At the end of each session they would put a lighted cigarette between the prisoner's swollen lips, but he'd not be able to hold it and would let it fall to the floor. Sitting in a heap on the chair, beneath the vertical cone of light in the basements of the fifth tier, he leans to one side and with his bloody hand searches around for the cigarette like a blind man. A black shoe steps on his hand, a fist smashes against his face again.

Prisoners who wake up in the morning in paddy wagons, the sound of waves dashing against the Campo de la Bota breakwater, and in Modelo a tall skinny man in blue overalls walking around the freshly hosed patio. His face would be swollen, with ash-gray bruises. Leaning against the wall, he bends over to pick up a butt. A hoarse, authoritarian voice from the tier of cells: "Lage Correa! Visitors!"

They were pushed into the visitors' room, their fingers clinging to the bars like hooks, amid a deafening din, with

Trini answering his questions: the boy's sick, pure air is what he needs, I'm the same as ever, sewing and doing day work, the house is so old it's falling in, who's going to repair the roof if you aren't there, darling, what's that on your face, what have they done to you, sweetheart?

"It's nothing" — and he would be reminded of the toothless mouth of his comrade writhing on the floor, two men in shirt-sleeves kicking him in the ribs, they say that the Guardia Civil had to hold him up by the armpits when he went before the firing squad: they shot him there, amid waterworn pebbles covered with moss, algae, and mussel shells rotting on the bloodstained beach. It must have been very close to the shore, because they say he sat down in a puddle, his legs wouldn't hold him up any longer. "Nothing's happened to me. I'll be out soon. But they've already buried Artemi, tell Uncle Juan that, Trini, tell him to buy Luisito that red-headed clown we saw one day on Paralelo, he knows which one, he'll know how to go about buying it."

It was that very active month, with bombs in the consulates of Brazil, Bolivia, and Peru. A cloud from the east, like phosphorus, came over the city, and the sun hid itself behind Montjuich. The warehouse-mansion of the baroness, in Sarria, the drawing room papered with fleurs de lis and the shutters nailed shut with wooden slats; the young girl lying on sacks of flour, her skirts pulled up to her belly and José María on top of her with fire in his groin. Menchu's eyes see the ceiling slowly come down on top of her, with its black light fixture and its four burned-out bulbs. The butt end of rifles must still ring out on that pavement, there must be a squeak of latches being shoved home all through the house and a circle of shadows surrounding them, phantoms of only yesterday, thin, moaning figures; an old lady with cigarette burns on her breasts, a naked man with a militiaman's cap walking about between blocks of quarried stone, a young man dangling a few inches off the soaking-wet floor, his hands pierced with hooks attached to the wall.

"Wouldn't you like paying salaries rather than receiving them, dearie?" — Master José María and his eagerness that ends in a fit of coughing. "Answer me."

She held back her rage between clenched teeth, and the spittle destined for the tubercular young man's face. Thinking, calculating.

"Yes. You're hurting me."

"Well then, say good-bye to my mother, because I've got an apartment in the Calle Casanovas. We're going to start up a business, honey, there are three of us partners; we're going to make a bundle."

"You're hurting me, you're hurting me."

A big gray car as long as a caterpillar. As Palau draws on the burning cigar with the red-hot tip, his face lights up for a moment in the darkness of the back seat. Navarro is at the wheel and "Taylor" is sitting next to him; they are parked on Paralelo, some twenty-five yards from the Teatro Cómico. In the rear-view mirror are the powerful cardboard thighs of Carmen de Lirio, parted above the main door of the theater, allowing crowds of people to flow between her calves. The contact was Ramón and he was waiting a little farther away, at the door of the moviehouse. Now, Navarro says, nudging Meneses in the ribs with his elbow. Meneses gets out of the car, thinking to himself: they might have chosen some other time and place, standing there in his new loose-fitting dark gray suit, walking away with his debonaire swagger that seemed to leave his buttocks behind. He faced into the March wind with his head down, his hand on his gray fedora. Suddenly, at his side, a couple dressed in their Sunday best begins to run, pushing him aside, and then a girl begins screaming, and immediately the crowd begins scattering in every direction. The first shot rings out, and he sees the grays leap out of the truck, running not toward him but in the direction where the contact is waiting for him. "Taylor" turns around and looking over his shoulder he sees the inspectors taking shelter in a doorway. He gets into the car.

"Wait," he says to Navarro. "They haven't spotted us. They're going after Quico's group."

"They got here just three days ago and the cops already are on to them?" Palau said clacking his tongue. "Hey, what'll we do? Ramón's disappeared."

Through the rear window he sees Pepe going back to the line of parked cars with his submachine gun down, crouching behind the corner of the moviehouse. Another one from the group, Larroy, is covering him. The people coming out of the afternoon show have thrown themselves down between the cars with their hands over their heads, making it harder for the police to take action, as Quico tries to distract their attention by shooting from the entrance to a cafeteria. The plump red-headed agent who has advanced the farthest into their territory suddenly finds himself with a pistol aimed at him by Pepe, who is shielding himself with the agent's body and keeps on shooting with the pistol, before putting a bullet through the agent's head and leaving him lying along the curb. With the smoking Colt .42 in his hand he runs toward his brother's car after removing the dead man's badge and his identification papers.

But Larroy was not covered by any of them. He turned on his heels there in no-man's-land, pointing his black revolver at the windswept gray sky, desperately searching for the straightest line back to the open door of the car that was already making a getaway. He stopped dead in his tracks on getting something like a slap on the forehead, bending violently backward, with a red cloud in his eyes. Navarro, who was watching him from a distance with his hand on the ignition switch of the other car, relived for a second his skinny, ungainly body in shirt sleeves rebelling against the terrible food and the bad treatment by the Senegalese, in that interminable summer of '39 that they suffered together amid fleas and the itch and barbed wire. With death already reflected in his eyes, Larroy took three more steps before a fan of bullets cut off his legs; he gyrated in the air and fell stiffly backward, his fingers like hooks, letting go of the revolver. Before he died he had time to see a hairdresser with red lips holding down her skirt as the wind blew it up, defenseless and terrified there on the corner: he went out of this world in good company, poor Larroy.

At a distance and without intervening, they sat there, with Navarro starting up the motor.

"Let's go" — Meneses, with his hat pulled down over his eyes.

"I'd swear that the cop they got was our man" — Navarro accelerating. "The one that Ramón was supposed to point out to you — what do you think?"

"Sure it was. Didn't you see his goddamned yellow skin? They've saved us the trouble. Luis will be happy when he finds out, and Artemi above all, there up yonder. But I'm sorry about Larroy."

"He'll soon be pushing up daisies," Palau said, putting an end to the conversation.

XII

B EFORE afternoon the pharmacy was already a nest of shadows. Behind the bars over the high little window that looked out on the street, legs sheathed in white stockings splashed about still in the dull, oblique rays of the sun, but around the caretaker and the nun, there inside, night was gaining whole minutes on the day as September went by. As she got up to turn on the light, the caretaker furtively filled his little liqueur glass, emptied it in one gulp, and filled it again. I see you, she said jokingly over her shoulder, and as he thought to himself, damn, she's got eyes in the back of her head, the door opened and a nurse's head peeked in; they want you in the office, she said, it seems there are relatives arriving. Getting to his feet, Ñito murmured it can't be, there aren't any relatives, as he went past the nun, who advised him to take a close look at her face: the left side, see if you can tell if it's her.

He didn't recognize her. It could be any of the older ones who were to remain old maids, Rosa, Muri, Isabel, any of them, thirty years older now. She was sitting there waiting on the edge of the bench as though about to get to her feet, her back very stiff, her yellowed hair tied back in a knot behind her little black hat, her hands crossed in her lap and between her fingers a printed form and the identity card. They'd already given her the two battered, badly damaged suitcases, tied around with rope, and they were there at her side, at the feet of three little girls dressed in dark clothes, lined up along the wall with a disinterested look on their faces, their eyes full of romantic mist. Ñito introduced himself to the woman, and an image painted by Sister Paulina during some conversation crossed his mind: an old maid like this one pushing the old man's wheelchair through the streets of the neighborhood, indifferent to the jokes of the hordes of little kids, the swampwater gaze hidden behind sunglasses and the left half of her face turned to a red and black crust, the color of wine. But it was not her.

There were a whole flock of visitors, the lines of the sick and injured in front of the consultation rooms were getting more crowded. The caretaker offered to accompany her to the morgue, but she said that she still had some formalities to go through, how complicated it all was, apparently the papers were lost? He didn't know, but he imagined so, the suitcases would have opened of course, but they'd recovered what they could, and in the end what did it matter, they wouldn't be needing identification papers. He sat down next to her: can you handle them by yourself, señora directress, pointing to the suitcases, do you want us to send them on to you? they weigh quite a bit because inside is what was contained in three or four of them, the others got ruined by the water. She corrected him: she was not the directress of the Casa de Familia, she was one of the assistants, no, they weren't in the Calle Verdi any more, it had been more than fifteen years since they moved, thanks to the generosity of Señor Galán, who turned into the benefactor of the parish after his mother's death. His mother had been the fairy godmother who'd fulfilled all the desires of deserving orphan girls, and he had gone on with this great work of charity. So his wife, Ñito commented, had been one of the girls from the Casa before she married? And afterwards too, she answered, always, even though they leave to have a family they still belong to the Casa, they keep up the contact and those who have made good marriages or had good luck in their work never forget their first home, Pilar for example helped us out with donations, poor thing, she may not have been happily married but there certainly was no lack of money, that was sure, the only thing her husband knew how to do was make money. . . . She interrupted herself to ask the caretaker if anyone else had come, some men, jewelers? yes, he said, but I didn't see them, I think they insisted on taking care of all the expenses, you can see that they thought a lot of him at work, he was a traveling jewelry salesman, wasn't that right, he must have been worth a lot. The woman sighed and rubbed her red eyelids, I'm sure of it, she said, but heaven knows that if I'm here it's because of her and the children, he made her suffer so much that she wouldn't move a finger for him, God forgive her.

Then as she sat there waiting for them to call her to the office, she let the conversation die out deliberately. She forced herself to do so, because the fate of certain persons, the misfortunes of her fellows in general and family conflicts in particular roused her natural talkativeness. That respectful, attentive, but dirty and ageless caretaker, whose ancient eyes seemed to search behind the words they exchanged, stood there silently at her side, reducing himself to a solicitous presence, but not for her and her grief but rather for some obscure grief of his own that time had not destroyed or lessened. And later, following his abrupt monkey-walk through the suffocating corridors on the way to the morgue, a wind from childhood struck her in the face, an odor of burned powder and a pencil-box, which memory was perhaps incapable of dredging up again. As they went through the foul-smelling basement of this vast hospital, something much worse than pain and old age and death surrounded them. Because how could this man live here, how could anybody bury himself alive, resign himself to this filth and this misery, lonelier than a dead person among other dead people? We knew each other when we were kids, he said without turning around, walking along stumblingly and all hunched over, almost as if he were oblivious to how he occupied his time, as though all he had sought from it was a refuge from a rain of outrages that had left him soaked to the soul. And when she saw him spit laboriously into the handkerchief, the woman, as though suddenly aware of a nameless degradation capable of infecting her, quickened her pace so as to be finished with the whole business as soon as possible.

Standing there in front of the twins she carefully crossed herself, remembering for an instant their games, their habits, and their character: how strange they were, she said, I never understood them, so well-behaved when separated, so normal and so harmless, but so bad, such liars, and so vindictive when they were together. And as she turned toward the dead woman, her eyes grew misty again and her hand tremblingly but resolutely, went out to the cold cheek to give it a few affectionate pats as she murmured Lord, Lord, poor child, poor Pilar. Was the autopsy necessary? and did they have to autopsy these two poor creatures too? That's the rule, ma'am, he answered from behind her, hugging the wall and not missing a thing. He was glad that he'd cleaned them up, dressed them, and combed their hair, and that she was gratified to see them that way.

As they left the room, he could have sworn she hadn't even looked at the dead man.

"I'll leave the suitcases," she decided. "Will you take care of having them sent to Pilar's apartment? The maid has already left, but I'll be there tomorrow."

"I'll bring them around myself," Ñito said.

As she rejoined the orphan girls in the corridor, the woman asked them for a pencil to note down the address, but the caretaker said there was no need, shaking his head from side to side with an amused look, I certainly won't lose my way.

Pilar? he thought as he went back to the dispensary, Pilarín.

She might be one of the ones that each Sunday crossed the neighborhood to Las Ánimas in pairs, with their cheap white mantillas and their prayer books, one of many in the double line of blue uniforms, little white ties, and rubber sandals, led by Señorita Moix; any one of the ones with braids and little pink ribbons and a cruel cold trapped between their eyelids, who used to stick their tongues out at people's commiseration, who flocked around the knife grinder in the Plaza del Diamante, who joked each morning with the young garbage collector, a boy with almost an old man's face and cat's eyes, or who ran to see the stills outside the Cine Verdi, this Saturday we're going to see *Boys' Town*, Pili, the ragpicker's in the third row, and how good-looking he is, just look. . . . Yes, one of the flock of them, with an anonymous face, as excited and lively as that of all the rest of them; a quiet one who never stood out much but whose eyes must have taken everything in, camouflaged among the rest so as to spy on him when he went to the Casa de Familia each Friday to fill his sack with wastepaper: you're coming with me today, kid.

"Haven't you ever been there, Itchy? Haven't you ever seen little orphan girls in their own sauce? You're coming with me today."

"I can just see you going in, you rascal: come to the parlor, girls!"

"Cut it out, don't be an asshole," Java said.

"Isn't there anything we can get from them then?"

"Not a thing. What did you think?"

The dark towering stairway with old warped steps, he thought, the first landing smelling of bums, the black door with the oval plaque of the Sacred Heart, a gift of the lieutenant. Wait, dummy. The girls looked through the peephole before opening the door, you can hear the laughter, the whispers, the running footsteps behind the door. You wait with your comic books in your hand, your sack on your shoulder, and your balance-scale in your belt, the one that opened the door was always a little tadpole on tiptoe who could hardly reach the latch, did you bring *The Man in the Iron Mask*, and runs off with her booty in her hand, the ragpicker, ma'am! A bow half in jest, good afternoon, señorita, do you have anything for me, papers, rags, bottles? The orphans flock around her, in excited little groups, peeking out, hiding themselves, and laughing: Fueguiña's sweetheart, the handsomest Lucifer in Las Ánimas parish. One of them had to be Pilar. None of your prudes here, even though they make them pray all the time: they dance with each other in the dormitories, they hide novels and song sheets under the covers, pictures of movie stars and singers, they know the words of "Bésame Mucho" and "Perfidia" by heart. From the roof terrace, there in the dark, on Saint John's Night or Saint Peter's Night they leap at the chance to hear the music from the neighboring terraces decorated with little lanterns and dance with each other, taking turns watching so that the directress doesn't catch them.

"They're fun."

On the terrace is a little room with laundry sinks, where they keep old rags and mountains of sheets of colored tissue paper, out of which they make the artificial flowers and the fringes that decorate the streets of the neighborhood when the September fiestas come round. One of the orphan girls always comes along with you so you don't cheat on the weight, Virginia or Fueguiña, and there's always time to rehearse for the play.

"Damn, you really make out, gummy-eyes."

"Cut it out, Itchy, cut it out."

"She's great-looking — don't deny it."

"There's another one I go for too, but she tries to make you think she's a prude. Pilarín. Do you know the one I mean? The serious type, more polite than the others, tall and very frail. Sometimes she comes along to watch that I don't cheat on the weight, but she won't let me touch one hair of her, though I think she's one of those who once she lets herself go. . . . "

And that's who it must have been. A svelte girl, very delicate, but with thick ankles, and big floppy tits.

"Yes, but isn't Fueguiña your sweetheart?"

"Sure, sure. Maria's something else. Those little tits like lemons. . . . "

"And you make it right there, on the floor of the roof terrace?"

"It's not like that, pal, you're always imagining more than what really happens."

The black cassocks hanging on hangers and swaying in the wind like tolling funeral bells, the surplices and altar cloths dripping water from the wire clotheslines, the wash of Las Ánimas drying in the sun and the cooing from the dovecote on the neighboring roof terrace. Java sitting leaning against the railing, Fueguiña at his side with the play book in her lap.

"Do you still want to rehearse some more?" she said. "What a laugh when you know even my part by heart. What a bore."

"You orphans are something," Java said. "What do you and Juanita do to get away and come to the shelter?"

"We've got a trick up our sleeves," she said, her eyes blinking in the sun. "Come on, get up. Do you see the little basket on the cord that's stretched from balcony to balcony, there above the street? Careful, don't get so close to the edge. That's what we call our ski lift. The balcony over there belongs to the lady who has the grocery store downstairs, do you see? That's where the Dondis live. Three terrific brothers. We pass each other messages and letters. The oldest one's got tuberculosis. Do you see the windowpane with a hole cut through it, there on the balcony, with the stovepipe coming out of it? — well, that's where he spends his time, in bed all the time, and day and night there's a pot boiling on the fire with water and eucalyptus; it smells great. . . . When we've read all the comic books you bring us, we give them to them, we send them over in the little basket, but they're ones we don't want anymore, because they come back with germs on them and I burn them."

When a girl wanted to sneak out she wrote her name on a

piece of paper, put it in the basket and pulled on the ropes to send it over to the next balcony; there was always one of the Dondi brothers keeping the invalid company; he took the message out of the basket and knew exactly what he had to do: go down to the grocery store, cross the street, and come up to the Casa and say: my mother says she'd like you to let so-and-so come over to do the cleaning. Sometimes it was true, and since she paid by giving the girls food...

"What about when it's a lie?"

"The Dondi brothers give us something so that the Señorita doesn't suspect, chocolate, a little sack of flour to make doughnuts, or something like that."

"In exchange for what, Fueguiña?"

"For a kiss. A quick one, nothing at all, downstairs at the door, in the dark."

"A kiss and that's all?"

"Juanita lets them pull up her skirt."

"What about you?"

"I manage to get away, stupid. Are you jealous?"

"Who, me? Come off it — it's not as though we were married. Come on over here...."

Toward the back of the roof terrace was a little garden from which white butterflies flew up around the wash hanging on the line: a passageway of black cassocks where they stood kissing each other without anyone being able to see them. The flock of pigeons was a white explosion in the blue of the sky. Fueguiña's breasts stood up in points. He puts his arms around her, caresses her body, suddenly round and languid, very soft, devoid of bones. Her blue uniform scrubbed a thousand times in the wash seems like a very delicate skin. Java doesn't even remember that he's famished. In the laundry room she held the sack open as he filled it with papers. He put his arms around her again.

"When are you going to marry me, Fueguiña?"

"You pig. Who knows why you're fooling around with me?"

"I'm serious."

"Tell that to Pilar. I don't go for things like that."

"I like you better, you heart-stealer. I've fallen in love with you. Don't try to wriggle away."

"Don't I look thin to you, little ragpicker?"

"Leave that cripple and we'll go away together.... When are you going to quit taking him for walks and cleaning up his snot and shit?"

"Never" — suddenly serious, wriggling out of his grasp. "Never, I hope" — not because she was disgusted by Señorito Conrado, and not at all because she was a prude. It simply seemed like a nervous reflex as the sadness suddenly welled up behind her half-open mouth with the missing teeth and her half-closed eyes: it was as though she were kissing him or prepared to let herself be kissed immediately.

That was when he got confused, when he intuited in this complacent young girl, even though her reactions were unpredictable, the same bottomless terror, the same terrible destiny that he saw one day in Ramona's skin, as dark and dirty as a stigma: in this ravaged body too, in these decayed teeth and in these dead eyes the mysterious rot of the city was at work, that indifference of a muddy puddle being pelted with successive rains of humiliations and disappointments. Maybe that was why Java asked: "Do you still have to take it out for him so he can pee?" — said with a smile.

She had her face turned to one side, the cripple caught her hesitant hand in the air and pulled her arm up behind her back, drawing her closer to him, playing: How come, if you know that your Conrado has plenty of strength in his hands, even though he's a paralytic?

"Tell me, how come you have to clean him up," Java said, "and then put it back and button him up? What a bore going there so early each morning, isn't it? what a bore to dress him there in bed, wash him, massage his legs...."

"It's no bother, I'm used to it. No, not that, no more now, somebody might come."

"You can get away if you want to, you can take your hands away. You can do it if you want to. . . . "

The guy has a neat time of it, Itchy had said, and Java: don't you believe it. Try to put yourself in his place: the pain wakes him up at exactly the same time every morning, she says, never later than eight o'clock. He likes to be taken care of without being babied, briskly. With one sweep of her hand she draws back the sheet and puts the bedpan under his buttocks: rubbing his chest with the soapy sponge, then his armpits, his knees, between his legs. Then turning him over and now his back, his buttocks, the backs of his knees. Cutting his toenails. Alcohol massages of his puny legs that get skinnier every day, and shorter too somehow, you'd almost think. When she heard him complain of lots of pain, she rubbed them without his even having to ask. He didn't even look at her: his eyes closed, face to the ceiling, still half asleep, as though dreaming, and rubbing the tips of his fingers on the towel all the time as if he were crumbling the close-woven threads. As she raised herself up trying to get away, her hands trembled a little.

"Don't stop, for heaven's sake; it feels better there. Ah, right there. And it has to be you, nobody but you: aren't you ashamed, a naked man?" Java said.

"Poor thing. He's had nurses, companions, practical nurses that come to give him shots, maids that his mother trusts. . . . But they didn't last three days. I did. He even prefers me to good Señor Justiniano, who's as faithful as a dog to him."

"Doesn't anybody come down from upstairs to help you?"

"I don't need anybody. His mother has a maid and a cook up there and now she wants to have a chauffeur again. But he wouldn't stand for anybody but Justiniano and me, he told the señora straight out. Why does he prefer me? I don't know, it's a knack I have maybe."

I've put myself in his shoes, gummy-eyes: a broken doll that lets himself be rocked and spoiled by a doll of an orphan, the limping little tin soldier who won the war, hard to please, a maniac, used to giving orders. She sits him on the bed, adjusts the pillows at his back, brings him his shaving things and leaves him as she goes to the kitchen to prepare his breakfast. Then she'll dust the wheelchair, and put a drop of oil on the axle that squeaks. And half an hour later, the little bell rings again from the bedroom: dress him, put on his feet whatever pair of boots he's chosen, take him in her arms, scented and his hair neatly combed, and sit him down in the chair. Until a year ago he could do that himself, leaning on his crutches, but his spine can no longer support him. It's wasted away, my girl, your job's a tough one.

"You don't need to be strong, just skillful," Fueguiña said. "He's lighter than a feather. Keep your hands to yourself, please, it's getting late. What if somebody should see us? What'll they think of a poor girl like me. . . . It's not good to get all excited like that."

"Some day you'll find him dead in his bed, like a little bird. It can't go on much longer."

"What do you mean? The señorito will live longer than all of us, if not forever. I felt sorry for him today, and I soaped him twice and gave him three massages: no, not there, please, sometimes it doesn't matter but today I can't," she begged but let his hand wander, burning with his secret fire. "Why, why, why do I have this feeling. . . . "

Then she pushed the wheelchair out into the hall, through a series of beveled glass doors opened wide, repeating each other as though in a mirror. They crossed the drawing room and reached the gallery, and before stopping at the round table his hand was already opening the newspaper. She will leave him facing the huge colored glass window set on fire by the sun, with his breakfast in front of him: his very strong coffee, his slices of toast, his marmalade and his butter. And she goes back again to her tasks, sweeping, emptying the ashtrays, making the bed, dusting. With her eyes lowered, briskly, her cheeks aflame, humming a popular song: inexplicably happy, Itchy, as happy as a lark.

I like that house, she said, her face aglow, how I do like it, kid. All the things in it. The standing wardrobes full of nicely folded clothes smelling of mothballs, the cases full of necklaces and fans, miniatures, ivory and mother-of-pearl crucifixes, and the candelabra in the salon and the blue light bulbs in the bedroom. Everything. Even the photograph of Mussolini, straddling an infernal motorcycle, autographed in his very own hand: "To Señor Galán, with a Roman embrace," on Conrado's desk, with a small photo of his father stuck in one corner of the frame. She even liked the paperweight with the bullets that they had extracted from Señor Conrado's spine, and the yellow scarf that his father had been wearing when he was killed. And she explained in a dreamy voice what the bathroom looked like: green tiles and a pink bathtub, gilt faucets in the form of fish with wide-open mouths and intertwined tails. And the big rug in the bedroom that is a famous picture, the señorito explained to me, laughing: don't sweep so hard with your broom; the blood stains aren't real, you little goose.

Tell me about the bedroom, Java said, and she described it as though it were a dream: the door covered in eggplant-colored velvet studded with nailheads, and the wide room and the very low bed, and the linen sheets, and the red bedspread, and the single pillow. On the ceiling, the gleaming crystal chandelier, an explosion of swans' necks, then the sofa with fringe and green striped upholstery, and the screen with cherubs and mother-of-pearl clouds, the thick silent rug and the dark carved chairs, on one of which there was always draped a purple sash with tassels and a cope with embroidered edges and a mysterious shield on the back. Several pairs of gleaming riding boots lined up at the foot of the standing wardrobe, the heavy honey-colored curtains and the two balcony windows that were always closed, without even a crack of daylight showing.

"How can you stand it month after month?"

"He doesn't move around so as not to be a burden, poor thing. How serious he seems at rehearsals, isn't that so? so haughty and disagreeable. Well, he's like a child at home, like a frightened child. He's afraid of being alone, of wetting himself, or catching cold. He doesn't let anybody see the hole in his throat, his war wounds, I'm the only one that's seen him, when I change the towel, he likes colored ones and it's not a whim; he's allergic to silk scarves; didn't you know that?"

Another summons and pushing the wheelchair to the library: he writes letters there, he telephones to the administrator in charge of the estate, he goes over his mother's accounts, the rent money to be collected. They say that almost all the houses in the neighborhood belong to his mother, besides the plots of land of Las Ánimas and Can Compte, estates that were confiscated during the war and that he's gotten back since. But Conradito has lots of troubles, people don't pay up, I hear him cursing on the telephone, shouting, threatening: he seems like another person then.

In midmorning the señora comes down to see him. She wants to know how he is, if he wants anything special for lunch. Sometimes she shows him her shopping list. After that he does whatever he likes, he reads plays, he copies out everybody's part on the typewriter, he decides on the cast and the costumes, and sometimes he calls me to ask me if I'd like this or that role, to rehearse, to try an outfit on me. He invents plots, getting his inspiration from poetry, from songs.

"You're awkward in that cloak. Take it off."

Leaning on the doorpost of the brothel, she watched the May night light up. With one hand on her hip, a cigarette in the other and a carnation in her hair, in a tight dress with polka dots and ruffles, sleeveless and low-cut. Men passed by and she smiled, until the horse halted at her door. Give me a light, mountain girl? She walks forward a few steps, allows the green cloak to slip from her shoulders. "Walk around arrogantly, keep your back straight, that's it, the cigarette isn't a pencil, your waist is a sheaf of wheat, stop, stick your hip out a little, put your legs together, that's the way. You'll have to sew up the lining, darn those stockings, dye those shoes green, tack on the heel, and the rest is all right. Come here now and I'll give you a light, don't be afraid you'll hurt my legs, that's right, please."

"I do better if I know the role by heart. . . ."

"Don't you have anything else underneath, Magnolia?"

"Not that. I'm afraid, little ragpicker."

"Will you give me a kiss until I collect the rest, woman, for I know that I'm on my way to my death today."

"Where did you girls get the clothes?"

"His mother gives us old dresses."

If his legs don't hurt him very much, he's happy. But the directress already told all of you that those songs are a sin, Java said. And what of it, he likes them and he says no, that you don't have to confess about them. Around noon she takes him to the elevator. If there's no current she leaves him sitting in an armchair and takes the wheelchair down the stairs, leaving it at the door. She goes upstairs again, wraps him in the shawl, takes him downstairs in her arms, and sits him in the wheelchair. If it's sunny out they take a walk, but with the weather like it is now they go around the block a few times, hugging the wall, avoiding the whirlwinds of dry leaves, talking together, rehearsing: We went out very late and walked about a Paris of yore, stained with moonlight. Laughter from her.

"Magnolia, forget this night and forget my name, and look for a man that you can love."

"Not so fast, not so fast."

"I beg your pardon, Magnolia, if the way I behave has turned your head for a few moments. Just remember that I am a soldier and you may never see me again."

They drink a sherry in some bar or other and when they return she leaves him with his mother on the third floor, that's where he eats lunch and spends the afternoon sometimes. After eating in the kitchen, she goes back to the Casa de Familia and the next morning it all begins over again.

"It's true that the days when it's rainy and damp are sad, he rests his chin on his chest, his back bends over like an old man's, the bullets must be moving inside him somewhere and tearing at his nerves. In the beginning I thought I could hear them moving, but it was his belly, his belly keeps rumbling all the time, it's the lack of exercise. Then he calls Señor Justiniano, they shut themselves up in the library and play chess, Señor Justiniano had endless patience with him and loves him like a son, he's heartbroken when the pain tortures him, I've seen him hiding and crying with his one eye."

"And what happens in the afternoon? Don't you ever go there in the afternoon?"

"Sometimes. To take him for an outing after lunch, but then right back to the house to wait for his friends; that's why he has me buy things along the way. They have supper together."

Java laughed, slipping his arm around her shoulders and drawing her toward him.

"And who are his friends, what do they do there, what have you seen?"

"Me? Nothing. I don't even go in, I leave him at the door. . . . "

"At his mother's apartment or his own?"

"His. He smiles at me and says thanks, Magnolia, you can go now."

"Do you remember one afternoon when he had you buy tuna pies, do you remember that I was there in the bar?"

"No."

"Are you stupid or just pretending to be, kid?"

"Let me go, you're tickling me. And finish weighing this stuff; it's late." She kept still as she watched him cram the papers in the sack with both hands, as she looked at the colored bandana around his neck, his black curly hair. And she added: "You mustn't think he's always like that, a cripple deserving people's pity; you mustn't think he doesn't have his fun. He has friends who telephone and visit him with their sweethearts or their friends, they tell him jokes and he laughs, do you know what they call him as a joke? the ex-future corpse, hi there corpse, they say when they arrive, but it isn't an insult — far from it, he explained to me, that's how they used to call him during the war. Sometimes they take him to the country in a car, and he has a circle of friends in the Oro del Rin, and he even . . . prepare yourself, this will knock you flat on your behind: I even found one of those dirty things in the toilet one day, a rubber. I was dumfounded, thinking this can't be, not him, it must have been one of his friends; I think he lends them the apartment on certain afternoons. An intimate friend of his also visits him a lot, the son of his mother's jeweler, and the administrator. But the one who comes most often is Señor Justiniano, who runs errands for him and tells him funny stories about a son of his who lives in the youth camps. And he laughs with them, he forgets his troubles. And the times I like best are when we have a rehearsal at Las Ánimas and go there in a taxi, the way he goes to mass on Sundays with his mother. He's another person when the pain lets up a little, really."

"Look what fair weight I'm giving you, so you'll tell the directress later."

"Come on, your scale doesn't have weights or anything, ragpicker, do you think we're dummies?"

And since you claim to know it all, to see everything, try to put yourself in Fueguiña's shoes and see where they pinch the worst, she keeps pushing the wheelchair, in the heat and in the cold, she takes him up and down what are really four floors, counting the gallery and the main floor; come on, you can imagine how much fun that is. But think too what a dream-life it is to share the festivities in the parish, Easter and Corpus Christi, when you push the chair along under a canopy, with him in his dress uniform and his gleaming boots, with the priest on his right and his mother on his left, all of them treading on the carpets of flowers and colored sawdust made up by the parishioners who kneel in the street the entire evening before, using lanterns and candles for light, think how nice it is to go with him under the canopy, surrounded by clouds of incense and hymns. Or the Way of the Cross on Good Friday, when he goes out onto the neighborhood streets every year, and even he bears the heavy cross on his shoulder during one station, the ninth one always: Jesus falls for the third time, because he knows that we are all sinners and thus sets an example, the beam weighs as much as he does even though the bearers give him a hand and Fueguiña pushes the wheelchair, everybody looks at him, all the neighbors out on their balconies and at the windows where they hang out purple and black bedspreads, they're impressed by his strength and each year they see that he's more feeble and wrinkled but nobody can take the ninth station away from him; in his uniform and his Sam Browne belt and his high boots he looks even braver beneath the cross, and everybody can look at him as much as they please as the retinue halts at each one of the altars set up in the doorways, and he knows all of them, they all owe him money and favors because the houses they live in belong to Señora Galán, they all kneel and beat their breasts when he passes by, Lord, Lord, forgive us. He knows that they're all there, that they notice his power and his strength, but he doesn't even look at them, he passes by very erect from the waist up, his arms crossed on his decorated chest and his eyes lowered, concentrating on some inner fury. And Fueguiña must experience still other exciting things, protected by his shadow, so it isn't strange that she appreciates him, pities him, and defends him, you'd defend him from our jokes too, Itchy, you too would let yourself be caressed by him sometimes and would get used to kissing the hand that orders you about and feels you up and beats you, because that's what it means to be an orphan, they're all that way: girls without a home and a family, aching for a home and a family.

XIII

THEY call me Tits, but it's also my real name: José Mari Tetas, at your service and God's, sir. It's probably because I'm fat, yes sir, a real fatty but don't laugh because it isn't because I eat too much, it's a sickness. I'm coming for Java's tobacco ration; he couldn't come. The card belonged to his brother who died, but the Tobacco Dispensary doesn't know that yet, and what's the harm in that, comrade? Everybody does it and what's more Java doesn't smoke, he sells it at the same price as the Dispensary and gives the money to his granny. I'm in a hurry, I have to go get communion wafers right away for the priest, far away, in a convent of nuns behind the cathedral, the nuns have a little machine there that makes them, they come out nice and round and sometimes they give me the little bits left over, I give them to my mother, it's the very best flour, yes, sir. . . . Me go to police headquarters? Whatever for, if I haven't done anything bad? Sit here and talk for a while? it says wet paint but it isn't, it's dry. I haven't done anything, don't beat me, sir, or whatever it is you want me to call you: comrade if you prefer, it's just that I'm not in the habit of calling you that, I beg your pardon. I don't know her, I've only heard about her, I swear on my mother's head. Me, a ruffian, a rowdy, a degenerate who molests girls in the neighborhood, playing doctor, Susana says, that girl from the big house says that we've done nasty things together in the basement of Las Ánimas, is that what that little snob is going around saying? If she went home crying it was on account of the cat, a cornered cat jumped on top of her. So her mother's complained, and the whole neighborhood is talking about us? The Red-Hot Iron? What are you saying? The Poisoned Host? I don't know anything about it, we didn't do anything bad with Susana, I swear, comrade, ow, don't hit me in the head, I've had pus in my ear since I was small. Of course I hear you, and I can tell you I'd like it very much to go to the youth camps and it'd please me very much to have a red beret and a machete with a leather sheath, that's the greatest, I know a kid who's got the Sam Browne belt and how proud he is of it. And how about my signing up to be an Arrow? Sure, I'd like that a whole lot, but my father won't let me. He's a laborer. Except that he's out of work now and in a sour mood, but he wasn't a Red, I give you my word, he wears the spider in his lapel just like you because he says that's the best thing you can do to get a job, he wants to take out a card as a member of the national labor union. . . . Along the Carmelo Highway. My father built the shack, there are seven of us kids; we came here from Cuevas, Almanzora: sure I understand Catalan, but I speak the language of the Empire, comrade, like we've been ordered to. I don't go to high school yet, my mother keeps telling me: one more year as an altar boy, José Mari, so sometimes they tease me, yes, sir. My mother's a real believer, and can be trusted, she sure can, we're all friends of the parish priest in our house, just ask, just ask. . . . That's true, comrade, I'm not just saying that, ow, don't hit me in the head, I've got a bad tumor, please, I've had it ever since I was born. . . . A sweet potato? I don't know anything about the dirty things they do to girls, you know me, you've seen me assist at mass in Señora Galán's private chapel, in her apartment, she knows me and knows that I'd tell her anything, but the fact is I don't know a thing, honest I don't. Well, yes, we were here with Susana, she likes acting in plays and sometimes we hold rehearsals and dress up in costumes in the dressing room of the crypt; we don't do anything bad but that day we had a stick of licorice, yes, one of the big fat ones that cost fifteen *céntimos*, Itchy brought it and we all sucked on it in turn, Susana too, otherwise I don't know anything about the Red-Hot Brand, and as for putting it up here there was nothing like that, do you think we run a torture chamber, comrade? It was just a plain old licorice stick to suck, what's so strange about that? Well, if she said we did dirty things, it's because she's a troublemaker and a liar, and it doesn't surprise me because her whole family's like that: did you know that her father wasn't even here when the Nationals entered, that he was hiding in the country with all his family? it's just a little thing, comrade, and please note that I don't like denouncing anybody. Are they rich, you ask? man, haven't you seen Susana? she always smells of tangerines and her hair is blond so blond and her eyes a vivid blue like rich people's, although to tell the truth they aren't as rich as all that: you can see it by the garbage that they put out, it's worse every day, comrade, just some skins from the sausages they get from the country from time to time, and lots of potatoes and chickpeas, nothing, misery and company, when all is said and done, I don't know, I think they don't have money now but at any rate they're people who are used to having it and it's as though they did: what I mean is that they'll have some again, you can see it coming, it can't help but be that way. Ow, pus is going to come out, I beg you in the name of my mother not to hit me there it hurts me a lot and makes me cry, seriously, I don't know anything about that whore, it's all due to Java and the trouble he stirs up, I don't know what Señora Galán asked him to do for the Congregation. Yes, Java spoke to Susana about it that day in the crypt, but I didn't see anything and I couldn't hear the questions he asked her, only her answers, she

191

screamed a lot, you'll see: Fueguiña made us sit all the time with our faces to the wall, we couldn't see anything, she and Itchy directed the play, Java lighted the candle and Susana protested in the beginning. . . . Sure she was wailing, sure she had to be tied to the back of the chair, it was her role of prisoner in the play, sure we heard her groan, but there was no marking her with the Red-Hot Brand, comrade, it wasn't like that at all, comrade, on the contrary: the martyrdom of Saint Susana, virgin and martyr, a story that Itchy invented. That we took her by force to the shelter, that we abducted her at the gate of the school by telling her lies? Not a chance, she came along because she wanted to, you don't know those stuck-up girls, comrade, they pretend to be prudes but they like the sweet potato. . . . Wait, don't beat me, everything I say is true, ow, ow, wait and let me think, what did she say, you ask, oh yes, that she didn't remember very much about her, that she'd been a maid in her house and that she had a sweetheart who died at the front and then she began to go out with soldiers, Mama scolded her and wanted to throw her out of the house, Susana said, and now you know everything, that we should please let her go home because it was late and she was afraid. She came because she wanted to, I swear, sir; are you coming to rehearse at Las Ánimas? Fueguiña said to her, would you like to be in our play? Susana was coming out of the School of the Esclavas de la Travesera and we just happened to be there on the sidewalk, I swear it. Before that we used to go spy on the girls at the gate of the school but we never touched so much as a hair of their heads, we hid behind the trees and the streetlamps to spy on them, we watched them saying goodbye and giving their little kisses in the courtyard covered with gravel, the way they hung on their mamas' necks when they went to get them, don't ask me why they went to get them, comrade, we looked at their pink pencil boxes, their spiral notebooks, and their boxes of Goya pastels, their little hats with the blue ribbon and their nice white socks, I don't know why we went to spy on them, I don't know, a mania, we didn't have anything special in mind. Tied to a bidet full of gunpowder, she said? What a liar. A sweet potato covered with hair was found in her pencil-box? That's a big fat lie, how can she say such awful things about her friends? If she liked that, if she laughed and joked with us, if we played guessing names of movies to get her over her fear: if a guy makes love to girls in Paris and London, what's the name of the movie, Susana? *Tail of Two Cities*, ha ha. And another one: the cops pick up hookers on Saturday night on the Ramblas, what do you call it? *Lost Whorizons*, ha ha, I already knew that one, she said laughing till she cried, she had a great time with us, even though she claims not to have now. Where did we get the gunpowder? well, it was made from sulphur and crushed coal and match-heads, Mingo makes it, what else do you want to know, comrade, it's God's own truth. What else, oh yes, one of those complicated puzzles that Java and Itchy like so much, something about her uncle who sometimes visited her in the house in town and scolded her for staying on there as a maid, Susana said, and when her papa and mama went off to the country and they stayed on alone in the house in town, when they came back they caught on to what they were up to: they were bringing men there to sleep, militiamen, she said, and Mama got very mad at Aurora and said it's better that you go away. But she cried and said where would I go, ma'am, I'm all alone in the world, and one day the other girl found herself pregnant, what a mess that was. Susana says that Aurora was always very affectionate with her; that that winter, at the time of the bombings, her mama had sent them to go sleep in the Fontana subway stop, that Aurora hugged her under the blanket and said don't cry, my little one, nobody's going to hurt you and your papa and mama will be back soon, but it was Aurora who was the one that was crying and trembling, Susana said, and cried herself to sleep and sweated a lot and had nightmares and cried out in her sleep: it's not that one, this one's his father, you've made a mistake, no! and woke up trembling and hiding her face between her hands. Then Java comes and asks her, that I did hear, he says to her: and did they rub him out, Susana, do you know if she saw it, if it was in a ditch, at night, in the light of headlamps of a car? and Susana, I don't know, those were the nightmares she had, don't ask me anything more. And the kid was sort of frightened then, comrade, because she said: I don't like this play, I'm not going to play anymore, let me go home because it's late.... What else, what else? ah, yes, that once there seemed to be no end to the bombings, her father and mother finally decided to go off to the country for an indefinite time and closed the house in town, and then they had to fire Aurora and the other maid. For good. And that since that day she'd never had anything more to do with them. It's the plain and simple truth, comrade, do you want me to swear it with my arm upraised, ow, you don't have to beat me for that, I'm not trying to crack jokes, ow, not in the head, my nose is bleeding, my mother says it's from weakness. Lots of sticks of licorice, is that what that little snob said? that's not right, sir, there was only one and we took turns sucking on it, her too, except that from time to time she started to moan and scream, it was her role and there's nothing surprising about that. But I wasn't able to see it, I've already said that we had our backs turned and the only thing we saw was their shadows on the wall, because Fueguiña was holding the candle in her left hand and working Susana over with her right. There was an argument at this point: no, kid, it's the other way around, Luis, who was next to me, said: haven't you noticed that Fueguiña is left-handed, haven't you seen licorice stains on her left hand when she brings us some to suck? well take a good look the next time. Shut up and don't look, you guys, Fueguiña shouted, I'll tell you when it's time to come rescue her. She came back with the licorice and I noticed then; it was after a scream from Susana, and she put it in our mouths very slowly, one after the other, we liked thinking about it, about it's being in Susana's, it still had the nice warm odor of her, because if she smells like tangerines outside, inside she smells like talcum powder and cologne, like a little baby; and it was her left hand, so Fueguiña is left-handed as well as being a little crazy in the head. No, sir, it wasn't a question of that at all, don't be a brute, ow (you shit) it was Martín who said laughingly: if only she doesn't pee, and we all laughed but nothing else happened and finally Mingo couldn't believe it, I don't know the whys and wherefores of the joke, comrade, Mingo made a disgusted face and asked if it was true and Itchy said yes, man, I saw it, can't you taste? Gracious, I said, I hadn't tumbled to what was going on. Then Java ordered them to untie Susana and the rehearsal was over, that's the whole truth and nothing but the truth, sir.... We aren't as big good-for-nothings as we're made out to be around the neighborhod. Yes, she came out to the street with us and threw a little handkerchief with licorice spots in the gutter. As she did, a black cat jumped on her face and we hunted it down with stones then, and just as we were getting ready to skin it she got sick to her stomach and went running home, that's why she was in tears when she got there. And that's all I know, can I go now? there'll be a line in the tobacco store and Java beats me up if I come back without the packets of to-bacco.... Sure, you say you'll let me go if I tell you one thing? Well, I did see her once, I remember now, I even spoke to her for a little while. It was on a bench in the Paseo de San Juan, she was getting some sun and I hadn't paid any attention to her but when she said hello, handsome, to me, I saw her face, it already shows that she's got tuberculosis, she's got makeup around her eyes like a mask, and I got scared. And Itchy was right; she was exactly the way he imagined her. From a dis-tance her hair seems very blonde, but close up it isn't as blonde as all that. It was a day like today, I was coming back from the tobacco place where Java'd sent me, I put the tobacco down on the bench and to distract her hands, she picked up a little pack-et of cigarette paper and took out a couple of leaves, as though it was part of a game, you're so little and yet you're smoking already? she said to me. No, ma'am, it's not for me, and she said with a bored look on her face, noting that I was looking at the packet of cigarette paper: don't worry, I'll put them back and nobody will notice. And to tell the truth she was very clever at it, because I went off for a minute to piss and when I came back all the papers were back in the packet and it looked just the same as before; yes, I had to piss in the pissoir that's close by because the broad was looking hard at me and I got choked up, because she suddenly burst out crying, very softly, looking at me, crying as though she was smiling at me, and her eye makeup started running, it was revolting to see her that way, to hear her say Mama, *madre mia*, I'd never seen a whore cry that way and I had to go piss. When I came back she'd calmed down, she still had the little packet of cigarette paper in her hands, and she gave it back to me and said, go on, they're probably waiting for you. I picked up the rest of the stuff and went running off to the junk shop, and that's the last I've ever seen of her. Can I go now? You're not taking me to the police station? that's fine, because if I find out anything more I'll tell you, one good turn deserves another, comrade, I swear it, I'm not fooling you, you don't have to beat me to make me remember to be good, ow (not in the mouth, you bastard, you political hack), I promise, you won't have any more complaints from the neighbors, I don't want to be locked up in Durán Asylum, anything but that, I'd really like being an Arrow but my mother needs what I get as an altar boy, we're poor, comrade, give me a blue shirt and some hobnailed boots and I'll never lie to you, sir, good-bye (you'll swallow anything you shitty one-eyed bastard), best of luck to you (I hope you rot)."

XIV

RAISE your skirt up, señorita."
They'd say something like that to her, without her
showing any bashfulness or shame, conscious perhaps of beginning a ritual of looks and desires that would lead her a long
way, ever higher and higher.

"Come on, Carmen, don't be silly. It's what's done," the
young pianist in a white drill suit alongside her said.

Menchu obeyed. The impresario's assistant said, yeah, that's
okay, and her two splendid thighs were trapped in the lenses of
his glasses.

"Come to rehearsal on Monday."

The blue light of the projector, followed by red and then
yellow, suddenly glided over the dreary unlighted stage set,
supposed to represent a newlywed's bedroom with the balcony
open onto a moonlit night. They were singing in a chorus line,
holding each other's hands behind their backs, with feathers
and sequins and net stockings, when I hear your voice that
invites me to dream, and your passionate words steal into my

heart, everything seems all peaches and cream, and everything's right from the very start.

She's in the grand finale with all the chorus girls, the middle-aged men in the first rows comment, she's the tallest one and she's got the blondest hair, to the right of the star of the show. Look at her, Muñoz, a Greek statue, sleep, sleep, baby of mine, she doesn't have a voice and doesn't know how to sing or wiggle her hips, but she's a real woman, a splendid woman, have a good look at her.

In the summer of '45, shortly after the French headquarters ordered the guerrilla units broken up. Sitting in the Oro del Rin every afternoon, with her legs crossed and a magazine in her hands, looking out at the Gran Vía with the air of expecting nothing and no one. Behind her, a coterie of ex-future corpses and businessmen lounging in leather armchairs look at her knees with iodine on them, her white shoes with cork soles, her platinum hair; they know that she no longer shows her thighs that drive you crazy on the runway at the Victoria and they've heard something from the waiters about her first lover in a sanitarium and the next one who abandoned her, a pianist in a cheap orchestra: she's having a bad time of it just now.

A hot afternoon in July, a man in a wine-colored sports jacket with yellow stripes sends her an open envelope via one of the waiters. It contains a blank bank check signed F. Muñoz. Carmen looks disdainfully at the check, snubs out her cigarette and uncrosses her knees, allowing them to twinkle quietly at the same height, spread a little bit too far apart. She indifferently asks the waiter for a pen, writes something on the check, puts it in the envelope, licks it, closes it and has it brought over to the sender.

She brought tobacco and magazines, candles, crullers, a book or two, a bottle of cologne, don't go out even at night she begged him, listen to me, one day they're going to pick you up on the sidewalk in one of these streets, you're so weak you might fall, wait a few years and everything will be over. She stretched out naked on the mattress, without blowing out the candle, she said this is something I only do with you, do you like it? with the others I do it in the dark. Or would you rather sleep?

"You sleep, if you can."

"What do you think about, all those hours here alone?"

Of the last holdup at Hispano Colonial; it was raining, the windshield wiper of the Ford measuring out the time they had yet to wait and the motor running, Jaime Viñas sitting at the wheel with his rod between his legs and his mind on some woman: he keeps talking to me about them, of love-fights with biting and fingernails digging into his back, at perhaps the most dangerous moments. Checking the big cartridge belt with the thirty-three bullets. Easy as pie: no alarms, not a shot. Four men in raincoats, unhurriedly coming out of the bank, the last one wiping his forehead with a handkerchief. Three hundred and fifty thousand in tax collections and Fusam with a cut on his forehead.

Having more arms at their disposal since the war ended, gotten from the French maquis and at auctions of the allied army. Maintaining irregular contacts with the other groups, exchanging men and arms and going into periods of inactivity so as to throw the police off the track. Discussions of the new line for guerrilla activities among the exiles in France. Infiltrations of little groups across the frontier had been frequent ever since the beginning of the year.

When Sendra came back from one of his trips to Toulouse, he spoke of his conversations with the secretary of defense on the Rue Belford and his visits to the Colonia Aymeric. Navarro and Fusam asked him about their wives and kids.

"Are they taken care of? Are they okay?"

"The Organization sees to everything. . . . Here, your wife gave me this, she's been making it since last winter."

It was a wool sweater. He added that Ramón, the contact in Barcelona, would bring more things for all of them. But Ramón also brought confirmation of what a number of them were afraid of:

"Your wife? Well, she's harvesting grapes. The Organization passes only insignificant amounts across the border, it's true. And lots of times the poor women have to ask for the money again and again. . . . "

Indignant but putting up with it, swallowing their protests in front of Sendra, especially Navarro, such a disciplined anarchist that he sleeps at attention, Palau used to say, who the hell can understand him? Yeah, the Central Committee takes care of everything: ha ha, he laughed: listen, brother, this isn't working. And yet they say that the Red Cross works very well.

That same day Palau was to hold up a jewelry store on the Calle Santa Ana, in Gracia, on his own, and two days later, along with Jaime and without the group finding out this time either, he got away with 400,000 pesos from the branch of the Banco de Bilbao on the Calle Mallorca. Through the contact, along with a note that said "We live with realities here," the take went to swell the funds of the Central Committee, minus a part that he and Jaime kept for themselves and another one that they sent to Navarro's and Fusam's wives, in Montpellier, without Ramón himself, the bearer, ever finding out.

A postcard squeezed in between two bananas comes through the cat-hole, after the plateful of lentils. A message written by Palau, that old idea of his: what a bunch of sissies; if you see a guy with a top hat in a big American car, have at him, stick the Parabellum in his kidneys with a clear conscience, what else could he be besides a Fascist. . . . And if you still go out at night to stretch your legs, come on Fridays to the Alaska Bar and we'll talk, there's lots to do in Rabassada.

Always joking, the brazen fool: the postcard is from the Conquerors of the Fatherland series and suggests an amusing experiment: Look fixedly at the portrait for thirty or forty seconds, and if you then look at the ceiling, you'll see the image of our late-lamented Founder. In person!

"Are you thinking of going?"

"Yes."

"You'll be a goner some night out there. . . . "

"Taylor" was sweating in his white shirt, it was soaked with sweat under the arms and the butt-ends of his pistols were adjusted so tightly to his armpits that he walked with his arms standing out from his body as though he were suffering from swollen glands. He went over to the table and wrapped the shoebox in newspaper. The little scorpion was hanging from his cuff and Sendra couldn't take his eyes off it, watching the golden reflections, the movements of the tail with its poison stinger. Be careful, he says to him. Then his eyes stare at Palau.

"When will we ever hear about all your capers, you brazen fool? Is it true that Marcos is helping you? How can you tell us that you aren't acting on your own?"

Palau is busy greasing the Parabellum:

"I'm only cleaning out German pigs. Word of honor."

But so what? His face hidden by the black bandana and his hat pulled down over his eyes, stopping the car on a turnoff along the highway to Rabassada. He sticks his arm through the window and puts the barrel of the gun to the driver's temple. A fat man with close-cropped gray hair. Hand it over quick, you. The wallet and the watch and everything you've got, hurry it up. Put the handbrake on first and put your feet up on the seat. Hurry it up.

"You're a German pig," Palau says to him. "I'd put money on it."

"No. . . . I'm from around here, from Sabadell, I swear."

Palau frowns above the edge of the handkerchief, and his supercilious grimace shows beneath the cloth pulled taut by the wind.

"But at least you're a Germanophile. How much do you want to bet?"

"No, I'm really not."

"Well, too bad you're not really anything. Hurry it up, bastard."

Crouched down in the seat, feet under his buttocks, the man

has handed over his leather wallet with 2500 pesos in it, his ten-carat watch, and his pen with a gold cap. At a sign from me he takes off the binoculars. Palau spies a package the size of a pencil-box wrapped in tissue paper and tied with a purple and gold ribbon lying on the back seat. A nice little present for one of our relatives? he says, and the man turns pale. Give it to me, hurry up. You can clear out of here now.

Sendra used to ride Palau hard for capers like that, and when he finished Bundó would start in on him, his hands on his hips. But Palau would cut him off short.

"Shut up, you asshole. I'm working at least."

"Yeah, if you call being a pickpocket working. Lifting wallets in the subway — that's how you're going to end up."

"You can go shove it, Bundó."

They mustn't use the same base very long, Sendra had said, so at the end of the summer they went back to the ice factory in Pueblo Nuevo. By the light of the bare bulb above the workbench, Fusam pushes the pistols toward me, come on let's get to work, looking at me as though I were a dead man come back to life. Why don't you get lost, we don't need you. All of them nervous except Palau and "Taylor." As he puts his jacket on, Bundó hits the light bulb with his hand and the shadows crouch down on the floor covered with sawdust and metal filings. Chewing that eternal sweetish smell of metal in a dry mouth. I drop my Browning, and a broken pane of glass leaning against the wall sends me back the dusty image of a greenish phantom hunched over, bare-chested and skinny, looking at me through dark glasses.

My nerves working on his.

"Be quiet, Marcos, damn it."

"Can you see him after living like a bat?"

"Nothing's wrong, I was never better."

Testing the arms to see if they work right. Meneses takes a last look at the contents of the shoebox, puts the cover on it, ties it with the cord and wraps it in the newspaper, his eyes questioning me: is it certain it won't be a dud this time?

You can start running when you throw it, I say to him. "Taylor" puts the box under his arm and Sendra pats him on the shoulder.

"Do you want me to go with you?"

"No, stick to your job. Good luck."

The scorpion sways on his wrist. With his dark gray suit, sitting on a bench in the Cataluña station on the Sarria line, the package and his hat on his knees, his black hair all slicked down with brilliantine and his petrified profile sniffing danger: he sees the Guardia Civil walking along the platform and he lowers his head and puts his hat on. As two young women in print dresses pass by, they notice the icy paleness underneath the hat-brim. Their stockings are bunched up at the backs of their knees, the folds looking like silkworms. He ducks his head down again, but the guard is heading toward him.

"What have you got in that package?"

"Bottles of liqueur."

The guard wants to check and his hand feels the newspaper. Taking off his gloves, he says in a low voice: come with me, we'll see outside. "Taylor" gets up and walks with the guard to the escalator. His right hand touching the knot in his tie suddenly slips down to his armpit and he takes out the revolver, shoots point-blank, and steps aside to let the body fall. He quickly reaches the escalator amid the screams of women. He stands there quietly with his feet together on the same stair, like a mannequin in a shop window, facing the crowd of people with his revolver in his hand. When he reaches the Avenida de la Luz he strolls along at a slow, indifferent pace, keeping close to the storefronts, elbowing his way through kids, maids, and soldiers. Two policemen come toward him with their submachine guns under their arm and he stops behind a column. Leaning against the counter of the cafeteria, a kid dressed in his first-communion suit is having his shoes shined. The authoritative shout of the Guardia Civil alerts people, who step away in a fan. The bullets of the submachine gun spatter the column, making chips of enamel fly up around his face. Sinking to his knees, the bootblack's arms fall and his mouth lands on the shiny leather shoe, a spot of blood growing larger on his back. "Taylor" lets go of the box, shifts his revolver from one hand to the other, takes the other revolver out of his armpit and shoots with both of them at once, running along hunched over to the next column. He notices a fierce burning sensation in his wrist, and hears the click as the love-bracelet hits the tiles. He slips and falls on one hip at the same time as the two policemen, but they don't get up and he begins running along the subterranean passageway that leads to the subway.

Her image trapped in a prison of mirrors repeating each other, with no possible escape, biting her tail: feeling that everything had been decided since the beginning of time. In her little whore's apartment she would have cretonne curtains, a bar and a bidet, a little terrace on the Paseo de San Juan with a blue and white striped awning and an orange-colored tubular veranda railing. On the mantelpiece of the living room she would have lots of crystal swans, a porcelain greyhound, a red enamel elephant, a glass picture frame with Tyrone Power and another one of her man: a guy with silky cheekbones and a gold-toothed smile. Standing naked in front of the mirror she would try on the new Persian lamb coat, reliving the far-off caress on her skin of other, less soft furs, because nothing had been forgotten: her years as a maid in so many houses, the warmth of the fireplace of her first little flat in the Calle Casanovas, the swift and dizzying prosperity of the trio of dealers in benzine, her ability to hit it off with the well-connected friends of the baroness, the Fiat 1100's and the Campsa tank trucks that were part of José María's operation, the happy nights at the Rigat, apéritifs at La Puñalada and La Navarra, the first abortion, the first irresistible impulse with the truck driver with blue eyes, the friendship with the director of the soccer club, her first reserved seat in the box at Las Corts, her negligence or guilt leading to José María's detention, dispossessed now of all his holdings and devoured by fever, his health and his business ruined, the second abortion, the bad period, the Barrio Chino and the rain boots, the first and only attempt to change her life, with a pianist in an orchestra, the Viennese waltzes, the runway at the Victoria and the net stockings, the sunny afternoons making herself desired on the terrace of the Oro del Rin, the signed blank check, her right move on returning it not with a figure and lots of zeroes following it, but with a stanza of "The Well-Kept Mistress," the good year or so living in the Ritz with her new platinum hair and her Pekingese, the happy wee hours of the morning in the Marfil Bar, the meeting again with the director of the Barcelona Soccer Club, his suntanned smile and his trucks loaded with tungsten passing clandestinely across the border into Portugal, having the box at Las Corts again and the Persian lamb coat, her dazzling ascent to the third floor of the Liceo with her famous naked shoulders and her jewels, the impresario with silky cheekbones always at her side and the invitations to the Tivoli, her new apartment on the Avenida Antonio María Claret 16, on the corner of the Paseo de San Juan, across from the Alaska Bar where she would drop in certain nights to have one last drink, alone, just a little bit drunk, swathed in furs on the high stool and hobnobbing with unknown midnight phantoms, ruined barflies, shadows of what they had once been, looking enviously at her jewels. Anyone could invite her to have a drink at that hour, I'm not finished, not yet anyway, she would go there with just anyone, walking around or drinking till dawn, perhaps in the old Ford in whose back seat, clutching a wooden mallet, there would be sitting the worn-out specter of ten years of useless and absurd resistance, the bloody stump of a corrupted ideology digging his own grave with a shovel in the wretched Can Compte vacant lot, at the foot of four palm trees that held up the starry vault of the sky on that cold night in January when she got herself murdered.

Since she was a high-class whore now, she was choosy about which dances and cocktail parties she went to so as not to meet old friends of the baroness, who according to what people said had taken refuge in Portugal as a result of the denunciation that provoked the fall of an official in the Treasury, and there was a rumor that she'd never been a baroness. Sure she was, her lover told her, she bought the baronetcy for two hundred carloads of wheat handed over to the civil government, I have it on good authority.

She had thought of not attending that cocktail party, but a police officer who had been on duty at the Hotel Ritz years before and was a commissioner now called her up to ask her to be sure to show up, that he had a nice surprise for her.

A mansion in Sarriá stuffed full of Louis XIV period furniture, more than would easily fit in the room and maybe even duplicated, though perhaps it was the effect of so many mirrors, which also multiplied all the urns, rugs, and statues. Two floors and three illuminated terraces full of guests. In the library, shielded in the smoke of their Havanas and their big round cognac glasses, three men buried in big leather armchairs talk of taxes and controls and a house full of underage girls, supposedly a dressmaking school. Red damask on divans and big cushions. A little man all dressed up, in boots and a white tie, gives a start in his armchair. What kind of a school, gentlemen? That blonde over there told me confidentially. . . .

In the drawing room, a woman with plump legs and varicose veins passes among the guests in a hat trimmed with fruit. A lieutenant of guards dressed in a peasant costume swallows grapes from Almería as he converses with the young wife of a car dealer. The hostess joins the group of ladies who are talking with a legion officer, shielded behind dark glasses, about the inauguration of a Social Assistance Home for the orphans of Republicans shot to death by firing squads. These children are not responsible, and we want them one day to be able to say without rancor: if Falangist Spain shot our fathers, they deserved it. The impresario delicately supports the elbow of the young girl with platinum hair. She turns to say hello to the police commissioner, and the dimples in her buttocks sheathed in silk wink in a silver sheen. Smiling, the police commissioner has the pleasure of informing her that the Brigade has recovered part of the jewels stolen from her some time before, among them a gold scorpion, and he hands Carmen a little box wrapped in tissue paper.

Next to the buffet a gentleman with bushy gray eyebrows collapses, dragging down with him a trayful of glasses and the strap of the dress of the middle-aged redhead who had been trying to hold him up. The guests laugh, two white-gloved waiters help him to his feet, what, the guest says, looking around for the hostess with bleary eyes but laughing, shaking a keychain in his hand, are we playing that game again of exchanging the keys of a car with a woman inside . . . ? Two fairies dressed as gypsies chase each other through the corridor with their skirts pulled up above their knees, mink stoles, and diamonds in their ears.

The silken-cheeked gentleman opens his gold cigarette case and offers his partner a cigarette. With a pout of distaste, the blonde suggests finishing the night at the Ritz Grill.

XV

IN those days she was a timid little fat girl with a hieratic bust, as stiff as cardboard, like a pouter pigeon, prefiguring the one she has today under her habit. She would never forget the night that she happened to discover the shelter and its secret way into the theater, one Sunday as she came home after attending a private dance in a friend's apartment: her blood was still musically tingling, with unconfessable desires of tenderness that had been frustrated once again.

Out of timidity she'd asked from the beginning to take care of the record player and the drinks, and when she tried to do something else there was no getting out of it. Get dolled up and come, Paulina, her girl friends had said to her, come on, you're sure to catch a man. It was her last dance, in her very last days as an old maid, in a dining room with torn wallpaper and unpleasant domestic odors where they'd pushed the table aside and taken the fringed lamp upstairs, and it only served to convince her of her innermost feelings about her future vocation. Her girl friends shoved little glasses of anisette into her sweaty hands and artificial flowers in her shapeless waist, conspiring together to change the reality of a figure that had no charm, a cheap dress, and the mocking indifference that she inspired in everyone; but she didn't find a partner this time either, and at the end her feet were aching from not moving and she felt an uncontrollable urge to cry. Somewhat lightheaded from the anisette, she did not expect anybody to offer to see her home and went down the muddy Calle Encarnación all by herself, skirting the puddles and zigzagging from one streetlight to the next so as to stay out of the dark spots.

There wasn't a single soul in the whole street, until a beggar suddenly appeared. He was walking along that same sidewalk, hunched over a bit, holding his beret on with his hand. Nothing about him attracted attention nor was there any reason to be afraid: he was simply a bum coming down the same sidewalk, holding his beret on his head. But twenty yards before she met up with him, she saw that his footsteps slowed down and he tended to lean toward the curb, slowly doubling up. He was probably not more than thirty years old, tall and skinny with a blind man's black glasses, a blue jacket, and broken-down espadrilles, without socks. His cheekbone hit squarely on one of the stones. Paulina hurried over to him, propped him against the wall, and cleaned the blood off his face with her handkerchief. He was breathing like a bellows. On his pale fingers were lots of bone rings. It's nothing, he reassured her; it's just that I feel weak. He tried to get up, and she saw that there was something peeking out between his chest and his dirty shirt: a silver candelabrum. Paulina recognized it, it was one of the four in the crypt of Las Ánimas along with other religious objects; she herself had stored them there after Holy Week.

"Where did you get that, my good man?"

The stranger muttered something, his eyes avoiding hers. He put his beret back on his head and started to leave, saying that he'd found it in a shelter where he sometimes slept, next to the church: it was getting ruined there, some kids had stuck it in a skull, it didn't belong to anybody, and that's why he'd taken it, he thought he might get a few *pesetas* for it.

Shortly thereafter, as the man went on his way, she went into the shelter. So they've dug a passageway into the crypt, she said to herself in surprise, prolonging her excitement, they're going to get it when I catch them. A candle was burning in a little recess on the left, but she didn't see the flame until she'd left behind the mud and the plank; it was guttering out in the little vaulted niche, above the wax drippings covering the skull, illuminating the tiny precincts of a recent secret conspiracy: you could still see the stones in a semicircle and on top of them the wigs for the devil, the three candelabra, the can with traces of gunpowder. She heard their voices from the passageway, but when she pushed the trunk aside she could see no one in the dressing room. Imagine, they're so well behaved at catechism, and just look, I must tell the priest.... She passed in front of a mirror, dirty water that her own form crossed like a phantom: a short, fat woman with her shoes in her hand and a ridiculous cloth flower in her waistband. I'll tell him tomorrow, when I go to confession. There was light on the other side of the burlap, on the stage: their footsteps, their voices resounded on the boards:

"You're dressed up as a man, with the tunic and the golden sash of Saint Michael, the cape and sword and helmet. But imagine that you're a girl, do you understand? what I mean is you're really a girl but you're passing yourself off as a man. And we don't know that."

"And this guy fights with you and the two of you fall to the floor, your helmet falls off and he can see your long girl's hair, like this, look, like in *The Iron Crown*, have you seen it?"

"No."

"Well, never mind. And *Suez*, have you seen that?"

"Yes, that one I've seen."

"Well, you know: there's a cyclone and you save him by tying him to a post, you've got the rope right here, see? Then imagine that the cyclone is about to carry you off, he's fainted and is tied to the post but he comes to and sees that you're lost, he holds you tightly in his arms but it's no use, an invisible force is impelling you, sweeping you off the ground, and taking you far away.... "

"No," María said. "I don't like movies, I hardly ever go to them."

"Well, then, what the Moors did to you, Fueguiña," José Mari said. "Let's rehearse that, how about it?"

"Again?"

Her stunned gaze penetrated to the very back of the stage, her eyes leaped from one horror to another: the chair with the rope hanging on the back of it, the Malayan Boot with the screw that breaks ankles, the Infernal Bell with the hammer and the iron rail, the bidet with trails of powder.... There was even an old radio in the form of a church chapel that if it had worked would surely have served to drown out the moans of the victims, like a real torture chamber. So I was right, Father, I told you once and I'll tell you again: something strange is happening, they've scared the girls to death and heaven only knows what they're up to, he'll see when I tell him tomorrow, he won't believe me: doing dirty things on the stage, I saw it with my own eyes, the girls half-naked and trembling with laughter and fear, María from Galicia and that nasty Virginia with her blonde braids, I spied them through one of the holes in the wall, I was sitting astride a tree trunk that had fallen on the floor, without their seeing me. I've been suspecting as much for some time, I saw it coming, I'll say to him, I said to him: you have to watch these youngsters, very odd things happen, they're as much at home as moles there, and the other day a girl from the Casa had rope marks on her wrists....

I should confess about the dance too, no, that is to say, it's all the same, one sin is connected with the other and it's as though I'll be confessing both of them at once: you see, Father, I'll say to him, I was feeling a little lightheaded coming back from the party and that's how I came to the shelter, and in that state of sin I saw everything. It was as though they were rehearsing for a play but that wasn't it, first it was bits and pieces of movies and the rest was made up, and then that torture that they'd rehearsed hundreds of times, with María forced at gunpoint to strip naked, until they made her laugh and cry at the same time. Pushing her, shaking her, making her rotten laughter, her abject, flowery tears fall as though from a tree, what a shameful thing, Father. When I saw her dressed up as the Archangel I thought they were really rehearsing, but I was immediately surprised not to see Señor Conrado there. There were four Moors in rags with blackened faces, they were brandishing belts with copper coins set in them and had Virginia tied to the ladder, with her arms and legs open like an X. I saw her naked back all tinged with red, God knows I'm not lying, Father, they looked like real lash marks. Then I heard a noise in the dressing room and I turned around: an ashen skull, floating in the void and looking at me, that poor sick Luisito, dressed as an Arrow with his feverish eyes in the middle of two purplish circles like a mask, or was he really wearing a mask? and I heard a scream and looked through the hole again just in time to see the Moors closing in, falling on top of her in the mud of the yard of the little farmhouse. She'd already lost her wooden shoes and the kerchief on her head, they were pulling up her skirts, I don't know if they've told you that the Regulars raped her after shooting her father and mother, and that they twisted her little brother's privates when he tried to defend her and whipped him on the back, I heard that later they cut them off and stuffed them in his mouth: but that's what they were acting out, Father, that little María was playing herself with real tears and that little hussy of a Virginia was playing the part of her brother, tied to the ladder with his back whipped raw, and the others had branches in their turbans and black beards and rifles pointing at them, three Regulars and an officer surrounding María Armesto, who was kicking and screaming, when her brother spat at them again.

" 'Tenant, let's us finish off her brother first," one of the Moors said. "He not going to let us rape her in peace."

"That's right. He-he. And meanwhile she gonna fix us up some nice hot tea, 'tenant."

"A couple pinches, peasant-girl."

"Silence!" the lieutenant said, going over to the boy who'd been whipped. Hands on his hips, provoking him. "You won't spit again. You've got no balls."

"Oh, I don't, do I?" — looking at him over his shoulder, the cheeky thing. "Grab hold of my fly and you'll see, you shitty fascist, here, touch: big and hard and stuck tight to my ass."

"You milisiaman, peasant," one of the Moors said. "But got no balls."

"Just feel, you filthy Moor."

"You just wait and see," the lieutenant said, cuffing him, and then: "You there, tie him up tighter. With this rope."

The Moor complied, laughing. And an even darker one, really black, with a little goat's beard, came over and planted his claws in her little bare lemon-yellow breasts, all full of mud, bitten lilies of light. Her legs opened even farther then, he was crucified there on the stairway, screaming as the officer poked around in his groin with his big ham-hand.

"Suai-suai," the Moors said laughing. "Jaudulilá, how soon he's going to faint!"

He twisted like a serpent, moaning and crying and laughing, and the officer, clenching his teeth, took a step backward and ordered the Moor to go on with it: squeeze, Moor, twist them, they're like rubber, that's right, squeeze them tightly with your fist and pull downward as though you were milking him, that's the way, and he began to hit him with his knees and his feet, as that cheeky girl made out as though she were fainting from pain or laughter. They all of them turned around to look at the girl from Galicia, who'd fallen to the ground, and in her eyes there was genuine terror and horror, Father, the same as back then, it's certain, and a vengeful, bloody anxiety. You have to stop them, I thought, get up and throw them out of here, but my legs wouldn't obey me. I turned my face away when three of them pinned her arms and legs down and the other one sat on her belly, I looked around for Luis at my back to help me but he wasn't in the dressing room and a surge of heat enveloped me, that was when I noticed something moving under me, in the cardboard tree trunk that I was straddling.

But she'd never have the courage to confess that, how could she if she wasn't sure what had happened, she must have dreamed it: that he'd glided into the tree trunk like a serpent, that he'd been coiled up there inside for some time, keeping himself from coughing and burning with fever the way they say that tubercular men burn when they're close to a woman; she also dreamed his dark mouth and his burning tongue, his poisoned breath passing through the cardboard seeking her out. Without being able to react, paralyzed by what she'd seen done on the stage: the dirtiest thing that degenerate Moors can do to a girl on the outskirts of a town devastated by machine-gun fire, I'll say that anyway, but how to confess the other part if it was an illusion of my senses, sitting astride the rough, scratchy tree trunk, with my bare feet and my shoes in my hand, my mind far away and my heart in my fist. . . . She ran home and I thought I'd tell you right away, Father, something's got to be done about those ruffians, it was the last dance of her youth, that had been so sad and such a bore, punish them or expell them and it won't happen again, they're corrupting everything but my vocation is even stronger now, may the Lord guide me, some kids, and at my age, how terribly embarrassing.

And Tits and Amén still slaving away: they went all over for funerals and masses dressed as altar boys, sometimes stopping in at the ragpicker's shop to find out what was going on — informed too late and badly. And Mingo was hopelessly lost now, especially on the days when he stayed over to eat in the jewelry store. On certain nights Luis went to a clandestine coffee-roasting shop, passing an iron sphere over beds of coals, and his mind was always somewhere else, drowsy as he was, with the good smell of coffee and burned sugar in his clothes;

but at least he was free in the daytime like Itchy and Martín and he would go with them to sell postcards or to the movies. They saw Java more often and for the moment they were up on everything that was going on, they didn't have to ask fucking questions like Amén:

"Did he finally find her, Itchy, did he really find her? I'm not in on things, man, I had a funeral, tell me," trotting around after him, trampling on his heels on the way to the Plaza Rovira. "Come on, what happened?"

"Don't be a drag. Java doesn't like the word to get around. Shall we grab the number 30 streetcar? Have you seen *On the Trail of the Dalton Brothers?* Or shall we go to the Delis?"

"I don't care. But listen, you fucker, you never tell me anything. Is it true that he went to the Barrio Chino?"

"Run for it!"

They hitched onto the back as the streetcar started down the straight stretch to Torrente de las Flores. For a good while all they heard was the bell ringing and the hissing of the trolley on the cable, and then the squeal of the wheels on the curve in front of the Delicias movie theater: hanging on to each other with their eyes closed, getting in the back of their necks the handfuls of sand that the conductor threw at them, his insults and his cuffs. Jump off when I tell you, Itchy said, now! The momentum made them run along for several yards, with their bodies bent backwards, their arms churning like fans and the soles of their boots hitting the pavement like pistons, right up to the vestibule of the theater. Martín and Luis were already there. Let's see if it's a nice bloody one because if it's one of those love stories I'm lighting out for the Iberia; they're showing *The Adventures of Marco Polo* there. We'll sneak in together, huh? Amén said; don't make me be the last one, it's always my turn.

They pretended to be looking at the stills. The doorman was sitting in his chair reading his newspaper. Behind the maroon curtain you could already hear the music for the ads. Luis bought a bag of peanuts and passed it around. They saw

Mianet the bum picking up cigarette butts from between the feet of the girls who were looking at the stills for next week's program: the old doorman was still watching. Was it here, Martín? Amén asked. Yes, Mianet said something as he looked at the pictures, he was right here just like now and Mingo happened to hear what he said and whistled to tell Java: I know where she is, gummy-eyes, they've seen her. And he went to see her with a lot of money, did he get money out of the señora, Amén asked. No, but he was just about to, Itchy said, you'll see, Java went to her and said, ma'am, this time I'm sure it's her, I've found out that she went out with an armed policeman and that surprised me at first, but then it turned out that he's a queer, just like her, and he's even got a scar on his chest, would you believe it, ma'am, he even made himself little dresses with a sewing machine that he later rented to her. They don't go out together any more, he hasn't seen her again, but he knows where she is and he's asking me for five *duros* to tell me. He's a poor fairy dying of hunger, on days when he's off duty he puts in hours in a body shop. He's a distant relation of the wife of the owner of the body shop, who was a kitchen-maid who's got a son whose father's a priest. This priest was the confessor of the orphans at the Casa de Familia before the war, until Aurora found out that he was feeling up the girls and told an uncle of hers who's an anarchist, and he kicked the priest out of the Casa, everybody on the Calle Verdi saw it and they all still remember it. I heard about it in a whores' bar that the gray dressed up as a girl from Andalucía frequented, he's already been kicked off the force, ma'am, so he couldn't be.... Well, anyway, he's asking me for five *duros,* ma'am, that's a lot of dough but I know that you'll give it to me, we mustn't miss this chance.

Itchy interrupted himself, his little eyes bulging like acorns as he watched the doorman: he folded his newspaper, got up out of his chair, and went to chat with the cashier. And what else, Amén said, did she give him the dough? Nope, things didn't turn out right. Itchy suddenly put his head between his shoulders as though he were going to attack and pushed Martín, who pushed Luis: now! come on, he's not watching . . . ! No, wait, don't move. And he had them doubled up with laughter. I don't understand, Amén said, taking advantage of the pause, how come a fairy? You numskull, Itchy replied, when are you ever going to catch on? the plan was to go back right away and not say anything, he fooled us, ma'am, fairies are treacherous, ma'am, he kept the five *duros* and it was all a lie, it wasn't her, you can't trust . . . Now! Inside!

They sneaked in, but before the music for the ads was over there was an electricity cut. Whistles and foot-stamping in the peanut gallery. The usher put two lighted candles at the foot of the screen. Martín and Luis threw handfuls of peanut shells and lighted matches at the stage, swept from time to time by the cone of light from the usher's flashlight. Amén smoked and kept up his barrage of questions: and where did Mianet say he saw Ramona? I don't know, stupid. But Mingo heard him and went running to tell Java? Yes. And what happened?

"You say they've seen her? Who?" Java asked.

"Mianet."

"Where is the old gaffer?"

"At the Delicias," Mingo said, "looking at the pictures outside."

The sun raised blinding glints on his old bum's shoes. He made the rounds of the vestibules of movie theaters in the neighborhood in his grimy, colorless army blouse and his basket, keeping close to the girls who were standing arm in arm spelling out the dialogue written on the sepia-colored stills, love-phrases or jokes mingled with the grinding of the projector in the booth, that could be heard even from the street. He stood out among them, with his bald, wrinkled, black tortoise head that gave off a metallic smell of tinned food, of empty cans. His nice face of an old monkey pretended a frank interest in the white-gloved tragedy in the photos, and he read aloud, because there was always some girl who stayed at his side to hear him: experience had taught him that not everyone knows how to read. Only a very sharp-eyed observer could catch on to the delicate maneuver: first his little head infected with misery swayed on his long neck, and there was a gentle, reverent winking as he watched his prey out of the corner of his eye; then immediately thereafter the slow, cautious displacement of his foot until it brushed hers; he humbly lowered his eyes then, tilting his head a little to one side, leaning forward with a certain caution, as though he were on the edge of a precipice, and the little mirror half hidden in the loose shoelaces of his shoe sent back to him those pale white, pink, or blue flashes as from the bottom of a well. At that point a beatific smile softened Mianet's face. He alternated the difficult process of focusing on the image in the mirror and the fervent, whispered reading of the dialogue, taking his prey from one photograph to the next, from a love scene to one showing jealousy, without ever dropping the appearance of spontaneous and gentle deference that he presented to the illiterate girl. And with precise movements of his foot, as the whirl of her skirt or her posture demanded, he patiently improved the perspective, glancing into that sort of penumbra that some day would cause his heart to stop with the joyous discovery: it just had to happen some day.

"When Java arrived, they'd already caught him," Itchy said, "and were beating up on him."

The doorman and an indignant spectator, a guy with a big double chin, imperious and full of wrath. They abruptly pushed him toward the street and he was muttering, having half fallen onto the ground, sweeping it with his muffler and his mattress. Peeking out from the open neck of his blouse were newspapers that protected him from the cold like a shirt. They called him a lousy pig, a dirty old man, a Red, they kicked him, broke his little magic mirrors to bits, threw his shoes far away, dented his lunch bucket, and he stumbled and fell with a melancholy sound of hardware. The pervert, they shouted, he ought to be locked up, spitting at him as the doorman and the spectator dragged him toward the street. Java intervened and got such a hard slap from the fat man that as he

crouched down like a feline his hand went, as swiftly as lightning, to his pocket with the razor. But he didn't take it out,
there was no need to: something in his eyes afflicted with
gummy secretions, sore and red, looking downward, made the
guy lose his balls, and he stepped back and allowed Java to help
Mianet, to put his shoes back on, to lift him up from the
ground and take him to a nearby bar. He sat him down and
said you're up to your old tricks again, you crazy old man, you
don't learn from experience and some day they're going to
beat you to death, why don't you go back to the villages and
try that, what are you waiting for in this city of bastards, for
them to do you in? They'll catch on to everything some day
and you'll end up with a mouthful of sand in the Campo de la
Bota, you stupid old geezer. Mianet took out his lunch bucket
and began to eat, offering Java a bit of canned meat and chewing lightly with his toothless gums. He said ha, villages, you
say? all the peasants give you nowadays are almonds and hazel-
nuts, nobody's got a cent and there's more hunger than around
here, a guy that raises a pig kills it in secret at night, with his
radio turned way up so that nobody hears the screaming,
they're tightfisted, son. And then laughing, more relaxed now:
hey, what's your granny up to, what's happened to the
sailor? ... Nothing. Where do you sleep now, Mianet? he
asked him, have you thrown away the sack, don't you want to
bring us paper? you remember that Granny always gave you
something. And he replied ha-ha, all that was over, he didn't
retin pans or fix umbrellas any more either, he did something
much better now, he sold love-bracelets in the Barrio Chino
and things were going pretty well for him, he had a clientele of
whores who wanted their names and the date engraved on
them. ... Yes, he'd seen her there just last week, in a bar on
Escudillers, she didn't buy anything from him, because she was
down to her last cent, that's how the poor thing is, son, people
who've seen her around still do, of course you've only known
her a little while, you've probably slept with her, you rascal,
but she's skinny as a beanpole and so scared, unknown, a face

that's all eyes; but what is there to do if she doesn't even have the strength left to put up with a guy on top of her, if she hardly talks, if she didn't even visit her Uncle Artemi so as not to go anywhere near Modelo, that's what people told me; but I went there, he was a friend and I took him something to eat when I could, we were together with Chepa during the Aragón offensive, ha, what shit, it never was a real offensive; poor Artemi's goose is cooked, he won't get out in thirty years. And what bar was that, Mianet? Java asked. Ah, you rascal, it could be any one of many, this one or that one, they're all the same to her, look along Escudillers and if you don't find her there, try La Maña: she's going through some bad times.

It was a Saturday night. Daytime has the disadvantage of being a time when they've got lots of work, but that's a guarantee that you'll find them. He walked through the entire Barrio Chino, all the houses, from La Maña to El Jardín and La Carola, all for nothing, they told him the same thing in all of them: we don't want sick people here, this isn't an asylum, we had to throw her out because she stank, really stank.

"So that's how it is, is it, pal?" Amén said, hunched over in the darkness of the moviehouse, greedily dragging on his stinking cigarette butt. "She's got a hopeless case of tuberculosis, has she? A wreck with a mustache and sagging tits? Don't men like her anymore, Itchy, doesn't she please them anymore?"

Itchy's eyes narrowed as he thought: no, he said. Do you remember the mummies that they took out of the door of the Salesian convent, in the Paseo de San Juan, that my father took us to see when we were kids, remember? Well, that's how she is, a mummy. Imagine. And very late one night he finally met up with her in a terrible dive, and what a surprise, kid: she was skinny as a rail, that's right, with skin that smelled of vinegar, a mummy but with lipstick on and her hair dyed, all dolled up and not feeling persecuted or terror-stricken at all, making eyes at two sailors at the bar counter, hotting 'em up even though it turned out that there was nothing doing, because they went off and she was left standing there with hot pants.

Just a touch of fear: she stepped backward when she saw him come in, saying, what, again, kid? A touch of fear: she'd hardly had two tricks all night long and it was Saturday, you could see failure written all over her face. Could it be on account of the scar, Itchy? He looked through the window and saw her buy herself a cup of coffee. He hadn't been able to get those five *duros* out of the lady, but he did get three bills from her, plus two that he already had. . . .

"I've got the money," he said, stopping her on the sidewalk. "Shall we go up to your place, Ramona?"

"Where are you trying to go, snot-nose, how did they let you in?"

"I'm not eighteen yet, but they think I am. Shall we go to your place?"

She gave a weary sigh and closed her eyes. Her purse hanging from her shoulder, her hands in the pockets of her gabardine coat, her legs dancing in her rain boots, as skinny as toothpicks. Let me alone, for heaven's sake, don't make trouble for me, sonny, quit bothering me. Suddenly he took her hand and put it down there, smiling: look how bad off I am. Look at the state you've got me in, Ramona. Quit it. If you like I'll tell Maruja and you can go up to her place with her, that's all I can do.

"No, with you."

"But I'm about to drop in my tracks, sonny. Have you taken a good look at me? It wouldn't work, not because I don't want to, I'll tell you that straight out." And she closed her eyes again, she closed her hand around his burning one, she closed her trembling legs, and her open mouth brushed his muffler. "But it's better not to. I don't want to have any dealings with you, I'll tell you that right now. 'Bye."

"Why not? I've got money" — she was walking away but he grabbed her by the arm. "Wait, listen. . . . "

"Tell the guy that sent you to go take a running jump. Tell him that."

"I won't say anything, I won't tell anybody I've met you."

Ramona stepped back on the sidewalk again, pulling her hand away and looking him straight in the eye. But all she said, in a voice he didn't recognize, with her face suddenly very different, a painted skull, was: "Oh, is that so? And why is that, sonny? Why would you do that for me?"

Java could not resist her look. What's happening? he thought. Naturally: that skeleton wasn't her, Itchy, it couldn't be her, he'd latched on to the wrong whore; that one wasn't hiding from anybody, so it couldn't be her, right? But it was her, and she was scared now, but she also wanted to, because remember: only a couple of tricks and maybe with doddering old men, think what it must be like for them, they've got the habit bad, kid, she was like a bitch in heat, you don't understand that yet but that's how life is, Amén, that's what vice is like. And I think it really was her, because she immediately added: "And why should I believe you if maybe you're more interested than he is? Do you think I'm a ninny or something, that I don't know that you'll denounce me?"

He explained to her, clinging to her arm as they walked along: that's not what I had in mind, stupid, don't you see that if I talk they'll take you to those Gerona nuns to redeem you and it'd be all over for me? That's killing the goose that laid the golden eggs, and that doesn't interest me; is that clear?"

"Well then," she said, stopping in her tracks, "what are you after, what do you want?"

"To go with you. That's all I want."

She thought it over for a while and then said: okay, let's go. They passed by two drunks acting up and clapping hands. It was very late by now and the bars were closing and the electric signs going out. Have you got money for the room? She was nervous, and stumbled. How time goes by, kid, he didn't even recognize me, she said, have I changed all that much, am I such a wreck as all that?

"There isn't much light here, and they're gas lamps."

"That's not it. It's been eight years, but what do eight years mean. . . . "

"You must have been almost a kid. You're a blonde now and you paint your face and you're so skinny. . . . "

"That's right, I'm ridiculous-looking."

"I like you."

"I've been sick. Okay. Have you got money for the room, yes or no?"

"Yes."

"What is there in the room, you ask, Amén? Well, a bed, a bidet, a little night table with an ashtray and that's all. Mirrors on the ceiling, satyrs and nymphs chasing each other on the walls. A red light, towels, pomades for your cock, nothing else. I've never been there, but hang on, here comes the good part: Java had never been there either. I can't believe it, Itchy. I'm telling you, kid, for all I know he might not even have lost his cherry yet. And as it happened, he couldn't do a thing, he couldn't even get it up. Heavens! Was that whore that bad, that fucked up? No, she looks like a beanpole but she's quite good-looking naked. What happened is that hookers like that always tell you their life story, you know, a dog's life with kids by an unknown father, and a pimp that beats them, and that makes you go down, way down to your feet, kid, and if you're not careful you end up crying, I've never been with one but that's the way it is. Damn, then it's better not to let them talk. That's precisely what I'm going to do when I go with one for the first time, Amén, but it depends on the hooker and if you cover up your ears it's great, just the way you thought it was going to be before you went: you lie in bed with her, smoking, feeling so great, so neat, as you can imagine, all you have to do is reach out your hand and there she is, kid, all naked and as nice and warm as a loaf of bread just out of the oven."

"Do they let you take their stockings off?"

"Yes, if they're in love with you. And their brassiere and panties."

But first the rain boots. Lying face up toward the ceiling, eyes fixed on a spider weaving a web or a crack that's spreading, he turned over for a moment to look at her kneeling on

223

the mattress like the first time in the bedroom at the apartment in Ensanche, tying her hair at the nape of her neck with a rubber band. Nice and peaceful, watching her body like a statue in the middle of a neglected garden, in the middle of a leafy memory that was not totally hers, looking at her little breasts marked with scars and little bite-marks and her rough thighs; thinking about the curious destiny of this flesh and his, united in a strange bed though not by chance, and not only out of hunger and need: the feeling of things that are now irreversible, like failure or death.

And if you treat her nicely she ends up starting to trust you, kid, and then you can ask her: how's life treated you, babe? and she tells you how and when it began, who the first guy was, where it was that she lost her virginity, if she bled, and so on. And it's exciting.

"He was an airplane mechanic, he worked in Can Elizalde. Very handsome, a bit brazen, and rebellious, one of Durruti's friends, like Uncle Artemi, he introduced him to me when he was a foreman."

"You were the directress of the Casa de la Familia, then," Java said. "You put on plays with the little orphans of Las Ánimas, is that right?"

"That was before, in the first year of the Republic. I took care of scrubbing and sweeping that top-floor apartment, but I slept in the Casa, when the war came and the directress lit out leaving the girls flat, the only money was the four *reales* that the oldest of us earned by going out and doing day-work, somebody had to take charge and I was the oldest. In fact I was never a directress of anything, Uncle Artemi and some women from the Party helped us a lot, and that lasted till they killed Pedro in Aragón."

She had sat down on the bed and was waiting for him, and he hung back by the bidet, lost in thought. He saw her get up, let me wash you, he saw her come over to him with bulging eyes, a smile that seemed like a grimace, let me do it.

"And you took them to mass when the Reds were in power?

did you take the orphans to communion at Las Ánimas, to pray and sing with the priest, in the middle of that mess with the Reds?" Java asked.

"Not to mass, of course, there wasn't any, the chapel was sacked and burned and there weren't any services till two years later. You mustn't think it was the same as now, we didn't spend the day chanting dirges, we spent it playing, learning solfège, or rehearsing plays. That winter the Casa was a temporary billet for some militiamen who gave the girls quite a few pairs of shoes, and they helped them set up camp in the garden, I can still see them around the bonfires carting around rifles, teetering back and forth in their high heels. . . . Everything was fine till I lost Pedro."

They always say the same thing: that their sweetheart pulled the wool over their eyes and mistreated them and then abandoned them. And if you press them, if you seem sympathetic, they'll tell you how it was, crying like Magdalenes as they remember it, disconsolate, kid, with their mascara getting ruined from their tears, and their rouge and lipstick; suddenly she's another whore altogether, another face: the face of a poor vice-ridden girl with no way out.

"Who could have ever told me that that would happen to me, to *me,* who helped my sweetheart take up collections for the Red Cross and go along the streets pasting up those posters that urged whores to abandon their profession, that the hour for their freedom had come. And just look at me now."

"What happened? How was it the first time, and where?"

"In a strange unmade bed. Before cleaning the apartment, because Pedro couldn't wait even a minute more. On some sheets that were still warm from him, the filthy pig. We took advantage of all the times when he wasn't in the apartment. But he caught on. He must have discovered us one day, and the pig didn't say a word, didn't do a thing, he just watched: months and months watching, spying on me as I dressed and undressed, seeing me there in his bed with my legs open, the miserable wretch, seeing me moan and cry with happiness, I know that today, just the way I know I'll never be happy again in this life. I idolized my Pedro, honey, I let him do whatever he wanted with me, it's not like now, do you know what I mean? it was real, true love. So that miserable guy went on rotting inside, crouching down behind a keyhole, and that's what he's still doing, rotting away by the day, and not only because of the machine-gun bullets he's got in his spine, corrupting everything he touches, his poor mother and you and others to come after you."

"And you didn't realize it? How long did it last?"

"Until one day when I couldn't get in the bathroom, it was always locked from inside and in order to scrub I had to carry buckets of water from the kitchen. How odd, I said to myself, but I was so dumb I didn't catch on. And he was so nice in other ways, so attentive to me and the girls from the Casa: one day he gave us a Ping-Pong table as a present and at night there was a doll in every orphan's bed, and he'd also begun giving me underwear as a gift. Do you know what I mean? darling things, the finest and most expensive ones, enough to get any girl hot. Do you see how he'd thought it all through, coming to me with those embroidered bras, those satin slips and transparent nightgowns, those lace garters? . . . And the bottles of cognac and anisette that he left within our reach on the little night table, so we'd get drunk, so we'd work ourselves up to doing what he must have liked the best? Until the day he forgot to lock the door."

It was shortly after Pedro went away, she said. She'd put her smock on and begun to empty the ashtrays, to shake the rug, to sweep and scrub. Every time she passed by the door of the bathroom with the bucket and the mop her hand went out automatically to the door handle — it was a conditioned reflex. And this time it opened. Surprised, and still not opening the door all the way, she saw light and heard the legs of the little stool creak as he moved back, then the sound of glass breaking and the trembling resistance behind the door. She opened it all the way, with a scream already in her throat. And there he was, leaning against the wall with his bathrobe slung over his shoulders, with his legs spread so as not to fall altogether, in the middle of a bunch of cigarette butts and broken glass and a perfumed puddle that smelled to high heaven, with the little room full of tobacco smoke and the unbreathable odor of sweat. And there he stood, kneading, crumpling the yellow towel with maniacal fingers. . . .

"And what did he do when he saw that you'd discovered him?"

"I was so scared. I wanted to go away but he wouldn't let me, he insisted on giving me an explanation. First he begged me, he crawled to my feet begging me: it was like a sort of sickness, he said, he said he couldn't help it and that what he did didn't hurt anybody, he begged me to forgive him, not to say anything to his mother. Then he realized that I was crying more than he was, that I was more frightened than he was, that I was still almost a kid, and he calmed down. I didn't know what to do. I wanted to go to the Casa and get in bed and cry, I remember that that night one of the little girls heard me and came on tiptoe to get in bed with me. I had to unburden myself to someone and I told her everything. We were dying of shame and rage and we cut the heads off all the orphan girls' dolls and the next day the fat directress raised a terrible fuss.

"Did you tell your sweetheart?"

"It would have killed him. I thought of telling him, but later, in those days there was shooting in the streets and I know that Pedro would have gone and killed him, him and Justiniano, who was the one who brought me the presents. Justiniano was his father's chauffeur and he used to come with the Hispano to get Conrado on the days when he ate with the family. He used to meet me sometimes in the street and would smile when he saw me, I can't say he ever misbehaved with me, but he was Conrado's confidant and his accomplice, and I think that was the one reason why I swore to do him dirt some day. . . . I also used to run into him in the top-floor apartment, brushing Conrado's clothes or shining his collection of riding boots, and I don't know why but it made me glad to see that great big man doing tasks like that, he looked like a happy dog wagging its tail, I could even have sworn that he licked the boots. Even though he must have been in on the whole thing, he'd never fooled around with me, not even as a joke. But one day when he brought drinks to the top-floor apartment when the señorito told him to and he found me there alone, scrubbing the hallway, he invited me to have a glass of cognac. It was the first time I'd ever seen him in his blue shirt. I didn't accept and he began to insist, he was in a good mood and cracking jokes, and as he was getting ready to uncork the bottle he tried to put his arms around me and in the scuffle, without meaning to, he hit me with the corkscrew, here and here, look. That made me anxious to talk to Pedro, but soon there wasn't time for anything, the war came along and Pedro went off to the front and because I was the oldest one in the Casa and we had no directress, I had to take charge of the littlest girls. Conrado went over to the Nationals with his father, they had already reached Pamplona, and then his mother left too, and the anarchist militia confiscated her apartment in Ensanche and they say, though I don't know if it's true, that for a time it was a torture chamber, I was never there. All I know is that Uncle Artemi never let them touch a single thing, not one piece of silverware was taken from that apartment and just look how they've paid me back for that. I never saw that miserable man again, and I haven't seen his mother either. . . . You still haven't kissed me on the mouth, do I turn your stomach or something? And I haven't felt your tongue either, my darling."

And the abortions they've had: they tell you about that too, kid. And how careful they are not to let themselves get excited, not to have too much pleasure, to distract themselves some way, by counting to a hundred in their minds, for instance. So as not to wear themselves out. Didn't you know that their pleasure-nerve is very sensitive and that in the end they ruin it? Don't you see that they couldn't bear it, with all the work they have, don't you see they'd end up with t.b.?

"But you've seen his father," Java said, noting her tongue in his groin, grabbing her peroxide head in his hands, perhaps with the idea of allaying a little that fever, that anxiety that was consuming him. "Wait. . . . You did see his father again, isn't that right?"

Ramona sat up with a sort of sadness in her eyes, pinching with trembling fingers a little hair stuck to the corner of her mouth. With a sigh she lay down beside him.

"Yes," she said. "Other people were taking care of the orphan girls by then and I was working as a maid again, this time in a mansion in La Salud that the owners left in my care for long stretches of time. I went out every night and ended up becoming a whore, that's the truth, I don't know how it could have happened but it did. I was in despair over the bombings, and I'm not making excuses, but it depressed me to go into the subway stations and the shelters. Balbina and I hung out at the Hotel Falcón, on the Ramblas."

"Looking for a lover?"

"Looking for company. Friends of Pedro's and my uncle's. The hotel was always full of militiamen on leave and their money burning a hole in their pockets, and sometimes we invited some of them to the mansion and they stayed the night. Balbina got pregnant and the señora fired her. But I went on living like that, I fell madly in love first with one and then with another, and you mustn't imagine that I was sad or bitter, no, I didn't realize what was happening, but my uncle did and one day he gave me a beating. Then I told him everything: that I liked it, that I couldn't do without it, that I'd never forget Pedro but that I needed a man and that it was all the fault of that guy who had watched. My uncle didn't say anything, he didn't want to know the details, only his name. Two months later some men from the Inspection Patrols came to look for me and took me to the Hotel Falcón in a car, I remember that it was spring and there was shooting in the street and barricades, you could see windows protected with sandbags and paper X's pasted over them, and my uncle's men were sitting there all preoccupied and silent with their rifles and their grenades and their red and black neckerchiefs; they were very young. There wasn't a soul to be seen on the Ramblas. In the hotel a militia-girl with her cap tilted to one side over her curly hair went in search of Uncle Artemi. You could hear laughter and soldiers' songs, the butt ends of rifles rang out on the pavement and there were lots of little girls collecting for the Red Cross. My uncle wasn't there, he'd gone to talk with somebody on the roof of the building opposite, above the Poliorama movie theater, do you see that cupola? they said to me, do you see that sniper with his head sticking out? I remember the profile of a skinny man, with his upright rifle poking him in the nose, reading a book. My uncle appeared at his side, offering him a bottle of beer. That's when I found out about the attack on the Telephone Center and they explained the situation to me: it was feared that there would be an attack on the places our side held, and they had to defend the hotel. You'll see, they said to me, but we waited for them and nothing happened, they decided to go back to the car and a little later we were hurrying down a highway on the outskirts of town. You'll have to identify him all by yourself, they said to me. We stopped on a curve and got out, night had already fallen and I was cold even though it was the month of May. Another car was waiting for us, with some men inside it who were smoking, the chauffeur was a hunchback, and all of them had leather hunting jackets and berets and drowsy faces. I didn't recognize his face behind the glass until he turned around, he didn't have handcuffs on and the agents watching over him weren't paying any attention to him. With his hair as carefully combed as ever and his little clipped mustache, he looked at me sadly but it all happened so fast they didn't even give me time to think. I'd seen him lots of times at Las Ánimas, along with the señora, and I supposed he was in Burgos or someplace else with the Nationals, I don't know how they found him but he was there and they shoved him out of the car; he was blinded by the headlights, and stood there looking at us at the edge of the ditch with his hands in the pockets of his leather jacket and his yellow scarf over his shoulder, so pale and thin, suddenly looking much older, stoop-shouldered all of a sudden and looking somehow even shorter. But we didn't hear him beg. Here he is, the man in charge said, and he took out his pistol and so did one of the F.A.I. men, but a voice said wait, when Navarro says to go ahead, not before. I tried to tell them they'd made a mistake but I was so scared I got all choken up, I couldn't manage to blurt out this isn't the one, this is the father, although my uncle's boys must have noticed something because they seemed to hesitate for a moment. But the S.I.M. agents were in a hurry, let's get this over with, come on, one of them said. The señor looked at me, hoping for a miracle maybe, he wasn't a bad sort, he and the señora were always nice to me. He didn't protest, he didn't put up the slightest resistance. In the silence of the preparations you could hear the night wind whispering in the pines. Even today I don't know if I managed to say, in a tiny little voice, what are you going to do or something like that, you're making a mistake, but they didn't hear me and didn't seem to be in any mood to turn back, they're all alike when they get a pistol in their hands, cruel and bloodthirsty, his hour's come and that's that, they said, and as the señor looked at me, certain now that he was going to die and I stood there saying no, not to kill him, that the one they were after was his son, somebody gave me a shove, saying turn your face this other way if you don't want to see it or better still go to the car, and I shut myself inside the car but I saw it all with my face pressed against the glass. They'd given him the order to walk and he was beginning to move along the edge of the ditch when the most decisive one caught up with him in two nimble strides and put two shots into the back of his neck, so close together that they seemed to be one. He shot him in the head with the pistol after he'd already fallen, and took his leather coat, his watch and his shoes off him. They moved the head with the bullet holes in it with the tips of their shoes. Then they drove over him with the car; the hunchback at the wheel looked back and asked, what shape have we left him in? and another man said: okay, he's ironed nice and flat. And they left him stretched out there on the edge of the ditch."

And they tell you everything, absolutely everything if you can earn their trust and their affection: like a sweetheart, but sadder and needing more real affection, do you know what I mean? more screwed by life. They're sentimental, I can tell you that. And then, when you've gotten in good with them, you see each other lots as though in secret and you can go to the movies or to dances, she invites you up to her nice warm apartment and you make meals, sharing what there is to eat, and if you're lucky she's like a mother to you. Did you know that from Can Compte, if you climb up on the wall you can almost see her in bed?

Java got up and went to look through the window. He parted the red curtains with green polka dots and saw the miserable vacant lot on the other side of the Calle Legalidad, the beginnings of a cultivated field once upon a time, after having passed through blood and fire to be so. He came back with his hands in his pockets, swaying from side to side: he didn't dare undress or feel or touch anything. It was the first time she'd invited him to her place, and he was losing his nerve.

"And how did the proprietress of the Continental talk you into it? How could you have gone to that apartment, how could you not have recognized the downstairs door? . . . "

Ramona hugged her knees with her interlocked fingers.

"I'd never been at the house on the Calle Mallorca, I only knew his bachelor apartment, the top-floor apartment on the Calle Cerdeña."

"How long have you lived here?"

"For a month" — taking off her bra, sitting on the edge of the miserable bed, kicking off the rain boots against the sewing machine. "Come on."

"And how come you've never brought me here till today?"

"I didn't want anybody to know" — her feet were cold: she

left her socks, her stockings, her black panties till last. "I share it with another girl who's going away soon and then I'm going to go to work."

The usual, Amén: a little room with ocher walls that are very damp, two couches that make into beds, a little table covered with oilcloth, three chairs, a brazier, a portable washstand, and flowerpots with geraniums in that window. And the Singer, a rented one to be sure. To Java much better than the best room on the Calle Robadors, the one they had been in the first time. If you look closely, even though it's the most perverted whore who lives there, even though the blanket is crawling with syphilis germs, you'll always find a little bit of the warmth of a real home, some detail that reminds you of a sister or a mother.

"Work, you say?"

"Yes. You see that sewing machine? I'm still paying for it. Come on, come closer."

With a smile Java evaded her request, that troubled urgency in her eyes and breasts. She clasped her belly: come on, hurt me.

"How about eating something first? Those beans look fine, and they're nice and warm. Have you got a few drops of oil around anywhere?"

"In a minute. Come on, you'll see how nice it is in bed, it's cold enough outside to freeze the balls off a brass monkey — smiling uncertainly, twisting about, pressing her thighs together as though she were about to pee, seriously, sometimes they can't wait, vice is something to make your hair stand on end, kid. "What's wrong?" — falling back onto the bed, calling to him with her arms and her legs open, seeing him standing there, still dressed, looking at her with his hands in his pockets. "Didn't you say you were dying to? Didn't you say that you've been looking for me for months and months just for this? I won't charge you anything, come on, I'll give it to you for a present. Get it while the getting's good, before I change my mind. It isn't the same as staging stuff for the cripple, there's not going to be any pretending that you like it here and you aren't even going to take the lead. . . . "

"That's right," Amén said, "let's go back to the Calle Robadors, to the first time."

"Come on, don't tell me you're bashful, it isn't possible, kid."

"That's not it. . . . "

"Well, well" — laughing as though she were almost dumfounded.

"Come on, let me wash you."

"I already washed, I don't need to."

"Just in case."

"No, I tell you" — suddenly furious. "Wash your own self, whore, you need it more than I do."

"It's okay, insult me as much as you like" — she saw that Java had lowered his eyes and was biting his lip. "It's because you're dying of shame, just look, almost a kid and already so perverted. But I'll help you, baby, come on, come with your Ramona, that's it, let me undress you, that's it. . . . "

His shaved head glistened, he was sweating in the half-shadow full of the red tips of cigarettes, and Amén was as rigid and tense as a bird of prey. But they had gotten tired of waiting and decided to leave; it was taking too long for the lights to come back on. They left the movie house kicking up a ruckus and went up Escorial to Legalidad like a guerrilla band. They jumped over the wall into the vacant lot and looked around, in vain once more, for bullets and buried grenades. From time to time they looked at the little windows with red curtains with green polkadots where two restless shadows came and went. They were cold, they made a fire and waited for it to get dark so as to join the others in the junk shop. From this same site, next to the wall and almost at the same hour, two years later, their eyes piercing the turbid glass pane of the real truth, it seemed to them they could see her naked in the window:

dressed in a ray of moonlight and a smile, walking with open arms toward someone that they could not quite make out. On his heels in front of the fire, Amén kept on asking questions and being amazed: and what about the scar? didn't he ask her how she got it? Some pimp probably gave it to her, and with his eyes staring at the firelight, Itchy went on endlessly, until Martín went over to him and said listen, why do you keep pulling the wool over the poor kid's eyes, can't you see he's just a kid, an altar boy? Well, that's why, because he's still just a youngster, what do you want me to tell him, the truth, the whole truth, and nothing but the truth? That whores aren't that nice or that affectionate, that they make fun of you and have no shame and no soul, that they suck you and then suck you some more, that she asked Java to give it to her again and again and cried as she licked him with her tongue from his toenails to the ends of his hair, crying like a poor crazy thing as though she were dying in pain, weeping and desperately sucking him so as to keep him there, so as not to be alone again, losing sight of her surroundings to the point that he got frightened and there was something like the taste of figs in his mouth, and then she gave up and huddled up at the foot of the bed and let herself slide off onto the rug, between the feet of the men shot by the firing squad, a bundle shaken by sobs on the cold sand at dawn, mingled with the men lined up with their hands tied behind their backs, as though she too were waiting for the shots from the death squad . . . ? What do you expect, the filthy truth, that she's a vice-ridden loser, a degenerate who's rotting away, with syphilis and the clap up to her eyebrows, used to anything and everything, from the front and from the back, a skinful of pus that can't find johns any more, who hardly has enough to eat and had to have Java buy her cones of cooked beans? . . . And what are *you* surprised at, what did you think? You ought to know that every love story, kid, however romantic they try to pass it off as, is nothing but a joke so as to camouflage with pretty phrases dirty things like

I'll kiss your cunt till you die sweetie or put it up me till it touches my heart, till the end of the world: things that can't be, man, making you want to slip away, especially in the case of a scared whore whose insides have been emptied out so that she doesn't have either feelings or ovaries left. And do you know what's left you in the end? a taste of codfish and a few little hairs for a souvenir in your mouth, and you're lucky if they're blond ones. That's what life is, love and purgatives, Amén. Did you want me to tell that to the kid, a dirty truth like that? He wouldn't have believed me, nobody believes me, and not even the one-eyed man will believe me the day he stops me on the street and asks me questions with the pretense that he's signing me up free for the youth camps the way he did with Tits. You'll see how it all turns out, I'm waiting for him now. . . .

"He'll ask you what we're doing in the shelter," Martín said. "Somebody's ratted."

"Yeah, it's high tide all right. But it doesn't matter. I've got my true lie all ready and one, two, three, out goes y, o, u, comrade, I'll say to him, take it or leave it. Yes, the bastard, I know how to deal with him, let him come whenever he likes.

XVI

W ATCH it, you can see your pistol under your jacket,
comrade, that scares people and rightly so, and then
you complain if they call you killers, I'll say to him. Me An-
toñito Faneca, at your service and God's, but nobody calls
me by my name, at first they called me the son of "The Pregnant Woman," and then "The Storyteller." Not the liar, but
the storyteller, that's something different that you don't know
anything about, imperial comrade, and don't be surprised:
politics doesn't leave you time for anything, you're always
walking in those streets wearing out your shoes and crossing
out names on your list of people who haven't paid up their
quota, I can see you now, always serving the fatherland that's
dawned, recruiting volunteers for the youth camps and collecting taxes in bars and shops, pursuing monopolists and retailers
who hike prices and turning in girls for illegal prostitution, a
sacrificial victim, an ex-prisoner, yes sir, a hero who gave an
eye for the cause, I'll say to him, but how much that black
patch becomes you, you look like Admiral Nelson in *Lady*

Hamilton; haven't you seen it? Well, don't miss it even though it's an English movie. No, I'm not fooling, really, I know you would have preferred to have a glass eye but they're very expensive, let's hope that some day they'll reward you for your many services that you don't say a word about, and as I was saying, that's what they used to call me but then they started pinning that name of Itchy on me, look at my hands and my head shaved bare, sir, look at how bad off I am, we're all very poor in my house; there's one with t.b., there's my grandfather who's crippled and who's got typhus, a sister who's a whore, and a brother who's in seminary. He got all confused in the head from the bombs, and there at least he has something hot to eat every day. From the south, yes, but honest people, from the province of Córdoba, but we came to Catalonia before the war, to a town with a weathervane, my father became an alcoholic and then here in Barcelona he kept hitting the bottle and he went on like that till he almost croaked, you knew him, they say he was a police informer but he was only a man who never had a single bit of good luck in his whole life. And my mother's a widow who scrubs floors, I was just about to go see her: on Mondays and Fridays she cleans the Rovira movie theater and sometimes they give her free tickets. . . . Well, I just stopped for a minute to see that garbage truck burning, how many people there are at the windows, look how high the flames are and what a lot of black smoke, they're reaching up to the balcony on the second floor and it's lucky that this Calle Verdi is pretty wide, look, they've unhitched the horse from it and are throwing buckets of water on it, it's quite a fire, sir, somebody threw a lighted cigarette butt on it, I'm sure, some gypsy or some poor beggar, who knows who. Stand back because there are sparks and what a stench there is from all that black smoke, and you can see that people eat shit these days. There have been quite a few fires in the neighborhood lately, though they were little ones, this is the biggest one I've seen, the other day somebody threw a lighted match into the dry cleaner's on the Calle Martí and there almost was a terrible explosion that would have burned down the entire block, they say, it must be some maniac....

How should I know, I'll say to him, I was just going to the movie house to see if they'd given any tickets to my mother and on the way I go into the bars to see if I can sell a few postcards. They're not dirty ones, they're just plain colored ones, look, five *céntimos* a half-dozen and the purple ones in relief are ten *céntimos* for fifteen, the customer can choose, they're nice to carry in your wallet or stick up on the wall with thumbtacks. I've also got some from "The Saviors of Spain" series, Mola, Varela, Yagüe, Queipo, the whole lot, and look at this one of the Founder, it's really neat: if you look at it for a long time and then look away, you'll see his face on the ceiling, it says so here in the instructions. And I've got a block of photographs where the Caudillo is saluting with his arm upraised, look, you flip through them very fast, like this, with your finger, and it's a movie with his arm going up and down saluting, look what a nice souvenir. Would you be interested in a real Parker pen, the cap's German gold, a bargain, I'll make you a price or better yet you tell me what you'd be willing to pay, I'm having a good day today, here, I'll give it to you as a gift, comrade, take it as a proof of my friendship and my respect. Ask me anything you like, I'll say, I've got nothing to hide. A girl in the dispensary with burns under her fingernails and marks from a leather belt on her back? I don't know a thing about it. Tortures, the Water Torture, the Infernal Bell, the Malayan Boot, the Death Pendulum? You've seen *The Drums of Fu-Manchu,* comrade, that sort of thing only happens in the movies and even then it's not for real, they're doubles, I'll say to him, we're real and we only go to Las Ánimas to learn our catechism and get the lunch they give us, and sometimes we rehearse, ask Señorito Conrado, who's our guide and benefactor. You say that fat catechism teacher has been spreading rumors, saying she saw us? But she's mentally retarded, comrade, she had a blood-clot when she was little, didn't you know that she doesn't have all her wits about her, poor thing, and that she's a bitter old maid who goes around saying that everybody's trying to rape her?

Ruffians, savages, degenerates — who, us, imperial comrade? The plague of Guinardó, uncontrollable, not in school, deserving being thrown into the Durán Asylum and getting the lash, heartless wretches with razors? search me, sir, I haven't even got a penknife on me, I'll say. That we sow terror in the neighborhood, that we brand girls, torture them, and do dirty things with them? Look, if some neighbor women have complained, you ought to know that it's not for that, it's on account of the stone fights and playing with gunpowder, bullets, and cans of gasoline. We've broken a few windows without meaning to and some woman may have gotten hit with a stone that wasn't intended for her, I don't deny it, but there's nothing to the rumor that we've whipped girls with a leather belt, and nobody can say they've seen us, that's what they say but it's all a pack of lies made up by those stuck-up kids from Los Luises and the Hermanos, fairies who can't stand us because they're so scared of us. . . . That we're all the same sort, that we're friends with those fancy-pants? not a chance, comrade, that will never be, we play with gunpowder and they play with silkworms. Clothespins on their tits, a raw sweet potato up their . . . , that we burn the hairs on their little . . . ? but what a thing to say, comrade, I'll say to him, what kind of a country are we living in anyway, it's all because of the damage done by the war and eating so much gruel that people have got diarrhea of the brain and see torture chambers everywhere. What a disgrace, what a scandal.

The ragpicker you say, Java looking for a whore and getting a good price for denouncing her, and that he knows where she is now but doesn't tell so as to keep on collecting? That's not exactly true, sir. I'll brand you, Ramona, even though you hide underground in the last place on earth I'll find you and brand you, that's what they say that Java solemnly promised in the shelter with his hand on the skull, and that that catechism teacher heard us second his oath, well that's just one big fat lie, we're not low-life from the Barrio Chino. I don't know anything about whores, either Reds or Blues, comrade, I'm an Arrow. But I'm one in secret, I don't like to show off, everybody shows off nowadays and they even paint spiders on the corners on Sundays in full daylight so that everybody will see them, the braggarts, but I like to do it at night by the light of the evening stars because the Founder deserves another style, right, comrad? that's the way I am, I'll say to him, and I always like to go to the first mass too so as not to make a big scene of it, and I take communion on the first Wednesday of each month, not on Friday, you're saved either way and it means you're less conceited, and what's more my uncle's in the Ministry of Supplies and a bearer in the Las Ánimas processions. . . . Word of honor, don't hit me, don't beat me, I'm the son of a widow! And what are you pushing me for now, where are you taking me, how come you're beating me up if I never touched those girls, please don't be mean because the girls from the Casa de Familia are watching, what'll they say if you beat me, look at Fueguiña there in the front row on the terrace so as not to miss out on a thing, she never misses a fire, ow, don't hit me on the head because it'll take the sulfur off and then Mama scolds me. . . .

That's right, yes of course he's seen her, I'll tell you if it interests you all that much, but only once and from a distance, you don't have to come around showing off the Star for me to sing: not what you imagine, because to tell the truth Java was looking for her for a reason that nobody knows anything about, comrade, I'm going to tell you something that I'm the only one to know. You'd never guess, no, you're cold, cold, I wouldn't fool around with a mutilated ex-combatant like you, I should say not, you're hot, hot, there you are: there's nobody hiding out in the junk shop, they say Java's brother died in France. He was one of those Pum guys that barely escaped by a hair after a rout during the war. And now we're coming to that thing that I'm the only one to know, but hang on, comrade, I don't want you to fall over from surprise: do you know the real reason why Java's been moving heaven and earth to locate a whore? not because somebody hired him to, no, not because kindhearted Señora Galán wants to redeem her former maid or because her son is interested in getting his revenge for something that she's involved in, they say, no, this is only the front he's been putting up, but what's behind that front? today it's all rumors and lies on top of denunciations and acts of revenge and even shootings every morning on the beach, they say, stuff invented by the Reds who are still around, comrade, you know, diarrhea of the brain of the powerless who are foaming at the mouth with rage at having lost everything in the war, they lost their dignity, the truth, their strength, good sense and even their real memory. No, I'll tell him: he was looking for her in order to take her to his brother when he was still here, sir, to keep him company from time to time in that dark hideout of his, do you see what I mean? it isn't easy to find a whore who's willing to work under those conditions and in fact it didn't matter to Java whether it was this one or some other one, but his brother had gotten the hots for Ramona and it had to be Ramona, see? And now listen carefully and don't interrupt me, I'm not a big-mouth, have a little patience, I'll say to him, okay?

Those news items that began to be converted into little paper birds day after day and night after night were the first thing that surprised me. Then on successive winter afternoons that were all alike and so gray you couldn't remember which was which, when the cold invited you to bury yourself in the mountain of paper warm with news, when our stories made us think that the ragpicker's shop was the navel of the world, then, above the sound of the rain and the far-off siren of a boat, we would hear the patient rasping of a file, footsteps on almond shells, repeated footsteps that were always the same, the pacing of a caged man, a tobacco cough that was terribly lonely, and if she was there, her nervous laugh all of a sudden, like a whip. How can they work in those conditions, and happily, how can a whore go to bed with so many corpses? Okay, we won't talk about that. Were you ever in the junk shop? I'll ask him, and maybe he'll say yes, it may be possible that they made a search some time ago: because you too have orders to look for her, but please do me the favor of putting two and two together, I'll tell him, everybody's after her for different reasons, but you add them up, comrade, put two and two together and you'll see: it seems like a plot, I'll bet.

Those walls peeling from the dampness and with bits and pieces of half-naked Republican women, strips of torn paper with rusty thumbtacks and fragments of the thighs of Margarita Carvajal or Laura Pinillos torn out of magazines, along with soccer players and boxers who've retired or are dead now, from the floor to the roof, behind the piles of paper and rags, that desperate and juvenile accumulation of idols in action and pretty girls in bathing suits, an exuberant joy of living fragmented and spread out on the walls like an exploded memory, in chaotic expansion, that's all that man left behind for us when he disappeared, with his chest that they say is tattoed and his eyes that would appear to be blue. Even though she climbed up on a chair, Granny couldn't get down the highest and prettiest pictures, almost under the ceiling, not even with a knife attached to the broom handle, scratching at the plaster until she got down to the brick: they'd have to destroy the house and bury the cellars underneath it and not even that way would they manage to destroy that poor personal memory that would continue to float amid the sickening dust of the debris, amid the ruins, the desolation, and the death of the cat and the rats crushed in their flight, the remains of a cornered consciousness, the unjustifiable massacre on top of which they would build the glorious future edifice, comrade.

Among those images still safe from the fingernails of fear there was one that obsessed us, a photo taken after the attack on a piece of private property, with figures out of focus, yellow, in distant poses: militiamen with a blurred, starved smile, with their overalls and rifles and espadrilles, lying on mattresses, and him almost unrecognizable, marked with an inked

243

cross above his head, with his eye sockets and cheeks devoured by a shadow, unshaven and uncombed, sprawling like a lazy bum on the striped upholstery with fringes, clutching a pistol and with his cap tilted at a jaunty angle. Smiling mockingly in the midst of the luxury, vengefully, an expression as though he were about to spit on something: the thick rug, the crystal chandelier with blinding swans' necks or the honey-colored drapes, he doesn't give a damn because he has the same hatred for all of this that isn't his and can never be his. A place, it seems like, converted into a gypsy camp: a dirty shirt hangs from the mother-of-pearl folding screen, a pair of tattered socks is drying on the wings of a marble angel and a red bandana on the high decorated back of a chair. There on the rug there can be seen, in a jumble, the big oil paintings and the gilded picture frames and cornucopias, sculptures of poly-chromed wood and silver dishes, the booty that the patrol was to carry away but that in the end they didn't, supposedly on account of the grandmother: at the last minute, one Nin, the leader, arrived and said leave everything just like it is, it'll serve as a trap to catch somebody that interests me. It's a blurred photograph, stained from the dampness, in which the shadows gain territory from the light day after day and attack your nostrils with an odor of mystery and the afterlife. The sacked palace of the bishop, Amén always says, spying it lying on the top of the pile of newspapers, the widow's apartment, Tits says, no the historic Palacete de la Moncloa, Mingo says, and we can never agree, comrade, but it doesn't matter: a photo of comradeship, a souvenir of impulsive, free youth, that's all, sir, when all is said and done he was a poor militia-man who was obeying orders. Said by Java with words or gestures from the grandmother: one day in the month of June of '37, when the destruction of the red bandanas was in progress, he disappeared from the map and the photo stayed here and this leaf from the calendar gathering dust, the only thing that the grandmother didn't try to tear off the walls.

Early one morning Martín and Tits were chasing a cat and

hung it on the gate of the Martinense soccer field. I got there just as they were skinning it and suggested they take it to Granny Javaloyes: cat tastes good with onions and roast potatoes, it's like rabbit if you put a few bay leaves in it, cheer up, Granny, we're going to lick our fingers today, I said to her. The old lady never smiles and usually she doesn't pay any attention to us, much less listen to what we have to say, but that day she told us by signs that the meal would be on Sunday at one o'clock. Martín and Tits couldn't go, but I did, all that morning I was at my comic-book stand on the Plaza del Norte and at one o'clock I went to the junk shop. Java wasn't there and the cat had disappeared: all that was left were the bones sucked very clean on two plates with remains of potatoes that the grandmother was emptying into the garbage can. Granny, did you and Java wolf it down all by yourselves, without waiting for me? I say to her, and she seemed surprised, she wasn't expecting me so early, what a dirty trick, Granny, I didn't deserve that, you haven't even left me the tail. Then I noticed the fork smeared with lipstick, and on the glass too, I'm very observant, comrade, I didn't say anything but suddenly everything was clear to me: those bone rings that Java sold and the little jeweler's files that Mingo brought him from the shop, so many crossword puzzles and so many little paper birds in the corners, the creak of the rocking chair and the prattling of the radio just at news time. . . .

Grumbling and in a worse humor than usual, Granny walked back and forth in the kitchen and finally almost threw me out in the street as she slipped a tangerine into my pocket, poor thing. That afternoon I was at the Center playing Ping-Pong after catechism and after I left, it was night already, I dropped by the junk shop again. I was thinking over all sorts of solutions of the mystery, comrade, and I remember that I got lost. Something strange sometimes happens to me, comrade: I know the city well but sometimes I get lost in my own neighborhood, I confuse the streets. Finally, as I rounded the corner of the Europa soccer field, I saw the taxi stopped in front of the door and I thought it was the widow with the lieutenant, but then I immediately saw Java heading for the junk shop as fast as he could run. The taxi had the door open and the motor didn't even stop, she was all set because she came out right away and Java helped her in; it was the only time that I saw her in person, comrade. I couldn't tell you what her face looks like, I didn't even catch a glimpse of it; blonde hair and a beret, a gray gabardine raincoat, a leather purse hanging from a wide strap over her shoulder, and a leg with a rain boot on it climbing quickly into the car. Java closed the door and stood there a while watching the car drive away. Hidden in an entryway, I waited for a few minutes and then went into the junk shop to see him: he was pushing the piles of newspapers and magazines up against the wall. What's up, he said, surprised to see me, and I said jokingly: did they know they were eating cat, gummy-eyes, did your granny tell them or did they believe it was really rabbit? But he answered evasively, the little bastard: how would you expect her to say anything if she's deaf and dumb, you animal, and I answered: by signs, man. And we burst out laughing. You know how to make your way around alone, Itchy, he said to me, but here in the neighborhood you get lost and you see visions in this junk shop.

So that was the reason, I'll tell him, that's why he kept looking for her till he found her, he'd already brought him others but she was the one he liked the most, what's so strange about that? Imagine what it must be like to be shut up in the dark for months and years all by yourself, how long can a Red go without fucking, comrade, if you'll pardon the expression? So that was why they saw each other, sometimes they shared lentil soup and a banana, and then they fornicated, sir, they fornicated.

Her long legs with black stockings showed above the garters, magnificent, scandalous. At a time when there was a scarcity of great whirlwind passions he placed his whore in the center of his dreams, of his nightmares and his deliriums of freedom: she would be his spy and his adventuress, his plati-

246

num blonde, his femme fatale, his sad little maidservant, his cheap whore and everything else that a resentful, extravagant, sleepless imagination could suggest to him. He never went to bed because he couldn't sleep anymore, he had a mattress with red and white striped ticking but he didn't use it, he leaned back in the rocking chair and sat there rocking for hours, pounding the floor with the iron tip of his cane, calling for another whore, always with the hope that it would be her or at least it would be someone who looked a little like her, ordering them to satisfy his urgent needs, new positions, new massages of his legs deformed from not moving, and so on. His life was one contemplated in a rear-view mirror, with her a few feet away from him, as though she weren't his. It appears that they had met a long time before, I'll tell him that people say, that he and other militiamen had had dealings with her when they were on leave and they may even have been lovers, she had lots of them, she began whoring around under a blanket when she was fifteen, they say. So you have the explanation of the whole thing now: once a month Java brought him some whore or other, no, I don't think she charged him anything, she must have done it out of friendship, I tell you: it was quite a romantic thing. Sure it's strange, that's certain, there aren't whores like her around any more, ow, I swear on the health of my mother, imperial comrade, it's absolutely true, ow, you're knocking the scales off my scalp.

All right, wait, I know more things but please note that I've told you the truth. Otherwise how can you explain the visits to the junk shop by the proprietress of the Continental Bar, that fox that traffics in whores? But there's more. In case you don't believe me, I'm going to tell you another version of the whole thing, another story of the man in hiding and the whore that everybody's chasing after, a rumor that's circulating around here and one that coincides with my true story in almost every detail and what's more it explains the scar. Did you know that she's got a scar on her left breast, comrade, right over her heart? Do you know how she got it and who did it to her, comrade? Well, they say that her uncle, when he was still a patrol leader, got her a pass one day to go to the front to visit her sweetheart, and decided to take advantage of the girl's trip to pass a very important secret message, a little piece of microfilm. Because he was afraid she might fall in the enemy's hands he had a doctor sew the film underneath her skin, some people say in her shoulder very close to her neck and others inside her left breast, no one knows which version is true but it doesn't matter, you'll see, because she was never able to pass the message to Durruti, and they say that's why he was murdered. When she got to the front, her sweetheart had died and the Nationals had retaken Fuendetodos, you guys swooped in as saviors and she couldn't make contact with another person in order to hand over the document, they say this person was Java's brother, whom Ramona had been screwing around with even while her sweetheart was alive, so she returned all alone and terrified to Barcelona but didn't see her uncle for a year, and when they tried to get the little piece of film out they couldn't find it. They opened her up but the celluloid had been traveling around her body under her skin all this time, going around without hurting or making any noise till nobody was able to tell where it was, and they even said to her: maybe it's near your heart and if so be careful, one day it'll pierce it and good-bye, to the cemetery with you. Just like Lieutenant Conrado, comrade, you know him very well: the machine-gun bullet is traveling around his body too, it's already paralyzed his legs and little by little it's destroying his cells and tissues, poor little hero, time is working against him and in just a little over thirty years it will devour him, what a tragedy for a victor over Bolshevism to be rotting away day after day on his throne with wheels, what a bitch of a life, we're nothing.

So finally one day Java met the maid who'd turned into just another hooker. His brother in hiding was planning his escape to France on a freighter and had decided to take that document with him, it's never too late and it can be useful to me, he thought, and it was that day that we saw the grandmother throwing cotton and bloodstained gauze into the garbage, and she reeked of alcohol: they took the celluloid out of her shoulder or her breast, no one knows for certain which, and it must have been right then, in that little walled-up room, that he happened to touch the little lump under her skin when he embraced her and decided to open her up there and then, and so she had another scar, that's what they say but I can't believe that story, comrade, I think he was only looking for company and going to bed with her and the little piece of celluloid is still under her skin, in some part of her battered whore's body, maybe it's traveled so far that it's in her leg or her other breast, who knows, it may be it's going round and round her waist and will keep on doing so forever. Every time I imagine her doing her job under some guy, I see lots and lots of hands running over her white skin and slowly feeling her up in search of the little lump, the sign, as if all the men who screwed her were spies, because we'll see, is that dumb thing so important that everybody is after it? I'll say to him, it all seems like some vague plot, sir, a very old act of revenge whose reasons have long since been forgotten by all the plotters.

And finally, it's been discovered that one day he decided to abandon his hiding place and embarked for Marseilles and ended up dying in a concentration camp in Algiers: he stuffed himself with chickpeas and raw flour, the poor man, he saw some sacks that were being distributed and couldn't contain his hunger, he grabbed up whole handfuls and fell to the ground right there with his stomach perforated. No, sir, my teeth aren't falling out because I'm lying, I'm not a kid anymore: it's for lack of calcium, it's from my weak constitution and the wine that my father had in his veins. But look, I've got a silver tooth that's never going to fall out on me. And if he starts beating me up the way he did Tits, wait, I'll say to him, and on top of that I'll give him a Parker, if I find out anything more I promise I'll tell you, I keep my ears open all the time. Ow, please let me go with my mom, she's waiting for me, I swear

I'll behave, sir, good-bye, I'll say to him, here's your damned pen, wretch, you're a lackey of the Nationalist crusade and I hope your glass eye rots if they ever give you one for the services you've done them, which I doubt, you bastard of a one-eyed man, and finally, comrade, there's just one thing I'd like to ask you before I go: will you let me see the Star and hold it a minute? Bang, bang, I sure wish I had one like it.

XVII

THE tobacco and the little booklet of cigarette paper appearing first and then a little later the wine and the food, potatoes with lentils or a cup of malt with crumbled bread, and sometimes the surprise of a banana, and two if there is a visitor. Your mouth waters when you hear the papers covering up the cat-hole being removed. Two bananas with the newspaper tucked between them, finally, let's see what lies it has in it today.

Reading: four subversives who had clandestinely crossed the border shot to death near Sant Llorens de Munt by forces of the Guardia Civil. During the shootout a ricocheting bullet gravely wounded a boy from the Youth Front camp in the vicinity. There were six of them. . . . And between the pages of foreign news, a message from Palau telling him to rendezvous at the usual place just past midnight.

"There were six of them, Marcos, and only two managed to escape" — Palau in the Alaska Bar. "It was the next day after crossing the frontier, on a little road that's not very well-known, skirting the mountain. I told Sendra repeatedly: don't take so many people, because you're sure to meet up with the Guardia Civil. . . . And just look what happened. Here's the picture now: Meneses with a bullet hole in his wrist for the last two months, Navarro sick, Lage still in Modelo, Sendra liquidated, and still no news of Ramón."

"I'm right to be careful," I said to her. "No need to worry, eat as much as you like but don't fool yourself, my girl: it's not rabbit. Pass me the wine."

"And so here we are, waiting" — Palau, poking at his teeth with the toothpick, his lips foaming with beer. "Some of them have been spending all their time passing English and Polish pilots across the border."

"Are they well paid?"

"I've got good friends in the English consulate."

"How much?"

"Three hundred a head. But that's coming to an end too. Did you see that they've landed in Normandy?" "But Juan Sendra was still alive then, wasn't he? At that time we couldn't see any end to the war yet, they hadn't even sent word to you about participating in that caper at the hotel for whores, what are you talking about, when was that?" "I don't remember, baby, it must have been before but I said to him: 'Do you think they'll come, Palau, is it worth holding out?' 'I don't hope for anything and I don't believe anything, I don't know a thing,' he said."

Palau was very excited and had an itchy trigger finger, so you're right, it must have been before the attack on the fancy hotel for whores, one of those nights of mine when I felt like stretching my legs, taking a nostalgic walk through the port or through the neighborhood, scaring kids without meaning to so as to land in the bar at the very last minute: I don't want anyone to say that I'm buried alive, that I'm forgetting my friends. But there wasn't anybody in the Alaska at that hour, only a drunk woman sitting on a stool in her fur coat, that blonde who was soon to be such friends with Viñas playing dice with him, she'd really tied one on, so lonely and bored and always trying to start a conversation, deaf to the pleading of the waiter who wanted desperately to close up, he'd already slammed down the iron grille but she paid no attention: kidding me about my tattoo and my bone rings, I'll buy all of them from you, sailor, she was having so much fun that she offered me peppermint drinks till past dawn, with the door closed and taking out bills from her ears even, she would have made a terrible ruckus if I hadn't accepted. And she kept endlessly telling the story of her life, from the age of fourteen when a soldier got her cherry, she says, till heaven knows when, nothing but work till she was thirty and began to live in luxury and then more fucking and who knows what else, till they knocked her off unexpectedly in that awful way, one winter night at the beginning of '49: her head bashed in with a wooden hammer in the back seat of a car and buried a few inches deep in a wretched vacant lot, doubtless in that same fur coat that's slipping off her bare shoulders and brushing the legs of the stool, with that same dark purple mouth and those silky knees twinkling, a little too far apart, who would ever have foreseen that?

They agreed that the Alaska Bar was a safe enough place to exchange views as they played dominoes or pretended to, always late at night. Wrapped in the blue jacket, his pale face hunched over between the lapels and in a beret and dark glasses, change chairs and sit with your back to the door, Mister Woolgatherer, I didn't think you'd come tonight.

"What do you want from me now, Palau?"

"Take it easy. We're all in on the big job, you'll be well covered." He looks at his watch, gets up, drains the beer, and wipes his lips with the back of his hand. "Let's go."

"Where?"

"To the hotel. It's turtledove time."

In the carpeted vestibule, four waiters with their arms raised to the ceiling, closely covered by Bundó and Fusam. The wall clock in the office said four-thirty A.M. As "Taylor" pockets the money in the cash register, Viñas watches the front door and Palau blocks the elevator. Fusam butts the waiters in the kidneys with the submachine gun, pushing them toward the little waiting room, the size of a candy box, and goes in with them. The others meet at the foot of the stairway, then scramble upstairs, and we separate.

At the shout of police, open up! the customer in 110 was to give a start in the bed, letting go of the fat redhead. As he fumbles around for his pants, the door hits him in the face and throws him violently to the floor. Navarro would have time to see the whore's buttocks trotting to the bathroom and he runs after her as Bundó points his gun at the guy, stay quiet and nothing will happen to you, opens the shower curtain and sees her crouching there, covering her face with her hands. He yanks the chain and the gold medal from around her neck, then comes back into the bedroom to empty the guy's wallet and pockets two rings, a brooch, the earrings and the wristwatch. The customer is standing next to the radiator; in order not to move he hasn't even put his pants on and drops of sweat are collecting on his bushy gray eyebrows.

Door number 206 has opened with the words Who is it? "Taylor" sticks his foot in it and pushes, thrusting in his hand with the revolver. Something hits the floor with a dull thud and as Pepe enters like a whirlwind he stumbles over a fat, suntanned man in shorts, kneeling there trembling. In the bed, covering herself with the sheet, is a girl with caramel-colored hair and pale, almost blue lips, and at her side an open box of candy. Don't anybody move or I'll blow you to kingdom come. Searching the clothes, "Taylor" finds two jackets, two pairs of pants, two shirts. . . . He exchanges rapid glances with his companion just as a bottle shatters in the bathroom. Pepe comes back in the room shifting his revolver from one hand to the other and taking another one out from his armpit: the wrinkled head and bulging eyes of an old man, and then his body, soaped all over, peek out of the bathroom door. He has red spots on his pubic hair and little trickles of pink water are running down his skinny legs. Pushing him out of his way,

Pepe enters the bathroom. In the tub is another girl all hunched over, half covered by the slightly red-tinted water, moaning in terror with her arms crossed over her eyes. Pepe sticks his revolver in the soaped back of the guy and forces him to sit down on the bidet with his hands on top of his head. On the floor are a bottle of champagne and four glasses, and in the washbasin is a bunch of gardenias with the stems wrapped in silver paper. The assailant cuts off a gardenia, sniffs it, and sticks it in his buttonhole.

Door number 333 doesn't have the bolt shut and Palau needs only to turn the handle. The bluish light falling like powder from the ceiling bathes a blonde lying naked in the bed. The black, curly head of a young kid is moving back and forth at the level of her genitals, there is a mirror on the ceiling and satyrs chasing nymphs on the walls. Her legs close abruptly, the youngster's back straightens as though someone had pinched him and he stammers what's happening? with his hands up. His girlfriend reaches her hand out toward the blanket. Just stay where you are, my girl, Jaime orders, and with a nod of his head he points out to me the clothes lying on the floor. Palau takes a look in the bathroom, comes back and empties the purse, and then the pockets of the Persian lamb coat. He gives a whistle as he shows the furs to Jaime, who says leave them, what would we do with them?

Searching the young kid's clothes, he throws aside a pair of shapeless pants, a worn gabardine coat and the Ritz Grill waiter's jacket. This sport doesn't even have a wallet, I say, looking at the kid. Meanwhile, sitting at the head of the bed, without covering herself and pretending not to be at all bothered, the whore doesn't take her eyes off the pistol that Jaime is pointing at her, a few inches away from her forehead. Jaime's getting impatient: hurry it up, sailor, but his eyes slowly take in the breasts, the taut belly, and the navel, the thighs. Kneeling on the bed, the kid has lowered his hands little by little. As he crosses them modestly over his genitals, Jaime discovers the watch on his wrist. He sweeps it off and looks at the gold scorpion. Palau takes it from him, says, well, would you look where this turned up? and pockets it. Jaime hits the guy with his pistol, quiet, you, forcing him to put his hands up again.

"Who gave you this, fellow?"

"Tell him somebody nicer than you," the girl says.

"That may be, cutie," Jaime says with a smile, nudging the kid with his pistol. "Don't be scared, man."

"Tell him we're not scared," she says. "Tell him."

Jaime looks at her haughtily and arrogantly, pretending scorn.

"You seem awfully brave. What's your name?"

"Guess."

"And how about this waiter?"

"He's a friend."

Palau spies the ring on the night table, the waiter sees what he is up to and tries to grab it, but the butt of the Parabellum hits him in the hand. Let go, snotnose, Palau says. The kid lowers his head in pain and the girl gives him a sad look and runs her hand through his curly hair. Do you like it that much? Jaime murmurs, sitting down on the bed and lowering the pistol. But Palau and I are already at the door. Come on, hotpants, Palau says, opening it, leave it for another day.

Going down the stairs four by four, Jaime asks for the scorpion. Come on, I'm onto you, Palau says, you want to give it back to the girl, and Jaime says you keep the brooch and share things with Marcos. Okay, Palau says, but not a word to "Taylor" and try to shake him right away, he's bad luck. Down in the vestibule, "Taylor" and Jesús with their guns trained on the waiters, there are five of them now, and the Wanderer outside the door with the motor running, and Fusam at the wheel. The last to climb in is Pepe, and a little before closing the door the lights of a car blocking the way blind him. An elegantly dressed man is driving, and at his side is a woman hiding her face between the lapels of her coat.

Pepe has leapt off the running board, unbuttoning his gabardine raincoat, the man comes over to him with the expression of somebody about to say what's going on here? and then suddenly he catches on, steps backward, and runs to his car; sticking his hand through the window he toots the horn again and again. Then he turns around but all he has time to see is Pepe opening his gabardine raincoat.

Standing there shooting the submachine gun, he looked like an epileptic. The other guy fell like an overcoat knocked off a coatrack.

XVIII

SLIDING down Escorial in the soapbox racers covered with broom was to make Señorita Paulina's catechism classes happy. Once the almond flowers had fallen, their green branches peeked even farther over the wall. Worn-out braziers thrown in the trash appeared on the corners. The little kids from Carmelo made gushers of water by putting their hands over the faucets of the public fountains, and put used cartridges and bottle caps on the streetcar rails, and the wheels then flattened them. Snowball bushes decked the paths of the Parque Güell in white, and in the dale next to Cottolengo, in the tiny gardens of the no-man's-land, men could be seen on Sundays digging in their streetcar workers' jackets with carnations tucked behind their ears. Spring never again smiled as it did that year.

"Come on, sing, come on," the cleaning women joked, humming: "We're going to tell lies, tra-la-la, come on, Nito."

He passed among them and their buckets of water with a bundle of clothes and flasks of formaldehyde in his basket, opened the dog cage and went in. The barks turned into almost human moans, into a painful panting. He put everything down on the floor, distributed the food, and the dogs began to eat, wagging their shaved tails. Poor things, the youngest scrubwoman said, it'd be better to kill them once and for all instead of injecting them with germs like that. They went inside, scrubbing the floor with brooms soaked in disinfectant. When the caretaker opened the basket and they saw the clothes, they clapped their hands in surprise. Ñito petted the dogs.

"Listen, I hope you don't get in trouble for doing us a favor. Are you sure the nuns know?"

"These things were all rotting in the trunks. I only took some of them."

"Why don't you bring more?"

Motionless, his eyes half-closed, as though he were sleeping on his feet, he spent long minutes watching the dogs. Dirty, skinny mongrels, of no special age or breed, tense on their hairless paws and full of sores, their jaws gaping open and leaking mucus. He could see their necks move as they swallowed ravenously, the tongues licking, their eyes not budging as they watched, waiting to see another hunk of food or a blow come from above them. Beyond the bars, beyond the vibration of the barbed wire singing in the open space, he could already see Sister Paulina asking tomorrow: what happened, you devil of a caretaker and why? They, the scrubwomen, would answer for him: that it was to do them a favor, that he wasn't such a bad sort after all; that he stood there quietly watching the puppies eat and the scrubwomen pawing through blouses and skirts, amazed at the quality, their minds elsewhere; that they would have forgotten that he was there, a little drunker than usual but without its being noticeable, except perhaps when at a certain moment he asked for fresh water to give his dogs a drink; they would also remember, if they wanted to be impartial, that at that moment he'd picked the basket up off the floor just in case; and that not even then, as he tried to close the door with one hand and didn't manage to budge it an inch, since it stuck on

259

the uneven cement, did he let go of his burden, the stubborn thing. The dogs leapt at his feet, almost made him fall, and made him spill the basket full of flasks of formaldehyde containing the dissected parts.

And then it was that spring that Luis Lage's father got out of jail and we ran to tell the kid. He was standing in line at the bakery on the Plaza Sanllehy and he refused to believe us, it's true, Luisito, run home, he's already there hugging your little sister and your mother; that day Java and the one-eyed man were sitting on a bench chatting aimiably, as though sharing confidences. What the fuck, Itchy, we've got no gunpowder and no shelter left. No, he can't do that to us, he's not a stool pigeon. And Luis left the line like a shot, his eyes were laughing as he ran, madly happy, and we all followed him, we even passed him because the poor thing has his tongue hanging out and was coughing after a hundred yards, that kid's going to die on us some day. As he rounded the corner he saw his father bragging and showing off in the middle of the neighbors who'd come out to say hello to him, he was standing with his hands on his hips, provocative and violent, his head shaved, the wide legs of his overalls held up by a rope around his waist. Luis ran toward him with his arms open wide, but when there were just ten yards left between them, his father, doubtless to impress his audience, to consolidate that prestige he had always enjoyed as a guy with real balls, suddenly put his knee to the ground in impeccable style, fleetingly contracted the muscles of his face as though pointing an imaginary machine-gun and emptied the cartridge belt at Luis as he went rat-a-tat-tat. The neighbors stepped back with fearful smiles. Luisito stopped short, took a step backward and put his back against the wall with his arms stretched out in a cross. Perhaps in order to continue with the joke, or perhaps because of his legs really wouldn't hold him up, he let himself slide down little by little to the ground, rolling up the whites of his eyes, doubling his head over on his chest, his face as white as paper. He made such a good show of it, if in fact he was pretending, that he irritated his father: it was a joke, you dummy, he said, shit, but more or less addressing the gallery, the neighbors: when the shoe is on the other foot you'll see what we'll do to some people I know, you'll see, they're all on the list. Luisito stared at him with his feverish eyes. Laughing, his father held him up against that blue sky and kissed him, but Luisito had began to cry silently and he put his arms around his neck saying don't go away, Papa, don't go away again. He must already have been quite sick.

It was this month or the next that Luisito signed up on the delegate's list to go to the youth camps; he swore that he already had the red beret and the machete and the shield that went with it, but he never showed them to us. They said that on Sundays Tits also wore the blue shirt with the spider embroidered on it under his altar boy's surplice. And little by little everything was changing.

"Your hair's grown a lot, Itchy, you can hardly see your crusts any more."

"Time cures everything, even the itch."

"Listen, were you for the Germans or the others?"

"Are you saying that because they lost, kid?"

"They're traitors and cowards."

"That's what the Japs are, they always attack by sinking their bayonets in their enemy's back. Haven't you seen *Guadalcanal?*"

"I'm hungry."

Martín asked what Java and Black Arrow could be up to sitting so close together there on that bench, and Tits said things aren't the same anymore, he's got the hots for Fueguiña and they spend their afternoons together on the roof-terrace of the Casa, petting. They go walking in the Parque Güell and do some heavy necking with each other, Amén added, and they've also been seen at the bumper cars on the Plaza Joanich and in the Delis. He's hooked, whoever would have thought it?

They had noted that he was beginning to isolate himself, to make the rounds of the billiard parlors with the big kids, to tumble down on the grass and look at the sky, all by himself. They'd seen his mysterious new ring, a skull with blue flames in the eyes, and they knew that he was trying to get himself hired as a clerk in a shop, a jewelry store apparently. His eyes squinting with exaggerated maliciousness, using up the last vestiges of a perception that was resisting ceasing to be childish, Itchy scrutinized his movements through the sun that flooded the square: Java was leaning back on the bench with his lazy, feline air, talking nonstop, and at his side the district delegate of the party with his arms crossed and leaning toward him a little bit, his good eye half-closed, apparently drowsing.

"They're smoking the peace pipe," he said. "What a sight to see! Black Arrow and Crazy Horse bosom buddies."

"I know a legionnaire," Martín said, "who at this distance could tell what they're saying by reading their lips. Better than Granny Javaloyes."

"Me too," Itchy said, "it's simple. Look, I just concentrate on their mouths and that's all there is to it. Silence. . . . He's biting his lip now, he's licking it and saying something like the tunnel, comrade, the big black tunnel where my brother got lost one day when he was running away in the rain — "

"And what does that mean?"

Then, what year was it exactly? there had been a great improvement in the quality of the garbage that the new maid in the mansion threw out on the corner, you could find chicken bones and fish heads in it, marmalade jars and even a few champagne bottles. One day Susana's tiny pink pencil box appeared amid tiny rotten tangerines. Java kept receiving from time to time, from the charity organizations of Las Ánimas or from the widow herself, packets of food and medicines for him and his granny, but he hadn't gotten any money out of the Señora Galán for some time. The last time he visited her, she thanked him for everything and said she didn't need him any longer, that the Congregation had decided not to take care of those poor wayward girls any longer; that other organizations were watching over them and thank heaven morality was returning to the country. Java probably came away all confused and in despair, and determined to tell the truth the next time: he doubtless understood that it was no longer a paying proposition to make things up, and that it made no sense to keep the place where Señora Galán's former maid now lived a secret, even supposing that she were still interested in the subject he could not be sure that it wasn't an open secret or hadn't once been one; what was more, he had more urgent projects on his mind, and because of them he doubtless would conclude that it was better to put an honorable end to the whole thing and leave a good impression by telling the really true truth.

Three days later, without having done so yet, he arrived late for his rendezvous on the second floor apartment in the Calle Mallorca. Like the garbage thrown away on the corner, the lunches in the little green drawing room had been getting better by the day: there were no longer stale sandwiches and little glasses of cold milk, but rather smoking cups of thick chocolate and slices of white bread, good butter and jam. But that day he didn't land in the little drawing room to be presented to the girl who was to be his partner, but rather was taken directly to the bedroom. He thought it was because he'd arrived late, but in the passageway, flanked by the silent clang of swords and the clamor of wheeling horses, he had a sudden suspicion.

"I don't know who it is today, son," the proprietress of the Continental Bar said. "They told me at the last minute not to come with Beni. They said they had another one. Apparently she's already here."

"Who is it?"

"I don't know. The only thing I can tell you is that you're going to get three times what you usually do."

"How come, ma'am?"

"Just shut up and take your pay, silly."

The first thing he saw after he'd closed the door to the bedroom behind him were the jewels sending out an affectionate gleam on the round table: a gold love bracelet, a medal with a beveled edge and a ring with a silver skull that had two aquamarines for eyes. Then on top of the Torrijos head, the wheat-colored shoes, shiny and elegant, with cherry-colored socks alongside. Hanging on the armchair was the blue silk shirt, the brown suit with white stripes, double-breasted, and the yellow tie. And on turning around he saw him on the bed, with the sheet pulled up to his waist, his smooth torso gleaming in the light from the gas lamp, one hand behind the nape of his neck and the other holding the cigarette, looking at him with indifferent complicity. He was a dead ringer for her: the same dark, silky skin, the same curly black hair, and the same eyes slanting to the temples like a cat's, along with that other resemblance to felines formed by his shoulders and the back of his neck: when he leaned forward slightly, he was mindful of a panther lying in wait.

Java glanced at the curtain out of the corner of his eye and it moved a little. He didn't balk at this new and unforeseen situation. The only thing he did was to get undressed behind the folding screen with the mother-of-pearl cherubim and leave the initiative to him.

With his head hanging out of the bed, biting his lip an inch from the rug, he must have thought about the slum kids then and the dark distance they were behind him, that perhaps they could never make up, willing boys who would never know incidents such as this, who would never have such an opportunity. And so he was probably more deeply aware of the vertigo of the takeoff, the anticipated emotion of the good-bye to so many things. Above the gaslight thrown on the carpet, he would doubtless try to concentrate on the capricious power of the man who was directing the scene and the expectant sound of the sea, on the arrogant acceptance of defeat looking past death, on the tenseness of the handcuffed fists and the livid faces showing the dryness of the bone, a stiff flesh that long before the shots rang out had already ceased to receive the flow of blood. One of the condemned men seemed not to be able to stand up. The beach was repeated in his eyes like a nameless desolation. Worn pebbles covered with moss, perhaps mussel shells rotting and spots of blood spattered on the sand. He would not be standing on his feet even at the count of three, his legs doubled up under him, and he would end up sitting in a puddle that the waves, in their ebb and flow, constantly kept filling. Far along in years or suddenly aged, bewildered, talking to himself, a ruin crowned by the snow of his hair and the bowler hat that he would not let go of, heaven only knows why. The Guardias Civiles would try everything to make him stand erect, but he kept falling down. The firing squad began to get nervous. The officer ordered them to hold him up by the armpits. But as they let go of him, at the very last moment he fell again, and the officer stopped insisting. The first volley caught him seated, his head between his legs, his tied hands splashing in the puddle, like a child playing on the seashore.

An hour later, as his unknown partner was still getting dressed, Java was already out in the passageway receiving the envelope from the hands of the woman. Yes, it was three times the usual amount. How did it go? she asked. Okay. Do you want to eat something, son? you don't look very good. No, I'm okay. Then he commented that the pay was right, she said yes, but that his partner had gotten twice as much as he had: they ordered me to leave the envelope downstairs by the door, she said, but I counted the money before I left it. Java said nothing for a while, and then he said: what's the other one's name, ma'am? and she said; well, didn't you ask? the envelope was marked Ado, her name must be Adoración.

He had an impulse that took him to the Oro del Rin Café that night, to the lieutenant's usual circle of friends. And amid that sound of conversations and tinkling of little spoons in thick cups, there was Ado, sitting in front of a chocolate milkshake next to the young man with a pale face and slicked-down hair, reading the paper. He also saw, on his right, the cripple chatting with some of his friends. A whole bunch of skinny, servile, sly waiters were circulating among the tables. He signaled to Ado without the others seeing him, and the kid got up, came over to him, and accompanied him to the bar. Don't let Alberto find out, please, don't let him see us together. Well, let's go downstairs, there's something we need to straighten out. And at the urinals he added, you got twice as much as me, kid, and that isn't right, divvy up with me or you'll go out of here in pieces. Double? how do I know that's true? the kid began to say with a smile but Java grabbed him by the lapels, raised him up three inches off the floor and shoved him into a corner; he was in a hurry; he stuck his knee in his fly, but he didn't see the smile playing about his lips till he spat at him, right square in the face, a nice compact gob, I'm not joking you fairy, he said, you're just going to have to believe me. Ado mumbled an apology, pale-faced, blinking fearfully: we shouldn't quarrel, dear, not here, if Alberto finds out you'll see what a row he'll kick up. He explained that his Alberto was a jeweler and a great friend of Conradito's, and that was why he didn't want the business this afternoon to come out; that when he said to him, Ado, why don't you come round to my house some day to have a drink, but don't tell Alberto, he didn't know that that was what it'd be for; that he'd never cheated on the jeweler, this is the first time and he'll kill me if . . . I'll kill you if you don't divvy up with me right now, Java cut in. Another kneeing and Ado trembled, stammering, wait, I'll give you this ring, do you like it? and Java put it in his pocket without looking at it but didn't let up on him.

He heard a little cough at his back: the jeweler was standing on the last stair, folding the newspaper carefully. Java let go of the kid, who went over to his friend with mournful eyes. The latter didn't even look at him and Ado slipped up the stairs. Very slowly, the jeweler came down the last step and came toward him, unbuttoning his pants. What you're asking for is fair, he said, come tomorrow afternoon and everything will be taken care of. Come on over here, don't you want to pee? I could hardly wait.

When he entered the café the next day he could see that life had gone on there as though nothing had happened; peaceful circles of bigshots and police officers, couples of nouveaux riches and ripe whores warming themselves in the sun behind the big glass windows that looked out on the Gran Vía. Nonetheless as he waited he saw a respectable client kick off from a sudden severe heart attack; it seemed impossible to stretch out one's legs on those leather sofas, on this bright April afternoon, surrounded by expensive whores and servile waiters, in that world that was so well off and spoiled. In the midst of the confusion that ensued, the jeweler arrived and offered him a cognac in the bar to help him over the shock he'd felt, and then he took him to his shop on the Ramblas to discuss a possible job for him.

But all of this, which is so easy to imagine and which I won't tell you because it shouldn't be told, didn't come to light until much later. He became sly and reserved, Sister. He didn't tell us anything; it wasn't to be told.

"You should have seen his close-fitting shirts and his suede shoes," he added, "his gold cuff links, his silk ties. It's certain he never took home less than fifty thousand a month. . . ."

"He doubtless worked long and hard," the nun said. "He surely earned the confidence of his superiors and saved his money. He chose a nice girl, got married, and was able to keep and multiply his god-given gifts. Just because you've ruined your life doesn't give you the right to think badly of other people," and her ivory cheeks glistened as her face broke into a broad smile or a pout, adding: "If he set out to prosper and enjoy good health, he surely did so, what with so many years of peace and penicillin."

"Except that that wasn't the way it was, Sister. You're too good."

"Who, me? If you only knew . . ."

"I know everything, kids, I can read his lips from here. He's saying to him: I look for you, Black Arrow, I smoke peace pipe with you, I tell you whole truth. . . ."

"Tell us more, Itchy, tell us more."

XIX

HE tells how they saw him enter the tunnel, but not come out: how it was the last news that there was of him, honest. I'm not pulling your leg, comrade, on the contrary, you have all my respect, I admire those who come out on top in life. When you were a private chauffeur you lost an eye, but you gained a post as district justice of the peace, and that's not bad if you ask me. That's right: Javaloyes, but almost nobody knows me by my full name. I'm bushed, what with the sack on my shoulder all day long; my cart's broken down on me and my granny's got a cold. I saw you stopping kids on the street and I kept asking myself what's he waiting for to ask me if I'd like to be an Arrow too. . . . No, we haven't ever heard from my brother and it's better that way, the land or the sea swallowed him up years ago, I swear, and as for the gang you can ask whatever you like, but please know that I can't sign up for the youth camps, I can't leave my granny alone and besides I've got other plans these days. Do you see this ring? It's pure silver, embossed. . . . No, I don't sell those awful bone jobs any more, no sir, they weren't made by anybody who's hiding out anywhere, they were made by Trini's husband when he was in Modelo, she passed them on to me and I sold them mostly to be doing him a favor. My work from now on is going to be quite different, I'll be starting any day now: in a jewelry store, but not like Mingo Palau, not fucking around in a dirty shop, it's a de luxe place with real bigwigs for customers, on the Ramblas, for the time being I'll be an errand boy but after a while I'll be a traveling salesman or a clerk, any one of these days, your honor, I swear. Wish me luck, man, I've always been a hard worker but this time I'm going to need all the luck in the world. Listen to this, comrade: I'm going to get ahead somehow, I want to shake off the lice and the filth of the junk shop and never see this sack or this scale again, forget this neighborhood and denunciations forever, the acts of revenge, the abuses, the intolerance of some people and the submissiveness of others and everybody's fear, you know what I mean. One of these days I'll pile all my ragged clothes in the middle of the street and throw gasoline on them and burn them and throw the ashes in the sewer, I'll do it in memory of my mother, comrade, so that I don't even have the memory of them left; and I'll pull this gummy stuff out of my sick eyes and light out of here and wear silk shirts and sky-blue jackets and suede shoes and gold cufflinks. I want you to know that that's a promise, sir, wish me luck.

I see that you talked with Itchy, that big-mouth. What can I tell you, comrade? Stuff like in the movies. What can you say of one of Itchy's stories that begins what can you say of a Red whore who begins by saying what can you say of the man I love who lives hidden several yards underground with his rocking-chair and his crossword puzzles and who says I won't ever see the sun again, Aurora, my brother will betray us? What to say of a rosary of lies that the touch of so many fingers and lips might end up turning into a rosary of truths, or the other way around? What to say of those damned stories that make the biggest kids laugh, and those stories of evil that begins to turn into good and of good that ends up being evil?

Couldn't the same thing perhaps be said of everybody in the neighborhood, comrade, maybe you yourself didn't begin by being a revolutionary of the evening stars and aren't just an errand-runner today who accepts everything out of convenience, and maybe even those fools in the underground have bowed to the evidence?

Yes, sir, he was there at home but one night he lit out for heaven knows where. He took away some bricks and made the cat-hole in the wall bigger, the ones that he himself put up years ago, and went out in the street with his beret, his sailor jacket that had never seen the sea, and those blind man's dark glasses that camouflaged his famous blue eyes. Bye, bye, brother, good sailing to you. He'd been there like a scared rat not since you people entered Barcelona, no indeed, he'd been there long before through the fault of the Bolsheviks and the Republic, you know the story: the other guy, Artemi Nin, who's probably still rotting in Modelo unless they've already shot him, those who'd like to find him alive would only find a skeleton, a man who's finished, walking along the beach without knowing he's going to die, having lost his wits, and insisting on dying with his bowler hat on; an old man who couldn't even stand up in front of the firing squad and who wouldn't be good even for the slaughterhouse. . . . I don't have hairs on my tongue, no sir, I'm not afraid to talk, and I've got nothing to hide, there's nothing that I haven't said already.

In fact, he *was* in there: what a bore, what a drag, comrade. Lying on the mattress for days and nights at a time, his eyes staring at the progress of a spider web or a crack getting bigger, he reconstructed the ruins of this neighborhood stone by stone, he smelled with his memory the hunger and the misery of these streets, the dreams of friends sleeping in the earth full of disappointments and machine-gun bullets, hope still unburied. The opposite of me, he wanted somehow to go back to the filth and the barricades, the itch and the hatred, he wanted to burn pulpits and altars again, to sack villas and the huge apartments of the rich and use for the last time the gunpowder and the fire that was to save us. That was not my brother, sir, I never thought that that dirty tatterdemalion could be my brother; a voice talking to itself, a memory in continual expansion, as vast and black as the night, going back in recollection and also getting ahead of it, stealing a march on it so as to see it arriving disfigured, belied, devoured by the vermin of forgetfulness and lies in the fearful memory of people. Like his granny's calendar that repeats the same date day after day, he manipulated a time that did not flow from the past but from the future, a sepulchral time that he saw coming and hurling itself upon him like a gravestone of silence. Who knows what will become of this voice tomorrow, comrade, I hope it rots and my sons never have to hear it, I hope that not a trace of it nor an echo of it remains for all time to come.

Yes sir, life seen through a hole. Imagine a dingy underground room lighted with a candle, with walls giving off a livid sweat and the floor covered with iron filings, half-done crossword puzzles, and little paper birds; a foul-smelling mattress and towels, piles and piles of magazines and newspapers, cigarette butts, a razor, and files. Can you imagine him, do you see him all alone there in the dark, coughing just to be aware of himself, smashing bottles onto the floor just to hear himself, are you able to imagine him poisoning himself with real and fancied images night and day, thinking of what? the whistling of machine-gun bullets, love moans, burning desires caressing the towel with feverish fingers and the two of them enveloped in the burning heat of his own impotence and his consuming desires for vengeance, smelling the massage spilled from the bottle that always, each time, had to break so that in his rat hole there would be mingled the fear and the desire of being discovered, that needed to empty itself out in some dark corner, like a peeing dog. Compassion for him, you say? yes, when on his sleepless nights he must have seen so many men lying face down in the mud, so many trenches like wells of corrupted flesh on the plain of Turia and so many women and children crushed beneath the bombs or machine-gunned on the outskirts of towns, so many dawns of fire and emerald, murdered peasants with their testicles in their mouths, girls with their heads shaved and a bullet in the neck, the crushed skulls of aristocrats, priests mowed down in the gutters and columns of ragged men crossing the border, running amid the tall grass toward the bomb that would go off many years afterward; spying their naked bodies embarking on the beach at dawn, among the men shot to death by the firing squad or laboring still in the bed, their mouths colliding and him crouching down behind the hole, still safe and sound, on wheels: a repugnant future under a refuge-canopy enveloped in puffs of incense and phantoms, lies and terror, the stink of his own urine and shit that in the end he was unable to control, a life with sad eyelids and silent pus in the pupil of his eye and a hole to look through, commanding the joys and the sorrows of others. Resembling more and more each day that portrait of his that his memory to come had in store for him, more and more each day and irremediably seeing his image correspond to that miserable image of tomorrow: a pale and bloated old man between two wheels, a mummy, an arthritic cripple blinking like a doll and stammering, pushed by a woman in mourning, gloved to the elbow and with a burned face. An endless defeat, irremediable, because the machine-gun bullet is traveling inexorably through his body and even though he may live thirty years more he will live rotted away, despised, cursed by most people.

Taking him a whore from time to time, the cheaper the better, I know how much sweat that's cost me, comrade. Sometimes he invited them to eat in there, by candlelight, and out of a desire to talk he told them of his life and his past prowessess. Why those mad desires to see her again? why precisely Ramona? He never told me, your honor, but you can imagine why: it must have been a sort of need, perhaps to settle accounts with her, the way you've done for your eye, perhaps only to recover that false freedom of movement of yesterday, to see her naked again at the foot of the bed. I don't know. I've always been simply one to take orders, but I don't believe that story about her being from the Pam or the Poum or whatever, if she was a poor whore who didn't even know how to explain what had happened to her, an unfortunate girl who lost her man and took to being a hooker and today feels sick and lonely. Where does she live? near here, but what does it matter, they don't mistreat her, don't be harsh with her. Make her appear for a simple interrogation, a medical examination, and then Señora Galán will take care of her, you'll get her into a redemption center? that's fine, of course, I've got nothing to say against it. What did I have in mind, you ask? How did I meet her? let me see: it was in the police headquarters in Travesera, the day they summoned me to report the business about my brother, she was there for the same thing but in her mind he was already only a vague memory, a love affair when she was young or something like that, I found her sitting on the bench in a little waiting room half-dead with fear, in the middle of some grim-faced guys, police informers capable of betraying their own mothers. Among them I thought I spied Itchy's father, may he rest in peace. None of them recognized her, they went away and we were there alone, she had her knees crossed and was looking at me suspiciously, I said to her it's for a confrontation, is that the word? and she smiled, she was still very good-looking then, she said I didn't think it would be with a kid and she took some delicious tuna pies out of her purse and asked me to share them. In the beginning there was nothing to make me think she was a whore, she had little shoes with tassels and a gabardine raincoat over her shoulders and she seemed like a simple housewife who's run down to the grocery store to buy something. She suggested that we should talk in a low voice because there were surely hidden microphones or a peekhole with a spy watching us. Her idea was: they want to know if we know each other from before, so pretend we don't because even if you don't remember me I remember you, I think, you look like somebody I once loved a whole lot. Oh, yes, I said in a whisper, but she put her fingers on my lips so I'd lower my voice. . . . That excited me. Her fingers smelled of tangerines. I'm ashamed to admit it, sir, but I want to be frank with you: they made us wait such a long time, we were so lonely there in that little waiting room, and so afraid we'd never see daylight again or that they'd beat us, and forced to talk in such an exciting whisper that we clung to each other to hear each other better, and she began to get me hot with her little pleated skirt and her darned stockings, and so we got to rubbing against each other, feeling each other up, and she ended up doing a certain thing for me out of sympathy, gratis, even though I offered her a *peseta* right away because I pitied her. No kidding: I think she liked me a little. One day, some time later, she took my head in both her hands and said to me: ah, if only you could go away and come back ten years earlier, ah, I think she was thinking not only of me but of the other guy too. Ever since that day at police headquarters she had the impression that they'd been looking at us through a keyhole, it must have been a mania of hers. She went in first to give her statement. I don't know if they beat her up like they did me; I didn't see her again. Some time later I met her at a matinee at the Roxy, in the last rows working more or less as a whore doing jerk-off jobs, but not really having made up her mind to be a whore yet, still with that fear of hers, that obsession that she was being spied on. I found her in terrible shape, she was going from bad to worse, she couldn't make up her mind to work that way and I'm sure she was much hungrier than I was. She told me again that I reminded her of somebody she'd loved a whole lot. I pitied her even more that day and I tried to invite her to have a vermouth with me, but she wouldn't and I lost sight of her again. And about that time Señora Galán's Congregation was interested in knowing her whereabouts and she herself had told me her story about being a maid, and about you being a chauffeur in the house and about your loyalty to the family, that was to cost you your eye in that mansion on San Gervasio converted into a torture chamber, when they tortured you by order of Artemi Nin, if I've gotten the story right, comrade, you proved you had real balls:

the Galáns had gone over into the National zone and left the apartments in your care, and one night Artemi's patrol caught you loading pictures and valuables into the Hispano, you of course were trying to join the Galáns, even though they tell another story in the neighborhood, as you know: envy and rancor; but at any rate they confiscated everything and detained you and then the militiamen occupied the third floor and profaned the private chapel, they even took a photo of themselves in the grand salon. And you were already a Falangist, right, you already had balls and you stood up under the torture and even managed to escape. And in the retina of your eye that got saved by a sheer miracle a bloodstained image remained engraved forever: Aurora Nin identifying you, insulting you, spitting in your face and calling you Señorito Conrado's dog, his foul accomplice, reminding you of I don't know what humiliations, mistreatment, and cruel mockery. But I know that you're good, generous, and self-sacrificing, and it goes without saying, comrade, that it isn't right that they haven't rewarded you for all your services, aside from the office of justice of the peace. A summary verdict and a cruel one, that Aurora was present at, along with other anarchists, one of whom might very well have been my brother, so you can see I'm not denying it. I don't know though: who are you really interested in, your honor, who have you been pursuing for years and years, him or her? Well anyway, what does it matter, the plot doesn't interest me, here's her address but I don't think it'll be any use interrogating her: she's at the end of her rope, poor thing. Don't harm her, what she needs is for somebody to give her work and their trust, let Señora Galán put her in the hands of those little nuns at Redención, sir, please, I swear she isn't a Red. . . .

Sorry to denounce her? this isn't a denunciation, but a work of charity. It's the best thing for her, it can cure her, they'll put an end to her fear, her memories, she'll be able to sleep at last. They'll root out that cursed voice of hers, that vengeful refrain of hers about something that was hers that she lost one day, something that for me, on the other hand, if fortune doesn't smile on me, will stay with me till the day I die. You can see I'm not doing it for money, but remind Señorito Conrado and his mother, they're friends of the owner of the jewelry store where I'm going to go to work and my unselfish help can be a guarantee of my good faith, right? we ought to do each other favors in times like these. . . . No sir, I'm not trying to get rid of her because she's not worth anything anymore, it's not that: I've fucked whores who were a worse mess than her. No, it's that I'm fed up with tears, fear, and misery. I can't stand defeated people, comrade, people who've been losers in life, who've fallen and aren't capable of getting up again, of adapting themselves to the pace of peace and being in the position that all of us are in here: how to explain that peace is turning out to be worse for them than war? So don't remind me any more about my brother, we're not anything alike, he always wore a red and black bandana knotted around his neck and even in that I'm different, look at mine, sir, multicolored, I'm spring itself that's smiling again, comrade, and that's no joke.

XX

THEY kept sending in pig bones, all nicely polished after swimming for a month in granny's pot, but there was really no reason to, since he didn't want to sell rings any more: he said he had other plans in mind. His indignant voice also rang out and there was a vengeful look in his eye, though all it could see was bare feet pushing the rocking chair back and forth: how long is this going to go on, sewer rat, he said, what are you waiting here for woolgathering, being in the way: I want to take Granny to an asylum, and he even talked of a fiancée. When are you going to make up your mind, go on, what are you afraid of, who's going to remember you after all this time. . . . And he saw him growing more impatient, it was noticeable in his voice that was already an adult's and in the fury in his eyes, he saw how time was making his fingernails of ambition and betrayal grow, he could see that every day he was a little better dressed and more pigheaded, wearing a macabre silver ring and a sky-blue flowered jacket like a lower-class dandy, dreaming about his job that he was about to get and even talking of getting married and about the situation not being able to last, something has to give somewhere.

On the night before the first of April they hung out bedspreads and flags on the balconies. The rogues climbed the acacias on the Avenida Virgen de Montserrat, like at a dress rehearsal. On the Plaza Sanllehy, before the exhausted eyes of passersby and old men with no work taking the sun, a young Arrow touches up the spider stamped on the wall with black paint as four companions guard his back in the position of sentinels, two on each side with their arms crossed, spoiling for a fight, bare-chested, arrogant, facing the onlookers: move on, damn it, move on.

The performance of Catalonian dances in the Parque Güell having been forbidden at the last moment, the plaza looked like an anthill of red berets from the hill of Las Tres Cruces.

"And I was thinking of going" — Margarita in the patio of her house, stroking her husband's hair. "I'd bought a pair of espadrilles."

"Last year, in the Plaza del Ayuntamiento" — "Taylor" shuffling the cards — "fifteen or twenty turned up and they began to beat them, they began to beat them, the bastards. . . . "

Swallowing the insult: whenever Margarita was around, he noted an amazement and a receding of his blood. Sunny Sundays under the trellis of the patio with the pink walls, that house on Torrente de las Flores where Margarita had sublet a room with kitchen privileges. To reach the patio you had to cross the dining room where an old man with a watchman's uniform rolled cigarettes with a little machine. Vermouth with olives and mussels with mayonnaise under the coolness of the trellis, the deck of cards in Jaime's carefully manicured hands, and Palau in the kitchen preparing the paella. Didn't Palau swear that day that they had marked the four bars on the arm of a young Catalan dancer with a machete and that the Falangist who did it was a snot-nosed kid who probably wasn't yet fifteen? and didn't Guillén talk of that other crazy man who

278

strolled down the Diagonal with his blue shirt open showing off three rows of medals pinned right to his bare flesh? The squirts of iced soda water and the thick green glasses on the marble table, the iridescent gleam of Jaime's new tie, Margarita's red mouth and the neighbor's radio: it seemed like Sundays in byegone days. The summer nights with dancing in the street, Navarro brought a watermelon and liters and liters of almond syrup, the whole neighborhood was an orchestra bubbling with mad dance pieces and forgetfulness. But Margarita advised caution: that year, for example, when the musicians' stage burned, she didn't let anybody go out to see it, or even look out the street door.

"On the way home I saw the justice of the peace talking with Luis's kid."

"It would appear that the old torture chamber on San Gervasio is in business again" — Palau eating a roast herring on a slice of bread with tomato. "As a consultate of I don't know what, claiming to be interceding in favor of the exiles. You can imagine what's going on."

"I can't believe it."

"Somebody ought to finish that bastard off."

"I know a kept woman who had dealings with him . . . ," Jaime Viñas said, remembering. "We could lay a trap for him."

Margarita warns: don't trust her, they're all confidants of his, and Jaime: why not, the poor thing had such a bad time at the beginning, they're treating her well now but Carmen isn't one to forget. What's more, she confides in me and doesn't know a thing about what we're up to.

At that time Viñas had already brought his brother-in-law the locksmith into the group, a man of few words and barely any education who scarcely made friends with anyone, and together they planned a new caper. The night that Palau asked me to go with him to another boxing match and I didn't go, they saw Jaime with her down at ringside, incognita, with a turban and the glasses with white frames, bundled up in the same Persian lamb coat that she was wearing when we met her perched on the stool in the Alaska Bar, the same coat they were to bury her in. It's certain she's already started inviting him up to her place, certain that she's fucked him, but don't let the F.A.I. guys find out, woolgatherer, let him make hay while the sun shines, people have a right to have a good time and she's a really nice kid, Palau will tell you.

Strutting around with a de luxe whore, going back little by little to his old calling as a pimp, Jaimito, who would have thought it. Even though you never lost your sense of reality, taking advantage of her to do everybody good turns certainly: thanks to her connections you managed to get Lage's situation in Modelo improved somewhat, and you got a lot more:

"When are you going to see the consul of Siam, Carmen? Did you talk to him about that Academy I told you about? I've got a friend who'd earn a few *duros'* commission . . . "

"Is it a place you can be sure of?"

"Absolutely. Girls thirteen years old."

"I don't think he'd be interested. Justiniano's a very upright man, in his own way. One of the old school. The one I've got almost talked into it is Don Joaquín, he's one who likes to cut the mustard."

In the reception room, next to the mahogany umbrella stand, the new client kissed the plump hand of Doña Rita, with her finger strangled by a diamond ring. The plaque on the door read "Dressmaking Academy." A huge dark apartment on the Calle Bailén with the hum of sewing machines and girls' laughter, the cheeping of birds in cages and a dreamlike purple glare in the gallery of crystal mirrors. The pupils' braids, their light gray uniforms, pins between their teeth, girls crawling on their knees around a wedding dress draped on a dressmaker's form, pedaling away at their Singers with their skirts halfway up their thighs, or grouped around the workbench with lengths of cloth and patterns.

They would make him wait in a little reception room, he was an elegantly dressed man with boots and a white tie who had heard tell, they gave me the address confidentially, they've told me that these girls, that little brunette with the braids sitting on her knees, what's your name, dear? that pale face and those little rat's eyes, those little breasts, alone in the anteroom leading to the bedroom. As she got up to close a window, she already had her uniform unbuttoned in the back and he could see the delicious cleft of her spinal column reaching down between her high little buttocks. As she slowly came back to his side, smiling, somewhere in the apartment, Viñas's friend was awaiting his chance, a father casually presenting himself to accompany his daughter back home, an indignant worker, yelling in the doorway, what is that pig doing with my daughter, I'll kill him, what does this mean, I'm going to denounce him as a corrupter of minors, the miserable wretch, and the directress behind him holding him back, begging the client's pardon, such a thing has never happened before, sir, the girl slips quickly away as the client buttons up with trembling fingers, everything could be arranged without any need for scandal, and the false father says no, we're going straight from here to the police station, wrathfully grabbing the client by the lapels, calling him filthy pig, I'll denounce you, the directress pleading for silence and let's see, please, take your daughter away and let me speak with this gentleman, we'll settle this between the two of us, we'll see that you're compensated in some way.

I wonder how all this can be: will they always be robbing, swindling, killing, and in the end fighting with each other, destroying themselves? That's the way I always see them in my head, that's the way they're living and that's the way they're dying each day with me with no possible way to escape, in a space even smaller than this dark rathole. If you could only imagine the capers they invented. Others were cleaner. Luis Lage, for example: he'd fought to the end in Asturias, he fought as a volunteer on the Aragón front and was wounded in the rear guard at Lérida, he worked in a war-matériel factory in Anglés and finally ended up moldering in Modelo, they've only just now let him out.

"And I'm ready to begin all over again. Let that be a warning to you, you whore."

His wife sitting in a rickety chair, muttering you've scared the child, you'll never change; the white patch of her thigh and the black garter, the radio on the sideboard saying the shameful Nuremberg trial has ended today and she gets up crying, puts the grease in the frying pan and takes a bit of bread with a fork, wets it in the melting grease and takes two precise bites out of it, her eyes staring at nothing, chewing blindly, weeping with no expression on her face. Lage with his fists clenched and standing in the center of the shack, looking at the blonde with contained fury, her saying how can you pay any attention to gossip, contradicting herself: how to bring a little meat home to your children by working at an honest job, what would you have done, tell me, sobbing.

"Taylor" attracts Lage's attention, pointing to the radio: "Have you heard? You can't expect anything from those people" — dwelling on the subject so as to avoid another marital quarrel. "Not one thing. They haven't come and they're never going to come."

Turning his back to his wife, postponing the fight, Lage sits down at the table.

"What did you expect? I've always said: they'll let us rot, what's the difference to them? But there's no reason to feel low just for that, what the hell, Meneses. Who's talking about a disappointment or anything? . . . I've decided you've lost your nerve, kid."

And what do you expect? What was there to do? How to root out that cancer, that gangrene, how to stop time: since Sendra's death there is probably no one who can control them or keep them in line, Quico would be slow at picking up the reins and all of them were beginning to look after their own interests, on the margin of group actions, intent on creating their own uproar: Navarro and Jaime involved in a scheme with minors, Fusam terrifying unscrupulous bakers, and even Ramón was soon to hold out several thousand *pesetas* of what he was supposed to send to the Central Committee, and so much for the little priest who kept his hands clean, and Palau remembers, even he has gone into a tailspin, he didn't even take the trouble to go wait for them at Rabassada: hopping into cars just as they are about to take off, on any old street, he sticks his pistol in the guy's ribs and forces him to drive to some deserted alley, and sometimes not even that.

"Did you know that his wife has kicked him out?" this from "Taylor," who for the first time does not hide a tiredness in his black velvet eyes, a heaviness in his eyelids: his craggy profile, repellent and beautiful, putting a calm face on things behind the smoke of his cigarette, behind the enervating vapors of that endless clandestine existence. "Yes. It appears that one of his favorite tricks was to follow his kid when he left the jewelry store, as he was about to go off on errands, it cost the poor kid his job and doubtless a stay in the reformatory. . . . In the end, Marcos is going to turn out to be the only reasonable one; I understand more and more why he's scared."

"Because of all the ones that got liquidated in the ditches."

"On account of just one. One whose name was Conrado Galán. But it isn't the same. Our activities these days really . . ."

He paced about restlessly in his new striped suit, repeating really this is the end, I tell you Luis, they've forgotten why they're fighting, nobody wants to know anything, and in the last analysis every country has the government it deserves, I'm beginning to think that's really true.

"Keep calm, kid. Everything is going to turn out all right. What's up with Ramón, he hasn't writtten, is he still in France?"

"He'll be here soon, I suppose, I don't know."

"Well, anyway, nobody here knows anything. You'll see when Quico gets back. How about his brother?"

"He's got his own men. He only calls on us from time to time, and not all of us even then. It's only natural: who can trust a bunch of pickpockets and thieves? I wish you could see the two new recruits that Viñas brought in, his brother-in-law and his son, what a pair of criminals."

I wish you could see them, they don't seem the same at all, all dressed up in their Sunday best and drinking in the bar of the Bolero with the whores, Palau clapping Navarro on the shoulder, the behinds of the girls when they turn away to go to the john. If you could only hear them talking of the comrades, making fun of us, calling me rat and yellow, I wouldn't have expected that from Palau:

"He's not even up to stealing candlesticks in churches at night now. That hooker's got him tied hand and foot, Navarrete, really, the kid's been a disappointment to me. . . ."

"Are you coming to the meeting tomorrow, Palau?" — the whores come back to the bar frantically waggling their hips inside their rumpled ankle-length dresses, and Palau avoids Navarro's eyes, saying what for, I don't trust Quico very far, he's a romantic and the oven isn't ready for anarchist rolls. And don't get offended, you anarchist, okay, I know you admire him and I know why.

Because he had real balls, that was for sure. He used taxis with the greatest possible sang-froid, he wore a red carnation in his button-hole and had a childish resoluteness in his little bird's eyes, he didn't turn a hair as he had himself driven to the Banco Central del Borne, kidding around with the taxi driver: wait for me at the door, pal.

"Hurry up because I don't want to hang around here."

"Don't worry, only as long as it takes to say hands up."

He has his raincoat hanging from his arm and a basket full of eggplants. He enters the bank, takes out the submachine gun hidden underneath the raincoat and points it at the cashier. A half-dozen customers raise their hands to the ceiling. He says to a big fat broad you can take your hands down, señora, you've got sweaty armpits. He puts the bundles of bills in the basket and covers them up with the eggplants, he walks backward to the door, he leaves a harmless firecracker with the fuse lit on the floor and goes out to the street. He climbs into the

284

taxi and half an hour later, when he gets out, he squares off with the taxi driver.

"I'm only going to give you the fifty *pesetas* on the meter. I'd give you more, but once when I gave seven thousand to a taxi driver, he couldn't wait to spill the beans to the cops."

Just like that, I swear. Look at Jaime on the other hand: parading around in his new overcoat and his hat shoved back onto the nape of his neck, drinking peppermint liqueur every night and playing dice in the Alaska Bar. Are you coming? I say to him, shall I wait for you in the car? Fusam's getting impatient, along with the rest of them in Hospitalet. . . .

"Have a drink with us first, sailor. I don't feel like working" — and then to her: "Carmen, this is Marcos. Your turn."

I know him, she said, one night he kept me company till they closed, he told me the story of his life and I told him mine weeping on his shoulder, from the time that I began as a maid till I got here after going through a whole lot of things, and so on.

"He's a good kid. He only comes out at night, like the moon" — Jaime, still kidding around, hanging loose, not hearing the car brake to a stop, not seeing the grays posting themselves in dark doorways with submachine guns under their arms and bunches of teargas grenades at their waists, not suspecting that the earth was already opening up under his feet. Fusam would not see anything either, bent over with the years and his hump that hurt from the dampness, entering a bakery shop on Gracia, flicking his lapel with his fingers: it isn't even a police badge, it's his own from when he was an agent of the Generalitat or passed himself off as one. The baker fearful, wiping his hands on his apron, and Fusam saying: denunciation for dealing in black-market flour, you'll be arrested and fined unless . . . A radio on in the back room saying this year will be the year for Argentine wheat.

And as he went out hours later to join the rest, that night that Jaime kept hanging around the bar of the Alaska, two cops would follow him at a distance, the wind in the Plaza del

Norte raising the loose pages of a comic book, a kid running after it with his arms raised and the blind man, hugging the wall of Los Luises, saying tickets for today like yesterday and like tomorrow, everything's still the same in the neighborhood. Everything was over many years ago and it's over still.

XXI

It rained for two days, the shelter was flooded and they went for a week without going into it. The sky with fat gray clouds hanging at the end of the street seemed like a cave of lightning flashes but it was the red sparks from the trolley of the streetcar along the electric wire. In front of the doughnut shop on the Plaza Rovira, Tits was taking up a collection to buy a sack of fried potatoes and Martín was taking down the comic-book stand. Mingo was running down Torrente de las Flores, then he stopped, panting, and said, key, kids, have you heard the news? Luisito's died. Tits finished dividing up the potatoes, blew up the paper sack and exploded it with his fist. Damn, he said, damn.

Old Mianet also died one spring day, they found him lying face up near the cave that he lived in on the side of the Montaña Pelada, surrounded by broom, a yellow sea in which the little mirrors on his shoes gleamed in the sun.

There were lots of people at Luis's funeral. For once Tits and Amén behaved like proper altar boys, with their eyes glistening with little tears. We all went in to see him stretched out

on the bedsprings, his lips were colorless and pressed tight together and his eyes were unevenly closed, his face white, and a
white rosary wound around his joined hands. They'd dressed
him up as an Arrow, with the machete and the red beret, and
he looked as though he were asleep. As he stood there in front
of him Java's carefully combed, brilliantined head almost
touched the ceiling. The shack smelled of boiled eucalyptus.
Neither flowers nor wreaths, only our armfuls of broom. We
could hardly believe he was dead, only yesterday we were
quite sure that he was still in a camp where he'd been invited
by Black Arrow. His mother, the pretty blonde dressed all in
black, was sitting in a chair crying and unwittingly showing a
little patch of thigh as white as snow. His little sister was playing in a doorway. We hadn't seen his father since the year
before, people said he'd been fighting with the blonde again.
Kneelings with our hands joined, following the example of
Señorita Paulina, pretending that we were praying. Mingo
murmured too bad about the machete, it won't be of any use to
him now, and Itchy crawled over on his knees to where
Martín was to call his attention to the marks on Luis's neck,
three little red spots under his ear, as transparent as wax; they
looked like mosquito bites. They really sucked him dry, he
whispered in Martín's ear, and Martín said what? and Itchy
said with his air of mystery: they sucked his blood, kid, why
did you think he was tubercular?

But he didn't explain clearly what he meant until the funeral
procession started out, walking behind the hearse. It was ten in
the morning, but they weren't hungry yet. For an instant they
spied the dark figure of "Taylor," mingling with the men at
the head of the procession. Because it was the last time they
saw him alive, they did not forget that tired look of sympathy
he gave them when he turned his head: his implacable eyes as
black as pitch, his very white, sound teeth, his ancient mouth
of a tango singer. He walked along not saying anything to
anybody, very slowly, his arms loose and separated from his
body, his head and his behind a little bit to one side.

They said that the blonde still made herself extra money in the afternoon sessions in the movie houses in the neighborhood, as a whore jerking guys off. We never believed that filthy lie that people invented out of the whole cloth and we never said anything about it to Luisito, who loved his mother so much; but when the little kids from Los Hermanos or Los Luises wanted to make the kid mad they told this tall story: of how one day Luis sat down next to one of those jerk-off experts in the darkness of the movie house, they said, and took her hand and that mother and son recognized each other by feel as he sat there with his fly already open. Those miserable liars say that his mother hauled off and gave him a rain of cuffs on the face right there and then and didn't stop till she'd kicked him all the way home. As told by Itchy, this story had doubled us up with laughter lots of times, but at Luis's funeral, when some neighbors remembered it and laughed softly, Itchy called them dirty liars and bastards and snot-nosed kids, at the top of his lungs, kicking up such a ruckus that the guy from the funeral parlor tried to kick him out.

Afterwards we remembered how good he was, a great kid even when he was so sick, a guy with balls, always doing his damnedest in order not to seem the weakest one: that's why he put on a bold front when old Mianet came back from wandering around the towns with those stories about kids they nabbed to suck their blood, Itchy said, do you remember? When his father disappeared for the second time, shortly after getting out of jail, his mother received a written notice from the consulate of Siam, brought to her by a locksmith from the Calle Industria: she was to present herself on such and such a day at such and such an hour of the night and they would give her news of a brother of hers who'd disappeared in the war. People said that this consulate maintained unofficial contact with a Republican organization in exile whose job it was to notify the families of the whereabouts or the fate of lots of the people on our side. The blonde wanted to go, but some friend of hers, "Taylor" doubtless, warned her not to go under any circumstances, that it was a trap laid by the cops, and tore up the little piece of paper. Luisito picked up the pieces, glued them together, screwed up his courage, and presented himself at the consulate of Siam. Night had long since fallen when he pushed the iron gate open: a mansion in San Gervasio, with two pointed towers that were lighted and soft exotic music; there was nothing to make a person suspect anything. There were some tall white shadows in the garden, statues that appeared to be covered with snow but were only covered with pigeon-shit. The secretary opened the door and Luis handed him the notice explaining that he'd come in his mother's stead, because she was sick. In a little waiting room he met men and women who were there for the same thing: they were looking at each other fearfully and saying over and over again that there was nothing to fear, that everything was over now, that the Nationals also know how to pardon and this was an official foreign center with diplomatic immunity, so we can talk without fear. There must have been another way out, because the visitors who were brought into the consul's office didn't come back out through this little waiting room. Half an hour later he was all alone in there and he began to be afraid that they'd forgotten him, he thought he heard the creak of bolts and groans, and he was so nervous it brought on a coughing fit that ended in his coughing up blood. The secretary hurried over, scared to death, he brought a towel and a glass of water, had him stretch out on the sofa and went away. A little later his head peeked in, he checked that Luis was better, disappeared, and came back with a bucket and a mop: please be kind enough to clean this up meanwhile, kid, his honor the consul will receive you immediately, look, the lavatory is at the end of that hall to the right. From above the ceiling there came the sound of rifle-butts hitting the floor, and in the lavatory as he was emptying the bucket, he heard the first scream: not exactly a scream of pain or terror, but of something that is dying of abandonment or despair, something that didn't even appear to be human. Then there were louder moans and the sound of weeping. He wasn't scared. He came out of the lavatory and opened another door: another hall but almost without light, with rooms that were cells to the right and the left, doors reinforced with planks and slats, window shutters nailed shut and with bars. The stench was unbearable. The floor was so wet with piss that you could almost make waves with your hand. Some rooms were so hermetically sealed that you couldn't see a thing; others had a little peephole: a naked old man with a paper cap on his head, giving a military salute, and in front of him a shadow beating him with a bull's pizzle; a young man covered with sweat and vomit, standing on his feet in a faint between four walls so close together that he couldn't fall to the floor; a man hung up on the wall with his arms outstretched, his thumbs pierced with hooks; a woman sitting on bricks on the pavement not knowing what to do with her bare, swollen feet without toenails, receiving a blow across the face that made blood gush from her nose as out of a broken water pipe, spattering the wallpaper. At the end of the hall a locksmith was installing iron peepholes in the doors, the same one who had come to give his mother the notice.

He stepped backwards and started running but when he got to the street door he found he couldn't open it. The secretary came out and ushered him into the office: it wasn't one, it was a big drawing-room with fleur-de-lys wallpaper, with the furniture shoved into the corners and sheets over them and the shutters nailed shut here too. An antique iron lamp was hanging from the ceiling, like a spider. There was music coming from a radio in the shape of a chapel, on full blast in order to drown out the screams of the victims. A scribe was pounding away on the black Erika with oval keys. And behind the big waxed rectangular table, not in front of it and not trembling like five years before, but behind it and with the back of his chair leaning against the wall, Señor Justiniano was looking pensively at Luis as though he were looking at himself through time, because Luis was standing there trembling on the same tile that he had been standing on when Marcos Javaloyes and

Aurora Nin had spat in his good eye that had been miraculously spared. You look better today, Artemi had said to him, and after his niece had identified him he remained there alone with him: let's go on, chauffeur, who did you get the order from to take possession of the Galán family's goods? Or were you thinking of taking it all to the National zone? How did you know that four foreign ships were unloading war matériel in the port of Vallcarca that morning?

"Lots of people besides me saw it and talked about it. I only wanted to say that the aviators from Mallorca were asleep on the job that time."

"Ingenious, but not convincing. And when the 'Canarias' bombarded and burned the Campsa installation in Tarragona, how did it know that the coastal batteries had slipped off the rails when they tried to open fire against the boat and fell into the hazelnut orchards?"

"Because there was lots of talk about it, even by the militiamen themselves. And there was no reason to go around with one's ears stopped up."

"And the number of cannon and their positions, the fortifications, etcetera, did they find this out from the militiamen too?"

"That's right."

"And who informed them about the tunnels with war matériel, Justiniano?"

"Anybody could have seen it. The train never went through the tunnels, and the mouths of them were guarded by sentinels. "

"You don't lack courage and you've demonstrated it. But what can I do? Admit that you're the military leader of a Century and that you were getting ready to pass through the lines to Burgos and join your master. Confess that you're a Franquist spy and you'll have a fair trial. If you don't you won't get out of here and you may lose your other eye."

"I know comrade Valdés. Just let me telephone him. . . . "

"Even God doesn't telephone from here. Strip."

Black Arrow stopped looking into the past and got up, went around the waxed table clacking his tongue, out of sorts. As before, his one eye didn't blink now either: there was still a glassy light in the retina, an obsessive gleam. It was he who was asking the questions now, it was he who decided who would go and who would stay. His assistants were awaiting their orders. There were seven of them in all and all of them were dressed in black, only one of them had a red beret and a machete at his waist, but Luis didn't even think that they might be what they seemed to be, that was to put people off the track, and he understood immediately what they were: vampires, kids, vampires disguised as Falangists and cops, lost sufferers from tuberculosis, mad suckers of blood, beyond redemption: either they sucked your blood or they died, there was no other way out. So the stories are true, the kidnappings, the disappearances of kids so as to take their blood and give it to victims of tuberculosis, it's the absolute truth, it's not a fairy tale. One of them seemed to be a desperate case, he was lying on a sofa with his greatcoat over him and shivering, as pale as a corpse: it was certain that the blood they took out tonight would be for him. At his side was a brazier and on top of it a pot with eucalyptus.

For a while nobody paid any attention to Luis. He had time to see how they interrogated a tall skinny man in shirt-sleeves who denied having been a priest, he denied fervently having been a Red priest as they said he'd been. And he could see how cleverly he was unmasked by Black Arrow:

"All right," he said, sticking out his massive jaw, adjusting the patch over his empty eye socket. "Since you're not the person we're looking for, you can go. We don't eat anybody here, all this is for your good and the good of your families. But please be kind enough to leave us your fingerprints, over here, come on."

The man obeyed. He left his fingerprints on the paper and was putting his jacket on when the one-eyed man said to him: if you'd like to wash your hands, you may, over there, pointing to the washbasin in the corner. The luckless man carefully rolled up his sleeves, put his hands in the water, and then they caught him, it was a really clever trick, that's how they recognized him, by the way priests have of washing their hands: so delicately, wetting just the tips of their fingers, as though they were afraid of catching germs, and with that humility of theirs, as though they'd never broken so much as a plate in their whole lives. And Señor Justiniano, who was standing at his side with the towel like Amén and Tits do at mass, burst out laughing and said I've got you, little priest, there's no use denying it. The man didn't deny it, but he still tried to save his neck:

"I'm a friend of Luys's," he said, "and I write for the Movement Press. Just ask . . . "

"Which Luys?"

"Luys with a *y*."

"Worse still. If it had been with an *i* . . . "

"And how about Ramona?" he asked without thinking.

The inquisitive gleam in the Falangist's eye grew brighter.

"Go on, go on. That bird interests me too. You said Luis and Ramona, right? Luis Lage . . . "

The man paled.

"What I meant to say was Marcos and Ramona. . . . A poor unfortunate girl. I know that they were lovers, but I didn't know them, my word of honor, I don't know anybody . . . " stammering, contradicting himself, getting himself in deeper and deeper until they put him in the Infernal Bell and started beating it with hammers and pieces of rail, and after a while he went mad from screaming and it was like he was deaf, and he confessed. Ramón Ginés, he said his name was, and he gave all the names as he covered his broken eardrums with his hands. But he refused to write a postcard from Toulouse as they wanted him to, and so they gave him the Five-Pointed Star.

"Strip" — and since he didn't react they ripped off his shirt and his pants. Slipknots at his neck, his wrists, and his ankles: five ropes tied to some wooden sawhorses forming a star and the unfortunate wretch in the middle, in a horizontal position, spread-eagled. The rope around his neck looser, if he didn't lower his head. And below him, only a few inches from his naked body, rubbing against his poor buttocks, a soft studio couch with feather pillows and a red silk bedspread, a jar with flowers on the night table, food, and a picture of Ginger Rogers dressed in lamé and lying on a sofa. So that he'd think: how well I'd eat and sleep here. The locksmith loosened the ropes two times, but the moment his body rested on the bed his torturer raised him up again. He groaned. Finally he said yes, please untie him for the love of God, and he agreed to write the postcard from Toulouse, cursing and weeping.

On the other hand he says that they treated him kindly enough: they also brainwashed him, the poor thing never remembered anything: they invited him to sit down, saying that he wasn't the one they wanted to talk to, it was his mother, and he says that they held out a crucifix to him, and he thought this is it, they're going to suck it out of me now, it must be as though they were emptying your insides. But now that he was there they wanted to ask him something: Was he the eldest son of Trinidad Sánchez Carmona, also known as "Blondie," born in Málaga, a subway ticket-taker by profession, domiciled in Carmelo? . . . Yes, sir. Why didn't she come herself? Are you sick, kid, don't you feel good? Not me, sir. Do you want a little milk? No, sir. Don't be scared, we don't eat anybody here. Is it true that your mother hangs out in certain moviehouses, trying to, let's say, fondle the kids? Of course not, that's a fairy story, sir, the neighbor women are envious because she's prettier than any of them. Does she have girlfriends who work at the same thing, do you know if she knows a certain Ramona or Aurora, have you heard of her, son, have you ever seen her? No. And how about your father, where's your father now? I don't know, he had a fight with Mama on account of all those scandalmongers and he left home. Wasn't your uncle Francisco a political commissar in Perchel? didn't he come to live with you here? wasn't he hiding out in your house? . . . The shack's so tiny not even a rat could hide out there, comrade vampire, not even an ant.

He said that they started boiling a knob of garlic in the pot and took water out of it with a rubber syringe and put it up his ass, but the boiling water perforated his intestines. It was a good remedy against ringworm. And that he'd heard something like a motor starting up and was horrified to see the roof slowly lowering above his head and they were going to crush him with the lighted green candelabrum, it was very close, closer and closer, and then they put him to sleep with an injection, he said, he thought he was in the hospital and while he was sleeping he noted more pricks, more suckings, they were like injections only the other way around: liquid didn't come in, instead they took it out. They emptied him, kids, and since then he's been a goner, he died for lack of blood, he was bound to end up that way, the poor thing, and so will all of us.

Police with heavy dark greatcoats climb out of a car whose radiator is smoking. And so close you almost stumble over them: clipped mustaches and dark eyelashes, dirty teeth chewing on toothpicks stained with nicotine and coffee. And you stood there without seeing anything, Jaime: a gray with his submachine gun peeking out of that doorway, I'd swear it, it's the second time tonight.

"You must have dreamed it, Marcos" — with the motor running, waiting for the rest of them in front of the Banco Hispano Colonial in Hospitalet. "There's not a soul around."

"Well, keep your eyes open."

"Bah. I wish I'd stuck around playing dice. . . . "

He never finished his sentence, blinded by the explosion of light from the headlamps and shouting jump! at me. The bullets pulverized the windows when he opened the door to escape, but he lost his footing and fell, he sank as though the Wanderer were really parked at the edge of a precipice, and disappeared in the darkness with a cry of surprise and pain.

Luis Lage came running with the suitcase, behind Pepe and

Fusam, running all hunched over, and behind Bundó, who was shooting blindly, screaming to himself it's your fault, you filthy hunchback, they've tailed you. "Taylor" had already replaced Jaime at the wheel, and as he accelerated he grabbed me by the arm and said where are you going? leave him, they won't find him. He'd rolled into a vacant lot with refuse and briars, we could hear him groaning there at the other end of it before we took off, no doubt he'd broken a leg.

Pepe was the last one to climb in, with a bullet in his shoulder, aided by Palau. As the car turned around, three cops fell face down on the sidewalk. Afterward, near the base in the suburb of La Torrasa, Bundó, who'd been shooting through the back window, silently slid over into the seat next to Lage. Get out of here, he said, and felt something like a warm bubble bursting in his chest.

"You're dying," Lage said, separating his fingers one by one to take the pistol away from him, whispering in his ear: "Miguel, Miguel."

Men with sandwich boards were walking up the Ramblas in Indian file, with weary footsteps. The last one turns his head and looks with dull blue eyes at the ashen façade of what had once been the Hotel Falcón.

Three months after Bundó's death Lage appears with a postcard from Toulouse: Trini's just received it but it's for you from Ramón, finally he's asking for a contact at the subway stop on the Calle Trafalgar Tuesday at six. Pepe grabs the postcard, looks for a long time at the cancellation, the trembling hand, the signature. It says my brother's coming, he said, it's about time, but Palau, greasing the pistol, replied: don't go, I've got a hunch you shouldn't.

"You're getting old, Palau," he answered. "There's nothing to be afraid of."

But he was not to have time even to think that Palau was right and that it was a trap. The wound in his shoulder ached and he went into the pharmacy near the streetcar stop. As he came out he was chewing the aspirin in his teeth, they say, and his hand was holding onto the tube in his pocket in a gesture that doubtless would be interpreted as taking out his pistol. The hail of submachine gun bullets hit the trunk of the tree first and then, raising chips from the sidewalk, it advanced like a cloud of dust to his shoes. He fell backward with his gabardine raincoat open and his hand still in his pocket.

And from that time on, vertigo, the lost notion of time, the silence: a Stern submachine gun and his loader falling onto the asphalt, bouncing slowly and noiselessly, as in a dream. Meneses bleeding on the wheel of a light van with a bullet in his head and another one in his back. The day before they'd attacked a factory on the outskirts of town: an attack for economic reasons, as he still liked to call it, doubtless believing that the group would be able to recover their former political morale thanks to the influence of the new leader, that man with Mongoloid eyes and greased hair at night who'd finally arrived, dreaming of avenging his brother. You'll see, Jaime, everything's going to change, you won't fuck up your ankle for lack of training from now on, this guy's really good, they say that one day he escaped from a stakeout by the Guardia Civil in a farmhouse by riding off amid the gunpowder and the shots on the back of a cow.... What didn't they say about him? On the day following the attack he was to rendezvous at the Plaza Molina, but when they arrived they noticed something strange about the atmosphere and decided to use the next point of contact, in the Calle Arenys. Shortly thereafter Quico arrived, not driving the Ford but a Renault 4-4 stolen right there on the Plaza Molina, where in fact they'd set up a trap.

"Everybody inside" — moving to one side, leaving "Taylor" at the wheel. "And get the hell out of here, as fast as you can," but there was barely enough room in the back; as the car abruptly accelerated, it threw Palau and Lage against the door that they hadn't had time to shut firmly, but at any rate they weren't to get very far. Quico thought they hadn't been followed, perhaps the only error that anyone remembers him committing. The first bullet broke the back window and grazed "Taylor" before it shattered the rear-view mirror. Something in the light that entered his eyes and flooded his head just then told him you're going to die. Behind them was a black car and soon two vans full of armed police would arrive. Navarro and Fusam shot out of the broken windows. "Taylor" shakes his head and lets go of the wheel, raising his hands to his ears. Hit in the rear wheel, the car hits the streetlight head on and suddenly all the doors fly open. An endless deserted sidewalk, without a tree, without a single doorway. Out, Navarro shouts. The rattling of the machine guns makes him tense and he leaps to the sidewalk out of an unconscious reflex. He feels the first shot a half-inch away from his forehead, the second gets him full in the face and chest and whirls him around. Taking "Taylor" on his shoulder, Jaime runs to the van, parked some fifteen yards away, as Palau shoots, using the car as cover. He notices "Taylor's" shudder as he gets another bullet in the back, and he lets him fall into the seat next to Quico, who is already accelerating. There is not a sign of Fusam anywhere, and Lage and Palau had few chances of catching the car that was already moving. Lage managed to, taking advantage of the lull as they picked up a cop wounded in the leg, and Palau, who was farther away, signaled to them not to stop. They had time to see his submachine gun bouncing on the pavement as he set out at a run for the corner.

They didn't stop till they reached the Cerdenyola highway, in the middle of a forest. Luis Lage got out first and went off without a word; he could not bear to see the death agony of a man dying like that: doubled over in the seat, with his left ear full of blood to the edges of his earlobe and his back soaked. His eyelids were heavy, but he didn't have time to close his eyes. As though Margarita were suddenly at his side, he noted an amazement and a gentle receding of his blood. When Jaime propped him up, he was already dead, and they left him that way, face down on the wheel as though he were asleep.

Giving up his plan to come out of hiding then, years without knowing anything about anybody. At the beginning of the

'60's the newspapers would report Quico's death. He never heard anything more of Luis Lage and Palau. If they were still alive, they might have read about Fusam's being arrested as he was digging in his miserable garden next to the train tracks, one Sunday morning. Suspected of having pretended to be an inspector of police using an old badge of an agent of the Generalitat, Andrés Soler Perarnau, alias Fusam, age 63, residing in Hospitalet, has been arrested. The night before he caused a ruckus in a bar with cocktail waitresses, where, drunk, he revealed this false identity and threatened two German customers with a plastic pistol. Apparently his mental faculties were disturbed. . . .

As for him, he would end up taking refuge at his sister and brother-in-law's. Getting more and more gray hairs and wrinkles, but gaining in good looks and authority over women. A compact, safe life in a working-class suburb, keeping books for the locksmith's shop on the Calle Industria. His only contact with the past, Carmen the blonde, stuck to her habit of frequenting the Alaska Bar at midnight, whenever she managed to get away from her lover. Drinking half-asleep on the tall stool, wrapped in her old fur coat, she claimed she'd passed thirty in the cold Christmas season of '49, and maybe it was true.

Those who knew her only because they saw her there, sitting on the same stool and at the very end of the bar every night, were to wonder how she managed to keep her jewelry with the life she was leading. And that might be the reason. The transparent eyes of someone who is disturbed fixed on the jewelry night after night. There were those who said it couldn't fail to happen some time: she always comes in half-tight and her lover has never seen us with her. Nobody will bother very much about a kept woman, they thought, she was well known but she isn't twenty any more, she's quite old, what are we waiting for, others here will attack her and leave her sleeping off her drunk naked, what are we waiting for? It's simple as pie, they would say: you wait for her in the Alaska that night as she was coming back from the movies at the Metropol with her lover, you invite her to have as many drinks as she wants to celebrate her birthday, then you suggest going there in a car to go on with the drunken spree and later, in some dark street, inside the Ford, somebody was to grab hold of the wooden mallet that they had all ready there in the back seat. The blonde would lean her head against the driver's shoulder, gaily humming, quite drunk, as usual. It seems that she still had enough strength left to turn around and scratch them and almost get the door open. She doubtless screamed till she lost her voice. They'd have to stop the car, and she would have managed to climb out, with her head all bloody, just as a night watchman ran over on seeing her stumble, but she lost consciousness and they got to her first, took her in their arms and made as though she'd hit herself on the windshield, as though she'd drunk too much and they were taking her to the clinic. Propped up bleeding in the seat, dying, she would be taken halfway across the city in the night and then be thrown into the vacant lot where the other guy was waiting for them, digging a hole at the foot of the palm trees. It would be necessary to finish her off with the shovel before burying her, and in their hurry they forgot to take the scorpion off her arm.

They left the blood-spattered car right there and it was discovered immediately. They took her out of the hole with her fur coat and her turban still on, her eyes and her mouth full of dirt, her cheekbones swollen with fury and terror.

XXII

T HE last vestiges of that fearless perception that refused to simply limp along, to limit its field of action to what was strictly palpable, still served to warn them that the fire, intentional or not, bore her trademark: a shitty little fire and an underground one at that, in the crypt; that is to say in the foundations of the church that had not been built yet, on the cement of the future church dedicated to the Expiation.

"Well, so what," Martín said. "You've always seen I-don't-know-what as far as the intentions of that chick are concerned."

"Anyway," Mingo chimed in, "it wasn't Fueguiña. She almost kicked off."

"And what does Java say?" Itchy grumbled. "Have you seen him?"

"He's almost never in the junk shop. But as you can see we know all about it. . . . "

"About what, bigmouth?" Itchy cut in without raising his eyes, frowning. "Who made you swallow a fairy story like that?"

"It's not a fairy story."

"You're behind the times, Itchy," Martín said. "You're on the moon."

"You're not thinking straight, kid, you're jerking off too much."

His eyes fixed on the floor, looking at a black lava that seemed to be still boiling, he heard their voices but avoided their eyes full of curiosity, their disappointed faces and their reproaches. For the first time they didn't believe him, they refused to accept his version of the facts, rejecting his authority, you're blind, Itchy, you've got a beam in your eye, how can you deny what we've seen with our own eyes. It all began, they explained to him, as Martín and Mingo were in the entryway of the Rovira: Margarita was climbing into a taxi with a bouquet of flowers for the cemetery, she was dressed all in mourning and they looked at her pretty legs encased in black stockings, allowing themselves to be dizzied by that black perfume of tragedy, when they heard people shouting fire! fire! in Las Ánimas. And they came at a run . . . do you hear, Itchy? Or don't you want to know what's up?

Sitting on the bidet, his elbows on his knees and his chin in his hands, a black spider stubbornly gazing at the scorched tatters of the sack and the board that had fallen down, burned to cinders along with the wooden benches that had held it up, looking at what remained of the curtain and the prompter's box, dozens of square feet turned to ashes, the vault blackened by the smoke. In the wings, the decorated stage flats were also turned to ashes, but the flames had not touched the unfurled backdrop, that splendid blue sky with white clouds sleeping above distant gray mountains covered with snow, that impossible horizon above the ravine with sparrows flying above the morning fog and the field that sometimes my mother crossed with armfuls of wheat and that still gleamed beyond memory. In the dressing room everything was also intact but with several inches of water and sawdust on the floor.

Amén and Tits were coming across the stage leaping from

bench to bench with their cassocks pulled up, did you see, Itchy? taking advantage of a free half-hour between a baptism and vespers, did you see what a catastrophe? They sat down on the trunks next to Mingo and Martín and formed a chorus. What you've missed out on, kid. Mingo distributed some Ideals and took out cigarette paper, he handed food around and said: Tits and Amén saw it all, have them tell you if I'm lying: they were watering with the hose in front of the sacristy as Java and Fueguiña strolled through the garden holding hands, a formal engagement, Itchy, what a nice couple the religious-minded prudes said, surrounding the directress, but what a face the girl made, what ill-humor in her eyes when she noticed that they were standing there gaping at her, you know, they turn to custard inside when one of the orphan girls catches a fiancé, they set the bells to ringing and sing te deums. So that was why they let Java come back and make his peace with everybody, because he was courting Fueguiña, though she hadn't dared to go back to Las Ánimas, and is probably still expelled the way we are, we were the ones who got punished, you'll see, they'll say the fire was our fault, that we left a candle lighted or else the gunpowder . . . You're crazy, Itchy said, but as Mingo sat there wetting the cigarette with saliva he smiled mockingly, certain that he would fascinate him: and they feted them, the priest was also there, and Señora Galán standing next to the faucet chatting, eating the couple up with her eyes, how cute they are, he'd put on a transparent nylon shirt and she had a carnation in her hair but it was all twisted and crumpled, he'd been petting with her, you could see that he was having a bad time of it, that being an official fiancé wasn't what he had in mind, you'll see why. . . .

"I can just see it now," Itchy said, recovering some of the authority that he'd lost. "On the roof terrace with the white butterflies and the cassocks hanging on the clothesline, she must have planned the whole thing, burning the theater with the lieutenant inside, and then going far away with her rag-picker, that was always a mania with her. . . ."

"No, Itchy, you don't know what's going on," Mingo said. "You're all wrong."

"You don't understand word one."

"It's been some time since you've been around here," Martín said, "and things have changed a lot, you can't be in on everything anymore these days."

"Shut up and let him talk," Amén protested. "Go on, I'm listening to you, Itchy."

"Well, this isn't a made-up story," Mingo warned, "so don't give me any bullshit."

"Even God doesn't know what's going on around here," Amén said disconsolately. "I was waiting for you so as to find out, I believe you, Itchy. Tell us."

"Yes, we were waiting for you" — this from Tits, patting him on the back and turning to the others: "Let him talk."

But he was still pensive, his eyes lowered, putting up with Mingo's mocking laughter: he's got bats in his belfry, he doesn't know what's going on, but we saw them kissing each other at the movies, with Juanita riding shotgun, and strolling through the park alone, and everybody knew it, it was an open secret.

"So what?"

Mingo smiled triumphantly: so despite this there was nothing doing with Fueguiña, because he's not her real sweetie, do you understand? he saw that clearly yesterday, let him tell you about it. Yes, Tits said, they were walking along so lovey-dovey, the devout prudes and the orphan girls, when suddenly she ups and asks where's Señorito Conrado, that's when it all began, she said Señorito Conrado's not here, I miss him, and she seemed to be on the point of bursting into tears or something. And one of the little girls helping me with the hose said he's on the stage waiting for the lights to go back on, and Fueguiña was suddenly furious; you took him there, when you don't know how to wheel the chair, when you might tip him over, you stupid she-ass, and don't you go doing it again, you dummy. A real tantrum. It was a strange thing.

"So what?"

"Nothing. But there's a reason for this whole furor, I thought."

"You think too much, kid."

They'd been rehearsing for a while: Fueguiña was standing in the middle of the stage holding the candelabrum, Amén explained, as the rest walked round with palm fronds and laurel branches, but the lights went out and they decided to go wait in the garden. In a little while, even though the lights hadn't gone back on yet, the lieutenant asked them to wheel him up onto the stage again. And you could see that he was sleepy as he sat there reading next to the candelabrum that she'd left on the floor, too near the curtains; yes, that's right, lately he's been falling asleep almost anywhere, don't laugh like that, he's become a sleepyhead again, like when he was little, they say it's his bad circulation and that he's rotting inside, you can notice that he hardly moves his right hand, you can see it when he says hello to somebody, it's Parkinson's disease, kid, everybody says so. That's just vicious gossip, Itchy said, they want him to kick off. Martín emphasized the fact that the lights hadn't come back on yet, and Fueguiña and Java were strolling through the garden, waiting, with him playing his role of her fiancée, with his hair carefully combed and his new shirt, and then . . . You're innocent kids, Itchy cut in, don't you see that she left the candelabrum there on purpose? No, Itchy, you're peeing outside the pot, wait a minute, shut up and listen.

"I'm hungry," they heard Amén say in a shrill voice. "Shall we go to the sacristy and get some hosts, Tits?"

But Tits was squatting on the trunk: never mind the hosts, Amén, he was listening to Itchy, all of them were: her fingers with wax stains on them, he said, did you see? and those white butterflies flying round her naked body there on the roof-terrace of the Casa, taking the sun with her sweetheart, come on, my little ragpicker, take me far away in your little cart, she said to him, far away from the orphans, from Las Ánimas, and from this neighborhood, can't you all understand that, is it as

306

hard as all that? Yes, but how about him? Well, he's going on with the same old malarky: I'll close up the junk shop, I'll put my granny in an asylum, and I've already got a job in that jewelry shop selling rings and bracelets, I'll have a car and I'll be a traveling salesman, and you'll be waiting for me at home in your apron and the kids will be there making cannelloni. The whole bit, mind you, a pair of turtledoves.

"Well, that's the reason it's so hard for you to understand the whole thing," Mingo said.

"Yes, that's the reason," Tits said excitedly, his eyes like saucers. "Because how can it be if she was so smitten with him she was suddenly so scared, how come she broke into a sweat when she saw the gleam behind the little window of the crypt, this one here, and let go of his hand and started running like a madwoman, screaming Conrado, Señorito Conradito?" What to make of her attack of nerves, the fainting fit that overcame her right there in the doorway as the smoke poured out, toppling over onto the ground and rolling around? Everybody saw her. She moaned like some sort of animal, as though she were the one who was getting burned, she was suffocating with terror and the whites of her eyes turned up like big Ping-Pong balls and her hands were like claws, can you imagine what a sensitive ear she has when it comes to her señorito: she was the only one who heard his cry for help, and she also heard the squeaking of his chair as he sat there surrounded by the fire, without being able to get down off the stage. She kept screaming Conrado Conrado, in a way that made your blood run cold, Java himself stood there rooted to the spot, not knowing what to do, and when he tried to hold her back she leaped at the door of the crypt. Amén was already running up with the hose, elbowing his way through the terrified bunch of devoted women parishioners. When she stopped because the smoke was blinding her, Java was able to grab hold of her and keep her back. Then she turned around, her blue-green eyes fell on him like two gusts of icy wind, she scratched his face, don't touch me she said, get away, and she bit him and kicked him

307

and did the same thing to the women, a wild beast, Itchy, let somebody who was there and saw it tell you: I couldn't believe it, Amén went on, her eyes were bloodshot and her mouth with the missing teeth spewed out insults and spit, right in Java's face and the faces of the women, until she rushed inside and the smoke swallowed her up. They sent us for help, but we nonetheless saw her from the doorway leaping on the benches onstage, protecting her hair with her arms; he had fallen alongside his wheelchair and the smoke enveloped the two of them. The flames from the board floor of the stage leaped up onto the sets with red twilights and moonlit nights. Yes, Itchy said, but it was a shitty little blaze, typical of her, all that stuff burned up because it was old and rotten. A shitty little blaze? Amén said, when they brought her out clinging to the cripple, and it was so hard to get her to let go that the skin on her hands peeled off and this whole side of her face was burned? She's in the hosptial. Nothing happened to him, because she wrapped him up in some clothes, what a thing, she bundled him up as though he were her kid, what a thing, huh?

"What a bunch of nonsense."

"They say it was her own clothes, that she took off her dress to protect him from the flames," Martin said.

"That's a lie."

"Isn't it strange that Itchy doesn't believe it? Isn't that right, Itchy? What's the matter with you?"

And Tits, just as concerned: make an effort, man, think about it: what should she get so hysterical for, why was she in such despair if fire doesn't scare her, if it's what she goes for. Why should she take off her clothes for him? It's not as if she were his mother, his wife, his . . . His what, kid, what were you saying? Mingo exclaimed, shake, Tits, you've just said it, his whore and if she isn't yet she will be, there's no other way out. And please note that I've been saying for ages that there's something going on there, that Fueguiña is as nice as anything, and if she isn't I dare anybody who saw her being put on the stretcher to say so, her breasts were all burned, there wasn't even a shred left of her petticoat, the only thing left was a little patch of panties and a few tatters instead of a skirt, explain that if you can, Tits: just remember the state she was in, and to think that every day she has to take his cock out so he can piss, and then she washes it and puts it back in his pants. . . . And Mingo, driving the nail home: elementary, my dear Tits, paralytics can get it up too, here, shake, you've sure learned a lot in a short while, kid.

"Of course not," Itchy said, but it was the voice of defeat and powerlessness. He looked like a fearful spider in his long pants that they'd never seen him in before, black ones, clinging to his very long skinny legs, a spider dragging on a cigarette, breathing out smoke and more smoke round about him in order to protect himself, thinking what's happening? All they can talk about is fucking and they only see the good side of it, ever since they've been playing billiards with the big kids that's all they can see, they simplify and falsify everything, what the fuck, and they don't even want my cough drops any more.

"Listen, kid, it's a fairy tale that they're good for coughs. Let me smoke in peace."

And they talked of him as though he weren't there: Itchy's out of it. Ever since his mother's been cleaning at the Clinic and the nuns have been giving him food and clothes, he's all confused. They want him to stay there next year to learn to be a male nurse. If he does he'll be sure to end up washing backsides like Fueguiña. And he could hardly believe his ears: she's not a virgin any longer, Itchy, I can tell you that, have you noticed the bandage she's got around her ankle? it's on account of the curse, she's a woman now and crazy about him, she plays dumb but she's not, she's always been like that, she's mad for his uniform and his riding boots and his black mustache, kneeling at his feet, ready for anything and everything, to carry him in her arms all his life and wash his ass and even lick it if he asks her to. . . . We saw it, we saw it. . . .

Itchy smiled to himself, threw away the cigarette, and rose

to his feet: "What a bunch of malarky. You kids only believe what you've seen."

"Well, we didn't make it up," Mingo said. "What's true is true, even though you don't like it. And you're hopping mad, it's plain to see, you fucking don't like the surprise we gave you. Look, here's the proof." He leaned over and pulled a broken black candelabrum, almost unrecognizable, out of the water. "Do you know what this is?"

"A prick cooked in vinegar."

"You're so mad you could burst because you didn't see it," Martín said.

"See what, you numskull? I've seen more things than you kids will ever see even if you live to be a hundred. You're jealous, that's what you are, jealous of Java because he went out with her. . . . Let me by, slaves. 'Bye."

They'd noticed that his voice had been shaky. Tucking up his cassock, Amén looked sadly at his back as he strode off, the caved-in stage, the water, and the ashes.

"And what now, Itchy?" he said. "Did you know they're going to close this place up? It's lucky we've still got the shelter left. . . . "

"They're going to shut it up soon," Itchy said from the door. "The asses. The bastards. We've got nothing left, pricks, nothing."

As he turned his head around before leaving once and for all, he could still see them walking about with their heads down amid the charred ruins. They were pulling away the cinders and the ashes looking for their can of gunpowder. They never found it again.

If you've spent your childhood in the country, you'll have a flowering almond tree in your heart your whole life long: this was what Ñito tried to express, without succeeding, as he tried to defend himself from Sister Paulina, who had once again called him an old fraud and a troublemaker. Most of us, the nun said, saw things as they were and asked ourselves why. But you people thought of things that never were and said to yourselves why not? You liked that little devil of a girl, didn't you? Hmmm, the caretaker said, and his eyes, that had been smiling mockingly, stared at some point that was invisible to her.

"Ah, Fueguiña!" he said all of a sudden in a fake, studied voice. "Ah Fueguiña, my beloved!"

"And why?" Sister Paulina retorted without paying any attention to him. "Why such wickedness? what was the sense of doing that?"

"It fell out of his hands, Sister, he didn't do it on purpose," the scrubwoman said, coming to his defense. "Isn't that right, Ñito? Come on, climb up here, you've really tied on a good one today."

"I know this fellow inside out," the nun said, turning around to look into the watchman's eyes as he sat there perched on the stool. "Let's see, look at me, raise up that head of yours and look at me."

"He didn't mean to, we saw him," the woman said in her usual indifferent voice, scattering disinfectant on the floor and scrubbing with the broom. "When he closed the door. Watch where you're walking, Sister, sit over here, we'll soon be through."

"Of course it was unintentional," the other scrubwoman insisted. "Don't scold him — it's not his fault, poor thing. How can those animals be kept tied up? They ate up everything in no time."

Smiling to himself, the watchman said, reeling:

"I've forgotten what it was I'm supposed to do."

Sister Paulina muttered something as she placed her feet on the rung of the chair, with the air of a little white elephant doing a balancing act, besieged by the scrubwomen's swift brooms. The greasy floor boiled with little bubbles.

"One lie on top of another, a rosary of lies, Ñito, that's what you are. What will Dr. Malet say, what are you going to do now?"

The yellow glare of the morning flooded the basement. The

watchman blew his nose in his handkerchief. The women came toward him with their skirts soaked with water and rags around their swollen knees. Out of here, you liar, in a low, conspiratorial tone of voice. Sister Paulina wasn't through scolding him, she was waiting for them to finish scrubbing the floor and leave, and for the moment she changed the subject: "And where are you going all dressed up like that?"

"I'm delivering the suitcases."

The caretaker avoided her eyes. He cast a rapid glance at the big pink bottle gleaming like a big caramel in the sun. Then he looked at the clock on the wall and the worn cuffs of his freshly laundered shirt. He drew his arms closer to his body, felt the twisted knot of his tie, and took out his clean handkerchief. The disinfectant tickled his nose. It wasn't ten o'clock yet and still it was very hot.

"I looked at the other girls who came to the funeral yesterday and I didn't see her," Sister Paulina said.

"The burn on her face might have been cured with the years, who knows, tissues do renew themselves."

"What do you mean? If you'd seen her face when she left the hospital . . . "

Last night I dreamed again about the ravine with the sparrows flying over the morning fog, he thought, they're on the right as you look from the window of the train going to Arboc. But he said:

"I didn't see her. That summer my mother sent me to town, and I worked like a dog for the first time in my life. With my uncle, on the ruins of the station. The bombs had left only the bare skeleton. There were some freight cars on abandoned tracks. . . . I earned almost fifteen *duros* in two months."

"And didn't you miss your friends, those wild beasts? "

"I couldn't say. We were just past the age when we were still kids. What I remember very well is the return to Barcelona, in the middle of August, because a girl fainted from the heat in the train, she fell on top of me with the whites of her

eyes showing. She had a cage with a parakeet in it. I do remember that, and coming back here with my mother to this
damned basement that I've never gotten out of since."

"Well, in any case you didn't have anywhere else to go,
they'd thrown all of you out of Las Ánimas."

"Except Tits and Amén."

Because they're altar boys and they need them, Itchy said,
crossing the parish garden for the last time, heading for the
street, behind Mingo and Martín, with dragging footsteps, as
the sacristan and the indignant lady parishioners still scolded
them from the door of the sacristy, get out of here, you bad
boys, out of here. The real hour of truth seemed to have
sounded for all of them: they had discovered the shelter and
the gunpowder, the tortures, the secret rehearsals with the
girls, the filthy things you all did to Susana, the whole thing,
you're revolting, you're pigs, clear out of here, go back to your
shacks, there's nothing to do with you, it's a waste of time
trying.

Because they can sing dirges, of course, Martín said. But
who could have ratted? Most likely Señora Galán.

"It wasn't her," Mingo said. "She says that somebody saw
us, and I believe her."

"Yes," Itchy said. "Someone discovered the shelter a long
time ago and spied on us from the dressing room. It was doubtless one of the catechism teachers, the clammy thing smelt of
incense, she was sitting right on top of my nose. . . . "

They tied him hand and foot underneath the tree-trunk so
that he wouldn't interrupt the rehearsal again, do you remember? Fueguiña and Virginia in the role of brother and sister
raped by the Moors. Itchy had wanted to keep them from staging torture scenes that night, claiming that it was dangerous,
that the rumor had gotten around and everybody knew about
the business with Susana, let's let it go for a while, he said. He
made such a pest of himself that they had to tie him up with a
rope and leave him in the dressing room underneath the tree-

trunk so that they could rehearse in peace. Itchy was insistent about certain details: he heard her footsteps first and then immediately afterward he saw her bare feet through the crack between the tree-trunk and the floor, and then her white high-heeled shoes that she left to one side and the edges of her bell-shaped skirt, she smelled as though she'd come from a dance, and sat down on top of the tree-trunk to spy on the scene through the hole in the wall. Lying there face up in the dark and unable to move, he knew that she was watching, panting, what you were doing with the girls, the Moors whipping Virginia with the belt, that must have excited her, that and what Fueguiña was letting them do to her in the farmyard, and even though she had panties on it was as though she didn't because the cloth was so thin and clung so to her pussy, and she went sliding down the trunk till her cunt was right over the hole I had to breathe through. All I had to do was stick my tongue out: it was like tasting a cake at first, the tip of it returning to my mouth with a few little grains of sugar or a bit of cream, and then the first prudent licks with my tongue, wetting the gauze till it was soaked, until it blended with her skin, that's the way it's done, kids, and then you note that it opens wider and wider and then you hear fingernails scratching the trunk, I didn't know what was happening to her, the sighs and the moans, I didn't know it could be that but then she let herself go all the way, she melted when the Moor shouted suaisuai and Fueguiña fainted with her arms stretched out in a cross.

"Good heavens . . . "

"You're crazy, Itchy, you're stark raving mad," Mingo said.

"I swear on the memory of my drunk father that it's true. "

"Jesus, Jesus."

"Come on, stop making up stories, you're quite a bit too old for that."

"I don't know who it was," he insisted. "I didn't see the face, but those eyes that took in everything denounced us to the priest and the parish prudes, you can be sure of that."

"You're crazy. That's enough."

"Jesus, my God," the nun's shoulders hunched over in front of him as though her belly ached, and her face contracted like paper. "Oh, sweet Jesus."

"Sister," he said, climbing quickly off the stool, his knees doubling up underneath him. "Sister, it's a joke; don't pay any attention. I made it all up, it was all a lie. . . . "

She brandished her pale fist between the folds of her habit for an instant, and pressed her belly with the other, pressed her insides. God has punished us, she said, as pale as death, humiliated and almost speechless, get out of here, you wretch, get out of here.

XXIII

THAT summer the locusts chirped madly amid the dusty stubble of Can Compte. The stench from the garbage heaps and pools of water there had never been so strong. The four palm trees riddled with bullets produced rotten, bitter dates. The ruins began to be populated by drowsy lizards that allowed you to catch them with your hand. A punishing sun took possession of the neighborhood and in the streets you seemed to hear a crackling of greasy paper and at times of soft crunching of little bones, as though a cat were destroying the spine of a little bird. There was no water in the houses, the lines at the public fountains were interminable and it wasn't certain whether the eyes that spied on the kids from the sewers belonged to rats or to humans.

In the afternoon of one of these exhausting days of the month of August three explosions, close together, could be heard from the Can Compte vacant lot.

It was the same day that they took Mingo to the Durán Asylum. The week before Tits had ceased to be an altar boy and demanded that they call him José Mari, and Martín was about to go off to live in Sabadell with his mother. It was already dark as they went up Escorial toward the billiard parlors, where they were hoping to meet up with Itchy.

"I'm girl-hungry," José Mari said. "When are we going to go to La Paloma, Martín?"

"Bah, that's a dancehall for whores," Amén said. "I'm hungry too — but for food. I wonder if Itchy's brought any country sausage?"

Three girls dressed in mourning brushed past them at a run, all excited. Slowly, feeling heavy and torpid for the first time, knowing beforehand that they would be defeated, they followed along after them, after the mournful and untouchable flights of their skirts, and when they reached the Calle Legalidad they saw the crowd of neighbors on the edge of the vacant lot and heard them talking about the disgraceful thing that had happened, disjointed words: a dead whore, head bashed in, platinum blonde. Mothers were holding back the kids in their laps and a Guardia Civil was pushing them toward the sidewalk. There was a police car and an ambulance with its headlights on, lighting up the most badly ruined section of the wall, the one the neighborhood used as a garbage dump. They saw Itchy among the group of onlookers surrounding the Ford, whose windows and seats were spattered with blood. A lock of blonde hair could be seen clinging to the door handle.

In the vacant lot, the beam of flashlights rent the night. Suddenly they realized who it was and remembered that Sunday when they'd climbed up on the wall and seen her for the last time: a shadowy figure pacing restlessly behind the window with red and green curtains, a phantom that made you unable to say whether she had a turban or a bandage on her head, since they'd interrogated her and shaved it bald. Itchy had emphasized that: they've caught up with her, he told them, for the moment all she's gotten is a beating but she knows they'll come back, she knows that she's lost, cornered, remembering that Java and Black Arrow had been yakking together on a bench in the Plaza Sanllehy. . . .

"What's happened?" Martin asked.

"I just got here," Itchy said. "But I know all about it. Come with me."

They exchanged skeptical looks but they listened to him: he'd found out what was up, he said, by going up to the groups of neighbors and keeping his ears open, and apparently a man had seen everything from his terrace, right above Ramona's window. When Señor Justiniano appeared on the corner accompanied by two men, she'd slipped out of her doorway just a few seconds before, running with an unknown man who was pulling her by the hand, with whom she jumped over the wall. They'd gone into the vacant lot alone and run to the other side, disappearing at intervals between the bushes near the fence, leaping into the ditches and reappearing on top of mountains of rubble and bricks, tripping, running, still holding hands, against a background of bombarded façades and black spiders in the Calle Encarnación, and had almost made it; they'd already left behind the barbed wire and the almond tree and had reached the palms, but then suddenly, as they jumped, they must have moved a stone that set the grenades off; they were blown several inches off the ground without letting go of each other's hand, and for a moment it seemed as though they were still fleeing together but in the air in the middle of a red and green fan of flames and grass.

"Damn."

"Follow me," Itchy said.

They went around the block to fool the guards and ran silently through the darkness toward the hole. They were digging her up and they could see her before they were kicked out of there: mouth up, with her open eyes full of dirt, blown up amid circles of dust like waves of water, with the open scar on her neck and her knee raised slightly, the inner surface of her thigh still trembling, flesh more pale than the rest of her, almost luminous. The turban torn and bloodstained, her shoes blown two yards away, her hand buried up to the wrist and the bracelet with the gold scorpion buried almost as deeply. The same thing had happened to him, though he had literally neither head nor feet left, it was the bloody remains of an unknown man without identity papers and no one was ever able to find out who it was. Perhaps her lover of the moment, perhaps a friend who tried to help her at the last minute.

The stretcher bearers carried her to the ambulance. The neighbor women crossed themselves and the men walked back and forth, excited, chewing a familiar taste of bombs. When they brought the body of the unknown man, Itchy came over so close to the stretcher that the shove the guard gave him almost threw him to the ground. The yellow headlights of the ambulance, as it maneuvered, threw his skinny silhouette on the wall, deformed grotesquely as, blinded by the light, he explained to his friends: It's him, it could only be him. They must have gone a long time without seeing each other, and it was his fault, not Ramona's. For some reason, perhaps because he'd gotten tired of her, because her fear and her misery depressed him till he couldn't stand it any more, or because when he was with her the danger increased by the day, he decided to keep her out of his hiding-place and his sleepless nights; it wasn't that he'd replaced her with another whore who was more complacent and prettier, because it wasn't at all easy to find trustworthy ones for work like that, and what was more, his brother refused to bring them around; and in fact it may be that he'd thrown her over because Java forced him to, since Java had been urging him to put a stop to that business and clean the rats out of the junk shop because he was going to live there after he was married. At any rate, and even though she knew that the trap was closing round her, the whore would manage to send the sailor her silvery kiss. One day as he was about to roll a cigarette after eating by candlelight, he found the urgent summons in his hands. Not on the cigarette paper that he took out but on the visible half of the next one, still stuck in the little booklet, a little leaf scribbled more with impatience than with the tip of the pencil, a handwriting jagged from despair, terror, and loneliness. An improvised message, taking advantage of who knows what opportunity. She is capable of doing anything out of fear, he thought, capable of destroying herself and destroying me. There were only seven words: if you abandon me, I'll kill myself, and signed Aurora. He put the loose tobacco in the paper, rolled the cigarette, wet it carefully with spit and lit it in the candle flame, when suddenly his blue eyes brimmed over with tears for her and for himself, for the two of them sharing the destiny of cornered rats, for his impossible love.

The next day his brother appeared at one point with his hair slicked down with brilliantine and his flowered jacket and said to him: your little friend is waiting for you, she wants you to come, it's very urgent, she was at the police station yesterday and she's afraid they'll come back for her and force her to spill something she doesn't want to. . . . He made up his mind then, he was sorry for her, and that night he shoved the mountain of papers aside with his hand and went out on the street with his blind man's glasses, his honey-colored beard and his beret that wouldn't hold back his blond curls. She had shut herself up in her room with the Singer and her shattered nerves, trembling, devoured by fever and presentiments; she showed him her shaved head, the marks of blows on her ribs, the kicks in the belly, the cigarette burns on her nipples and the blows on her eyes that her blue makeup hid a little, like a mask. I can't stand any more, she said, what shall we do? He'd hurried to her side in such an unconscious way that only then did he doubtless stop to consider that they could have let her go so as to let the two of them meet and kill two birds with one stone. She was standing next to the window, looking out at the street: you must go far away from here, right away, Aurora, he said, it doesn't matter where, luckily this time my bastard of a little brother has behaved decently and brought me your message. . . . What message, she said, when I haven't seen him for two months? and he said: what do you mean, what message? . . . But he caught on too late; from the window he could already see them rounding the corner: the one-eyed man and behind him two guys from the Vice Squad, not counting the other one who'd taken up his post at the end of the street. He made up his mind quickly, and taking her by the hand he almost lifted her off the floor as he began running down the stairs. They went out onto the street, jumped over the wall and flew past the flowering almond tree without even seeing it, they didn't see the chassis of the Ford abandoned in the grass or the operating table, they didn't notice a thing. Holding hands they ran through this devastated, sepulchral plot of ground, they left the ruins and the ashes behind and reached the palm trees, disappearing, for a moment they'd made it, swallow me up, earth, his dream became a reality and it was as if they had become one with the late afternoon and the world had finally forgotten them. . . .

"Well, I don't know," José Mari said absentmindedly, his eyes following one of the girls dressed in mourning. "It might be, but . . . "

The story was only a truth like any other, heard once too often. A story also reconstructed with debris, lived by the intrepid sons of memory.

"Well," Martin said, clacking his tongue, patting Itchy on the back with a certain amount of sympathy, "let's clear out, there's nothing to see here."

The ambulance and the police had gone, people were filing away, and Itchy slowly stalked over to the almond tree and sat down, hugging his knees as though he were biting them. Amén and José Mari tried to ingratiate themselves with him, to cheer him up by suddenly pointing their pistol-finger in his back and saying hands up! but he didn't even blink. Go on, clear out of here, he said, if you don't want to listen to me, and he stayed there, all curled up in a ball there under the flowering almond tree, and there was no way of getting him away.

There never was any flowering almond tree in that filthy vacant lot, the nun muttered with a persistent, resentful pout: never as far as I know. The caretaker, she explained, was suffering from something that was as if it had rained a lot in his

memory and there had been earth-slides: "That famous almond tree that sheltered your lonely years is doubtless the one
in Penedés, but your memory has transplanted it and you do
the same thing with people and with what they say. Lord, lord,
there's more disorder in that head of yours than in this storeroom, and that's saying a lot."

"Don't be cross with me, Sister."

It took almost three weeks for Sister Paulina to make up
with him, feeling obliged to do so not so much because of the
kindliness of age or the force of habit as out of vast curiosity,
so as to find out if he'd already done his job and delivered the
suitcases and what happened, what the apartment's like, who
opened the door: the same assistant who came with the orphan
girls? The same one, but much more willing to reveal things;
he reported that she showed him into the reception room, but
didn't leave the suitcases there, she said please follow me if you
will, I'll open them up in the boys' bedroom and I wouldn't be
able to lift them — I'm sorry to bother you.

"At your service, señora. What a big apartment."

"That way, be careful, everything is rather a mess."

With a suitcase in each hand the caretaker threaded his way
through the movers' baskets, following her down the hall with
carved walls and a carved ceiling, still with a few cornucopias,
two crossed swords, a marble bust and various antiques, but
without any paintings or armor, and without that din of battle.
The woman walked along with her sleeves rolled up and her
little black hat on, like a visiting relation who is helping out a
little with the household tasks, ready to leave at any minute.

"We're almost finished. Come, this way." They passed by
the little reception room, where three maids were wrapping
the dishes in newspapers, arrived at the door that was no
longer padded with wine-colored velvet, and entered. "Everything was in such good order, poor Pilar. Come in, put them
here on the bunk, the lower one."

"Was this the boys' room? How nice it is, isn't it, señora?"

The walls were papered with little white horses adorned

with plumes, pink elephants balancing on multicolored balls, giraffes, bears, clowns, and doves, the world of innocence covering from floor to ceiling walls that had seen so many humiliations, so much ignominy. The crystal lamp hanging from the ceiling, opening out into dozens of swans' necks, but not a trace of the drapes, the folding screen with the cherubim, the rug whose design reproduced a famous painting, nor the bed with the red bedspread.

"Are these pieces of rope yours?" she asked. "If they are, untie the suitcases and take them with you."

"How big these old rooms are, aren't they?" Ñito commented. "Did they always live here?"

"Since the owner's death. Her son moved upstairs and sold this apartment to a jeweler who was a friend of his, who rented it to Pilar's husband. The first decent home she ever had, imagine; the first one was in a junk shop. He was a bad man, and never loved her."

"Were you on very intimate terms with him?"

"I hardly ever saw him, thank heaven. He made her very unhappy, terribly unhappy, may the Lord have pardoned him. He was a hard worker, very much appreciated at the place where he worked, I must say, but still a bad lot."

But why, he thought, why would he have married her, when she was a poor orphan who had nothing, an ignorant, defenseless kid, why if he was looking for exactly the opposite traits, if he'd left Fueguiña, perhaps even before she'd rejected him when her face got disfigured, if he'd seemed ready to do anything to make a career for himself, why if he was already on the most direct and easiest path to what he wanted?

"Why did he marry her if he didn't love her?" Ñito asked, slowly rolling up the ropes in the palm of his hand.

"Why would he have?" the woman sighed, emptying the first suitcase. "He got her pregnant. Señorito Conrado forced him to face up to what he'd done and he got scared, at heart he was a miserable wretch. He must have thought that in any event Pilar was good-hearted, very long-suffering, and obedi-

323

ent, and that a wife like that would be useful to him, if not for any other reason, at least to put up a good front, I don't know if you understand what I mean. . . . And I don't want to talk about it anymore, because I might say something that's non-sense. "

On the track of a cushy job gotten through pull, marrying in a hurry and running around with a little ninny who wouldn't ask questions, who would prefer not to know. Living temporarily in the junk shop, but he wasn't a ragpicker any more and there was no question of his ever being one again, and no question of Granny Javaloyes, who was little by little wasting away in the old folks' home on the Calle San Salvador. A job in the jewelry store on the Ramblas and his first errands as a messenger boy, his first trips in the provinces and his first sales, the first fruits after five years of lowering his pants. He was a rather indifferent fairy, in fact, he never really got into that scene, he never consented out of pleasure or weakness, only to make his way in the world. He only wanted to assure his future and prosper in his work, because he'd inherited an almost physical fear of misery and hunger: he immediately began to wear fancy suits with wide shoulders, his furious curls were carefully combed, and there were fine little chains of gold tangled in the hair on his chest, that in summer he showed off by wearing an unbuttoned white shirt. Those who still were on friendly terms with him in the neighborhood saw him turn into a very attractive, talkative man, animated and yet hard to pin down, practiced at hiding the fact that he didn't want to talk or didn't have anything to say.

And one fine day he took off, closed the junk shop and went away forever without once looking back; without saying good-bye to the neighbors, without remembering anybody, without one glance at the garbage that was still piled up on the corner or at the smoke-blackened broken panes that could still be seen in the windows of so many houses. He came back a year later driving a Renault 4-4, it was Saint John's Night; he opened the junk shop, full of nothing but spiderwebs and dust, and stayed there inside for over two hours. When the bonfire that the kids had made in the street was reduced to embers, they saw him walk up to it pushing the little cart full to overflowing with junk: piles of yellow papers and old magazines, a cane with an ivory handle, a red beret and a machete with its sheath, a chipped folding screen with cherubim and little mother-of-pearl clouds, a purple sash with fringe, a set of springs, a rocking chair, a mattress and a urinal, mended sacks full of tattered clothes and dusty cans of rations, some rotted cartridge belts, moth-eaten armchairs, a brazier, dozens of candle ends, wedding rings made of bones and dolls without heads, a blue fisherman's jacket, a multicolored neckerchief, and a balance-scale. The childish shouts of "Everything old into the fire!" resounded like an echo at the end of the streets as they did every year, as he slowly took off his suit coat, which he gave to a kid to hold. And in shirtsleeves with gold cuff links at his wrists, wearing a heaven-blue vest that was very tight at the waist, without turning a single hair on his head, plastered down with abundant brilliantine, he proceeded to unload the cart and threw everything into the bonfire, including the cart, and then he stood there, contemplating the flames with his hands in his pockets. The thick black smoke rose in the night like a mantle of furious stars, the air was full of ashes, of the smell of a wooden pencil box and pencil varnish, and the flames reached above the branches of the acacias. And he stood there motionless in front of the blaze, his eyes fixed on the fire until, scarcely moving his hand, he snapped his fingers for his suit coat. He put it on, took a comb out of his pocket, passed it through his hair, turned around and left. Kids from other streets came running and long past midnight, when he'd driven off in his car never to return again and the fire was dying, they jumped over the flames one after the other letting out war-whoops.

Ñito lingering, rolling the ropes up in his hands, dully asking questions, and as though hardly interested in the replies, his eyes staring at the floor: but how about her? A saint, the woman said with a sigh, her one thought was the baby that was going to be born, and not wanting it to lack a father the way she had. That's why she got married. But there are disappointments in life, and the baby was stillborn. And then almost twenty years without children, the worst thing that she could imagine, worse than the other. And what do you know, the doctor was wrong when he told her she'd never have any more children. They were God's blessing, the twins, and now that she'd raised them, after so many hardships, look what happened. . . . Lord, Lord.

She went on putting away the things from the suitcase that she'd emptied out on the bed, when suddenly she covered her eyes with her hand. In her other hand, together with a reprint of The Shadow Walks, discolored by iodine and salt and the photograph of the twins that had come loose from the dashboard of the Simca, was a square of cardboard that was also ruined by the sea water. Despite the Don't Speed, Papa, he thought, hurriedly bringing over a chair for the sorrowing woman, please don't cry, you persisted in speeding, gummy-eyes, you never stopped speeding ever since the night you threw all your past into the fire, calm yourself, señora, sit down for a while, what can we do, poor wretches that we are, these are the sorrows of life. . . .

"No, no," she answered, pulling herself together. "Not with the work I have to do. I beg your pardon. Was this all that was able to be saved, did all the suitcases fall open? We'll have to wash these things right away or they'll be ruined. Rosita!"

One of the girls hurried in, yes, señorita, listening intently; she took the clothes and went out, looking at the caretaker out of the corner of her eye, almost in fun. He put the rolled-up ropes in his pocket. How mischievous they are, he said as he bade her good-bye, like those in the old days. The woman rummaged around in her purse, said wait my good man, counted out a dozen or so coins one by one and then said: oh, I almost forgot, a week from today there is going to be a funeral in the parish, and since you say you knew each other as children ... Here you are, and thank you for helping me.

"You're welcome" — taking the tip. "Don't bother to see me out — I know the way."

And he tells how the next week he finally saw her, coming out of the funeral, and how in fact he wouldn't have recognized her. At that moment he wasn't even thinking about her, he confessed to the nun: he was going down the steps of the church, blinded by the sun, among the girls from the Casa, who were folding their white mantillas, and he went down Escorial in the shade of the old acacia trees, drying the sweat on his neck with his handkerchief. He stopped for a moment and turned around to look at the somber bulk of the church that was so firmly anchored, so solid on its miserable and violent yesterdays. First it was as though a shadow carefully slipping along had brushed past him, leaving a silky tatter, a black spiderweb hanging on some part of his body. He turned around again, and a few yards farther on, she had stopped pushing the chair and was looking at him expectantly. But the caretaker didn't understand. Not a single word, a single expression came to take the place of that meaning that escaped him, until his hand encountered the mantilla and he understood. It had caught on his shoulder as she passed, on the tip of a bit of horsehair sticking out of the padding of his coat. With his head down, with liquid in his eyes and in his words, he returned the mantilla to her, begging her pardon, and she murmured her thanks and went on her way.

A woman in long gloves up to her elbows despite the heat, in dark glasses and a lilac scarf knotted under her chin, tall, with a severe elegance. Clinging tightly to the wheelchair, pushing it with the ample bulk of corseted flesh that is still youthful, not using her hands, lying inertly at her sides, so that she seemed to be not so much pushing the chair as being dragged along with it, without the ability to maneuver it nor the will to react. United in a confused way with the organic paralysis that preceded her and carried her along without her belly's losing contact with the back of the seat at any moment, a dependency or an unconscious surrender, the ruin of her face ill-concealed, the great rough spot that peeked out from beneath the lilac kerchief making her mouth twist in a bitter grin, there was nonetheless a trace of furious submission, a tense acceptance of defeat in her terrible gloved hands hanging at her sides. She who was the salt of our adventures, the warm sun of our corners.

As for him, he was a bald old man, with sagging cheeks and eyes that blinked like a doll's. His arthritic hand, on indicating the terrace of the bar where probably he wanted to have a cool drink, repeated as though in dreams that firm gesture that in his youth brandished a whip and wielded power, and above his tortoise neck he still raised a face abused by the years, insomnia, and memory. But what sad eyelids, what silent pus in the pupils of his eyes. The machine-gun bullet had accompanied him for more than thirty years and of course it had corrupted him with more meticulous precision than Aurora Nin had in a second. Everything was reduced, finally, to a vexatious survival of corruption and pain, to a macabre waste of time.

Leaning over him, his companion murmured something to him; convincing him that it would be better to go on walking or go home, she covered his legs with the shawl and with her black silk glove smoothed the sparse hair at the nape of his neck, and he agreed by bowing his head.

XXIV

THEY recognized each other and pounded each other on the shoulders beneath a battered umbrella, on an afternoon smudged by a gray drizzle, hugging the wall of the Pompeya Church where the posters half-scraped away and the spider half-erased by time seemed like prehistoric messages. They exchanged exuberant greetings and their old wrists feigned jubilant blows beneath the belt, how many years has it been, Palau, I was sure you were dead or in Modelo, that's what I thought about you, but you'll see, a bad penny always turns up. Casually the two of them went off to catch the subway and they crossed Diagonal, Lage looking down the broad gray avenue where the double row of plane trees finally joined at the end, amid a thick cloud of carbon monoxide, staring far off in time:

"Do you remember when we took over this street for our own?" he asked.

Palau stifled a bitter-tasting cough or nasal laughter, enveloped it in a gob of spittle, cleared his throat and spat on the pavement.

"It just won't stop raining," he said. "It's endless."

They went down to the platform. Sitting there on a bench, they let several trains go by as they discharged crowds of people, exchanging questions, names, and dates, putting that tunnel of twenty-five years that they'd left behind in order: it wasn't the little girl who'd died on them in '46, Lage said, it was the boy, don't you remember? Trini's okay, and our daughter has already made us grandparents, and did you know that Esteban Guillén died of typhus some fifteen years ago? , I stopped seeing him when he went back to his old job as a traveling salesman, poor thing, in the end he turned out to be a rake and a sponger. . . . Lage was clutching a worn brown leather briefcase to his side, brandishing in the other hand the closed umbrella and tracing lines in the wet floor with the tip of it. He nodded thoughtfully, squinting his eyes in the glare of memory, cursing as though they'd stolen something from him: what he'd most regretted in those days was not being able to attend his own son's funeral, that was all. After the death of "Taylor" and Navarro, he added, he'd gone off to Bilbao, where Guillén had relatives, he'd hidden out for a time and then worked five years in the shipyards, and when he came back here "Blondie" was no longer waiting for him but they made up with each other, I had a job with the subway system until they replaced them with buses and let me go, and now I collect bills of exchange at people's homes, it's nothing, cowshit, just to make ends meet, and how about you?

"Well, you know me" — teary yellow eyes looked at him from beneath a peasant cap. "I don't work for those guys, damn it, I don't feel like it. Balls, Palau's not going to give an inch."

"Don't tell me you still live off your take," Lage said laughing. "Look what happened to the sailor, he pushed matters so far he didn't know that the junk shop was about to be demolished and one day they say they found a crushed skeleton along with the cat and the rats, for all I know he stayed there for twenty years. . . . "

He stopped laughing, adding: listen, you can take my word for it, I'm telling you in all seriousness: It's not good to live on memories. Palau blinked, kneading his cheeks covered with gray stubble, breathing with difficulty, sticking out his asthmatic chest full of resonances: Marcos Javaloyes? he said, he joined the other group, in '59 I think it must have been, and they killed them all. No, man, Lage broke in, he ended up in a bad way long before that, it seems that he went around here picking up cigarette butts with a young girl; they sat down for a while in a vacant lot and got blown up, he didn't even know what hit him, poor thing, it must have been a Laffite that hadn't gone off during the war. Palau shook his head, his grimy smile showing all his teeth in his horse face: years ago, a whole lot of years ago, one Sunday when my kid went to the beach with his friends they saw a poor beggar stealing like a rat into the Montgat tunnel. I for my part would swear that one day I saw him as a sandwich-man on the Ramblas, but . . . He paused, and then he added: sometimes I like to think that he may still be hiding out somewhere, wool-gathering.

"He wouldn't be the only one, that's for sure."

"You see, all that fighting — and for what?"

They probably talked of arms that never arrived and of obscure disappointments, of that feeling of being abandoned and that obstinate loneliness of a hiding place weaving labyrinths in one's memory, of friends tortured and shot to smithereens; they doubtless talked of the cause that was to end up buried beneath a dirty code of assailants and swindlers, of an ideal whose origin they could almost not identify now, of an illusion that the years corrupted. They would evoke men as solid as towers who collapsed, companions who would never return from their sleep, of whom not so much as a memory remained, not so much as an image: not even the position in which they fell, riddled with bullets, would remain.

And reviewing a long list of phantoms, they stopped at the blonde who'd been murdered, it was in the papers, who would ever have said that Jaimito would end up like that, the brother-in-law and his son must have stirred him up, and the latter finally ended up cozying up to her behind the back of her lover and even of Jaime Viñas, didn't you read it, Palau? the crime on the Calle Legalidad, there where there's a big tall apartment house now that belongs to the Savings Association, it's changed a lot, all that's left are the four palm trees. And how soon they caught them, Jaime in bed in a hotel for whores, he poisoned himself with cyanide and left a paper that said life is a dream, what nonsense, didn't you read that either? No, Palau said, I don't read the papers that those guys write, balls on them, it's all propaganda, pure fairy-tales. . . .

And nonetheless, he could still see the palm trees, alive and swaying, the girls' names written with the tip of a razor, he could see the barbed wire fences and the chassis of the car rotting in the grass, he could see the open field and the blonde hair streaming, like the hair of a drowned woman, in the maelstrom of a quarter of a century. We'll never know what happened, he said, just like so many other things. He looked down at his old hands lying quietly on his knees, and his liquid eyes blinked slowly: amateurs, he added, wretched no-accounts paid by someone higher up, we've seen that before. That's what I think, Luis Lage said, a settling of accounts. Because if it was for the jewels, how come they forgot the bracelet? The locksmith turned out to be an old friend of the justice of the peace, that wretched bastard, and that woman knew too much, of course, she was one of the cheapest whores around who ended up being the mistress of bigwigs. . . .

"She didn't climb that high or sink that low," Palau said. "She wasn't all that much of a platinum blonde, and she wasn't a whore who didn't have a pot to piss in. She was just one of many."

Lage sighed, then smiled nostalgically.

"And speaking of those whores, do you know that sometimes I still think of them?"

"What, you too?" Palau said, shaking his head slowly, with a sudden light in his eyes. "The best part was when they washed it for you with soap in the bidet. That terrible soap of those days, that itched so . . . I'd go back just for that."

Coughing between his bursts of laughter he draws his legs in to let a woman dressed in purple by, and taking advantage of the momentum, he gets up. Lage is going to the Ramblas, it's all the same to Palau, and don't look at me as though I was a pickpocket, you bastard, in the end who is it that's taught us how to live on our take, the ones in power. It's true that before I used to be pretty light-fingered in the streetcars, and if it weren't for my asthma I'd take out my old Parabellum again, this can't last, they don't know what to do any more, but I'm stifling, Lage, I need air, some day I'll burst in this subway but to hell with those that are left, well anyway, good-bye and my regards to "Blondie."

He coughed, clenching his hernia, and as he saw the cars pulling up full to the gunwales, they're like sheep, he said, and that's exactly what they are. Patting Lage on his back shaking with his cough, he accompanied him to the door, listen, Palau, it's not for nothing, and with the time of it that you've had you're going to laugh, but tell me something, did you ever hear that story about "Blondie" going to the movies and doing it in the back rows? . . . And Palau, clearing his throat, well, just look what he comes out with, what do you expect, people say so many things, come on, come on, good-bye, good luck.

The automatic door closes between the two of them and Lage waves goodbye with his hand to the face that's going off pressed against the window, that blinks, that opens its mouth as though panting for air. Palau is crushed by people and not able to move, that big heavy body surrounded by people's backs and the napes of their necks without being able to find a place for himself or make one, who would have said it of him a while ago, we all thought then this can't last and here are people who still think this can't last, it's got to end some day, it can't go on, without knowing that these words would reach the deaf ears of their sons and grandsons with the emptiness of an echo: they were so far from seeing themselves taking arms once again, so blind, in fact that they couldn't even imagine themselves doing that, their minds couldn't even stop to see themselves with their faces muffled in a balaclava helmet and a pistol in their hand, pushing open the revolving door of a bank or placing an explosive.

Men of iron, tested in so many battles, dreaming like children.